Praise for Sophie Kinsella's Novels

TWENTIES GIRL

"[Kinsella] is a chick-lit maven with more than one delightful modern-day heroine up her stylish sleeves."
—*USA Today*

"Think *Topper*, that impossibly sophisticated and goofy 1937 ghost tale of blithe spirits bugging the only living soul who can hear them. Kinsella creates an equally vexing and endearing shade [in this] most delicious and delightful romp. . . . Kinsella [is] a master of comic pacing and feminine wit." —*Publishers Weekly*

"Kinsella . . . is in her element with scattered, wisecracking Lara, and Sadie (and her outfits) are fabulous."
—*Kirkus Reviews*

"Kinsella juggles romance, mystery, and a spirited spirit with . . . thoroughly charming results." —*Booklist*

"[A] must-have beach read." —*Boston Herald*

"Sophie Kinsella's got the knack. Her latest novel has a delightfully executed sense of humor and a mastery of character idiosyncrasies." —*The Roanoke Times*

"[Kinsella] delivers yet another entertaining story—this time about trust, friendship, and the discovery of true relationships." —*Toledo Blade*

REMEMBER ME?

"Kinsella delights again. . . . Winning . . . keeps things fresh and frothy with workplace politicking, romantic intrigue and a vibrant . . . cast. . . . Readers will be rooting for Lexi all along." —*Publishers Weekly*

"Buoyed by Kinsella's breezy prose, this winning offering boasts a likable heroine and an involving story." —*Booklist*

"A delicious page-turner, filled with both hearty chuckles and heartache . . . [Kinsella] finds a way to make losing one's memory seem refreshingly funny." —*USA Today*

"Comfort food for the brain . . . A perfect pick for a spring-break read." —*Fort Worth Star-Telegram*

"Kinsella is a witty writer and the novel is consistently funny." —*Rocky Mountain News*

"A lively new novel . . . a breezy blend of romantic comedy and cautionary fairy tale . . . Kinsella is hilarious." —*New York Post*

THE UNDOMESTIC GODDESS

"Kinsella is at the top of the chick-lit game. . . . [She] skewers high-powered city life while delivering a romantic comedy anyone who subsists on takeout will appreciate. . . . Light yet filling." —*New York Post*

"*The Undomestic Goddess* is a fast, fun read that delves a little deeper." —Cleveland *Plain Dealer*

"A delightful, fluffy novel of great charm and wit. Take it along on your next trip for several diverting hours."
—*Contra Costa Times*

"Another charming winner from the delightful Kinsella."
—*Booklist*

"Kinsella has given her heroine enough charm to make you care enough to stick with her through her trials, intrigues and romances." —New York *Daily News*

CAN YOU KEEP A SECRET?

"Venturing beyond Saks and Barneys, the bestselling author of *Confessions of a Shopaholic* and *Shopaholic Ties the Knot* entertains readers with backstabbing office shenanigans, competition, scandal, love and sex. . . . Kinsella's down-to-earth protagonist is sure to have readers sympathizing and doubled over in laughter."
—*Publishers Weekly*

"Chick lit at its lightest and breeziest . . . filled with fabulous clothes, stalwart friends and snotty enemies waiting to be taken down a peg." —*Orlando Sentinel*

"[Kinsella's] dialogue is sharp, even her minor characters are well drawn, and her parody of the marketing world is very funny." —*The Washington Post Book World*

"[A] comedic frenzy of ill-fated events . . . punchy . . . fast-moving." —*Rocky Mountain News*

"Kinsella's witty take on mundane office and family life will really make you laugh out loud. . . . Move over, Bridget [Jones]!" —*Evening Chronicle* (UK)

"Hilarious." —*The Sun* (UK)

"Kinsella's light touch keeps this very funny look at life and relationships flying along and builds Emma into a genuinely endearing character. Romantic, but refreshingly witty." —*Sunday Mirror* (UK)

"Like a riotous gossip with your best friend—it'll have you laughing, cringing and hopelessly engrossed from the first page." —*Daily Record & Sunday Mail* (Scotland)

PRAISE FOR SOPHIE KINSELLA'S SHOPAHOLIC NOVELS

"A hilarious tale . . . hijinks worthy of classic *I Love Lucy* episodes . . . too good to pass up." —*USA Today*

"[Sophie Kinsella] gives chick-lit lovers a reason to stay home from the mall." —*Entertainment Weekly*

"Kinsella's Bloomwood is plucky and funny. . . . You won't have to shop around to find a more winning protagonist." —*People*

"Don't wait for a sale to buy this hilarious book." —*Us Weekly*

"Perfect for anyone wishing that bank statements came in more colours than just black and red." —*Mirror* (London)

"If a *crème brûlée* could be transmogrified into a book, it would be *Confessions of a Shopaholic*."—*The Star-Ledger*

"Kinsella's heroine is blessed with the resilience of ten women, and her damage-limitation brain waves are always good for a giggle."   —*Glamour* (UK)

"A have-your-cake-and-eat-it romp, done with brio and not a syllable of moralizing . . . Kinsella has a light touch and puckish humor."   —*Kirkus Reviews*

"For anyone with a love-hate relationship with their flexible friend."   —*Company* (UK)

"This book is an indulgence that's definitely worth every penny."   —*New Woman* (UK)

"Never has so much been bought by one woman as by shopaholic Rebecca."   —*Hello!* (UK)

ALSO BY SOPHIE KINSELLA

Sophie Kinsella

TWENTIES GIRL

a novel

DELL BOOKS
New York

Sale of this book without a front cover may be unauthorized.
If this book is coverless, it may have been reported to the publisher
as "unsold or destroyed" and neither the author nor the publisher
may have received payment for it.

Twenties Girl is a work of fiction. Names, characters, places,
and incidents either are the product of the author's imagination
or are used fictitiously. Any resemblance to actual persons,
living or dead, events, or locales is entirely coincidental.

2010 Dell Mass Market International Edition

Copyright © 2009 by Sophie Kinsella

All rights reserved.

Published in the United States by Dell,
an imprint of The Random House Publishing Group,
a division of Random House, Inc., New York.

DELL is a registered trademark of Random House, Inc.,
and the colophon is a trademark of Random House, Inc.

Originally published in hardcover in the United Kingdom
by Bantam Press, an imprint of Transworld Publishers,
a division of the Random House Group Limited, London,
and subsequently published in hardcover in the United States
by The Dial Press, an imprint of The Random House Publishing Group,
a division of Random House, Inc., in 2009.

ISBN: 978-0-440-29632-4

Cover design: Belina Huey
Cover illustration: Anne Keenan Higgins

Printed in the United States of America

www.bantamdell.com

4 6 8 9 7 5 3

To Susan Kamil,
who inspired me years ago with the remark:
"You should write a ghost story one day."

TWENTIES GIRL

ONE

The thing about lying to your parents is, you have to do it to *protect* them. It's for their own good. I mean, take my own parents. If they knew the unvarnished truth about my finances/love life/plumbing/council tax, they'd have instant heart attacks and the doctor would say, "Did anyone give them a terrible shock?" and it would all be my fault. Therefore, they have been in my flat for approximately ten minutes and already I have told them the following lies:

1. L&N Executive Recruitment will start making profits soon, I'm sure of it.
2. Natalie is a fantastic business partner, and it was a really brilliant idea to chuck in my job to become a headhunter with her.
3. Of course I don't just exist on pizza, black cherry yogurts, and vodka.
4. Yes, I did know about interest on parking tickets.
5. Yes, I did watch that Charles Dickens DVD they gave me for Christmas; it was great, especially that lady in the bonnet. Yes, Peggotty. That's who I meant.
6. I was actually *intending* to buy a smoke

alarm at the weekend, what a coincidence
they should mention it.
7. Yes, it'll be nice to see all the family again.

Seven lies. Not including all the ones about Mum's
outfit. And we haven't even mentioned The Subject.

As I come out of my bedroom in a black dress and
hastily applied mascara, I see Mum looking at my
overdue phone bill on the mantelpiece.

"Don't worry," I say quickly, "I'm going to sort that
out."

"Only, if you don't," says Mum, "they'll cut off
your line, and it'll take ages for you to get it installed
again, and the mobile signal is so patchy here. What if
there was an emergency? What would you do?" Her
brow is creased with anxiety. She looks as though this
is all totally imminent, as though there's a woman
screaming in labor in the bedroom and floods are rising outside the window and how will we contact the
helicopter? *How?*

"Er . . . I hadn't thought about it. Mum, I'll pay the
bill. Honest."

Mum's always been a worrier. She gets this tense
smile with distant, frightened eyes, and you just know
she's playing out some apocalyptic scenario in her head.
She looked like that throughout my last speech day at
school; afterward she confessed she'd suddenly noticed
a chandelier hanging above on a rickety chain and became obsessed by what would happen if it fell down on
the girls' heads and splintered into smithereens?

Now she tugs at her black suit, which has shoulder
pads and weird metal buttons and is swamping her. I
vaguely remember it from about ten years ago, when
she had a phase of going on job interviews and I had to

teach her all the really basic computer stuff like how to use a mouse. She ended up working for a children's charity, which doesn't have a formal dress code, thank goodness.

No one in my family looks good in black. Dad's wearing a suit made out of a dull black fabric which flattens all his features. He's actually quite handsome, my dad, in a kind of fine-boned, understated way. His hair is brown and wispy, whereas Mum's is fair and wispy like mine. They both look really great when they're relaxed and on their own territory—like, say, when we're all in Cornwall on Dad's rickety old boat, wearing fleeces and eating pasties. Or when Mum and Dad are playing in their local amateur orchestra, which is where they first met. But today, nobody's relaxed.

"So are you ready?" Mum glances at my stockinged feet. "Where are your shoes, darling?"

I slump down on the sofa. "Do I *have* to go?"

"Lara!" says Mum chidingly. "She was your great-aunt. She was one hundred and five, you know."

Mum has told me my great-aunt was 105 approximately 105 times. I'm pretty sure it's because that's the only fact she knows about her.

"So what? I didn't know her. None of us knew her. This is so stupid. Why are we schlepping to Potters Bar for some crumbly old woman we didn't even ever meet?" I hunch my shoulders up, feeling more like a sulky three-year-old than a mature twenty-seven-year-old with her own business.

"Uncle Bill and the others are going," says Dad. "And if they can make the effort . . ."

"It's a family occasion!" puts in Mum brightly.

My shoulders hunch even harder. I'm allergic to

family occasions. Sometimes I think we'd do better as dandelion seeds—no family, no history, just floating off into the world, each on our own piece of fluff.

"It won't take long," Mum says coaxingly.

"It will." I stare at the carpet. "And everyone will ask me about . . . things."

"No, they won't!" says Mum at once, glancing at Dad for backup. "No one will even mention . . . things."

There's silence. The Subject is hovering in the air. It's as though we're all avoiding looking at it. At last Dad plunges in.

"So! Speaking of . . . things." He hesitates. "Are you generally . . . OK?"

I can see Mum listening on super-high-alert, even though she's pretending to be concentrating on combing her hair.

"Oh, you know," I say after a pause. "I'm fine. I mean, you can't expect me just to snap back into—"

"No, of course not!" Dad immediately backs off. Then he tries again. "But you're . . . in good spirits?"

I nod assent.

"Good!" says Mum, looking relieved. "I knew you'd get over . . . things."

My parents don't say "Josh" out loud anymore, because of the way I used to dissolve into heaving sobs whenever I heard his name. For a while, Mum referred to him as "He Who Must Not Be Named." Now he's just "Things."

"And you haven't . . . been in touch with him?" Dad is looking anywhere but at me, and Mum appears engrossed in her handbag.

That's another euphemism. What he means is, "Have you sent him any more obsessive texts?"

"No," I say, flushing. "I haven't, OK?"

It's so unfair of him to bring that up. In fact, the whole thing was totally blown out of proportion. I only sent Josh a few texts. Three a day, if that. Hardly any. And they weren't obsessive. They were just me being honest and open, which, by the way, you're *supposed* to be in a relationship.

I mean, you can't just switch off your feelings because the other person did, can you? You can't just say, "Oh right! So your plan is, we never see each other again, never make love again, never talk or communicate in any way. Fab idea, Josh, why didn't I think of that?"

So what happens is, you write your true feelings down in a text simply because you want to share them, and next minute your ex-boyfriend changes his phone number and tells your parents. He's such a sneak.

"Lara, I know you were very hurt, and this has been a painful time for you." Dad clears his throat. "But it's been nearly two months now. You've got to move on, darling. See other young men . . . go out and enjoy yourself . . ."

Oh God, I can't face another of Dad's lectures about how plenty of men are going to fall at the feet of a beauty like me. I mean, for a start, there aren't any men in the world, everyone knows that. And a five-foot-three girl with a snubby nose and no suntan isn't exactly a beauty.

OK. I know I look all right sometimes. I have a heart-shaped face, wide-set green eyes, and a few freckles over my nose. And to top it off, I have this little bee-stung mouth which no one else in my family has. But take it from me, I'm no supermodel.

"So, is that what you did when you and Mum broke

up that time in Polzeath? Go out and see other people?" I can't help throwing it out, even though this is going over old ground. Dad sighs and exchanges glances with Mum.

"We should never have told her about that," she murmurs, rubbing her brow. "We should *never* have mentioned it—"

"Because if you'd done that," I continue inexorably, "you would never have got back together again, would you? Dad would never have said that he was the bow to your violin and you would never have got married."

This line about the bow and the violin has made it into family lore. I've heard the story a zillion times. Dad arrived at Mum's house, all sweaty because he'd been riding on his bike, and she'd been crying but she pretended she had a cold, and they made up their fight and Granny gave them tea and shortbread. (I don't know why the shortbread is relevant, but it always gets mentioned.)

"Lara, darling." Mum sighs. "That was very different; we'd been together three years, we were engaged—"

"I know!" I say defensively. "I know it was different. I'm just saying, people do sometimes get back together. It does *happen*."

There's silence.

"Lara, you've always been a romantic soul—" begins Dad.

"I'm not romantic!" I exclaim, as though this is a deadly insult. I'm staring at the carpet, rubbing the pile with my toe, but in my peripheral vision I can see Mum and Dad, each mouthing vigorously at the other to speak next. Mum's shaking her head and pointing at Dad as though to say, "You go!"

"When you break up with someone," Dad starts

again in an awkward rush, "it's easy to look backward and think life would be perfect if you got back together. But—"

He's going to tell me how life is an escalator. I have to head him off, quick.

"Dad. Listen. Please." Somehow I muster my calmest tones. "You've got it all wrong. I don't want to get back together with Josh." I try to sound as if this is a ridiculous idea. "That's not why I texted him. I just wanted *closure*. I mean, he broke things off with no warning, no talking, no discussion. I never got any answers. It's like . . . unfinished business. It's like reading an Agatha Christie and never knowing whodunnit!"

There. Now they'll understand.

"Well," says Dad at length, "I can understand your frustrations—"

"That's all I ever wanted," I say as convincingly as I can. "To understand what Josh was thinking. To talk things over. To communicate like two civilized human beings."

And to get back together with him, my mind adds, like a silent, truthful arrow. *Because I know Josh still loves me, even if no one else thinks so.*

But there's no point saying that to my parents. They'd never get it. How could they? They have no concept of how amazing Josh and I were as a couple, how we fit together perfectly. They don't understand how he obviously made a panicked, rushed, boy-type decision, based on some nonexistent reason probably, and how if I could just *talk* to him, I'm sure I could straighten everything out and we'd be together again.

Sometimes I feel streets ahead of my parents, just like Einstein must have done when his friends kept saying, "The universe is straight, Albert, take it from us," and inside he was secretly thinking, "I know it's curved. I'll show you one day."

Mum and Dad are surreptitiously mouthing at each other again. I should put them out of their misery.

"Anyway, you mustn't worry about me," I say hastily. "Because I have moved on. I mean, OK, maybe I haven't moved on *totally*," I amend as I see their dubious expressions, "but I've accepted that Josh doesn't want to talk. I've realized that it just wasn't meant to be. I've learned a lot about myself, and . . . I'm in a good place. Really."

My smile is pasted on my face. I feel like I'm chanting the mantra of some wacky cult. I should be wearing robes and banging a tambourine.

Hare hare . . . I've moved on . . . hare hare . . . I'm in a good place. . . .

Dad and Mum exchange looks. I have no idea whether they believe me, but at least I've given us all a way out of this sticky conversation.

"That's the spirit!" Dad says, looking relieved. "Well done, Lara, I knew you'd get there. And you've got the business with Natalie to focus on, which is obviously going tremendously well. . . ."

My smile becomes even more cultlike.

"Absolutely!"

Hare hare . . . my business is going well . . . hare hare . . . it's not a disaster at all. . . .

"I'm so glad you've come through this." Mum comes over and kisses the top of my head. "Now, we'd better get going. Find yourself some black shoes, chop chop!"

With a resentful sigh I get to my feet and drag myself into my bedroom. It's a beautiful sunshiny day. And I get to spend it at a hideous family occasion involving a dead 105-year-old person. Sometimes life really sucks.

As we pull up in the drab little car park of the Potters Bar Funeral Center, I notice a small crowd of people outside a side door. Then I see the glint of a TV camera and a fluffy microphone bobbing above people's heads.

"What's going on?" I peer out the car window. "Something to do with Uncle Bill?"

"Probably." Dad nods.

"I think someone's doing a documentary about him," Mum puts in. "Trudy mentioned it. For his book."

This is what happens when one of your relations is a celebrity. You get used to TV cameras being around. And people saying, when you introduce yourself, "Lington? Any relation to Lingtons Coffee, ha ha?" and them being gobsmacked when you say, "Yes."

My uncle Bill is *the* Bill Lington, who started Lingtons Coffee from nothing at the age of twenty-six and built it up into a worldwide empire of coffee shops. His face is printed on every single coffee cup, which makes him more famous than the Beatles or something. You'd recognize him if you saw him. And right now he's even more high profile than usual because his autobiography, *Two Little Coins,* came out last month and is a bestseller. Apparently Pierce Brosnan might play him in the movie.

Of course, I've read it from cover to cover. It's all about how he was down to his last twenty pence and bought a coffee and it tasted so terrible it gave him the idea to run coffee shops. So he opened one and started a chain, and now he pretty much owns the world. His nickname is "The Alchemist," and according to some article last year, the entire business world would like to know the secrets of his success.

That's why he started his Two Little Coins seminars. I secretly went to one a few months ago. Just in case I could get some tips on running a brand-new business. There were two hundred people there, all lapping up every word, and at the end we had to hold two coins up in the air and say, "This is my beginning." It was totally cheesy and embarrassing, but everyone around me seemed really inspired. Personally speaking, I was listening hard all the way through and I *still* don't know how he did it.

I mean, he was twenty-six when he made his first million. Twenty-six! He just started a business and became an instant success. Whereas I started a business six months ago and all I've become is an instant head case.

"Maybe you and Natalie will write a book about your business one day!" says Mum, as though she can read my mind.

"Global domination is just around the corner," chimes in Dad heartily.

"Look, a squirrel!" I point hastily out the window. My parents have been so supportive of my business, I *can't* tell them the truth. So I just change the subject whenever they mention it.

To be strictly accurate, you could say Mum wasn't *instantly* supportive. In fact, you could say that when I first announced I was giving up my marketing job and taking out all my savings to start a headhunting company, having never been a headhunter in my life or knowing anything about it, she went into total meltdown.

But she calmed down when I explained I was going into partnership with my best friend, Natalie. And that

Natalie was a top executive headhunter and would be fronting the business at first while I did the admin and marketing and learned the skills of headhunting myself. And that we already had several contracts lined up and would pay off the bank loan in no time.

It all sounded like such a brilliant plan. It *was* a brilliant plan. Until a month ago, when Natalie went on holiday, fell in love with a Goan beach bum, and texted me a week later to say she didn't know exactly when she'd be coming back, but the details of everything were in the computer and I'd be fine and the surf was fabulous out here, I should really visit, big kisses, Natalie xxxxx.

I am never going into business with Natalie again. Ever.

"Now, is this off?" Mum is jabbing uncertainly at her mobile phone. "I can't have it ringing during the service."

"Let's have a look." Dad pulls in to a parking space, turns off the engine, and takes it. "You want to put it on silent mode."

"No!" says Mum in alarm. "I want it off! The silent mode may malfunction!"

"Here we are, then." Dad presses the side button. "All off." He hands it back to Mum, who eyes it anxiously.

"But what if it somehow turns itself back on while it's in my bag?" She looks pleadingly at both of us. "That happened to Mary at the boat club, you know. The thing just *came alive* in her handbag and rang, while she was doing jury duty. They said she must have bumped it, or touched it somehow. . . ."

Her voice is rising and becoming breathless. This is where my sister, Tonya, would lose patience and snap,

"Don't be so stupid, Mum, of course your phone won't turn itself on!"

"Mum." I take it gently from her. "How about we leave it in the car?"

"Yes." She relaxes a little. "Yes, that's a good idea. I'll put it in the glove compartment."

I glance at Dad, who gives me a tiny smile. Poor Mum. All this ridiculous stuff going on in her head. She really needs to get things in proportion.

As we approach the funeral center, I hear Uncle Bill's distinctive drawl carrying on the air, and sure enough, as we make our way through the little crowd, there he is, with his leather jacket and permatan and springy hair. Everyone knows Uncle Bill is obsessed about his hair. It's thick and luxuriant and jet black, and if any newspaper ever suggests that he dyes it, he threatens to sue them.

"Family's the most important thing," he's saying to an interviewer in jeans. "Family is the rock we all stand on. If I have to interrupt my schedule for a funeral, then so be it." I can see the admiration pass through the crowd. One girl, who's holding a Lingtons takeaway cup, is clearly beside herself and keeps whispering to her friend, "It's really him!"

"If we could leave it there for now . . ." One of Uncle Bill's assistants approaches the cameraman. "Bill has to go into the funeral home. Thanks, guys. Just a few autographs . . ." he adds to the crowd.

We wait patiently at the side until everyone has got Uncle Bill to scribble on their coffee cups and funeral programs with a Sharpie, while the camera films them.

Then, at last, they melt away and Uncle Bill heads over our way.

"Hi, Michael. Good to see you." He shakes Dad's hand, then immediately turns back to an assistant. "Have you got Steve on the line yet?"

"Here." The assistant hastily hands Uncle Bill a phone.

"Hello, Bill!" Dad is always unfailingly polite to Uncle Bill. "It's been a while. How are you doing? Congratulations on your book."

"Thank you for the signed copy!" puts in Mum brightly.

Bill nods briefly at all of us, then says straight into the phone, "Steve, I got your email." Mum and Dad exchange glances. Obviously that's the end of our big family catch-up.

"Let's find out where we're supposed to be going," murmurs Mum to Dad. "Lara, are you coming?"

"Actually, I'll stay out here for a moment," I say on impulse. "See you inside!"

I wait until my parents have disappeared, then edge closer to Uncle Bill. I've suddenly hatched a demon plan. At his seminar, Uncle Bill said the key to success for any entrepreneur was grabbing every opportunity. Well, I'm an entrepreneur, aren't I? And this is an opportunity, isn't it?

When he seems to have finished his conversation, I say hesitantly, "Hi, Uncle Bill. Could I talk to you for a moment?"

"Wait." He lifts a hand and puts his BlackBerry to his ear. "Hi, Paulo. What's up?"

His eyes swivel to me and he beckons, which I guess is my cue to speak.

"Did you know I'm a headhunter now?" I give a nervous smile. "I've gone into partnership with a friend. We're called L&N Executive Recruitment. Could I tell you about our business?"

Uncle Bill frowns at me thoughtfully for a moment, then says, "Hold on, Paulo."

Oh wow! He's put his phone call on hold! For me!

"We specialize in finding highly qualified, motivated individuals for senior executive positions," I say, trying not to gabble. "I wondered if maybe I could talk with someone in your HR department, explain our services, maybe put a pitch together—"

"Lara." Uncle Bill lifts a hand to stop me. "What would you say if I put you in touch with my head of recruitment and told her: 'This is my niece, give her a chance'?"

I feel an explosion of delight. I want to sing "Hallelujah." My gamble paid off!

"I'd say thank you very much, Uncle Bill!" I manage, trying to stay calm. "I'd do the best job I could, I'd work 24/7, I'd be so grateful—"

"No," he interrupts. "You wouldn't. You wouldn't respect yourself."

"Wh-what?" I stop in confusion.

"I'm saying no." He shoots me a dazzling white smile. "I'm doing you a favor, Lara. If you make it on your own, you'll feel so much better. You'll feel you've *earned* it."

"Right." I swallow, my face burning with humiliation. "I mean, I *do* want to earn it. I *do* want to work hard. I just thought maybe . . ."

"If I can come from two little coins, Lara, so can you." He holds my gaze for a moment. "Believe in yourself. Believe in your dream. Here."

Oh no. Please no. He's reached in his pocket and is now holding out two ten-pence pieces to me.

"These are your two little coins." He gives me a deep, earnest look, the same way he does on the TV ad. "Lara, close your eyes. Feel it. Believe it. Say, 'This is my beginning.' "

"This is my beginning," I mumble, cringing all over. "Thanks."

Uncle Bill nods, then turns back to the phone. "Paulo. Sorry about that."

Hot with embarrassment, I edge away. So much for grabbing opportunities. So much for contacts. I just want to get through this stupid funeral and go home.

I head around the building and through the front glass doors of the funeral center to find myself in a foyer with upholstered chairs and posters of doves and a subdued air. There's no one about, not even at the reception desk.

Suddenly I hear singing coming from behind a pale wood door. Shit. It's started. I'm missing it. I hurriedly push the door open—and, sure enough, there are rows of benches filled with people. The room is so crowded that, as I edge in, the people standing at the back have to jostle to one side, and I find myself a space as unobtrusively as possible.

As I look around, trying to spot Mum and Dad, I'm overwhelmed by the sheer number of people here. And the flowers. All down the sides of the room there are gorgeous arrangements in shades of white and cream. A woman at the front is singing *Pie Jesu,* but there are so many people in front of me, I can't see. Near me, a couple of people are sniffing, and one girl has tears streaming openly down her face. I feel a bit chastened. All these people, here for my great-aunt, and I never even knew her.

I didn't even send any flowers, I realize in sudden mortification. Should I have written a card or something? God, I hope Mum and Dad sorted it all out.

The music is so lovely and the atmosphere is so emotional that suddenly I can't help it, I feel my eyes pricking too. Next to me is an old lady in a black velvet hat, who notices and clicks her tongue sympathetically.

"Do you have a handkerchief, dear?" she whispers.

"No," I admit, and she immediately snaps open her large, old-fashioned patent bag. A smell of camphor rises up, and inside I glimpse several pairs of spectacles, a box of mints, a packet of hairpins, a box labeled *String,* and half a packet of digestive biscuits.

"You should always bring a handkerchief to a funeral." She offers me a packet of tissues.

"Thanks," I gulp, taking one. "That's really kind. I'm the great-niece, by the way."

She nods sympathetically. "This must be a terrible time for you. How's the family coping?"

"Er . . . well . . ." I fold up the tissue, wondering how to answer. I can't exactly say "No one's that bothered; in fact, Uncle Bill's still on his BlackBerry outside."

"We all have to support each other at this time," I improvise at last.

"That's it." The old lady nods gravely as though I've said something really wise, as opposed to straight off a Hallmark card. "We all have to support each other." She clasps my hand. "I'd be glad to talk, dear, anytime you want to. It's an honor to meet any relative of Bert's."

"Thank you—" I begin automatically, then halt.
Bert?

I'm sure my aunt wasn't called Bert. In fact, I know she wasn't. She was called Sadie.

"You know, you look a lot like him." The woman's surveying my face.

Shit. I'm in the wrong funeral.

"Something about the forehead. And you have his nose. Did anyone ever tell you that, dear?"

"Um . . . sometimes!" I say wildly. "Actually, I've just got to . . . er . . . Thanks so much for the tissue. . . ." I hastily start making my way back toward the door.

"It's Bert's great-niece." I can hear the old lady's voice following me. "She's very upset, poor thing."

I practically throw myself at the pale wooden door and find myself in the foyer again, almost landing on Mum and Dad. They're standing with a woman with woolly gray hair, a dark suit, and a stack of leaflets in her hand.

"Lara! Where were you?" Mum looks in puzzlement at the door. "What were you doing in there?"

"Were you in Mr. Cox's funeral?" The gray-haired woman looks taken aback.

"I got lost!" I say defensively. "I didn't know where to go! You should put signs on the doors!"

Silently, the woman raises her hand and points at a plastic-lettered sign above the door: BERTRAM COX— 1:30 p.m. Damn. Why didn't I notice that?

"Well, anyway." I try to regain my dignity. "Let's go. We need to bag a seat."

TWO

Bag a seat. What a joke. I've never been at anything as depressing as this, my whole entire life.

OK, I know it's a funeral. It's not supposed to be a riot. But at least Bert's funeral had lots of people and flowers and music and atmosphere. At least that other room *felt* like something.

This room has nothing. It's bare and chilly, with just a closed coffin at the front and SADIE LANCASTER in crappy plastic letters on a notice board. No flowers, no lovely smell, no singing, just some Muzak piped out of speakers. And the place is practically empty. Just Mum, Dad, and me on one side; Uncle Bill, Aunt Trudy, and my cousin Diamanté on the other.

I surreptitiously run my gaze over the other side of the family. Even though we're related, they still seem like a celebrity magazine come to life. Uncle Bill is sprawled on his plastic chair as though he owns the place, typing at his BlackBerry. Aunt Trudy is flicking through *Hello!*, probably reading about all her friends. She's wearing a tight black dress, her blond hair is artfully swept around her face, and her cleavage is even more tanned and impressive than last time I saw her. Aunt Trudy married Uncle Bill twenty years ago, and I swear she looks younger today than she does in her wedding pictures.

Diamanté's platinum-blond hair sweeps down to her bum, and she's wearing a minidress covered with a skull print. Really tasteful for a funeral. She has her iPod plugged in and is texting on her mobile and keeps looking at her watch with a sulky scowl. Diamanté is seventeen and has two cars and her own fashion label called Tutus and Pearls, which Uncle Bill set up for her. (I looked at it online once. The dresses all cost four hundred pounds, and everyone who buys one gets their name on a special "Diamanté's Best Friends" list, and half of them are celebs' kids. It's like Facebook, but with dresses.)

"Hey, Mum," I say. "How come there aren't any flowers?"

"Oh." Mum immediately looks anxious. "I spoke to Trudy about flowers, and she said she would do it. Trudy?" she calls over. "What happened about the flowers?"

"Well!" Trudy closes *Hello!* and swivels around as though she's quite up for a chat. "I know we discussed it. But do you know the price of all this?" She gestures around. "And we're sitting here for, what, twenty minutes? You've got to be realistic, Pippa. Flowers would be a waste."

"I suppose so," Mum says hesitantly.

"I mean, I don't begrudge the old lady a funeral." Aunt Trudy leans toward us, lowering her voice. "But you have to ask yourself, 'What did she ever do for us?' I mean, I didn't know her. Did you?"

"Well, it was difficult." Mum looks pained. "She'd had the stroke, she was bewildered a lot of the time—"

"Exactly!" Trudy nods. "She didn't understand anything. What was the point? It's only because of Bill that we're here." Trudy glances at Uncle Bill fondly.

"He's too softhearted for his own good. I often say to people—"

"Crap!" Diamanté rips out her earphones and looks at her mother scornfully. "We're only here for Dad's show. He wasn't planning to come 'til the producer said a funeral would 'massively up his sympathy quotient.' I heard them talking."

"Diamanté!" exclaims Aunt Trudy crossly.

"It's true! He's the biggest hypocrite on earth and so are you. And I'm supposed to be at Hannah's house right now." Diamanté's cheeks puff out resentfully. "Her dad's, like, having this big party for his new movie and I'm missing it. Just so Dad can look all 'family' and 'caring.' It's so unfair."

"Diamanté!" says Trudy tartly. "It's your father who paid for you and Hannah to go to Barbados, remember? And that boob job you keep talking about—who's paying for that, do you think?"

Diamanté draws in breath as though mortally offended. "That is so unfair. My boob job's for *charity*."

I can't help leaning forward with interest. "How can a boob job be for charity?"

"I'm going to do a magazine interview about it afterward and give the proceeds to charity," she says proudly. "Like, half the proceeds or something?"

I glance at Mum. She looks so speechless with shock, I almost burst into giggles.

"Hello?"

We all look up to see a woman in gray trousers and a clerical collar, heading up the aisle toward us.

"Many apologies," she says, spreading her hands. "I hope you haven't been waiting too long." She has cropped salt-and-pepper hair, dark-rimmed glasses, and a deep, almost masculine voice. "My condolences on your loss." She glances at the bare coffin. "I don't know if you were informed, but it's normal to put up photographs of your loved one. . . ."

We all exchange blank, awkward looks. Then Aunt Trudy gives a sudden click of the tongue.

"I've got a photo. The nursing home sent it on."

She rummages in her bag and produces a brown envelope, out of which she draws a battered-looking Polaroid. As she passes it over, I take a look. It shows a tiny, wrinkled old lady hunched over in a chair, wearing a shapeless pale-mauve cardigan. Her face is folded over in a million lines. Her white hair is a translucent puff of candy floss. Her eyes are opaque, as though she can't even see the world.

So that was my great-aunt Sadie. And I never even met her.

The vicar looks at the print dubiously, then pins it onto a big notice board, where it looks totally sad and embarrassing all on its own.

"Would any of you like to speak about the deceased?"

Mutely, we all shake our heads.

"I understand. It can often be too painful for close family." The vicar produces a notebook and pencil from her pocket. "In which case I'll be glad to speak on your behalf. If you could perhaps just give me some details. Incidents from her life. Tell me everything about Sadie that we should be celebrating."

There's silence.

"We didn't really know her," Dad says apologetically. "She was very old."

"One hundred and five," Mum puts in. "She was one hundred and five."

"Was she ever married?" the vicar prompts.

"Er . . ." Dad's brow is wrinkled. "Was there a husband, Bill?"

"Dunno. Yeah, I think there was. Don't know what he was called, though." Uncle Bill hasn't even looked from his BlackBerry. "Can we get on with this?"

"Of course." The vicar's sympathetic smile has frozen. "Well, perhaps just some small anecdote from the last time you visited her . . . some hobby . . ."

There's another guilty silence.

"She's wearing a cardigan in the picture," ventures Mum at last. "Maybe she knitted it. Maybe she liked knitting."

"Did you never visit her?" The vicar is clearly forcing herself to stay polite.

"Of course we did!" says Mum defensively. "We popped in to see her in . . ." She thinks. "In 1982, I think it was. Lara was a baby."

"*1982?*" The vicar looks scandalized.

"She didn't know us," puts in Dad quickly. "She really wasn't all there."

"What about from earlier in her life?" The vicar's voice sounds slightly outraged. "No achievements? Stories from her youth?"

"Jeez, you don't give up, do you?" Diamanté rips her iPod speakers out of her ears. "Can't you tell we're only here because we have to be? She didn't do anything special. She didn't achieve anything. She was nobody! Just some million-year-old nobody."

"Diamanté!" says Aunt Trudy in mild reproof. "That's not very nice."

"It's true, though, isn't it? I mean, look!" She gestures scornfully around the empty room. "If only six people came to my funeral, I'd *shoot* myself."

"Young lady." The vicar takes a few steps forward,

her face flushing with anger. "No human on God's earth is a *nobody*."

"Yeah, whatever," says Diamanté rudely, and I can see the vicar opening her mouth to make another retort.

"Diamanté." Uncle Bill lifts a hand quickly. "Enough. Obviously I myself regret not visiting Sadie, who I'm sure was a very special person, and I'm sure I speak for all of us." He's so charming, I can see the vicar's ruffled feathers being smoothed. "But now what we'd like to do is send her off with dignity. I expect you have a tight schedule, as do we." He taps his watch.

"Indeed," says the vicar after a pause. "I'll just prepare. In the meantime, please switch off your mobile phones." With a last disapproving look around at us all, she heads out again, and Aunt Trudy immediately turns in her seat.

"What a nerve, giving us a guilt trip! We don't *have* to be here, you know."

The door opens and we all look up—but it's not the vicar, it's Tonya. I didn't know she was coming. This day just got about a hundred percent worse.

"Have I missed it?" Her pneumatic drill of a voice fills the room as she strides down the aisle. "I just managed to scoot away from Toddler Gym before the twins had a meltdown. Honestly, this au pair is worse than the last one, and that's saying something. . . ."

She's wearing black trousers and a black cardigan trimmed with leopard print, her thick highlighted hair pulled back in a ponytail. Tonya used to be an office manager at Shell and boss people around all day. Now she's a full-time mum of twin boys, Lorcan and Declan, and bosses her poor au pairs around instead.

"How are the boys?" asks Mum, but Tonya doesn't notice. She's totally focused on Uncle Bill.

"Uncle Bill, I read your book! It was amazing! It changed my life. I've told *everyone* about it. And the photo is wonderful, although it doesn't do you justice."

"Thanks, sweetheart." Bill shoots her his standard yes-I-know-I'm-brilliant smile, but she doesn't seem to notice.

"Isn't it a fantastic book?" She appeals around to the rest of us. "Isn't Uncle Bill a genius? To start with absolutely nothing! Just two coins and a big dream! It's so inspiring for humanity!"

She's such a suck-up, I want to hurl. Mum and Dad obviously feel the same way, as neither of them answers. Uncle Bill isn't paying her any attention either. Reluctantly, she swivels around on her heel.

"How are you, Lara? I've hardly seen you lately! You've been hiding!" Her eyes start focusing in on me with intent as she comes nearer and I shrink away. Uh-oh. I know that look.

My sister, Tonya, basically has three facial expressions:

1) Totally blank and bovine.

2) Loud, showy-offy laughter, as in "Uncle Bill, you kill me!"

3) Gloating delight masked as sympathy as she picks away at someone else's misery. She's addicted to the Real Life channel and books with tragic, scruffy kids on the cover, called things like *Please, Grammy, Don't Hit Me with the Mangle.*

"I haven't seen you since you split up with Josh. What a shame. You two seemed so perfect together!" Tonya tilts her head sorrowfully. "Didn't they seem perfect together, Mum?"

"Well, it didn't work out." I try to sound matter-of-fact. "So anyway . . ."

"What went wrong?" She gives me that doe-eyed, fake-concerned look she gets when something bad happens to another person and she's really, *really* enjoying it.

"These things happen." I shrug.

"But they don't, though, do they? There's always a reason." Tonya is relentless. "Didn't he say anything?"

"Tonya," Dad puts in gently. "Is this the best time?"

"Dad, I'm just *supporting* Lara," Tonya says, in affront. "It's always best to talk these things through! So, was there someone else?" Her eyes swivel back to me.

"I don't think so."

"Were you getting on OK?"

"Yes."

"Then why?" She folds her arms, looking baffled and almost accusing. "Why?"

I don't know why! I want to scream. *Don't you think I've asked myself that question a bazillion times?*

"It was just one of those things!" I force a smile. "I'm fine about it. I've realized that it wasn't meant to be, and I've moved on and I'm in a good place. I'm really happy."

"You don't look happy," Diamanté observes from across the aisle. "Does she, Mum?"

Aunt Trudy surveys me for a few moments.

"No," she says at last, in definitive tones. "She doesn't look happy."

"Well, I am!" I can feel tears stinging my eyes. "I'm just hiding it! I'm really, really, really happy!"

God, I hate all my relatives.

"Tonya, darling, sit down," Mum says tactfully. "How did the school visit go?"

Blinking hard, I get out my phone and pretend to be checking my messages so no one bothers me. Then, before I can stop it, my finger scrolls down to photos.

Don't look, I tell myself firmly. *Do* not *look.*

But my fingers won't obey me. It's an overwhelming compulsion. I have to have one quick look, just to keep me going . . . my fingers are scrabbling as I summon up my favorite picture. Josh and me. Standing together on a mountain slope, arms around each other, both with ski tans. Josh's fair hair is curling over the goggles thrust up on his head. He's smiling at me with that perfect dimple in his cheek, that dimple I used to push my finger into, like a toddler with Play-Doh.

We first met at a Guy Fawkes party, standing around a fire in a garden in Clapham that belonged to a girl I knew at university. Josh was handing out sparklers to everyone. He lit one for me and asked me what my name was and wrote *Lara* in the darkness with his sparkler, and I laughed and asked his name. We wrote each other's names in the air until the sparklers went dead, then edged closer to the fire and sipped mulled wine and reminisced about fireworks parties of our childhoods. Everything we said chimed. We laughed at the same things. I'd never met anyone so easygoing. Or with such a cute smile. I can't imagine him being with anyone else. I just can't . . .

"All right, Lara?" Dad is glancing over at me.

"Yes!" I say brightly, and jab off the phone before he can see the screen. As organ Muzak begins, I sink back in my chair, consumed with misery. I should never have come today. I should have made up an excuse. I hate my family and I hate funerals and there isn't even any good coffee and—

"Where's my necklace?" A girl's distant voice interrupts my thoughts.

I glance around to see who it is, but there's no one behind me. Who was that?

"Where's my *necklace*?" the faint voice comes again. It's high and imperious and quite posh-sounding. Is it coming from the phone? Didn't I turn it off properly? I pull my phone out of my bag—but the screen is dead.

Weird.

"Where's my *necklace*?" Now the voice sounds as though it's right in my ear. I flinch and look all around in bewilderment.

What's even weirder is, no one else seems to have noticed.

"Mum." I lean over. "Did you hear something just now? Like . . . a voice?"

"A voice?" Mum looks puzzled. "No, darling. What kind of voice?"

"It was a girl's voice, just a moment ago . . ." I stop as I see a familiar look of anxiety coming over Mum's face. I can almost see her thoughts, in a bubble: *Dear God, my daughter's hearing voices in her head.*

"I must have misheard," I say hastily, and thrust my phone away, just as the vicar appears.

"Please rise," she intones. "And let us all bow our heads. Dear Lord, we commend to you the soul of our sister, Sadie. . . ."

I'm not being prejudiced, but this vicar has the most monotonous voice in the existence of mankind. We're five minutes in and I've already given up trying to pay attention. It's like school assembly; your mind just goes numb. I lean back and stare up at the ceiling and tune out. I'm just letting my eyelids close when I hear the voice again, right in my ear.

"Where's my necklace?"

That made me jump. I swivel my head around from side to side—but, again, there's nothing. What's wrong with me?

"Lara!" Mum whispers in alarm. "Are you OK?"

"I've just got a bit of a headache," I hiss back. "I might go and sit by the window. Get some air."

Gesturing apologetically, I get up and head to a chair near the back of the room. The vicar barely notices; she's too engrossed in her speech.

"The end of life is the beginning of life . . . for as we came from earth, so we return to earth. . . ."

"Where's my *necklace*? I *need* it."

Sharply, I turn my head from side to side, hoping to catch the voice this time. And then suddenly I see it. A hand.

A slim, manicured hand, resting on the chair back in front of me.

I move my eyes along, incredulously. The hand belongs to a long, pale, sinuous arm. Which belongs to a girl about my age. Who's lounging on a chair in front of me, her fingers drumming impatiently. She has dark bobbed hair and a silky sleeveless pale-green dress, and I can just glimpse a pale, jutting chin.

I'm too astonished to do anything except gape.

Who the hell is that?

As I watch, she swings herself off her chair as though she can't bear to sit still and starts to pace up and down. Her dress falls straight to the knee, with little pleats at the bottom, which swish about as she walks.

"I need it," she's muttering in agitation. "Where is it? Where *is* it?"

Her voice has a clipped, pinched accent, just like in old-fashioned black-and-white films. I glance wildly

over at the rest of my family—but no one else has noticed her. No one has even heard her voice. Everyone
else is sitting quietly.

Suddenly, as though she senses my gaze on her, the
girl wheels around and fixes her eyes on mine. They're
so dark and glittering, I can't tell what color they are,
but they widen incredulously as I stare back.

OK. I'm starting to panic here. I'm having a hallucination. A full-on, walking, talking hallucination. And
it's coming toward me.

"You can see me." She points a white finger at me,
and I shrink back in my seat. "You can see me!"

I shake my head quickly. "I can't."

"And you can hear me!"

"No, I can't."

I'm aware of Mum at the front of the room, turning
to frown at me. Quickly, I cough and gesture at my
chest. When I turn back, the girl has gone. Vanished.

Thank God for that. I thought I was going crazy. I
mean, I know I've been stressed out recently, but to
have an actual *vision*—

"Who are you?" I nearly jump out of my skin as the
girl's voice punctuates my thoughts again. Now suddenly she's striding down the aisle toward me.

"Who are you?" she demands. "Where is this? Who
are these people?"

Do not reply to the hallucination, I tell myself
firmly. *It'll only encourage it.* I swivel my head away,
and try to pay attention to the vicar.

"Who are you?" The girl has suddenly appeared
right in front of me. "Are you real?" She raises a hand
as though to prod my shoulder, and I cringe away, but
her hand swishes straight through me and comes out
the other side.

I gasp in shock. The girl stares in bewilderment at her hand, then at me.

"What are you?" she demands. "Are you a dream?"

"Me?" I can't help retorting in an indignant undertone. "Of course I'm not a dream! You're the dream!"

"I'm not a dream!" She sounds equally indignant.

"Who are you, then?" I can't help shooting back.

Immediately I regret it, as Mum and Dad both glance back at me. If I told them I was talking to a hallucination, they'd flip. I'd be incarcerated in the Priory tomorrow.

The girl juts her chin out. "I'm Sadie. Sadie Lancaster."

Sadie . . . ?

No. No *way*.

I can't quite move. My eyes are flicking madly from the girl in front of me . . . to the wizened, candy-floss-haired old woman in the Polaroid . . . and then back again to the girl. I'm hallucinating my dead 105-year-old great-aunt?

The hallucination girl looks fairly freaked out too. She turns and starts looking around the room as though taking it in for the first time. For a dizzying few seconds, she appears and reappears all over the room, examining every corner, every window, like an insect buzzing around a glass tank.

I've never had an imaginary friend. I've never taken drugs. What is *up* with me? I tell myself to ignore the girl, to blank her out, to pay attention to the vicar. But it's no good; I can't help following her progress.

"What is this place?" She's hovering by me now, her eyes narrowing in suspicion. She's focusing on the coffin at the front. "What's that?"

Oh God.

"That's . . . nothing," I say hastily. "Nothing at all! It's just . . . I mean . . . I wouldn't look too closely if I were you. . . ."

Too late. She's appeared at the coffin, staring down at it. I can see her reading the name SADIE LANCASTER on the plastic notice board. I can see her face jolt in shock. After a few moments she turns toward the vicar, who is still droning on in her monotone:

"Sadie found contentment in marriage, which can be an inspiration to us all. . . ."

The girl puts her face right up close to the vicar's and regards her with disdain.

"You *fool*," she says scathingly.

"She was a woman who lived to a great age," the vicar carries on, totally oblivious. "I look at this picture"—she gestures at the photo with an understanding smile—"and I see a woman who, despite her infirmity, led a beautiful life. Who found solace in small things. Knitting, for example."

"*Knitting?*" the girl echoes incredulously.

"So." The vicar has obviously finished her speech. "Let us all bow our heads for a final moment of silence before we say farewell." She steps down from the podium, and some organ Muzak begins.

"What happens now?" The girl looks around, suddenly alert. A moment later she's by my side. "What happens now? Tell me! Tell me!"

"Well, the coffin goes behind that curtain," I murmur in an undertone. "And then . . . er . . ." I trail off, consumed by embarrassment. How do I put it tactfully? "We're at a crematorium, you see. So that would mean . . ." I wheel my hands vaguely.

The girl's face blanches with shock, and I watch in discomfiture as she starts fading to a weird, pale, translucent state. It almost seems as if she's fainting—but even more so. For a moment I can almost see right through her. Then, as though making some inner resolution, she comes back.

"No." She shakes her head. "That can't happen. I need my necklace. I need it."

"Sorry," I say helplessly. "Nothing I can do."

"You have to stop the funeral." She suddenly looks up, her eyes dark and glittering.

"What?" I stare at her. "I can't!"

"You can! Tell them to stop!" As I turn away, trying to tune her out, she appears at my other side. "Stand up! Say something!"

Her voice is as insistent and piercing as a toddler's. I'm frantically ducking my head in all directions, trying to avoid her.

"Stop the funeral! *Stop it!* I must have my necklace!" She's an inch away from my face; her fists are banging on my chest. I can't feel them, but I still flinch. In desperation, I get to my feet and move back a row, knocking over a chair with a clatter.

"Lara, are you all right?" Mum looks back in alarm.

"Fine," I manage, trying to ignore the yelling in my ear as I sink down into another seat.

"I'll order the car," Uncle Bill is saying to Aunt Trudy. "This should be over in five."

"Stop it! Stop-it-stop-it-stop-it!" The girl's voice rises to the most penetrating shriek, like feedback in my ear. I'm going schizophrenic. Now I know why people assassinate presidents. There's no way I can ignore her. She's like a banshee. I can't stand this any longer. I'm clutching my head, trying to block her out, but it's no good. "Stop! Stop! You have to stop—"

"OK! OK! Just . . . shut up!" In desperation, I get to my feet. "Wait!" I shout. "Stop, everybody! You have to stop the funeral! STOP THE FUNERAL!"

To my relief, the girl stops shrieking.

On the downside, my entire family has turned to gape at me as if I'm a lunatic. The vicar presses a button in a wooden panel set in the wall, and the organ Muzak abruptly stops.

"Stop the *funeral*?" says Mum at last.

I nod silently. I don't feel quite in control of my faculties, to be honest.

"But why?"

"I . . . um . . ." I clear my throat. "I don't think it's the right time. For her to go."

"Lara." Dad sighs. "I know you're under strain at the moment, but really . . ." He turns to the vicar. "I do apologize. My daughter hasn't been quite herself lately. *Boyfriend trouble,*" he mouths.

"This is nothing to do with that!" I protest indignantly, but everyone ignores me.

"Ah. I understand." The vicar nods sympathetically. "Lara, we'll finish the funeral now," she says, as though I'm a three-year-old. "And then perhaps you and I will have a cup of tea together and a little talk, how about that?"

She presses the button again and the organ Muzak resumes. A moment later, the coffin starts moving creakily away on its plinth, disappearing behind the curtain. Behind me I hear a sharp gasp, then—

"Noooo!" comes a howl of anguish. "Nooo! Stop! You have to stop!"

To my horror, the girl runs up onto the plinth and starts trying to push the coffin back. But her arms don't work; they keep sinking through.

"Please!" She looks up and addresses me desperately. "Don't let them!"

I'm starting to feel a genuine panic here. I don't know why I'm hallucinating this or what it means. But it feels real. Her torment looks real. I can't just sit back and witness this.

"No!" I shout. "Stop!"

"Lara—" Mum begins.

"I mean it! There's a just cause and impediment why this coffin cannot be . . . fried. You have to stop! Now!" I hurry down the aisle. "Press that button or I'll do it myself!"

Looking flustered, the vicar presses the button again, and the coffin comes to a standstill.

"Dear, perhaps you should wait outside."

"She's showing off, as usual!" says Tonya impatiently. " 'Just cause and impediment.' I mean, how on earth could there be? Just get on with it!" she bossily addresses the vicar, who bristles slightly.

"Lara." She ignores Tonya and turns to me. "Do you have a reason for wanting to stop your great-aunt's funeral?"

"Yes!"

"And that is . . ." She pauses questioningly.

Oh God. What am I supposed to say? Because a hallucination told me to?

"It's because . . . er . . ."

"Say I was murdered!" I look up in shock, to see the girl right in front of me. "Say it! Then they'll have to put off the funeral. Say it!" She's beside me, shouting in my ear again. "Say it! Say-it-say-it-say-it—"

"I think my aunt was murdered!" I blurt out in desperation.

I have seen my family looking at me, gobsmacked,

on a number of occasions in my time. But nothing has ever provoked a reaction like this. They're all turned in their seats, their jaws hanging in incomprehension like some kind of still-life painting. I almost want to laugh.

"*Murdered?*" says the vicar at last.

"Yes," I say forthrightly. "I have reason to believe there was foul play. So we need to keep the body for evidence."

Slowly, the vicar walks toward me, narrowing her eyes, as though trying to gauge exactly how much of a time-waster I am. What she doesn't know is, I used to play staring matches with Tonya, and I always won. I gaze back, perfectly matching her grave, this-is-no-laughing-matter expression.

"Murdered . . . how?" she says.

"I'd rather discuss that with the authorities," I shoot back, as though I'm in an episode of *CSI: Funeral Home*.

"You want me to call the police?" She's looking genuinely shocked now.

Oh *God*. Of course I don't want her to call the bloody police. But I can't backtrack now. I have to act convincing.

"Yes," I say after a pause. "Yes, I think that would be best."

"You can't be taking her seriously!" Tonya explodes. "It's obvious she's just trying to cause a sensation!"

I can tell the vicar is getting a bit pissed off with Tonya, which is quite useful for me.

"My dear," she says curtly, "that decision does not rest with you. Any accusation like this has to be followed up. And your sister is quite right. The body would have to be preserved for forensics."

I think the vicar's getting into this. She probably watches TV murder mysteries every Sunday evening. Sure enough, she comes even farther toward me and says in a low voice, "Who do you think murdered your great-aunt?"

"I'd rather not comment at this time," I say darkly. "It's complicated." I shoot a significant look at Tonya. "If you know what I mean."

"What?" Tonya's face starts turning pink with outrage. "You're not accusing *me*."

"I'm not saying anything." I adopt an inscrutable air. "Except to the police."

"This is bullshit. Are we finishing this or not?" Uncle Bill puts his BlackBerry away. "Because, either way, my car's here and we've given this old lady enough time already."

"More than enough!" chimes in Aunt Trudy. "Come on, Diamanté, this is a farce!" With cross, impatient gestures, she begins to gather up her celebrity magazines.

"Lara, I don't know what the hell you're playing at." Uncle Bill scowls at Dad as he passes. "She needs help, your daughter. Bloody lunatic."

"Lara, darling." Mum gets out of her seat and comes over, her brow crinkled in worry. "You didn't even know your great-aunt Sadie."

"Maybe I didn't, maybe I did." I fold my arms. "There's a lot I don't tell you."

I'm almost starting to believe in this murder.

The vicar is looking flustered now, as though this is all getting out of her league. "I think I'd better call the police. Lara, if you wait here, I think everyone else should probably leave."

"Lara." Dad comes over and takes my arm. "Darling."

"Dad . . . just go." I muster a noble, misunderstood air. "I have to do what I have to do. I'll be fine."

Shooting me various looks of alarm, outrage, and pity, my family slowly files out of the room, followed by the vicar.

I'm left alone in the silent room. And it's as if the spell has suddenly broken.

What the bloody hell did I just do?

Am I going mad?

Actually, it would explain a lot. Maybe I should just get admitted to some nice, peaceful mental home where you do drawing in a jumpsuit and don't have to think about your failing business or ex-boyfriend or parking tickets.

I sink into a chair and exhale. At the front of the room, the hallucination girl has appeared in front of the notice board, staring at the photo of the little hunched old woman.

"So, *were* you murdered?" I can't help saying.

"Oh, I shouldn't think so." She's barely acknowledged me, let alone said thank you. Trust me to have a vision with no manners.

"Well, you're welcome," I say moodily. "You know. Anytime."

The girl doesn't even seem to hear. She's peering around the room as if she doesn't understand something.

"Where are all the flowers? If this is my funeral, where are the flowers?"

"Oh!" I feel a squeeze of guilt. "The flowers were . . . put somewhere else by mistake. There were lots, honestly. Really gorgeous."

She's not real, I tell myself fervently. This is just my own guilty conscience speaking.

"And what about the people?" She sounds perplexed. "Where were all the people?"

"Some of them couldn't come." I cross my fingers behind my back, hoping I sound convincing. "Loads wanted to, though—"

I stop as she disappears into thin air, right as I'm talking to her.

"Where's my *necklace*?" I jump in fright as her voice comes urgently in my ear again.

"I don't know where your bloody necklace is!" I exclaim. "Stop bugging me! You realize I'll never live this down? And you haven't even said thank you!"

There's silence and she tilts her face away, like a caught-out child.

"Thank you," she says at last.

"'s OK."

The hallucination girl is fidgeting with a metal snake bracelet entwined around her wrist, and I find myself eyeing her more closely. Her hair is dark and shiny, and the tips frame her face as she tilts her head forward. She has a long white neck, and now I can see that her huge, luminous eyes are green. Her cream leather shoes are tiny, size 4 maybe, with little buttons and Cuban heels. I'd say she's about my age. Maybe even younger.

"Uncle Bill," she says at last, twisting the bracelet around and around. "William. One of Virginia's boys."

"Yes. Virginia was my grandmother. My dad is Michael. Which makes you my great-aunt—" I break off and clutch my head. "This is crazy. How do I even know what you *look* like? How can I be hallucinating you?"

"You're not hallucinating me!" She jerks her chin up, looking offended. "I'm real!"

"You can't be real," I say impatiently. "You're dead! So what are you, then—a *ghost*?"

There's a weird beat of silence. Then the girl looks away.

"I don't believe in ghosts," she says disparagingly.

"Nor do I." I match her tone. "No way."

The door opens and I start in shock.

"Lara." The vicar comes in, her face pink and flustered. "I've spoken to the police. They'd like you to come down to the station."

THREE

$\mathcal{I}$t turns out they take murder quite seriously at police stations. Which I suppose I should have guessed. They've put me in a little room with a table and plastic chairs and posters about locking your car. They've given me a cup of tea and a form to fill in, and a policewoman told me a detective would be along in a moment to talk to me.

I want to laugh hysterically. Or climb out the window.

"What am I going to say to a detective?" I exclaim, as soon as the door has closed. "I don't know anything about you! How am I going to say you were murdered? With the candlestick in the drawing room?"

Sadie doesn't even seem to have heard me. She's sitting on the window ledge, swinging her legs. Although when I look more closely, I notice that she's not actually *on* the ledge, she's floating about an inch above it. Following my gaze, she sees the gap and flinches with annoyance. She adjusts her position carefully until she looks as though she's sitting right on the ledge, then insouciantly starts swinging her legs again.

She's all in my mind, I tell myself firmly. Let's be rational here. If my own brain has conjured her up, then my own brain can get rid of her.

Go away, I think as strongly as I can, holding my

breath and clenching my fists. *Go away, go away, go away*—

Sadie glances over at me and gives a sudden giggle.

"You *do* look peculiar," she says. "Do you have a pain in your stomach?"

I'm about to make a retort when the door opens— and my stomach really does twinge. It's a detective, wearing plainclothes, which makes it almost more scary than if he was in uniform. Oh God. I am in such trouble.

"Lara." The detective holds out his hand. He's tall and broad, with dark hair and a brisk manner. "DI James."

"Hi." My voice is squeaky with nerves. "Nice to meet you."

"So." He sits down in a businesslike way and takes out a pen. "I understand you stopped your great-aunt's funeral."

"That's right." I nod with as much conviction as I can muster. "I just think there was something suspicious about her death."

DI James makes a note, then looks up. "Why?"

I stare blankly back at him, my heart pounding. I have no answer. I should have made something up, very quickly. I'm an *idiot*.

"Well . . . don't *you* think it suspicious?" I improvise at last. "Her just *dying* like that? I mean, people don't just die out of the blue!"

DI James regards me with an unreadable expression. "I believe she was one hundred and five years old."

"So what?" I retort, gaining confidence. "Can't people of a hundred and five be murdered too? I didn't think the police were so *ageist*."

DI James's face flickers, whether with amusement or annoyance I can't tell.

"Who do you think murdered your great-aunt?" he says.

"It was . . ." I rub my nose, playing for time. "It's . . . rather . . . complicated . . ." I glance helplessly up at Sadie.

"You're useless!" she cries. "You need a story or they won't believe you! They won't delay the funeral any longer! Say it was the staff at the nursing home! Say you heard them plotting."

"No!" I exclaim in shock before I can help myself.

DI James gives me an odd look and clears his throat.

"Lara, do you have a genuine reason for believing something was amiss with your great-aunt's death?"

"Say it was the staff at the nursing home!" Sadie's voice is in my ear like a screeching brake. "Say it! *Say it!* SAY IT!"

"It was the staff at the nursing home," I blurt out in desperation. "I think."

"What grounds do you have for saying this?"

DI James's tone is even, but his eyes are alert. In front of him, Sadie is hovering, glowering at me and wheeling her hands around, as though to crank the words out of me. The sight is totally freaking me out.

"I . . . er . . . I overheard them whispering in the pub. Something about poison and insurance. I thought nothing of it at the time." I swallow feebly. "But the next moment, my great-aunt's dead."

I've lifted this entire plot from a daytime soap opera that I watched last month when I was off sick, I abruptly realize.

DI James gives me a penetrating look. "You would testify to this."

Oh God. *Testify* is one of those very scary words, like *tax inspector* and *lumbar puncture*. I cross my fingers under the table and gulp, "Ye-es."

"Did you see these people?"

"No."

"What's the name of the nursing home? What area is it in?"

I stare back at him steadily. I have no idea. I glance up at Sadie, who has her eyes closed as though recalling something from a long, long way away.

"Fairside," she says slowly. "In Potters Bar."

"Fairside, Potters Bar," I repeat.

There's a short silence. DI James has finished writing and is flicking his pen backward and forward.

"I'm just going to consult with a colleague." He stands up. "I'll be back in a minute."

The moment he's left the room, Sadie gives me a contemptuous look.

"Is that the best you could do? He'll never believe you! You were supposed to be *helping* me."

"By accusing random people of *murder*?"

"Don't be such a goose," she says dismissively. "You didn't accuse anyone by name. In fact, your story was utterly hopeless. Poison? Whispered conversations in pubs?"

"You try making something up on the spot!" I reply defensively. "And that's not the point! The point is—"

"The point is, we need to delay my funeral." She's suddenly about two inches away from me, her eyes intense and pleading. "It can't happen. You can't let it. Not yet."

"But—" I blink in surprise as she disappears right before my eyes. God, this is annoying. I feel like I'm Alice in Wonderland. Any minute she'll reappear with a flamingo under her arm, shouting, "Off with her head!"

Leaning gingerly back in my chair, half expecting that to disappear too, I blink a few times, trying to process everything. But it's too surreal. I'm sitting in a police station, inventing a murder, being bossed around by a nonexistent phantom girl. I never even got any lunch, it occurs to me. Maybe this is all due to low blood sugar. Maybe I'm diabetic and this is the first sign. My mind feels like it's tying itself up in knots. Nothing makes any sense. There's no point trying to work out what's going on. I'll just have to go with the flow.

"They're going to pursue it!" Sadie appears again, speaking so fast I can barely follow her. "They think you're *probably* deluded, but they're going to follow it up anyway, just in case."

"Really?" I say incredulously.

"That policeman's been talking to another policeman," she explains breathlessly. "I followed them. He showed him your notes and said, 'Got a right one here.'"

"A 'right one'?" I can't help echoing indignantly.

Sadie ignores me. "But then they started talking about some other nursing home where there *was* a murder. Sounds *too* ghastly. And one policeman said maybe they should put in a phone call just in case, and the other agreed. So we're all right."

All *right*?

"You may be all right! But I'm not!"

As the door swings open, Sadie adds quickly, "Ask the policeman what's going to be done about the funeral. Ask him. Ask him!"

"That's not *my* problem—" I begin, then hastily stop as DI James's head appears around the door.

"Lara, I'm going to ask a detective constable to take a statement from you. Then we'll decide how to progress."

"Oh. Er . . . thanks." I'm aware of Sadie glaring meaningfully at me. "And what will happen to . . ." I hesitate. "How does it work with the . . . body?"

"The body will be kept at the mortuary for now. If we decide to proceed with an investigation, it will remain there until we file a report to the coroner, who will demand an inquest, should the evidence be sufficiently credible and consistent."

He nods briskly, then heads out. As the door closes I subside. I'm suddenly feeling shaky all over. I've invented a murder story to a real policeman. This is the worst thing I've ever done. Even worse than the time I ate half a packet of biscuits aged eight and, rather than confess to Mum, hid the whole biscuit tin in the garden behind the rosebush and had to watch her search the kitchen for it.

"You realize I've just committed perjury?" I say to Sadie. "You realize they might *arrest* me?"

" 'They might arrest me,' " Sadie echoes mockingly. She's perched on the window ledge again. "Have you never been arrested before?"

"Of course I haven't!" I goggle at her. "Have you?"

"Several times!" she says airily. "The first time was for dancing in the village fountain one night. It was *too* funny." She starts to giggle. "We had some mock handcuffs, you know, as part of a fancy dress costume, and while the policeman was hauling me out of the pond, my friend Bunty locked her handcuffs round him as a lark. He was livid!"

She's in paroxysms of laughter by now. God, she's annoying.

"I'm sure it was hilarious." I shoot her a baleful look. "But, personally, I'd rather not go to jail and catch some hideous disease, thank you."

"Well, you wouldn't have to if you had a better story." Her laughter stops. "I've never seen such a ninny. You weren't credible *or* consistent. At this rate they won't even proceed with the investigation. We won't have any time."

"Time for what?"

"Time to find my *necklace,* of course."

I drop my head down on the table with a clunk. She doesn't give up, does she?

"Look," I say at last, raising my head an inch. "Why do you need this necklace so badly? Why this one particular necklace? Was it a present or something?"

For a moment she's silent, her eyes distant. The only movement in the room is her feet, swinging rhythmically back and forth.

"It was a present from my parents for my twenty-first birthday," she says at last. "I was happy when I wore it."

"Well, that's nice," I say. "But—"

"I had it all my life. I wore it all my life." She sounds suddenly agitated. "No matter what else I lost, I kept that. It's the most important thing I ever had. I *need* it."

She's fidgeting with her hands, her face tilted down so all I can see is the corner of her chin. She's so thin and pale, she looks like a drooping flower. I feel a pang of sympathy for her, and am about to say, "Of course I'll find your necklace," when she yawns elaborately, stretching her skinny arms above her head, and says, "This is *too* dull. I wish we could go to a nightclub."

I glare at her, all my sympathy gone. Is this the gratitude I get?

"If you're so bored," I say, "we can go and finish your funeral if you like."

Sadie claps a hand over her mouth and gasps. "You *wouldn't*."

"I might."

A knock at the door interrupts us, and a jolly-looking woman in a dark shirt and trousers puts her head around it. "Lara Lington?"

An hour later, I've finished giving my so-called "statement." I've never had such a traumatic experience in my life. What a shambles.

First I forgot the name of the nursing home. Then I got my timings all wrong and had to convince the policewoman it had taken me five minutes to walk half a mile. I ended up saying I was training to be a professional speed walker. Just thinking about it makes me cringey and hot. There's no *way* she believed me. I mean, do I *look* like a professional speed walker?

Then I said I'd been to my friend Linda's before visiting the pub. I don't even *have* a friend called Linda; I just didn't want to mention any of my real friends. She wanted Linda's surname, and I blurted out "Davies" before I could stop myself.

Of course, I'd read it off the top of the form. She was DC Davies.

At least I didn't say "Keyser Söze."

To her credit, the policewoman didn't flicker. Nor did she say whether they would proceed with the case.

She just thanked me politely and found me the number of a cab firm.

I'll probably go to jail now. Great. All I need.

I glower at Sadie, who's lying full length on the desk, staring up at the ceiling. It really didn't help having her in my ear the whole time, constantly correcting me and adding suggestions and reminiscing about the time two policemen tried to stop her and Bunty "racing their motors over the fields" and couldn't catch up with them; it was "*too* funny."

"You're welcome," I say. "Again."

"Thank you." Sadie's voice drifts idly over.

"Right, well." I pick up my bag. "I'm off."

In one quick movement, Sadie sits up. "You won't forget my necklace, will you?"

"I doubt I will, my entire life." I roll my eyes. "However hard I try."

Suddenly she's in front of me, blocking my way to the door. "No one can see me except you. No one else can help me. Please."

"Look, you can't just say, 'Find my necklace!'" I exclaim in exasperation. "I don't know anything about it, I don't know what it looks like. . . ."

"It's made of glass beads with rhinestones," she says eagerly. "It falls to here. . . ." She gestures at her waist. "The clasp is inlaid mother-of-pearl—"

"Right." I cut her off. "Well, I haven't seen it. If it turns up, I'll let you know."

I swing past her, push the door open into the police-station foyer, and take out my phone. The foyer is brightly lit, with a grubby linoleum floor and a desk, which right now is empty. Two huge guys in hoodies are having a loud argument while a policeman is trying to calm them down, and I back away to what looks like a safe corner. I get out the minicab firm number DC Davies gave me and start keying it into my phone. I can see there are about twenty voice messages on there, but I ignore them all. It'll just be Mum and Dad, stressing away. . . .

"Hey!" A voice interrupts me and I pause midway through. "Lara? Is that you?"

A guy with sandy hair in a polo neck and jeans is waving at me. "It's me! Mark Phillipson? Sixth-form college?"

"Mark!" I exclaim, suddenly recognizing him. "Oh my God! How are you doing?"

The only thing I remember about Mark is him playing bass guitar in the college band.

"I'm fine! Great." He comes across with a concerned expression. "What are you doing at the police station? Is everything OK?"

"Oh! Yes, I'm fine. I'm just here for a . . . you know." I wave it off. "Murder thing."

"*Murder?*" He looks staggered.

"Yeah. But it's no big deal. I mean, obviously it *is* a big deal. . . ." I correct myself hastily at his expression. "I'd better not say too much about it. . . . Anyway, how are you doing?"

"Great! Married to Anna, remember her?" He flashes a silver wedding ring. "Trying to make it as a painter. I do this stuff on the side."

"You're a policeman?" I say disbelievingly, and he laughs.

"Police artist. People describe the villains, I draw them; it pays the rent. . . . So how about you, Lara? Are you married? With somebody?"

For a moment I just stare back with a rictus smile.

"I was with this guy for a while," I say at last. "It

didn't work out. But I'm fine about it now. I'm in a really good place, actually."

I've clenched my plastic cup so hard, it's cracked. Mark looks a bit disconcerted.

"Well . . . see you, Lara." He lifts a hand. "Will you be OK getting home?"

"I'm calling a cab." I nod. "Thanks. Nice to bump into you."

"Don't let him go!" Sadie's voice in my ear makes me jump out of my skin. "He can help!"

"Shut up and leave me alone," I mutter out of the corner of my mouth, shooting an even brighter smile at Mark. "Bye, Mark. Give my love to Anna."

"He can draw the necklace! Then you'll know what you're looking for!" She's suddenly right in front of me. "Ask him! Quickly!"

"No!"

"Ask him!" Her banshee voice is coming back, piercing my eardrum. "Ask-him-ask-him-ask-him—"

Oh, for God's sake, she's going to drive me insane.

"Mark!" I call, so loudly that the two guys in hoodies stop fighting and stare at me. "I've got this tiny favor to ask you, if you have a moment. . . ."

"Sure." Mark shrugs.

We go into a side room, with cups of tea from the machine. We pull up chairs to a table and Mark gets out his paper and artist's pencils.

"So." He raises his eyebrows. "A necklace. That's a new one."

"I saw it once at an antiques fair," I improvise. "And I'd love to commission one like it, but I'm so bad at drawing things, and it suddenly occurred to me that maybe you could help. . . ."

"No problem. Fire away." Mark takes a sip of tea,

his pencil poised over the paper, and I glance up at Sadie.

"It was made of beads," she says, holding up her hands as though she can almost feel it. "Two rows of glass beads, almost translucent."

"It's two rows of beads," I say. "Almost translucent."

"Uh-huh." He nods, already sketching circular beads. "Like this?"

"More oval," says Sadie, peering over his shoulder. "Longer. And there were rhinestones in between."

"The beads were more oval," I say apologetically. "With rhinestones in between."

"No problem . . ." Mark is already rubbing out and sketching longer beads. "Like this?"

I glance up at Sadie. She's watching him, mesmerized. "And the dragonfly," she murmurs. "You mustn't forget the dragonfly."

For another five minutes, Mark sketches, rubs out, and sketches again, as I relay Sadie's comments. Slowly, gradually, the necklace comes alive on the page.

"That's it," says Sadie at last. Her eyes are shining as she gazes down. "That's my necklace!"

"Perfect," I say to Mark. "You've got it."

For a moment we all survey it in silence.

"Nice," says Mark at last, jerking his head at it. "Unusual. Reminds me of something." He frowns at the sketch for a moment, then shakes his head. "No. Lost it." He glances at his watch. "I'm afraid I have to dash—"

"That's fine," I say quickly. "Thanks so much."

When he's gone, I pick up the paper and look at the necklace. It's very pretty, I have to admit. Long rows of

glassy beads, sparkling rhinestones, and a big orna-
mental pendant in the shape of a dragonfly, studded
with even more rhinestones.

"So this is what we're looking for."

"Yes!" Sadie looks up, her face full of animation.
"Exactly! Where shall we start?"

"You have to be joking!" I reach for my jacket and
stand up. "I'm not looking for anything now. I'm going
home and having a nice glass of wine. And then I'm
having a chicken korma with naan. Newfangled modern food," I explain, noticing her bemused expression.
"And then I'm going to bed."

"So what shall I do?" says Sadie, suddenly looking
deflated.

"I don't know!"

I head out of the side room, back into the foyer. A
taxi is offloading an elderly couple onto the pavement
outside, and I hurry out, calling, "Taxi? Can you take
me to Kilburn?"

As the taxi moves off, I spread out the sketch on my
lap and look at the necklace again, trying to imagine it
in real life. Sadie described the beads as a kind of pale
yellow iridescent glass. Even in the drawing, the rhinestones are sparkling all over. The real thing must be
stunning. Worth a bit too. Just for a moment I feel a
flicker of excitement at the thought of actually *finding* it.

But an instant later, sanity checks back into my
brain. I mean, it probably doesn't exist. And even if it
did, the chances of finding some random necklace be-
longing to a dead old lady who probably lost it or
broke it years ago are approximately . . . three million
to one. No, three billion to one.

At last I fold the paper and tuck it in my bag, then flop back on my seat. I don't know where Sadie is and I don't care. I close my eyes, ignoring the constant vibrations of my mobile phone, and let myself doze off. What a day.

FOUR

The next day the sketch of the necklace is all I have left. Sadie has disappeared and the whole episode feels like a dream. At eight-thirty I'm sitting at my desk, sipping coffee and staring down at the picture. What on earth got into me yesterday? The entire thing must have been my brain cracking up under the strain. The necklace, the girl, the banshee wailing . . . It was obviously all a figment of my imagination.

For the first time, I'm starting to sympathize with my parents. *I'm* worried about me too.

"Hi!" There's a crash as Kate, our assistant, swings open the door, knocking over a bunch of files, which I'd put on the floor while I got the milk out of the fridge.

We don't have the biggest office in the world.

"So, how was the funeral?" Kate hangs up her coat, leaning right back over the photocopier to reach her hook. Luckily, she's quite gymnastic.

"Not great. In fact, I ended up at the police station. I had this weird mental flip-out."

"God!" Kate looks horrified. "Are you OK?"

"Yeah. I mean, I think so. . . ." I have to get a grip. Abruptly, I fold up the necklace sketch, thrust it into my bag, and zip it shut.

"Actually, I knew something was up." Kate pauses

halfway through twisting her blond hair into an elastic. "Your dad called yesterday afternoon and asked me if you'd been particularly stressed recently."

I look up in alarm. "You *didn't* tell him about Natalie leaving."

"No! Of course not!" Kate has been well trained in what to divulge to my parents—i.e., nothing.

"Anyway," I say with more vigor. "Never mind. I'm fine now. Were there any messages?"

"Yes." Kate reaches for her notebook with a super-efficient manner. "Shireen kept calling all yesterday. She's going to call you today."

"Great!"

Shireen is our one piece of good news at L&N Executive Recruitment. We recently placed her as operations director at a software company, Macrosant; in fact, she's about to start the job next week. She's probably just calling to thank us.

"Anything else?" I say, just as the phone rings. Kate checks the caller ID and her eyes widen.

"Oh yes, another thing," she says hurriedly. "Janet from Leonidas Sports called, wanting an update. She said she was going to ring at nine a.m. sharp. This'll be her." She meets my panicky eyes. "Do you want me to answer?"

No, I want to hide under the desk.

"Um, yes, you'd better."

My stomach is bubbling with nerves. Leonidas Sports is our biggest client. They're a massive sports equipment company with shops all over the UK, and we've promised to find them a marketing director.

Rephrase that. *Natalie* promised to find them a marketing director.

"I'll just put you through," Kate is saying in her best

PA voice, and a moment later the phone on my desk rings. I glance desperately at Kate, then pick it up.

"Janet!" I exclaim in my most confident tones. "Good to hear from you. I was just about to call."

"Hi, Lara," comes Janet Grady's familiar hoarse voice. "Just phoning for an update. I was hoping to speak to Natalie."

I've never met Janet Grady face-to-face. But in my head she's about six foot three with a mustache. The first time we ever spoke, she told me the team at Leonidas Sports are all "tough thinkers," "hard players," and have an "iron grip" on the market. They sound terrifying.

"Oh right!" I twist the phone cord around my fingers. "Well, unfortunately Natalie's still . . . er . . . poorly."

This is the story I've been spinning ever since Natalie didn't make it back from Goa. Luckily, you just have to say "She's been to India," and everyone launches into their own My Horrendous Traveling Illness story without asking any more questions.

"But we're making great headway," I continue. "Really marvelous. We're working through the long list, and there's a file of very strong candidates right here on my desk. We'll be looking at a top-class short list, I can assure you. All tough thinkers."

"Can you give me any names?"

"Not right now!" My voice jumps in panic. "I'll fill you in nearer the time. But you'll be very impressed!"

"OK, Lara." Janet is one of those women who never waste time on small talk. "Well, as long as you're on top of it. Best to Natalie. Good-bye."

I replace the receiver and meet Kate's eyes, my heart

thumping. "Remind me, who do we have as possibles for Leonidas Sports?"

"The guy with the three-year gap in his résumé," says Kate. "And the weirdo with the dandruff. And . . . the kleptomaniac woman."

I wait for her to continue. She gives a tiny apologetic shrug.

"That's *all*?"

"Paul Richards pulled out yesterday," she says anxiously. "He's been offered a position at some American company. Here's the list." She hands me the sheet of paper and I stare at the three names in total despair. They're all no-hopers. We *can't* send this list in.

God, headhunting is hard. I had no idea. Before we started up the company, Natalie always made it seem so exciting. She talked about the thrill of the chase, "strategic hiring" and "upskilling" and "the tap on the shoulder." We used to meet every few weeks for a drink, and she was full of such amazing stories about her work, I couldn't help feeling envious. Writing promotional website copy for a car manufacturer seemed really dull in comparison. Plus there were rumors we were going to have big layoffs. So when Natalie suggested a start-up, I jumped at the chance.

The truth is, I've always been a bit in awe of Natalie. She's so glossy and confident. Even when we were at school, she always had the latest slang and could blag us into pubs. And when we first started off the company, it all worked brilliantly. She brought in some big bits of business for us at once and was constantly out networking. I was writing our website and supposedly learning all the tricks from her. It was all going in the right direction. Until she disappeared and I realized I hadn't actually learned any tricks at all.

Natalie's really into business mantras, and they're all on Post-its around her desk. I keep sidling over and studying them, as if they're the runes to some ancient religion, trying to divine what I'm meant to do. For example, *The best talent is already in the market* is stuck up above her computer. That one I do know: It means you're not supposed to go through the résumés of all the bankers who were fired from an investment bank last week and try to make them sound like marketing directors. You're supposed to go after *existing* marketing directors.

But how? What if they won't even speak to you?

After doing this job for several weeks on my own, I have a few new mantras, which go as follows: *The best talent doesn't answer the phone itself. The best talent doesn't ring back, even if you leave three messages with its secretary. The best talent doesn't want to move into sports retail. When you mention the fifty percent employee discount on tennis rackets, the best talent just laughs at you.*

I pull out our original crumpled, coffee-stained long list for the millionth time and flick through it gloomily. Names glitter off the page like shiny sweeties. Employed, bona fide talent. The marketing director of Woodhouse Retail. The European marketing head at Dartmouth Plastics. They can't all be happy at their jobs, surely. There *must* be someone out there who would love to work for Leonidas Sports. But I've tried every single name and got nowhere. I glance up to see Kate standing on one foot, surveying me anxiously, the other leg wrapped around her calf.

"We have precisely three weeks to find a tough-thinking, hard-hitting marketing director for Leonidas Sports." I'm trying desperately to stay positive. Natalie landed this deal. Natalie was going to woo all the starry candidates. Natalie knows how to do this. *I don't.*

Anyway. No point dwelling on that now.

"OK." I slap my hand on the desk. "I'm going to make some calls."

"I'll make you a fresh coffee." Kate springs into action. "We'll stay here all night if we have to."

I love Kate. She acts like she's in a film about some really thrusting multinational company, instead of two people in a ten-foot-square office with moldy carpet.

"Salary, salary, salary," she says as she sits down.

"You snooze, you lose," I respond.

Kate got into reading Natalie's mantras too. Now we can't stop quoting them at each other. The trouble is, they don't actually tell you how to do the job. What I need is the mantra telling you how to get past the question "May I ask what it is in connection with?"

I swing my chair over to Natalie's desk to get out all the Leonidas Sports paperwork. The cardboard file has fallen off its hangers inside her drawer, so with a muttered curse I gather all the papers together and pull them out. Then suddenly I stop, as I notice an old Post-it which has somehow attached itself to my hand. I've never seen this before. *James Yates, mobile* is written in faded purple felt-tip. And then a number.

A mobile number for James Yates. I don't believe it! He's marketing director at Feltons Breweries! He's on the long list! He'd be perfect! Whenever I've tried his office, I've been told he's "abroad." But wherever he is, he'll have his mobile, won't he? Trembling with excitement, I push my chair back to my own desk and dial the number.

"James Yates." The line is a little crackly but I can still hear him.

"Hi," I say, trying to sound as confident as possible. "It's Lara Lington here. Can you talk?" This is what Natalie always says on the phone; I've heard her.

"Who is this?" He sounds suspicious. "Did you say you're from Lingtons?"

I give an inward sigh.

"No, I'm from L&N Executive Recruitment, and I was phoning to see if you'd be interested in a new position, heading up marketing in a dynamic, growing retail company. It's a very exciting opportunity, so if you'd like to discuss it, perhaps over a discreet lunch at a restaurant of your choice . . ." I'm going to die if I don't breathe, so I stop and gasp for air.

"L&N?" He sounds wary. "I don't know you."

"We're a relatively new outfit, myself and Natalie Masser—"

"Not interested." He cuts me off.

"It's a marvelous opportunity," I say quickly. "You'll have a chance to expand your horizons; there's a lot of exciting potential in Europe—"

"Sorry. Good-bye."

"And a ten percent discount on sportswear!" I call desperately down the dead phone.

He's gone. He didn't even give me a chance.

"What did he say?" Kate approaches, her hands clutched hopefully around a coffee cup.

"He hung up." I slump in my chair as Kate puts down the coffee. "We're *never* going to get anyone good."

"Yes, we will!" says Kate, just as the phone starts ringing. "Maybe this is some brilliant executive who's longing for a new job...." She hurries back to her desk and picks up the phone with her best assistant's manner. "L&N Executive Recruitment . . . Oh, Shireen! Great to hear from you! I'll put you through to Lara." She beams at me and I grin back. At least we've had one triumph.

I suppose strictly speaking it was Natalie's triumph, since she made the placement, but I've been doing all the follow-up work. Anyway, it's a *company* triumph.

"Hi, Shireen!" I say cheerfully. "All set for the new job? I just know it's going to be a great position for you—"

"Lara." Shireen interrupts tensely. "There's a problem."

My stomach plunges. No. No. Please no problems.

"Problem?" I force myself to sound relaxed. "What kind of problem?"

"It's my dog."

"Your *dog?*"

"I'm intending to take Flash into work every day. But I just phoned human resources about setting up a basket for him, and they said it was impossible. They said it wasn't their policy to allow animals in the offices, can you believe it?"

She clearly expects me to be as outraged as she is. I stare at the phone in bewilderment. How has a dog suddenly entered the picture?

"Lara? Are you there?"

"Yes!" I come to. "Shireen, listen to me. I'm sure you're really fond of Flash. But it's not usual to take dogs into the workplace—"

"Yes, it is!" she interrupts. "There's another dog in

the building. I've heard it every time I've been in. That's why I assumed it would be fine! I never would have taken this job otherwise! They're discriminating against me."

"I'm sure they're not discriminating," I say hurriedly. "I'll call them straightaway." I put down the phone, then quickly dial the HR department at Macrosant. "Hi, Jean? It's Lara Lington here, from L&N Executive Recruitment. I just wanted to clarify a small point. Is Shireen Moore permitted to bring her dog to work?"

"The whole building has a no-dog policy," says Jean pleasantly. "I'm sorry, Lara, it's an insurance thing."

"Of course. Absolutely. I understand." I pause. "The thing is, Shireen believes she's heard another dog in the building. Several times."

"She's mistaken," Jean says after the tiniest of beats. "There are no dogs here."

"None at all? Not even one little puppy?" My suspicions have been aroused by that pause.

"Not even one little puppy." Jean has regained her smoothness. "As I say, there's a no-dog policy in the building."

"And you couldn't make an exception for Shireen?"

"I'm afraid not." She's polite but implacable.

"Well, thanks for your time."

I put the phone down and tap my pencil silently on my notepad for a few seconds. Something's up. I bet there is a dog there. But what can I do about it? I can't exactly phone Jean back and say, "I don't believe you."

With a sigh, I redial Shireen's number.

"Lara, is that you?" She picks up straightaway, as though she's been sitting by the phone, waiting for an answer, which she probably has. She's very bright,

Shireen, and very intense. I can picture her now, drawing that endless crisscross of squares which she obsessively doodles everywhere. She probably *needs* a dog, just to stay sane.

"Yes, it's me. I called Jean and she says no one else in the building has a dog. She says it's an insurance thing."

There's silence as Shireen digests this.

"She's lying," she says at last. "There *is* a dog in there."

"Shireen . . ." I feel like banging my head against the desk. "Couldn't you have mentioned the dog before? At one of the interviews, maybe?"

"I assumed it would be OK!" she says defensively. "I heard the other dog barking! You can tell when there's a dog in a place. Well, I'm not working without Flash. I'm sorry, Lara, I'll have to pull out of the job."

"Nooo!" I cry out in dismay before I can stop myself. "I mean . . . please don't do anything rash, Shireen! I'll sort this out, I promise. I'll call you soon." Breathing heavily, I put the phone down and bury my head in my hands. "Crap!"

"What are you going to do?" ventures Kate anxiously. She clearly overheard the whole thing.

"I don't know," I admit. "What would Natalie do?"

Both of us instinctively glance toward Natalie's desk, gleaming and empty. I have a sudden vision of Natalie sitting there: her lacquered nails tapping on the desk, her voice raised in some high-octane call. Since she's been gone, the volume level in this office has dropped by about eighty percent.

"She might tell Shireen she *had* to take the job and threaten to sue her if she didn't," says Kate at last.

"She'd definitely tell Shireen to get over herself." I

nod in agreement. "She'd call her unprofessional and flaky."

I once heard Natalie tearing a strip off some guy who had second thoughts about taking up a position in Dubai. It wasn't pretty.

The deep-down truth, which I don't want to admit to anyone, is that now I've got to know the way Natalie thinks and does business . . . I don't really relate to a lot of it. What appealed to me about this job was working with people, changing lives. When we used to meet up and Natalie would tell me her stories of finding talent, I was always just as interested in the story behind the deal as the deal itself. I thought it must be so much more satisfying to help people's careers than to sell cars. But that aspect doesn't seem to feature highly on our agenda.

I mean, OK, I know I'm a novice. And maybe I am a bit idealistic, like Dad always says. But your job is one of the most important things in your life, surely. It should be *right* for you. Salary isn't everything.

There again, that'll be why Natalie's the successful headhunter with loads of commission under her belt. And I'm not. And right now we need commission.

"So what we're saying is, I should ring Shireen back and give her a hard time," I say reluctantly. There's silence. Kate looks as pained as I feel.

"Thing is, Lara," she says hesitantly, "you're not Natalie. She's away. So you're the boss. So you should do things *your* way."

"Yes!" I feel a surge of relief. "That's true. I'm the boss. So what I say is . . . I'll think about it for a while first."

Trying to look as though this is a decisive piece of action instead of a cop-out, I push the phone aside and

start leafing through the post. A bill for office paper.
An offer to send all my staff on a team-building trip to
Aspen. And, at the bottom of the pile, *Business People*,
which is like the celebrity magazine of business. I open
it and start flipping through the pages, trying to find
someone who would make a perfect marketing director for Leonidas Sports.

Business People is essential reading for a headhunter. It's basically endless photo spreads of thrusting,
super-groomed types who have massive offices with
plenty of space to hang up their coats. But God, it's depressing. As I turn from one highflier to another, my
spirits sink lower and lower. What's wrong with me? I
only speak one language. I haven't been asked to chair
any international committees. I don't have a working
wardrobe which pairs Dolce & Gabbana trouser suits
with quirky shirts from Paul Smith.

Dolefully, I close the magazine and slump back,
staring at the grimy ceiling. How do they all do it? My
uncle Bill. Everyone in this magazine. They decide to
run a business and it's instantly a success, and it looks
so easy. . . .

"Yes . . . yes . . ." Suddenly I become aware of Kate
making semaphore signals across the room. I look up
to see her face all pink with excitement as she talks on
the phone. "I'm sure Lara would be able to make space
for you in her schedule, if you could just hold on a moment. . . ."

She presses Hold and squeaks, "It's Clive Hoxton!
The one who said he wasn't interested in Leonidas
Sports?" she adds, at my blank look. "The rugby guy?
Well, he might be after all! He wants to have lunch and
talk about it!"

"Oh my God! Him!" My spirits shoot back up.

Clive Hoxton is marketing director at Arberry Stores and used to play rugby for Doncaster. He couldn't be more perfect for the Leonidas Sports job, but when I first approached him he said he didn't want to move. I can't believe he's got in touch!

"Play it cool!" I whisper urgently. "Pretend I'm really busy interviewing other candidates."

Kate nods vigorously.

"Let me just see. . . ." she says into the phone. "Lara's schedule is very packed today, but I'll see what I can do. . . . Ah! Now, what a stroke of luck! She unexpectedly has a vacancy! Would you like to name a restaurant?"

She grins broadly at me and I give her an air high-five. Clive Hoxton is an A-list name! He's tough-thinking *and* hard-playing! He'll totally make up for the weirdo and the kleptomaniac. In fact, if we get him, I'll ax the kleptomaniac, I decide. And the weirdo isn't *that* bad, if we could just get rid of his dandruff. . . .

"All fixed up!" Kate puts the phone down. "You're having lunch today at one o'clock."

"Excellent! Where?"

"Well, that's the only thing." Kate hesitates. "I asked him to name a restaurant. And he named—" She breaks off.

"What?" My heart starts to thump anxiously. "Not Gordon Ramsay. Not that posh one in Claridge's."

Kate winces. "Worse. Lyle Place."

My insides shrivel. "You have to be kidding."

Lyle Place opened about two years ago and was instantly christened the most expensive restaurant in Europe. It has a massive lobster tank and a fountain, and loads of celebrities go there. Obviously I've never been there. I've just read about it in the *Evening Standard*.

We should never, never, *never* have let him name the restaurant. I should have named it. I would have named Pasta Pot, which is around the corner and does a set lunch for £12.95 including a glass of wine. I daren't even *think* how much lunch for two at Lyle Place is going to be.

"We won't be able to get in!" I say in sudden relief. "It'll be too busy."

"He said he can get a reservation. He knows some people. He'll put it in your name."

"Damn."

Kate is nibbling at her thumbnail anxiously. "How much is in the client entertainment kitty?"

"About 50P," I say in despair. "We're broke. I'll have to use my own credit card."

"Well, it'll be worth it," says Kate resolutely. "It's an investment. You've got to look like a mover and a shaker. If people see you eating at Lyle Place, they'll think, *Wow, Lara Lington must be doing well if she can afford to take clients here!*"

"But I *can't* afford it!" I wail. "Could we phone him up and change it to a cup of coffee?"

Even as I'm saying it, I know how lame this would look. If he wants lunch, I have to give him lunch. If he wants to go to Lyle Place, we have to go to Lyle Place.

"Maybe it isn't as expensive as we think," says Kate hopefully. "I mean, all the newspapers keep saying how bad the economy is, don't they? Maybe they've reduced the prices. Or got a special offer."

"That's true. And maybe he won't order very

much," I add in sudden inspiration. "I mean, he's sporty. He won't be a big eater."

"Of course he won't!" agrees Kate. "He'll have, like, one tiny bit of sashimi and some water and dash off. And he *definitely* won't drink. Nobody drinks at lunch anymore."

I'm feeling more positive about this already. Kate's right. No one drinks at business lunches these days. And we can keep it down to two courses. Or even one. A starter and a nice cup of coffee. What's wrong with that?

And, anyway, whatever we eat, it can't cost *that* much, can it?

Oh my God, I think I'm going to faint.

Except I can't, because Clive Hoxton has just asked me to run through the specs of the job again.

I'm sitting on a transparent chair at a white-clothed table. If I look to my right, I can see the famous giant lobster tank, which has crustaceans of all sorts clambering around on rocks and occasionally being scooped out in a metal net by a man on a ladder. Over to the left is a cage of exotic birds, whose cheeping is mingling with the background whooshing sound from the fountain in the middle of the room.

"Well." My voice is quite faint. "As you know, Leonidas Sports has just taken over a Dutch chain. . . ."

I'm talking on autopilot. My eyes keep darting down to the menu, printed on Plexiglas. Every time I spot a price, I feel a fresh swoop of horror.

Ceviche of salmon, origami style £34.

That's a starter. A *starter.*

Half a dozen oysters £46.

There's no special offer. There's no sign of any hard times. All around, diners are merrily eating and drinking as if this is all totally normal. Are they all bluffing? Are they all secretly quailing inside? If I stood on a chair and yelled, "It's too expensive! I'm not going to take this anymore!" would I start a mass walkout?

"Obviously the board wants a new marketing director who can oversee this expansion. . . ." I have no idea what I'm blabbering about. I'm psyching myself up to peek at the main courses.

Fillet of duck with three-way orange mash £59.

My stomach lurches again. I keep doing mental math and reaching three hundred and feeling a bit sick.

"Some mineral water?" The waiter appears at the table and proffers a blue-tinted Plexiglas square to each of us. "This is our water menu. If you like a sparkling water, the Chetwyn Glen is rather fun," he adds. "It's filtered through volcanic rock and has a subtle alkalinity."

"Ah." I force myself to nod intelligently, and the waiter meets my eyes without a flicker. Surely they all get back into the kitchen, collapse against the walls, and start snorting with laughter: "She paid fifteen quid! For water!"

"I'd prefer Pellegrino." Clive shrugs. He's a guy in his forties with graying hair, froggy eyes, and a mustache, and he hasn't smiled once since we sat down.

"A bottle of each, then?" says the waiter.

Noooo! Not *two* bottles of overpriced water!

"So, what would you like to eat, Clive?" I smile. "If you're in a hurry, we could go straight to main courses. . . ."

"I'm not in any hurry." Clive gives me a suspicious look. "Are you?"

"Of course not!" I backtrack quickly. "No hurry at all!" I wave a generous hand. "Have whatever you'd like."

Not the oysters, please, please, please not the oysters . . .

"The oysters to begin with," he says thoughtfully. "Then I'm torn between the lobster and the porcini risotto."

I discreetly whip my eyes down to the menu. The lobster is £90; the risotto, only £45.

"Tough choice." I try to sound casual. "You know, risotto is always *my* favorite."

There's silence as Clive frowns at the menu again.

"I love Italian food," I throw in with a relaxed little laugh. "And I bet the porcini are delicious. But it's up to you, Clive!"

"If you can't decide," the waiter puts in helpfully, "I could bring you both the lobster *and* a reduced-size risotto."

He could *what*? He could *what*? Who asked him to interfere, anyway?

"Great idea!" My voice is two notes shriller than I intended. "Two main courses! Why not?"

I feel the waiter's sardonic eye on me and instantly know he can read my thoughts. He knows I'm skint.

"And for madam?"

"Right. Absolutely." I run a finger down the menu with a thoughtful frown. "The truth is . . . I went for a big power breakfast this morning. So I'll just have a Caesar salad, no starter."

"One Caesar salad, no starter." The waiter nods impassively.

"And would you like to stick to water, Clive?" I desperately try to keep any hint of hope out of my voice. "Or wine . . ."

Even the *idea* of the wine list makes my spine feel all twingey with fear.

"Let's see the list." Clive's eyes light up.

"And a glass of vintage champagne to start, perhaps," suggests the waiter, with a bland smile.

He couldn't just suggest champagne. He had to suggest *vintage* champagne. This waiter is a total sadist.

"I could be persuaded!" Clive gives a sort of lugubrious chuckle, and somehow I force myself to join in.

At last the waiter departs, having poured us each a zillion-pound glass of vintage champagne. I feel a bit giddy. I'm going to be paying off this lunch for the rest of my life. But it'll be worth it. I have to believe that.

"So!" I say brightly, raising my glass. "To the job! I'm *so* glad you've changed your mind, Clive—"

"I haven't," he says, swigging about half of his champagne down in one gulp.

I stare at him, unnerved. Am I going mad? Did Kate take down the message wrong?

"But I thought—"

"It's a possibility." He starts to break up a bread roll. "I'm not happy with my job at the moment, and I'm considering a move. But there are drawbacks to this Leonidas Sports gig too. Sell it to me."

For a moment I'm too choked with dismay to answer. I'm spending the price of a small car on this man and he might not even be interested in the job? I take a sip of water, then look up, forcing my most professional smile. I can be Natalie. I can sell this to him.

"Clive. You're not happy in your current post. For a

man with your gifts, this is a criminal situation. Look at you! You should be in a place which will *appreciate* you."

I pause, my heart thumping hard. He's listening attentively. He hasn't even buttered his bread roll yet. So far, so good.

"In my opinion, the job at Leonidas Sports would be the perfect career move for you. You're a former sportsman—it's a sporting goods company. You love to play golf—Leonidas Sports has a whole golfwear line!"

Clive raises his eyebrows. "You've done your research on me, at any rate."

"I'm interested in people," I say honestly. "And knowing your profile, it seems to me that Leonidas Sports is exactly what you need at this stage. This is a fantastic, unique opportunity to—"

"Is that man your lover?" A familiar clipped voice interrupts me, and I jump. That sounded just like—

No. Don't be ridiculous. I take a deep breath and resume.

"As I was saying, this is a fantastic opportunity to take your career to the next level. I'm sure that we could achieve a very generous package—"

"I said, 'Is that man your lover?' " The voice is more insistent, and before I can stop myself, I swivel my head.

No.

This can't be happening. She's back. It's Sadie, perched on a nearby cheese trolley.

She's not in the green dress anymore; she's wearing a pale pink one with a dropped waistband and a matching coat over the top. There's a black band around her head, and from one of her wrists dangles a little gray silk bag on a beaded chain. The other hand is resting on a glass cheese dome—apart from her fingertips, which have sunk into it. She suddenly notices and pulls them out sharply, carefully positioning them on top of the glass.

"He's not terribly handsome, is he? I want some champagne," she adds imperiously, her eyes lighting on my drink.

Ignore her. It's a hallucination. It's all in your head.

"Lara? Are you OK?"

"Sorry, Clive!" I hastily turn back. "Just got a bit distracted there. By the . . . cheese trolley! It all looks so delicious!"

Oh God. Clive doesn't seem amused. I need to get things back on track, quick.

"The real question to ask yourself, Clive, is this." I lean forward intently. "Will an opportunity like this come along again? It's a unique chance to work with a great brand, to use all your proven talents and admired leadership skills—"

"I want some *champagne*!" To my horror, Sadie has materialized right in front of me. She reaches for my glass and tries to pick it up, but her hand goes through it. "Drat! I can't pick it up!" She reaches again, and again, then glares at me crossly. "This is so irritating!"

"*Stop it!*" I hiss furiously.

"I'm sorry?" Clive knits his heavy brows.

"Not you, Clive! Just got something caught in my throat . . ." I grab my glass and take a gulp of water.

"Have you found my necklace yet?" Sadie demands accusingly.

"No!" I mutter from behind my glass. "Go *away*."

"Then why are you sitting here? Why aren't you looking for it?"

"Clive!" I desperately try to focus back on him. "I'm so sorry about that. What was I saying?"

"Admired leadership skills," says Clive, without cracking a smile.

"That's right! Admired leadership skills! Um . . . so the point is . . ."

"Haven't you looked anywhere?" She thrusts her head close to mine. "Don't you *care* about finding it?"

"So . . . what I'm trying to say is . . ." It's taking every ounce of willpower to ignore Sadie and not bat her away. "In my opinion, this job is a great strategic move; it's a perfect springboard for your future, and furthermore—"

"You've got to find my necklace! It's important! It's very, very—"

"Furthermore, I know the generous benefits package will—"

"Stop ignoring me!" Sadie's face is practically touching mine. "Stop talking! Stop—"

"Shut up and leave me alone!"

Shit.

Did that just come out of my mouth?

From the shell-shocked way Clive's froggy eyes have widened, I'm guessing the answer is yes. At two neighboring tables, conversations have come to a halt, and I can see our supercilious waiter pausing to watch. The buzz of clashing cutlery and conversation seems to have died away all around. Even the lobsters seem to be lined up at the edge of the tank, watching.

"Clive!" I give a strangled laugh. "I didn't mean . . . obviously I wasn't talking to *you*. . . ."

"Lara." Clive fixes me with a hostile gaze. "Please do me the courtesy of telling me the truth."

I can feel my cheeks staining red. "I was just . . ." I clear my throat desperately. What can I say?

I was talking to myself. No.

I was talking to a vision. No.

"I'm not a fool." He cuts me off contemptuously. "This isn't the first time this has happened to me."

"It isn't?" I peer at him, bemused.

"I've had to put up with it in board meetings, in directors' lunches . . . it's the same everywhere. Black-Berries are bad enough, but these hands-free sets are a bloody menace. You know how many car accidents people like you cause?"

Hands-free—Does he mean . . .

He thinks I was on the phone!

"I wasn't—" I begin automatically, then stop myself. Being on the phone is the most sane option available to me. I should go with it.

"But this really is the pits." He glowers at me, breathing heavily. "Taking a call during a one-to-one lunch. Hoping I might not notice. It's fucking disrespectful."

"I'm sorry," I say humbly. "I'll . . . I'll switch it off now." With a fumbling hand, I reach up to my ear and pretend to switch off an earpiece.

"Where is it, anyway?" He frowns at me. "I can't see it."

"It's tiny," I say hastily. "Very discreet."

"Is it the new Nokia?"

He's peering more closely at my ear. Shit.

"It's actually . . . um . . . embedded in my earring." I hope I sound convincing. "New technology. Clive, I'm really sorry I was distracted. I . . . I misjudged the situation. But I am very sincere about wanting to place you with Leonidas Sports. So if I could maybe just recap on what I was trying to say—"

"You have to be joking."

"But—"

"You think I'm going to do business with you now?" He gives a short, unamused laugh. "You're as unprofessional as your partner, and that's saying something." To my horror, he pushes back his chair and gets to his feet. "I was going to give you a chance, but forget it."

"No, wait! Please!" I say in panic, but he's already striding away, between the tables of gawping diners.

I feel hot and cold as I stare at his empty chair. With a still-shaky hand, I reach for my champagne and take three deep gulps. So that's that. I've fucked up. My best hope is gone.

And, anyway, what did he mean, I'm "as unprofessional as my partner"? Has he heard about Natalie disappearing off to Goa? Does everyone *know*?

"Will the gentleman be returning?" My trance is interrupted by the waiter approaching the table. He's holding a wooden platter bearing a dish with a silver dome on it.

"I don't think so." I stare at the table, my face burning with humiliation.

"Shall I return his food to the kitchen?"

"Do I still have to pay for it?"

"Unfortunately, madam, yes." He gives me a patronizing smile. "Since it has been ordered, and everything is cooked from fresh—"

"Then I'll have it."

"*All* of it?" He seems taken aback.

"Yes." I lift my chin mutinously. "Why not? I'm paying for it; I might as well eat it."

"Very good." The waiter inclines his head, deposits the platter in front of me, and removes the silver dome. "Half a dozen fresh oysters on crushed ice."

I've never eaten oysters in my life. I've always thought they looked gross. Close up they look even grosser. But I'm not admitting that.

"Thanks," I say curtly.

The waiter retreats, and I stare fixedly at the six oysters in front of me. I'm determined to see this stupid lunch out. But there's a tight pressing feeling behind my cheekbones, and my bottom lip would be trembling if I allowed it.

"Oysters! I *adore* oysters." To my disbelief, Sadie appears in front of my eyes again. She sinks into Clive's vacated chair with a languid sideways movement, looks around, and says, "This place is rather fun. Is there a cabaret?"

"I can't hear you," I mutter savagely. "I can't see you. You don't exist. I'm going to the doctor and getting some drugs and getting rid of you."

"Where's your lover gone?"

"He wasn't my lover," I snap in low tones. "I was trying to do business with him, and it's all spoiled because of you. You've ruined everything. *Everything.*"

"Oh." She arches her eyebrows unrepentantly. "I don't see how I could do that if I don't exist."

"Well, you did. And now I'm stuck with these stupid oysters that I don't want and can't afford, and I don't even know how to eat them. . . ."

"It's easy to eat an oyster!"

"No, it isn't."

I suddenly notice a blond woman in a print dress at the next table nudging the perfectly groomed woman next to her and pointing at me. I'm talking to thin air.

I look like a lunatic. Hastily I reach for a bread roll and start to butter it, avoiding Sadie's eye.

"Excuse me." The woman leans over and smiles at me. "I couldn't help overhearing your conversation. I don't mean to interrupt, but did you just say your phone is embedded in your earring?"

I stare back at her, my mind scrabbling for an answer other than "yes."

"Yes," I say at last.

The woman claps a hand to her mouth. "That's amazing. How does it work?"

"It has a special . . . chip. Very new. Japanese."

"I have to get one." She's gazing at my Claire's Accessories £5.99 earring, awestruck. "Where do they sell them?"

"Actually, this is a prototype," I say hurriedly. "They'll be available in a year or so."

"Well, how did *you* get one, then?" She gives me an aggressive look.

"I . . . um . . . know Japanese people. Sorry."

"Could I see?" She holds out her hand. "Could you take it out of your ear for a moment? Would you mind?"

"A call's just coming in," I say hastily. "It's vibrating."

"I can't see anything." She's peering incredulously at my ear.

"It's very subtle," I say desperately. "They're microvibrations. Er, hello, Matt? Yes, I can talk."

I mime apologies to the woman and reluctantly she returns to her meal. I can see her pointing me out to all her friends.

"What are you talking about?" Sadie's eyeing me disdainfully. "How can a telephone be in an earring? It sounds like a riddle."

"I don't know. Don't you start quizzing me too." I prod an oyster with little enthusiasm.

"Do you really not know how to eat an oyster?"

"Never eaten one before in my life."

Sadie shakes her head disapprovingly. "Pick up your fork. The shellfish fork. Go on!" Casting her a suspicious look, I do as she says. "Ease it around, make sure it's detached from the shell. . . . Now give it a squeeze of lemon and pick it up. Like this." She mimes picking up an oyster, and I copy. "Head back and swallow the whole thing. Bottoms up!"

It's like swallowing a piece of jellified sea. Somehow I manage to slurp down the whole thing, grab my glass, and take a swig of champagne.

"You see?" Sadie is watching me greedily. "Isn't that too delicious?"

"'s OK," I say reluctantly. I put my glass down and survey her silently for a moment. She's reclining on the chair as though she owns the place, one arm flung to the side, her beaded bag dangling down

She's all in my head, I tell myself. My subconscious has invented her.

Except . . . my subconscious doesn't know how to eat an oyster. Does it?

"What is it?" She juts out her chin. "Why are you looking at me like that?"

My brain is edging very slowly to a conclusion. To the only possible conclusion.

"You're a ghost, aren't you?" I say at last. "You're not a hallucination. You're a proper, real-live ghost."

Sadie gives a remote shrug, as though she's really not interested in this conversation.

"*Aren't* you?"

Again, Sadie doesn't reply. Her head is tilted and

she's examining her fingernails. Maybe she doesn't want to be a ghost. Well, too bad. She is.

"You are a ghost. I know you are. So, what, am I *psychic*?"

My head is prickling all over as this revelation hits me. I feel a bit shivery. I can talk to the dead. Me, Lara Lington. I always *knew* there was something different about me.

Think of the implications. Think what this means! Maybe I'll start talking to more ghosts. Lots of ghosts. Oh my God, I could have my own TV show. I could go around the world. I could be famous! I have a sudden vision of myself on a stage, channeling spirits while an audience watches avidly. With a surge of excitement, I lean across the table.

"Do you know any other dead people you could introduce me to?"

"No." Sadie folds her arms crossly. "I don't."

"Have you met Marilyn Monroe? Or Elvis? Or . . . or Princess Diana? What's she like? Or Mozart!" I feel almost dizzy as possibilities pile into my head. "This is mind-blowing. You have to describe it! You have to tell me what it's like . . . *there.*"

"Where?" Sadie tosses her chin.

"*There.* You know . . ."

"I haven't been anywhere." She glares at me. "I haven't met anybody. I wake up and it's as though I'm in a dream. A very bad dream. Because all I want is my necklace, but the only person who can understand me refuses to help me!" She looks so accusing, I feel a surge of indignation.

"Well, maybe if you didn't come along and ruin everything, that person might *want* to help you. Did you think of that?"

"I didn't ruin everything!"

"Yes, you did!"

"I taught you how to eat an oyster, didn't I?"

"I didn't want to know how to eat a bloody oyster! I wanted my candidate not to walk out!"

For a moment, Sadie looks cornered—then her chin juts out again. "I didn't know he was your candidate. I thought he was your lover."

"Well, my business is probably sunk now. And I can't afford any of this stupid food. It's all a disaster and it's *all your fault*."

Morosely, I reach for another oyster and start poking at it with my fork. Then I glance at Sadie. All her spirit seems to have evaporated, and she's hugging her knees with that droopy-headed-flower look. She meets my eyes, then drops her head down again.

"I'm sorry." Her voice is barely above a whisper. "I apologize for causing you so much trouble. If I could communicate with anyone else, I would do so."

Now, of course, I feel bad.

"Look," I begin. "It's not that I don't *want* to help—"

"It's my final wish." As Sadie looks up, her eyes are dark and velvety and her mouth is in a sad little O shape. "It's my only wish. I don't want anything else; I won't ask you for anything else. Just my necklace. I can't rest without it. I can't—" She breaks off and looks away as though she can't finish the sentence. Or doesn't want to finish it, maybe.

I can tell this is a bit of a sensitive area. But I'm too intrigued to let it go.

"When you say you 'can't rest' without your necklace," I venture delicately, "do you mean *rest* as in sit down and feel relaxed? Or do you mean *rest* as in pass on to . . . *there*?" I catch her stony gaze and amend hastily, "I mean, the Other . . . I mean, the Better . . . I mean, the *After*—" I rub my nose, feeling hot and bothered.

God, this is a minefield. How am I supposed to put it? What's the politically correct phrase, anyway?

"So . . . how does it work, exactly?" I try a different tack.

"I don't *know* how it works! I haven't been given an instruction pamphlet, you know." Her tone is scathing, but I can see an insecure flash in her eye. "I don't *want* to be here. I've just found myself here. And all I know is, I need my necklace. That's all I know. And for that . . . I need your help."

For a while there's silence. I swallow another oyster, uncomfortable thoughts jabbing at my conscience. She's my great-aunt. This is her one and only last wish. You should make an effort with someone's one and only last wish. Even if it is totally impossible and stupid.

"Sadie." At last I exhale sharply. "If I find your necklace for you, will you go away and leave me in peace?"

"Yes."

"For good?"

"Yes." Her eyes are starting to shine.

I fold my arms sternly. "If I look for your necklace as hard as I can but can't find it because it was lost a zillion years ago or, more likely, never existed . . . will you still go away?"

There's a pause. Sadie looks sulky.

"It *did* exist," she says.

"Will you?" I persist. "Because I'm not spending all summer on some ridiculous treasure hunt."

For a few moments, Sadie glowers at me, clearly trying to think of some put-down. But she can't.

"Very well," she says at last.

"OK. It's a deal." I lift my champagne glass toward her. "Here's to finding your necklace."

"Come on, then! Start looking!" She darts her head around impatiently, as though we might start searching right here and now in the restaurant.

"We can't just go randomly looking! We have to be *scientific*." I reach into my bag, pull out the necklace sketch, and unfold it. "All right. Think back. Where did you last have it?"

FIVE

Fairside Nursing Home is in a leafy residential road: a red-brick, double-fronted building with net curtains in every single window. I survey it from the other side of the road, then turn to look at Sadie, who has been following me in silence ever since Potters Bar station. She came with me on the tube, but I barely saw her: She spent the whole time flitting along the carriage, looking at people, popping up to ground level and down again.

"So, that's where you used to live," I say with an awkward brightness. "It's really nice! Lovely . . . garden." I gesture at a couple of mangy shrubs.

Sadie doesn't answer. I look up and see a line of tension in her pale jaw. This must be strange for her, coming back here. I wonder how well she remembers it.

"Hey, how old are you, anyway?" I say curiously, as the thought occurs to me. "I mean, I know you're a hundred and five really. But now. As you are . . . here." I gesture at her.

Sadie looks taken aback by the question. She examines her arms, peers at her dress, and thoughtfully rubs the fabric between her fingers.

"Twenty-three," she says at last. "Yes, I think I'm twenty-three."

I'm doing mental calculations in my head. She was 105 when she died. Which would mean . . .

"You were twenty-three in the year 1927."

"That's right!" Her face suddenly comes alive. "We had a pajama party for my birthday. We drank gin fizzes all evening and danced 'til the birds started singing. . . . Oh, I miss pajama parties." She hugs herself. "Do you have many pajama parties?"

Does a one-night stand count as a pajama party?

"I'm not sure they're *quite* the same—" I break off as a woman's face glances out of a top-floor window at me. "Come on. Let's go."

I head briskly across the road, up the path to the wide front door, and press the security buzzer.

"Hello?" I call into the grille. "I don't have an appointment, I'm afraid."

There's the sound of a key in a lock, and the front door opens. A woman in a blue nurse's uniform beams at me. She looks in her early thirties, with her hair tied back in a knot, and a plump pale face.

"Can I help you?"

"Yes. My name's Lara, and I'm here about a . . . a former resident." I glance at Sadie.

She's gone.

I hurriedly scan the whole front garden—but she's totally disappeared. Bloody hell. She's left me in the lurch.

"A former resident?" The nurse prompts me.

"Oh. Er . . . Sadie Lancaster?"

"Sadie!" Her face softens. "Come in! I'm Ginny, senior staff nurse."

I follow her into a linoleum-floored hall smelling of beeswax and disinfectant. The whole place is quiet, apart from the nurse's rubber shoes squeaking on the floor and the distant sound of the TV. Through a door I glimpse a couple of old ladies sitting in chairs with crocheted blankets over their knees.

I've never really known any old people. Not really, *really* old.

"Hello!" I wave nervously at one white-haired lady who is sitting nearby, and her face immediately crumples in distress.

Shit.

"Sorry!" I call quietly. "I didn't mean to . . . er . . ."

A nurse comes over to the white-haired lady, and in slight relief I hurry after Ginny, hoping she didn't notice.

"Are you a relation?" she asks, showing me into a little reception room.

"I'm Sadie's great-niece."

"Lovely!" says the nurse, flicking on the kettle. "Cup of tea? We've been expecting someone to call, actually. Nobody ever picked up her stuff."

"That's what I'm here about." I hesitate, gearing myself up. "I'm looking for a necklace which I believe once belonged to Sadie. A glass-bead necklace, with a dragonfly set with rhinestones." I smile apologetically. "I know it's a long shot and I'm sure you don't even—"

"I know the one." She nods.

"You know the one?" I stare at her stupidly. "You mean . . . it exists?"

"She had a few lovely bits." Ginny smiles. "But that was her favorite. She wore it over and over."

"Right!" I swallow, trying to keep calm. "Could I possibly see it?"

"It'll be in her box." Ginny nods again. "If I can get you to fill in a form first . . . Do you have any ID?"

"Of course." I scrabble in my bag, my heart racing. I can't believe it. This was so easy!

As I fill in the form, I keep looking around for Sadie, but she's nowhere to be seen. Where's she gone? She's missing the great moment!

"Here you are." I thrust the form at Ginny. "So, can I take it away? I'm nearly next of kin. . . ."

"The lawyers said the next of kin weren't interested in having her personal effects," says Ginny. "Her nephews, was it? We never saw them."

"Oh." I color. "My dad. And my uncle."

"We've been holding on to them in case they changed their minds. . . ." Ginny pushes through a swing door. "But I don't see why you can't take them." She shrugs. "It's nothing much, to be honest. Apart from the bits of jewelry . . ." She stops in front of a pin board and gestures fondly at a photo. "Here she is! Here's our Sadie."

It's the same wrinkled old lady from the other photo. She's wrapped in a pink lacy shawl, and there's a ribbon in her white candy floss hair. I feel a slight lump in my throat as I gaze at the picture. I just can't relate this tiny, ancient, folded-up face to Sadie's proud, elegant profile.

"Her hundred and fifth birthday, that was." Ginny points to another photo. "You know, she's our oldest ever resident! She's had telegrams from the queen!"

A birthday cake is in front of Sadie in this photo, and nurses are crowding into the picture with cups of tea and wide smiles and party hats. As I look at them, I feel a crawling shame. How come we weren't there?

How come she wasn't surrounded by me and Mum and Dad and everyone?

"I wish I'd been there." I bite my lip. "I mean . . . I didn't realize."

"It's difficult." Ginny smiles at me without reproach, which of course makes me feel a million times worse. "Don't worry. She was happy enough. And I'm sure you gave her a wonderful send-off."

I think back to Sadie's miserable, empty little funeral and feel even worse.

"Er . . . kind of—Hey!" My attention is suddenly drawn by something in the photograph. "Wait! Is that *it*?"

"That's the dragonfly necklace." Ginny nods easily. "You can have that photo, if you like."

I take down the photo, light-headed with disbelief. There it is. Just visible, poking out of the folds of Great-Aunt Sadie's shawl. There are the beads. There's the rhinestone-studded dragonfly. Just as she described it. It's real!

"I'm so sorry none of us could make the funeral." Ginny sighs as we resume walking down the corridor. "We had such staff problems this week. But we toasted her at supper. . . . Here we are! Sadie's things."

We've arrived at a small storeroom lined with dusty shelves, and she hands me a shoe box. There's an old metal-backed hairbrush inside, and a couple of old paperbacks. I can see the gleam of beads coiled up at the bottom.

"Is this *all*?" I'm taken aback, in spite of myself.

"We didn't keep her clothes." Ginny makes an apologetic gesture. "They weren't really hers, so to speak. I mean, she didn't choose them."

"But what about stuff from earlier in her life? What about . . . furniture? Or mementos?"

Ginny shrugs. "Sorry, I've only been here five years, and Sadie was a resident for a long while. I suppose things get broken and lost and not replaced."

"Right." Trying to hide my shock, I start unpacking the meager things. Someone lives for 105 years and this is all that's left? A shoe box?

As I reach the jumble of necklaces and brooches at the bottom, I feel my excitement rising. I untangle all the strings of beads, searching for yellow glass, for a flash of rhinestones, for the dragonfly. . . .

It's not there.

Ignoring a sudden foreboding, I shake the tangle of beads out properly and lay them straight. There are thirteen necklaces in all. None of them is the right one.

"Ginny. I can't find the dragonfly necklace."

"Oh dear!" Ginny peers over my shoulder in concern. "It should be there!" She lifts up another necklace, made from tiny purple beads, and smiles at it fondly. "This was another favorite of hers—"

"I'm really after the dragonfly necklace." I know I sound agitated. "Could it be anywhere else?"

Ginny looks perplexed. "This is strange. Let's check with Harriet. She did the clear-out." I follow her back down the corridor and through a door marked *Staff*. Inside is a small, cozy room in which three nurses are sitting on old floral armchairs, drinking cups of tea.

"Harriet!" says Ginny to a pink-cheeked girl in glasses. "This is Sadie's great-niece Lara. She wants that lovely dragonfly necklace that Sadie used to wear. Have you seen it?"

Oh God. Why did she have to put it like that? I sound like some horrible grasping person out of Scrooge.

"I don't want it for me," I say hastily. "I want it for . . . a good cause."

"It isn't in Sadie's box," Ginny explains. "Do you know where it could be?"

"Is it not?" Harriet looks taken aback. "Well, maybe it wasn't in the room. Now you mention it, I don't remember seeing it. I'm sorry, I know I should have taken an inventory. But we cleared that room in a bit of a rush." She looks up at me defensively. "We've been so stretched. . . ."

"Do you have any idea where it could have gone?" I look at them helplessly. "Could it have been put somewhere; could it have been given to one of the other residents . . ."

"The jumble sale!" pipes up a thin dark-haired nurse sitting in the corner. "It wasn't sold by mistake at the jumble sale, was it?"

"What jumble sale?" I swivel around to face her.

"It was a fund-raiser, two weekends ago. All the residents and their families donated stuff. There was a bric-a-brac stall with lots of jewelry."

"No." I shake my head. "Sadie would never have donated this necklace. It was really special to her."

"Like I say." The nurse shrugs. "They were going from room to room. There were boxes of stuff everywhere. Maybe it was collected by mistake."

She sounds so matter-of-fact, I suddenly feel livid on Sadie's behalf.

"But that kind of mistake shouldn't happen! People's stuff should be safe! Necklaces shouldn't just *disappear*!"

"We do have a safe in the cellar," Ginny puts in anxiously. "We ask residents to keep anything of real value in that. Diamond rings and so forth. If it was valuable, it should really have been locked up."

"It wasn't valuable exactly, I don't think. It was just . . . important." I sit down, rubbing my forehead, trying to organize my thoughts. "So can we track it down? Do you know who was at this jumble sale?" Doubtful looks are exchanged around the room, and I sigh. "Don't tell me. You have no idea."

"We do!" The dark-haired nurse suddenly puts down her cup of tea. "Have we still got the raffle list?"

"The raffle list!" says Ginny, brightening. "Of course! Everyone who came to the sale bought a raffle ticket," she explains to me. "They all left their names and addresses in case they won. The star prize was a bottle of Baileys," she adds proudly. "And we had a Yardley gift set—"

"Do you have the list?" I cut her off. "Can you give it to me?"

Five minutes later I'm clutching a four-page photocopied list of names and addresses. There are sixty-seven in all.

Sixty-seven possibilities.

No, *possibilities* is too strong a word. Sixty-seven outside chances.

"Well, thanks." I smile, trying not to feel too daunted. "I'll investigate this lot. And if you *do* come across it . . ."

"Of course! We'll all keep an eye out, won't we?" Ginny appeals around the room, and there are three nods.

I follow Ginny back through the hall, and as we approach the front door she hesitates.

"We have a visitors' book, Lara. I don't know if you'd like to sign it?"

"Oh." I hesitate awkwardly. "Er . . . yes. Why not?"

Ginny takes down a big red-bound book and leafs through it.

"All the residents have their own page. But Sadie never had very many signatures. So now that you're here, I thought it would be nice if you signed, even though she's gone. . . ." Ginny flushes. "Is that silly of me?"

"No. It's sweet of you." I feel a renewed guilt. "We should have visited more."

"Here we are." Ginny's flipping through the cream pages. "Oh, look! She did have one visitor this year! A few weeks ago. I was on holiday, so I missed it."

Charles Reece, I read, as I scrawl *Lara Lington* across the page, nice and big to make up for the lack of other entries. "Who's Charles Reece?"

"Who knows?" She shrugs.

Charles Reece. I stare at the name, intrigued. Maybe he was Sadie's dearest friend from childhood. Or her lover. Oh my God, yes. Maybe he's a sweet old man with a cane who came to hold his dear Sadie's hand just one more time. And now he doesn't even know she's dead and he wasn't invited to the funeral. . . .

We really are a crap family.

"Did he leave any contact details, this Charles Reece?" I look up. "Was he really old?"

"I don't know. I can ask around, though." She takes the book from me, and her face lights up as she reads my name. "Lington! Any relation to the coffee Lington?"

Oh God. I really cannot face it today.

"No." I smile weakly. "Just a coincidence."

"Well, it's been a real pleasure to meet Sadie's great-niece." As we reach the front door, she gives me a friendly hug. "You know, Lara, I think you have a little of her in you. You both have the same spirit. And I can sense the same kindness."

The nicer this nurse is to me, the crappier I feel. I'm not kind. I mean, *look* at me. I never even visited my great-aunt. I don't do cycle rides for charity. OK, I do buy *The Big Issue* sometimes, but not if I'm holding a cappuccino and it's too much hassle to reach for my purse. . . .

"Ginny." A red-haired nurse beckons her. "Can I have a quick word?" She draws her to one side and murmurs under her breath. I just catch the odd word . . . *strange . . . police.*

" . . . *police?*" Ginny's eyes have widened in surprise.

" . . . don't know . . . number . . ."

Ginny takes the slip of paper, then turns to smile at me again. I manage a rictus grin, totally paralyzed with horror.

The police. I'd forgotten about the police.

I told them Sadie was murdered by the staff at the home. These lovely saintly nurses. Why did I say that? What was I *thinking*?

This is all Sadie's fault. No, it's not. It's my fault. I should have kept my big trap *shut.*

"Lara?" Ginny peers at me in alarm. "Are you all right?"

She's going to be accused of homicide, and she has no idea. And it's all my fault. I'm going to ruin everyone's career and the home will be shut and boarded up and all the old people will have nowhere to go. . . .

"Lara?"

"I'm fine," I manage at last, in a grainy voice. "Fine. But I have to go." I start backing out of the front door on wobbly legs. "Thanks so much. Bye."

I wait until I'm down the path and safely back on the pavement, then whip out my phone and speed-dial DI James's number, almost hyperventilating in panic. I should never have accused anyone of murder. I am never, ever, ever doing that again. I'm going to confess everything, tear up my statement—

"DI James's office." A woman's crisp voice interrupts my thoughts.

"Oh, hello." I try to sound calm. "This is Lara Lington speaking. Could I speak to DI James or DC Davies?"

"I'm afraid they're both out on calls. Can I take a message? If it's urgent—"

"Yes, it's very, very urgent. It's to do with a murder case. Could you please tell DI James I've had a . . . a . . . a realization."

"A realization," she echoes, obviously writing it down.

"Yes. About my statement. Quite a crucial one."

"I think perhaps you should talk to DI James personally—"

"No! This can't wait! You have to tell him it wasn't the nurses who murdered my great-aunt. They didn't do a thing. They're wonderful, and it was all a terrible mistake, and . . . well . . . the thing is . . ."

I'm psyching myself up to bite the bullet and admit I invented the whole thing—when suddenly I'm brought up short by a horrible thought. I *can't* confess everything. I can't admit I made the whole thing up. They'll instantly resume the funeral. I have a flashback to Sadie's anguished cry at the funeral service, and feel a shiver of anxiety. I can't let that happen. I just can't.

"Yes?" says the woman patiently.

"I . . . um . . . the thing is . . ."

My mind is doing double backflips trying to work out a solution that involves both being honest and buying time for Sadie. But I can't find one. There isn't one. And the woman's going to give up waiting in a minute and put the phone down. I have to say *something*.

I need a red herring. Just to distract them for a while. Just while I find the necklace.

"It was someone else," I blurt out. "A . . . man. It was *him* I overheard in the pub. I got confused before. He had a plaited goatee beard," I add randomly. "And a scar on his cheek. I remember it really clearly now."

They'll never find a man with a plaited goatee and a scar on his cheek. We're safe. For now.

"A man with a plaited beard . . ." The woman sounds as if she's trying to keep up.

"And a scar."

"And, I'm sorry, what is this man supposed to have done?"

"Murdered my great-aunt! I gave a statement, but it was wrong. So if you could just cancel it out . . ."

There's a rather long pause—then the woman says, "Dear, we don't just cancel out statements. I think DI James will probably want to talk to you himself."

Oh God. The thing is, I really, *really* don't want to talk to DI James.

"Fine." I try to sound cheery. "No problem. As long

as he knows the nurses definitely didn't do it. If you could write that message on a Post-it or something? *The nurses didn't do it.*"

" 'The nurses didn't do it,' " she repeats dubiously.

"Exactly. In big capitals. And put it on his desk."

There's another, even longer pause. Then the woman says, "Can I take your name again?"

"Lara Lington. He'll know who I am."

"I'm sure he will. Well, as I say, Miss Lington, I'm sure DI James will be in touch."

I ring off and head down the road, my legs weak. I think I just about got away with it. But, honestly, I'm a nervous wreck.

Two hours later, I'm not just a nervous wreck. I'm exhausted.

In fact, I'm taking a whole new jaded view of the British populace. It might seem like an easy project, phoning a few people on a list and asking if they'd bought a necklace. It might seem simple and straightforward, until you actually tried it yourself.

I feel like I could write a whole book on human nature, and it would be called: *People Are Really Unhelpful.* First of all, they want to know how you got their name and phone number. Then, when you mention the word *raffle,* they want to know what they won and even call out to their husband, "Darren, we won that raffle!" When you hastily tell them, "You didn't win anything," the mood instantly turns suspicious.

Then, when you broach the subject of what they bought at the jumble sale, they get even more suspicious. They get convinced you're trying to sell them something or steal their credit card details by telepathy.

At the third number I tried, there was some guy in the background saying, "I've heard about this. They phone you up and keep you talking. It's an Internet scam. Put the phone down, Tina."

"How can it be an Internet scam?" I wanted to yell. "We're not *on* the Internet!"

I've only had one woman so far who seemed keen to help: Eileen Roberts. And actually she was a total pain because she kept me on the line for ten minutes, telling me about everything she bought at the jumble sale and saying what a shame it was and had I thought of making a replacement necklace as there was a wonderful bead shop in Bromley?

Argh.

I rub my ear, which is glowing from being pressed against the phone, and count the scribbled-out names on my list. Twenty-three. Forty-four to go. This was a crap idea. I'm never going to find this stupid necklace. I stretch out my back, then fold the list up and put it in my bag. I'll do the rest tomorrow. Maybe.

I head into the kitchen, pour myself a glass of wine, and am putting a lasagna in the oven when her voice says, "Did you find my necklace?" I start, crashing my forehead against the oven door, and look up. Sadie's sitting on the sill of the open window.

"Give me some *warning* when you're going to appear!" I exclaim. "And, anyway, where were you? Why did you suddenly abandon me?"

"That place is deathly." She tosses her chin. "Full of old people. I had to get away."

She's speaking lightly, but I can tell she was freaked out by going back there. That must be why she disappeared for so long.

"*You* were old," I remind her. "You were the oldest

one there. Look, that's you!" I reach in my jacket pocket and produce the picture of her, all wrinkled and white-haired. I see the briefest of flinches on Sadie's face before she brushes a scornful glance across the image.

"That's not me."

"It is! A nurse at the home gave it to me, she said it was you on your hundred and fifth birthday! You should be proud! You got telegrams from the queen and everything—"

"I mean, it's not *me*. I never felt like that. No one feels like that inside. This is how I felt." She stretches out her arms. "Like this. A girl in my twenties. All my life. The outside is just . . . cladding."

"Well, anyway, you could have warned me you were leaving. You left me all alone!"

"So did you get the necklace? Do you have it?" Sadie's face lights up with hope, and I can't help wincing.

"Sorry. They had a box of your stuff, but the dragonfly necklace wasn't in there. Nobody knows where it's gone. I'm really sorry, Sadie."

I brace myself for the tantrum, the banshee screaming . . . but it doesn't come. She just flickers slightly, as though someone turned the voltage down.

"But I'm on the case," I add. "I'm calling everyone who came to the jumble sale, in case they bought it. I've been on the phone all afternoon. It's been quite hard work, actually," I add. "Quite exhausting."

I'm expecting some gratitude from Sadie at this point. Some nice little speech about how brilliant I am and how appreciative she is of all my effort. But she sighs impatiently and wanders off, through the wall.

"You're welcome," I mouth after her.

I head into the sitting room and am flicking through the TV channels when she appears again. She seems to have cheered up immensely.

"You live with some very peculiar people! There's a man upstairs lying on a machine, grunting."

"What?" I stare at her. "Sadie, you can't spy on my neighbors!"

"What does 'shake your booty' mean?" she says, ignoring me. "The girl on the wireless was singing it. It sounds like nonsense."

"It means . . . dance. Let it all out."

"But why your booty?" She still looks puzzled. "Does it mean wave your shoe?"

"Of course not! Your booty is your . . ." I get up and pat my bum. "You dance like this." I do a few "street" dance moves, then look up to see Sadie in fits of giggles.

"You look as though you've got convulsions! That's not dancing!"

"It's modern dancing." I glare at her and sit down. I'm a bit sensitive about my dancing, as it happens. I take a gulp of wine and look critically at her. She's peering at the TV now, watching *EastEnders* with wide eyes.

"What's this?"

"*EastEnders*. It's a TV show."

"Why are they all so angry with one another?"

"Dunno. They always are." I take another gulp of wine. I can't believe I'm explaining *EastEnders* and "shake your booty" to my dead great-aunt. Surely we should be talking about something more meaningful?

"Look, Sadie . . . what *are* you?" I say on impulse, zapping the TV off.

"What do you mean, what am I?" She sounds affronted. "I'm a girl. Just like you."

"A dead girl," I point out. "So, not *exactly* like me."

"You don't have to remind me," she says frostily.

I watch as she arranges herself on the edge of the sofa, obviously trying to look natural despite having zero gravity.

"Do you have any special superhero powers?" I try another tack. "Can you make fire? Or stretch yourself really thin?"

"No." She seems offended. "Anyway, I *am* thin."

"Do you have an enemy to vanquish? Like Buffy?"

"Who's Buffy?"

"The Vampire Slayer," I explain. "She's on TV; she fights demons and vampires—"

"Don't be ridiculous," she cuts me off tartly. "Vampires don't exist."

"Well, nor do ghosts!" I retort. "And it's not ridiculous! Don't you know anything? Most ghosts come back to fight the dark forces of evil or lead people to the light or something. They do something *positive*. Not just sit around watching TV."

Sadie shrugs, as though to say, "What do I care?"

I sip my wine, thinking hard. She's obviously not here to save the world from dark forces. Maybe she's going to shed light on mankind's plight or the meaning of life or something like that. Maybe I'm supposed to learn from her.

"So, you lived through the whole twentieth century," I venture. "That's pretty amazing. What was . . . er . . . Winston Churchill like? Or JFK! Do you think he really was killed by Lee Harvey Oswald?"

Sadie stares at me as though I'm a moron. "How would I know?"

"Because!" I say defensively. "Because you're from

history! What was it like living through World War Two?" To my surprise, Sadie looks quite blank.

"Don't you *remember* it?" I say incredulously.

"Of course I remember it." She regains her composure. "It was cold and dreary and one's friends got killed, and I'd rather not think about it."

She speaks crisply—but that little hesitation has pricked my curiosity.

"Do you remember your whole life?" I ask cautiously.

She must have memories spanning more than a hundred years. How on earth can she keep hold of them all?

"It seems like . . . a dream," murmurs Sadie, almost to herself. "Some parts are hazy." She's twirling her skirt around one finger, her expression distant. "I remember everything I need to remember," she says at last.

"You choose what to remember," I offer.

"I didn't say that." Her eyes flash with some unfathomable emotion and she wheels away from my gaze. She comes to rest in front of the mantelpiece and peers at a photo of me. It's a tourist gimmick from Madame Tussauds and shows me grinning next to the waxwork of Brad Pitt.

"Is *this* your lover?" She turns around.

"I wish," I say sardonically.

"Don't you have any lovers?" She sounds so pitying, I feel a bit piqued.

"I had a boyfriend called Josh until a couple of months ago. But it's over. So . . . I'm single at the moment."

Sadie looks at me expectantly. "Why don't you take another lover?"

"Because I don't want to just take another lover!" I say, nettled. "I'm not ready!"

"Why not?" She seems perplexed.

"Because I loved him! And it's been really traumatic! He was my soul mate; we completely chimed—"

"Why did he break it off, then?"

"I don't know. I just don't know! At least, I have this theory. . . ." I trail off, torn. It's still painful talking about Josh. But, on the other hand, it's quite a relief to have someone fresh to download to. "OK. Tell me what *you* think." I kick off my shoes, sit crosslegged on the sofa, and lean toward Sadie. "We were in this relationship and it was all going great—"

"Is he handsome?" she interrupts.

"Of course he's handsome!" I pull out my phone, find the most flattering picture of him, and tilt it toward her. "Here he is."

"Mmm." She makes a so-so gesture with her head.

Mmm? Is that the best she can do? I mean, Josh is absolutely, definitely good-looking, and that's not just me being biased.

"We met at this bonfire party. He's in IT advertising." I'm scrolling through, showing her other pictures. "We just clicked, you know how you do? We used to spend all night just talking."

"How dull." Sadie wrinkles her nose. "I'd rather spend all night gambling."

"We were getting to know each other," I say, shooting her an offended look. "Like you *do* in a relationship."

"Did you go dancing?"

"Sometimes!" I say impatiently. "That wasn't the point! The point was, we were the perfect match. We talked about everything. We were wrapped up in each other. I honestly thought this was The One. But then . . ." I pause as my thoughts painfully retread old paths. "Well, two things happened. First of all, there was this time when I . . . I did the wrong thing. We were walking past a jewelers' shop and I said, 'That's the ring you can buy me.' I mean, I was *joking*. But I think it freaked him out. Then, a couple of weeks later, one of his mates broke up from a long-term relationship. It was like shock waves went through the group. The commitment thing hit them and none of them could cope, so they all ran. All of a sudden Josh was just . . . backing off. Then he broke up with me, and he wouldn't even talk about it."

I close my eyes as painful memories start resurfacing. It was such a shock. He dumped me by email. By *email*.

"The thing is, I *know* he still cares about me." I bite my lip. "I mean, the very fact he won't talk proves it! He's scared, or he's running away, or there's some other reason I don't know about. . . . But I feel so powerless." I feel the tears brimming in my eyes. "How am I supposed to fix it if he won't discuss it? How can I make things better if I don't know what he's thinking? I mean, what do *you* think?"

There's silence. I look up to see Sadie sitting with her eyes closed, humming softly.

"Sadie? *Sadie?*"

"Oh!" She blinks at me. "Sorry. I do tend to go into a trance when people are droning on."

Droning on?

"I wasn't 'droning on'!" I say with indignation. "I was telling you about my relationship!"

Sadie is surveying me with fascination.

"You're terribly *serious*, aren't you?" she says.

"No, I'm not," I say at once, defensively. "What does that mean?"

"When I was your age, if a boy behaved badly, one simply scored his name out from one's dance card."

"Yes, well." I try not to sound too patronizing. "This is all a bit more serious than dance cards. We do a bit more than dance."

"My best friend, Bunty, was treated terribly badly by a boy named Christopher one New Year. In a taxi, you know." Sadie widens her eyes. "But she had a little weep, powdered her nose again, and tally-ho! She was engaged before Easter!"

"Tally-ho?" I can't keep the scorn out of my voice. "That's your attitude toward men? Tally-ho?"

"What's wrong with that?"

"What about proper balanced relationships? What about commitment?"

Sadie looks baffled. "Why do you keep talking about commitment? Do you mean being committed to a mental asylum?"

"No!" I try to keep my patience. "I mean . . . Look, were you ever married?"

Sadie shrugs. "I was married for a spell. We had too many arguments. So wearing, and one begins to wonder why one ever liked the chap in the first place. So I left him. I went abroad, to the Orient. That was in 1933. He divorced me during the war. Cited me for adultery," she adds gaily, "but everyone was too distracted to think about the scandal by then."

In the kitchen, the oven pings to tell me my lasagna's ready. I wander through, my head buzzing with all this new information. Sadie was divorced. She played around. She lived in "the Orient," wherever that's supposed to be.

"D'you mean Asia?" I hoick out my lasagna and tip some salad onto my plate. "Because that's what we call it these days. And, by the way, we *work* at our relationships."

"Work?" Sadie appears beside me, wrinkling her nose. "That doesn't sound like any fun. Maybe that's why you broke up."

"It isn't!" I feel like slapping her, she's so annoying. She doesn't understand anything.

"*Count On Us*," she reads off my lasagna packet. "What does that mean?"

"It means it's low fat," I say, a little reluctantly, expecting the usual lecture that Mum gives me about processed diet foods and how I'm a perfectly normal size and girls these days are far too obsessed about weight.

"Oh, you're on a *diet*." Sadie's eyes light up. "You should do the Hollywood diet. You eat nothing but eight grapefruit a day, black coffee, and a hard-boiled egg. And plenty of cigarettes. I did it for a month and the weight *fell* off me. A girl in my village swore she took tapeworm pills," she adds reminiscently. "But she wouldn't tell us where she got them."

I stare at her, feeling a bit revolted. "Tapeworms?"

"They gobble up all the food inside one, you know. Marvelous idea."

I sit down and look at my lasagna, but I'm not hungry anymore. Partly because visions of tapeworms are now lodged in my mind. And partly because I haven't talked about Josh so openly for ages. I feel all churned up and frustrated.

"If I could just talk to him." I spear a piece of cucumber and stare at it miserably. "If I could just get inside his head. But he won't accept my calls, he won't meet up—"

"*More* talking?" Sadie looks appalled. "How are you going to forget him if you keep talking about him? Darling, when things go wrong in life, this is what you do." She adopts a knowledgeable tone. "You lift your chin, put on a ravishing smile, mix yourself a little cocktail—and out you go."

"It's not as simple as that," I say resentfully. "And I don't *want* to forget about him. Some of us have hearts, you know. Some of us don't give up on true love. Some of us . . ."

I suddenly notice Sadie's eyes have closed and she's humming again.

Trust me to get haunted by the flakiest ghost in the world. One minute shrieking in my ear, the next making outrageous comments, the next spying on my neighbors . . . I take a mouthful of lasagna and chew it crossly. I wonder what else she saw in my neighbors' flats. Maybe I could get her to spy on that guy upstairs when he's making a racket, see what he's actually doing—

Wait.

Oh my God.

I nearly choke on my food. With no warning, a new idea has flashed into my mind. A fully formed, totally brilliant plan. The plan that will solve everything.

Sadie could spy on Josh.

She could get into his flat. She could listen to his conversations. She could find out what he thinks about everything and tell me, and somehow I could work out what the problem is between us and solve it.

This is the answer. This is it. *This* is why she was sent to me.

"Sadie!" I leap to my feet, powered by a kind of

giddy adrenaline. "I've worked it out! I know why you're here! It's to get me and Josh back together!"

"No, it's not," Sadie objects at once. "It's to get my necklace."

"You can't be here just for some crummy old necklace." I make a brushing-aside gesture. "Maybe the real reason is you're supposed to help me! *That's* why you were sent!"

"I wasn't *sent*!" Sadie appears mortally offended at the very idea. "And my necklace isn't crummy! And I don't want to help you. You're supposed to be helping *me*."

"Who says? I bet you're my guardian angel." I'm getting carried away here. "I bet you've been sent back to earth to show me that actually my life is wonderful, like in that movie."

Sadie looks at me silently for a moment, then surveys the kitchen.

"I don't think your life's wonderful," she says. "I think it's rather drab. And your haircut's atrocious."

I glare at her furiously. "You're a crap guardian angel!"

"I'm *not* your guardian angel!" she shoots back.

"How do you know?" I clutch at my chest determinedly. "I'm getting a very strong psychic feeling that you're here to help me get back together with Josh. The spirits are telling me."

"Well, I'm getting a very strong psychic feeling that I'm *not* supposed to get you back together with Josh," she retorts at once. "The spirits are telling *me*."

She's got a nerve. What would she know about spirits? Is she the one who can see ghosts?

"Well, I'm alive, so I'm boss," I snap. "And I say

you're supposed to help me. Otherwise, maybe I won't have time to look for your necklace."

I didn't mean to put it quite as bluntly as that. But then, she forced me into it by being so selfish. I mean, honestly. She should *want* to help her own great-niece.

Sadie's eyes flash angrily at me, but I can tell she knows she's caught out.

"Very well," she says at last, and her slim shoulders heave in a huge, put-upon sigh. "It's a terrible idea, but I suppose I have no choice. What do you want me to do?"

SIX

$\mathcal{Q}$ haven't felt as zippy as this for weeks. For months. It's eight o'clock the next morning, and I feel like a brand-new person! Instead of waking all depressed, with a picture of Josh clutched in my tearstained hand, a bottle of vodka on the floor, and Alanis Morissette playing on a loop . . .

OK. That was only the one time.

But anyway. Just look at me! Energetic. Refreshed. Straight eyeliner. Crisp stripy top. Ready to face the day and spy on Josh and get him back. I've even booked a cab, to be efficient.

I head into the kitchen to find Sadie sitting at the table in yet another dress. This one is mauve, with panels of tulle and a draping effect at the shoulders.

"Wow!" I can't help gasping. "How come you have all these different outfits?"

"Isn't it glorious?" Sadie looks pleased with herself. "And it's very easy, you know. I just imagine myself in a particular frock and it appears on me."

"So was this one of your favorites?"

"No, this belonged to a girl I knew called Cecily." Sadie smooths down the skirt. "I always coveted it."

"You've pinched another girl's outfit?" I can't help giggling. "You've stolen it?"

"I haven't *stolen* it," she says coldly. "Don't be ridiculous."

"How do you know?" I can't resist needling her. "What if she's a ghost too and she wants to wear it today and she can't? What if she's sitting somewhere, crying her eyes out?"

"That's not how it works," says Sadie stonily.

"How do you know what works? How do you know—" I break off as a sudden brilliant thought hits me. "Hey! I've got it! You should just *imagine* your necklace. Just picture it in your head and then you'll have it. Quickly, close your eyes, think hard—"

"Are you always this slow-witted?" Sadie interrupts. "I've tried that. I tried to imagine my rabbit-fur cape and dancing shoes as well, but I couldn't get them. I don't know why."

"Maybe you can only wear ghost clothes," I say after a moment's consideration. "Clothes that are dead too. Like, that have been shredded up or destroyed or whatever."

We both look at the mauve dress for a few moments. It seems sad to think of it being shredded up; in fact, I wish I hadn't mentioned it.

"So, are you all set?" I change the subject. "If we go soon, we can catch Josh before he leaves for work." I take a yogurt out of the fridge and start spooning it into my mouth. Just the thought of being near Josh again is making me feel fizzy. I can't even finish my yogurt, I'm so excited. I put the half-eaten pot back in the fridge and dump the spoon in the sink.

"Come on. Let's go!" I pick up my hairbrush from its place in the fruit bowl and tug it through my hair. Then I grab my keys and turn to see Sadie studying me.

"*Goodness*, your arms are plump," she says. "I hadn't noticed before."

"They're not plump," I say, offended. "That's solid muscle." I clench my biceps at her and she recoils.

"Even worse." Complacently, she looks down at her own slender white arms. "I was always renowned for my arms."

"Yeah, well, these days, we appreciate a bit of definition," I inform her. "We go to the gym. Are you ready? The taxi'll be here in a minute." The buzzer goes and I lift the receiver.

"Hi! I'm just coming down—"

"Lara?" comes a familiar muffled voice. "Darling, it's Dad. And Mum. Just popped round to check you're all right. We thought we'd catch you before work."

I stare at the speakerphone in disbelief. Dad and Mum? Of all the times. And what's all this with the "popping round," anyway? Mum and Dad never "pop round."

"Um . . . great!" I try to sound breezy. "I'll be right down!"

I emerge from my building to find Mum and Dad standing on the pavement. Mum is holding a potted plant and Dad is clutching a full Holland & Barrett bag, and they're talking in low voices. As they see me, they come forward with fake smiles as though I'm a mental patient.

"Lara, darling." I can see Dad's worried eyes scanning my face. "You haven't replied to any of my texts or messages. We were getting worried!"

"Oh, right. Sorry. I've been a bit busy."

"What happened at the police station, darling?" asks Mum, attempting to sound relaxed.

"It was fine. I gave them a statement."

"Oh, Michael." Mum closes her eyes in despair.

"So you really believe Great-Aunt Sadie was murdered?" I can tell Dad is as freaked out as Mum.

"Look, Dad, it's no big deal," I say reassuringly. "Don't worry about me."

Mum's eyes snap open. "Vitamins," she says, and starts rooting in the Holland & Barrett bag. "I asked the lady at the shop about . . . behavioral—" She stops herself. "And lavender oil . . . and a plant can help with stress—you could talk to it!" She tries to give me the potted plant, and I thrust it away again impatiently.

"I don't want a plant! I'll forget to water it and it'll die."

"You don't have to have the plant," says Dad in soothing tones, glancing warningly at Mum. "But you've obviously been very stressed, what with the new business . . . and Josh. . . ."

They are so going to change their tune. They are so going to realize I was right all along, when Josh and I get back together and get married. Not that I can say this right now, obviously.

"Dad." I give him a patient, reasonable smile. "I told you, I don't even think about Josh anymore. I'm just getting on with life. It's you who keeps bringing him up."

Ha. That was quite clever. I'm just about to tell Dad that maybe *he's* obsessed with Josh, when a taxi pulls up beside us on the pavement and a driver leans out.

"Thirty-two Bickenhall Mansions?"

Damn. OK, I'll just pretend I didn't hear him.

Mum and Dad are exchanging looks. "Isn't that where Josh lives?" says Mum tentatively.

"I don't remember," I say carelessly. "Anyway, it's for someone else—"

"Thirty-two Bickenhall Mansions?" The driver has leaned farther out of his cab, his voice raised higher. "Lara Lington? You book taxi?"

Bugger.

"Why are you going to Josh's flat?" Mum sounds beside herself.

"I'm . . . not!" I flounder. "It must be some car I booked months ago, finally turning up! They're always late. You're six months late! Go away!" I shoo at the bemused driver, who eventually puts the car into gear and drives away.

There's a kind of tense silence. Dad's expression is so transparent it's endearing. He wants to believe the best of me. On the other hand, the evidence is all point-ing one way.

"Lara, do you swear that taxi wasn't for you?" he says at last.

"I swear." I nod. "On . . . Great-Aunt Sadie's life."

I hear a gasp and look around to see Sadie's eyes beaming fury at me.

"I couldn't think of anything else!" I say defensively.

Sadie ignores me and walks right up to Dad. "You're fools," she says emphatically. "She's still smit-ten with Josh. She's about to spy on him. And she's making *me* do her dirty work."

"Shut up, you sneak!" I exclaim before I can stop myself.

"Sorry?" Dad stares at me.

"Nothing." I clear my throat. "Nothing! I'm fine."

"You're a lunatic." Sadie swivels around pityingly.

"At least I'm not *haunting* people!" I can't help re-torting.

"Haunting?" Dad is trying to follow me. "Lara . . . what on earth . . ."

"Sorry." I smile at him. "Just thinking aloud. In fact . . . I was actually thinking about poor Great-Aunt Sadie." I sigh, shaking my head pityingly. "She had such sad little twiggy arms."

"They're not twiggy!" Sadie glares back.

"She probably thought they were really attractive. Talk about deluded!" I laugh gaily. "Who wants pipe cleaners for arms?"

"Who wants pillows for arms?" Sadie shoots back, and I gasp in outrage.

"They're *not* pillows!"

"Lara . . ." says Dad faintly. "What's not pillows?"

Mum looks like she wants to cry. She's still clutching on to her potted plant and a book entitled *Stress-Free Living: You CAN Achieve It.*

"Anyway, I have to get to work." I give Mum a huge hug. "It's been brilliant to see you. And I'll read your book and take some vitamins. And I'll see you soon, Dad." I hug him too. "Don't worry!"

I blow them both kisses and hurry off along the pavement. When I reach the corner, I turn to wave— and they're both still standing there like waxworks.

I do feel sorry for my parents, I really do. Maybe I'll buy them a box of chocolates.

Twenty minutes later I'm standing outside Josh's building, feeling bubbly with exhilaration. Everything's going according to plan. I've located his window and explained the layout of the flat. Now it's up to Sadie.

"Go on!" I say excitedly. "Walk through the wall! This is so cool!"

"I don't *need* to walk through the wall." She shoots me a disparaging look. "I'll simply imagine myself inside his flat."

"OK. Well . . . good luck. Try to find out as much as you can. And be careful!"

Sadie disappears, and I crane my neck to survey Josh's window, but I can't see anything. I feel almost sick with anticipation. This is the nearest I've been to Josh in weeks. He's in there right now. And Sadie's watching him. And any minute she'll come out and—

"He's not there." Sadie appears in front of me.

"Not there?" I stare at her, affronted. "Well, where is he? He doesn't usually leave for work 'til nine."

"I've no idea." She doesn't sound remotely interested.

"What did the place look like?" I can't help probing for details. "Is it a real mess? Like, with old abandoned pizza boxes and beer bottles everywhere? Like he's been letting himself go? Like he doesn't really care about life anymore?"

"No, it's very tidy. Lots of fruit in the kitchen," Sadie adds. "I noticed that."

"Oh. Well, he's obviously taking care of himself, then." I hunch my shoulders, a bit discouraged. It's not that I *want* Josh to be an emotional wreck on the brink of meltdown, exactly, but . . .

Well. You know. It would be quite flattering.

"Let's go." Sadie yawns. "I've had enough of this."

"I'm not just leaving! Go in again! Look around for clues! Like . . . are there any photographs of me or anything?"

"No," says Sadie at once. "None. Not a single one."

"You haven't even looked." I glare at her resentfully. "Search on his desk. Maybe he's in the middle of writing a letter to me or something. Go on!" Without thinking, I try to push her toward the building, but my hands sink straight through her body.

"Urgh!" I recoil, feeling squeamish.

"Don't do that!" she exclaims.

"Did it . . . hurt?" I can't help glancing at my hands, as though they really have just plunged through her innards.

"Not exactly," she says grudgingly. "But it's not pleasant to have someone's hands poking through my stomach."

She whisks off again. I try to damp down my agitation and wait patiently. But this is totally unbearable, being stuck outside. If it were me searching, I'd find something, I know I would. Like a diary full of Josh's thoughts. Or a half-written email, unsent. Or . . . or *poetry*. Imagine that.

I can't help sliding into a fantasy about Sadie coming across a poem scrawled on some cast-aside piece of paper. Something really simple and direct, just like Josh himself.

It Was All A Mistake

God, I miss you, Lara.
I love your—

I can't think of anything to rhyme with *Lara*.

"Wake up! *Lara?*" I jump and open my eyes to see Sadie in front of me again.

"Did you find something?" I gasp.

"Yes. As a matter of fact, I did!" Sadie looks triumphant. "Something rather interesting and extremely relevant."

"Oh my God. What?" I can hardly breathe as tantalizing possibilities flash through my mind. A photo of me under his pillow . . . a diary entry resolving to get back in touch with me—

"He's having lunch with another girl on Saturday."

"What?" All my fantasies melt away. I stare at her, stricken. "What do you mean, he's having lunch with another girl?"

"There was a memorandum pinned up in the kitchen: *twelve-thirty lunch with Marie.*"

I don't know anyone called Marie. Josh doesn't know anyone called Marie.

"Who's Marie?" I can't contain my agitation. "Who's Marie?"

Sadie shrugs. "His new girlfriend?"

"Don't say that!" I cry in horror. "He hasn't got a new girlfriend! He wouldn't have! He said there wasn't anyone else! He said . . ."

I trail off, my heart thumping. It never even occurred to me that Josh might be seeing another girl already. It never even crossed my mind.

In his breakup email, he said he wasn't going to rush into anything new. He said he had to take time out to *think about his whole life.* Well, he hasn't thought for very long, has he? If I was going to think about my whole life, I'd take *ages* longer than six weeks. I'd take . . . a year! At least! Maybe two or three.

Boys treat thinking like sex. They think it takes twenty minutes and then you're done and there's no point talking about it. They have *no idea.*

"Did it say where they're having lunch?"

Sadie nods. "Bistro Martin."

"Bistro Martin?" I think I'm going to hyperventilate.

"That's where we had our first date! We always used to go there!"

Josh is taking a girl to Bistro Martin. A girl called Marie.

"Go in again." I wave my hands agitatedly at the building. "Search around! Find out more!"

"I'm not going in again!" objects Sadie. "You've found out all you need to know."

Actually, she has a point.

"You're right." Abruptly, I turn and start walking away from the flat, so preoccupied that I nearly bump into an old man. "Yes, you're right. I know which restaurant they're going to be at, and what time; I'll just go along and see for myself—"

"No!" Sadie appears in front of me, and I stop in surprise. "That's not what I meant! You *can't* be intending to spy on them."

"I have to." I look at her, perplexed. "How else am I going to find out if Marie's his new girlfriend or not?"

"You *don't* find out. You say, 'Good riddance,' buy a new dress, and take another lover. Or several."

"I don't want several lovers," I say mulishly. "I want Josh."

"Well, you can't have him! Give up!"

I'm so, so, *so* sick of people telling me to give up on Josh. My parents, Natalie, that old woman I got talking to on the bus once . . .

"Why should I give up?" My words fly out on a swell of protest. "Why does everyone keep telling me to give up? What's wrong with sticking to one single goal? In every other area of life, perseverance is *encouraged*! It's *rewarded*! I mean, they didn't tell Edison to give up on lightbulbs, did they? They didn't tell Scott to forget about the South Pole! They didn't say,

'Never mind, Scotty, there are plenty more snowy wastes out there.' He kept trying. He refused to give up, however hard it got. And he made it!"

I feel quite stirred up as I finish, but Sadie is peering at me as though I'm an imbecile.

"Scott didn't make it," she says. "He froze to death."

I glare at her resentfully. Some people are just so negative.

"Well, anyway." I turn on my heel and start stumping along the street. "I'm going to that lunch."

"The worst thing a girl can do is trail after a boy when a love affair is dead," Sadie says disdainfully. I stump faster, but she has no problem keeping up with me. "There was a girl called Polly in my village— *frightful* trailer. She was convinced this chap Desmond was still in love with her and followed him around everywhere. So we played the most ripping joke on her. We told her that Desmond was in the garden, hiding behind a bush as he was too shy to talk to her directly. Then, when she came out, one of the boys read out a love letter, supposed to be from him. We'd written it ourselves, you know. Everyone was hiding behind the bushes, simply rocking."

I can't help feeling a reluctant interest in her story.

"Didn't the other guy sound different?"

"He said his voice was high from nerves. He said her presence reduced him to a trembling leaf. Polly replied that she understood, because her own legs were like aspic." Sadie starts giggling. "We all called her Aspic for ages after that."

"That's so mean!" I say in horror. "She didn't realize it was a trick?"

"Only when the bushes all started shaking around

the garden. Then my friend Bunty rolled out onto the grass, she was laughing so hard, and the game was up. Poor Polly." Sadie gives a sudden giggle. "She was foaming. She didn't speak to any of us all summer."

"I'm not surprised!" I exclaim. "I think you were all really cruel! And, anyway, what if their love affair *wasn't* dead? What if you ruined her chance of true love?"

"True love!" echoes Sadie with a derisive laugh. "You're so old-fashioned!"

"*Old-fashioned?*" I echo incredulously.

"You're just like my grandmother, with your love songs and your sighing. You even have a little miniature of your beloved in your handbag, don't you? Don't deny it! I've seen you looking at it."

It takes me a moment to work out what she's talking about.

"It isn't a miniature, actually. It's called a mobile phone."

"Whatever it's called. You still look at it and make goo-goo eyes and then you take your smelling salts out of that little bottle—"

"That's Rescue Remedy!" I say furiously. God, she's starting to wind me up. "So you don't believe in love, is that what you're saying? You weren't ever in love? Not even when you were married?"

A passing postman shoots me a curious look, and I hastily put a hand to my ear as though adjusting an earpiece. I must start wearing one as camouflage.

Sadie hasn't answered me, and as we reach the tube station I stop dead to survey her, suddenly genuinely curious. "You were really never in love?"

There's the briefest pause, then Sadie flings her arms out with a rattle of bracelets, her head thrown back. "I

had fun. That's what I believe in. Fun, flings, the sizzle . . ."

"What sizzle?"

"That's what we called it, Bunty and I." Her mouth
curves in a reminiscent smile. "It starts as a shiver,
when you see a man for the first time. And then he
meets your eye and the shiver runs down your back
and becomes a sizzle in your stomach and you think *I
want to dance with that man*."

"And then what happens?"

"You dance, you have a cocktail or two, you
flirt. . . ." Her eyes are shining.

"Do you—"

I want to ask, "Do you shag him?" but I'm not sure
it's the kind of question you ask your 105-year-old
great-aunt. Then I remember the visitor from the nursing home.

"Hey." I raise my eyebrows. "You can say what you
like, but I know there was someone special in your
life."

"What do you mean?" She stares at me, suddenly
tense. "What are you talking about?"

"A certain gentleman by the name of . . . Charles
Reece?"

I'm hoping to provoke a blush or gasp or something, but she looks blank.

"I've never heard of him."

"Charles Reece! He came to visit you in the nursing
home? A few weeks ago?"

Sadie shakes her head. "I don't remember." The
light in her eyes fades as she adds, "I don't remember
much about that place at all."

"I suppose you wouldn't. . . ." I pause awkwardly.
"You had a stroke, years ago."

"I *know.*" She glares at me.

God, she doesn't have to be so touchy. It's not my fault. Suddenly I realize my phone is vibrating. I pull it out of my pocket and see that it's Kate.

"Hi, Kate!"

"Lara? Hi! Um, I was wondering . . . are you coming into work today? Or not?" she adds quickly, as though she might have offended me by asking. "I mean, either way is great, everything's fine. . . ."

Shit. I've been so absorbed in Josh, I'd almost forgotten about work.

"I'm on my way in," I say hastily. "I was just doing a bit of . . . er . . . research at home. Is anything up?"

"It's Shireen. She wants to know what you've done about her dog. She sounded quite upset. In fact, she was talking about pulling out of the job."

Oh God. I haven't even *thought* about Shireen and her dog.

"Could you phone her back and say I'm on the case and I'll call her really soon? Thanks, Kate."

I put my phone away and massage my temples briefly. This is bad. Here I am, out on the street, spying on my ex, completely abandoning my work crisis. I need to reorder my priorities. I need to realize what's important in life.

I'll leave Josh until the weekend.

"We have to go." I reach for my Oyster card and start hurrying toward the tube. "I've got a problem."

"Another man problem?" asks Sadie, wafting effortlessly along beside me.

"No, a dog problem."

"A *dog?*"

"It's my client." I march down the tube steps. "She wants to take her dog to work, and they're saying no, it's not allowed, but she's convinced there's another dog in the building."

"Why?"

"Because she heard barking, more than once. But, I mean, what am I supposed to do about it?" I'm almost talking to myself now. "I'm totally stuck. The human-resources department is denying there's any other dog, and there's no way to prove they're lying. I can't exactly get into the building and search every office—"

I stop in surprise as Sadie appears right in front of me.

"Maybe not." Her eyes sparkle. "But I can."

SEVEN

Macrosant is housed in a massive block on Kingsway, with big steps and a steel globe sculpture and plate-glass windows. From the Costa Coffee across the road, I have a pretty good view of it.

"Anything doglike," I'm instructing Sadie, behind an open copy of the *Evening Standard*. "The sound of barking, baskets under desks, dog toys . . ." I take a sip of cappuccino. "I'll stay here. And thanks!"

The building's so massive, I could be waiting here awhile. I flick through my *Evening Standard* and slowly nibble my way through a chocolate brownie, and I've just ordered a fresh cappuccino when Sadie materializes in front of me. Her cheeks are flushed and her eyes are shining and she's glowing all over. I pull out my mobile phone, smile at the girl at the next table, and pretend to dial a number.

"So?" I say into the phone. "Did you find a dog?"

"Oh, that," Sadie says, as though she'd forgotten all about it. "Yes, there's a dog, but guess what—"

"Where?" I cut her off in excitement. "Where's the dog?"

"Up there." She gestures. "In a basket under a desk. It's the *dearest* little Pekingese—"

"Can you get a name? An office number? Anything like that? Thank you!"

She vanishes and I sip my new cappuccino, hugging myself. Shireen was right all along! Jean lied to me! Wait until I get on the phone with her. Just wait. I'm going to demand a full apology and full office rights for Flash and maybe a new dog basket as a goodwill gesture. . . .

I glance through the window and suddenly spot Sadie drifting along the pavement, back toward the coffee shop. I feel a tiny spike of frustration. She doesn't seem in any hurry at all. Doesn't she realize how important this is?

I'm ready with my mobile out as soon as she enters. "Everything OK?" I demand. "Did you find the dog again?"

"Oh," she says vaguely. "Yes, the dog. It's on floor fourteen, room 1416, and its owner is Jane Frenshew. I've just met the most *delicious* man." She hugs herself.

"What do you mean, you've met a man?" I'm scribbling it all quickly on a piece of paper. "You can't meet a man. You're dead. Unless—" I look up with a sudden thrill. "Ooh. Have you met another ghost?"

"He's not a ghost." She shakes her head impatiently. "But he's divine. He was talking in one of the rooms I walked through. Just like Rudolph Valentino."

"Who?" I say blankly.

"The film star, of course! Tall and dark and dashing. Instant sizzle."

"Sounds lovely," I say absently.

"And he's just the right height," Sadie continues, swinging her legs on a bar stool. "I measured myself against him. My head would rest on his shoulder perfectly if we went dancing together."

"Great." I finish writing, grab my bag, and stand up. "OK. I need to get back to the office and sort this out."

I head out of the door and start hurrying toward the tube, but to my surprise Sadie blocks my way.

"I want him."

"I'm sorry?" I peer at her, flicking my mobile open out of habit.

"The man I just met. I felt it, right here. The sizzle." She presses her concave stomach. "I want to dance with him."

Is she joking?

"Well, that would be nice," I say at last, in placatory tones. "But I've really got to get to the office—"

As I move forward, Sadie thrusts a bare arm across my path and I stop, taken aback.

"Do you know how long it's been since I've danced?" she says with sudden passion. "Do you know how long it's been since I've . . . shaken my booty? All those years, trapped in an old woman's body. In a place with no music, with no life . . ."

I feel a rub of guilt inside as I remember the picture of Sadie, ancient and wrinkled in her pink shawl.

"OK," I say quickly. "Fair enough. So, let's dance at home. We'll put on some music, dim the lights, have a little party—"

"I don't want to dance at home to the wireless!" she says scornfully. "I want to go out with a man and enjoy myself!"

"You want to go on a *date,*" I say disbelievingly, and her eyes light up.

"Yes! Exactly! A date with a man. With him." She points at the building.

What exactly is it about being a ghost that she doesn't understand?

"Sadie, you're *dead.*"

"I know!" she says in irritation. "You don't have to keep reminding me!"

"So you can't go on a date. Sorry. That's the way it is." I shrug and start walking on again. Two seconds later, Sadie lands in front of me once more, her jaw set.

"Ask him for me."

"What?"

"I can't do it on my own." Her voice is fast and determined. "I need a go-between. If you go out with him on a date, I can go out with him on a date. If you dance with him, I can dance with him too."

She's serious. I almost want to burst out laughing.

"You want me to go on a date for you," I say, to clarify. "With some random guy I don't know. So you can have a dance."

"I just want one last little burst of fun with a handsome man while I still have the chance." Sadie's head falls forward and her mouth pouts into the sad little O shape again. "One more whirl around a dance floor. That's all I ask before I disappear from this world." Her voice descends to a low, pitiful whisper. "It's my last desire. My final wish."

"It's not your final wish!" I say, a bit indignantly. "You've already had your final wish! It was searching for your necklace, remember?"

For an instant Sadie looks caught out.

"This is my other final wish," she says at last.

"Look, Sadie." I try to sound reasonable. "I can't just ask a stranger on a date. You'll have to do without this one. Sorry."

Sadie is surveying me with such a silent, quivering, wounded expression that I wonder if I somehow stepped on her foot.

"You're really saying no," she says at last, her voice cracking as though with emotion. "You're really refusing me. One last innocent wish. One tiny request."

"Look—"

"I was in that nursing home for years. Never any visitors. Never any laughter. Never any life. Just old-ness . . . and loneliness . . . and misery . . ."

Oh God. She can't do this to me. It's not fair.

"Every Christmas, all alone, never a visitor . . . never a present . . ."

"It wasn't my fault," I say feebly, but Sadie ignores me.

"And now I see the chance of a sliver of happiness. A morsel of pleasure. Yet my own callous, selfish great-niece—"

"OK!" I stop in my tracks and rub my forehead. "OK! Whatever! Fine! I'll do it."

Everyone in my life thinks I'm a lunatic anyway. Asking a stranger on a date will make no difference; in fact, my dad will probably be delighted.

"You're an angel!" Sadie's mood has instantly flipped to giddy excitement. She whirls around on the pavement, the panels on her dress flying out. "I'll show you where he is! Come on!"

I follow her toward the massive steps and push my way into the huge double-height foyer. If I'm going to do this, I need to do it very quickly, before I change my mind.

"So where is he?" I look around the echoing marble chamber.

"In a room upstairs! Come on!" She's like a puppy straining the leash.

"I can't just walk into an office building!" I hiss

back, gesturing at the electronic security barriers. "I need a plan. I need an excuse. I need . . . *aha.*"

In the corner is a stand with the sign *Global Strategy Seminar*. A pair of bored-looking girls are sitting behind a table of name badges. They'll do.

"Hi." I approach briskly. "Sorry I'm late."

"No problem. They've only just started." One of the girls sits up and reaches for her list, while the other stares resolutely at the ceiling. "And you are . . ."

"Sarah Connoy," I say, grabbing a name badge at random. "Thanks. I'd better get going."

I hurry to the security barriers, flash my name badge at the guard, and hurry through into a wide corridor with expensive-looking artwork on the walls. I have no idea where I am. The building holds about twenty different companies, and the only one I've ever visited is Macrosant, which is on floors 11–17. "Where's this guy, then?" I murmur to Sadie out of the side of my mouth.

"Twentieth floor."

I head for the lifts, nodding in a businesslike way at all the other passengers. At floor 20 I get out of the lift and find myself in another massive reception area. Twenty feet away from where I'm standing is a granite-colored desk manned by a scary-looking woman in a gray suit. A plaque on the wall says *Turner Murray Consulting*.

Wow. Turner Murray are the really brainy ones who get asked to sort out big businesses. This guy must be pretty high-powered, whoever he is.

"Come on!" Sadie is dancing ahead toward a door with a security panel. A pair of men in suits stride past, and one of them gives me a curious look. I hold my phone up to my ear to discourage conversation, and follow the men. As we reach the door, one of the men punches in a code.

"Thanks." I nod in my most businesslike way and follow them in. "Gavin, I've told you the European figures don't make sense," I say into my phone.

The taller man hesitates as though he's going to challenge me. Shit. I hastily increase my speed and walk straight past them.

"I have a meeting in two minutes, Gavin," I say hastily. "I want those updated figures on my Black-Berry. Now I have to go and talk about . . . er . . . percentages."

There's a ladies' room on the left. Trying not to run, I hurry into it and duck into a marble-clad cubicle.

"What are you doing?" Sadie demands, materializing right in the cubicle with me. Honestly. Does she have no idea of privacy?

"What do you think I'm doing?" I reply under my breath. "We need to wait a bit."

I sit it out for three minutes, then head out of the ladies'. The two men have disappeared. The corridor is empty and quiet, just a long stretch of pale-gray carpet and occasional water machines and blond-wood doors leading off on either side. I can hear the hum of conversation and occasional small computer sounds.

"So where is he?" I turn to Sadie.

"Hmm." She's peering around. "One of these doors along here . . ."

She heads along the corridor and I follow cautiously. This is surreal. What am I doing roaming around a strange office building, looking for a strange man?

"Yes!" Sadie appears by my side, glowing. "He's in

there! He has the most *penetrating* eyes. Absolutely shiversome." She points to a solid wooden door labeled *Room 2012*. There isn't a window or even a tiny glass panel. I can't see anything inside.

"Are you sure?"

"I've just been inside! He's there! Go on! Ask him!" Her hands are trying to push me.

"Wait!" I take a few steps away, trying to think this all through. I can't just blunder in. I have to make a plan.

1) Knock and enter strange guy's office.
2) Say hello in natural, pleasant manner.
3) Ask him out on date.
4) Almost die of embarrassment as he calls security.
5) Leave very, very swiftly.
6) Do not give my name under any circumstances. That way I can run away and blank the whole thing from my memory and nobody will ever know it was me. Maybe he'll even think he dreamed it.

The whole thing will take thirty seconds max and then Sadie will have to stop pestering me. OK, let's get it over with. I approach the door, trying to ignore the fact that my heart is suddenly galloping with nerves. I take a deep breath, raise my hand, and knock gently.

"You didn't make any sound!" exclaims Sadie behind me. "Knock harder! Then just walk in. He's in there! Go on!"

Squeezing my eyes, I rap sharply, twist the door handle, and take a step inside the room.

Twenty suited people seated around a conference table all turn to look at me. A man at the far end pauses in his PowerPoint presentation.

I stare back, frozen.

It's not an office. It's a conference room. I'm standing

in a company I don't belong to, in a great big meeting I don't belong to, and everyone's waiting for me to speak.

"Sorry," I stammer at last. "I don't want to interrupt. Carry on."

Out of the corner of my eye I've noticed a couple of empty seats. Barely knowing what I'm doing, I pull a chair out and sit down. The woman next to me eyes me uncertainly for a moment, then pushes along a pad of paper and pen.

"Thanks," I murmur back.

I don't quite believe this. No one's told me to leave. Don't they realize I don't belong here? The guy at the front has resumed his speech, and a few people are scribbling notes. Surreptitiously, I look around the table. There are about fifteen men in this room. Sadie's guy could be any of them. There's a sandy-haired guy across the table who looks cute. The man giving the presentation is quite good-looking too. He has wavy dark hair and pale blue eyes and the same tie I bought Josh for his birthday. He's gesturing at a graph and talking with an animated voice.

". . . and client satisfaction ratings have increased, year-on-year—"

"Stop right there." A man standing at the window, whom I hadn't even noticed before, turns around. He has an American accent, a dark suit, and chestnut-colored hair brushed straight back. There's a deep V-shaped frown between his eyebrows, and he's looking at the wavy-haired guy as though he represents some great personal disappointment to him. "Client satisfaction ratings aren't what we're about. I don't want to perform work that a client rates as an A. I want to perform work that *I* rate as an A."

The man with wavy hair looks wrong-footed, and I feel a stab of sympathy for him.

"Of course," he mumbles.

"The emphasis in this room is all wrong." The American guy frowns around the table. "We're not here to perform tactical quick fixes. We should be influencing strategy. Innovating. Since I've been over here . . ."

I tune out as I notice Sadie sliding into the chair next to me. I scribble *WHICH MAN?* and push my pad across.

"The one who looks like Rudolph Valentino," she says, as though surprised I even need to ask.

For God's sake.

HOW WOULD I KNOW WHAT BLOODY RUDOLPH VALENTINO LOOKS LIKE? I scribble. *WHICH ONE?*

I'm betting on the wavy-haired man. Unless it's the blond guy sitting right at the front; he looks quite nice. Or maybe that chap with the goatee?

"Him, of course!" Sadie points to the other side of the room.

THE MAN GIVING THE PRESENTATION? I write, just to confirm it.

"No, silly!" She giggles. "Him!" She appears in front of the American man with the frown, and gazes at him longingly. "Isn't he a dove?"

"Him?"

Oops. I spoke out loud. Everyone turns to look at me, and I hastily try to sound as though I'm clearing my throat: "Hmrrrm hrrrmm."

SERIOUSLY, HIM? I write on my pad of paper as she returns to my side.

"He's delicious!" she says in my ear, sounding affronted.

I survey the American guy dubiously, trying to be fair. I suppose he is quite good-looking in that classic preppy way. His hair springs up from a broad, square brow, he has the hint of a tan, and dark wrist hair is visible inside his immaculate white cuffs. And his eyes *are* penetrating. He's got that magnetic quality that leaders always seem to have. Strong hands and gestures. As he speaks, he commands attention.

But honestly. He's so totally not my sort. Too intense. Too frowny. And everyone else in the room seems terrified of him.

"Speaking of which." He picks up a plastic folder and skims it deftly across the table toward the goatee-beard guy. "Last night I put together some points with regard to the Morris Farquhar consultation. Just a memo. Might help."

"Oh." Goatee-beard guy looks utterly taken aback. "Well . . . thanks. I appreciate it." He flips through wonderingly. "Can I *use* this?"

"That's the general idea," says the American guy, with a smile so wry and brief you'd miss it if you blinked. "So, regarding the final point . . ."

From my place at the back, I can see goatee-beard guy leafing through the typed pages, agog. "When the hell did he have time to do this?" he mutters to his neighbor, who shrugs.

"I have to go." The American guy suddenly consults his watch. "My apologies for hijacking the meeting. Simon, please continue."

"I have just one question." The sandy-haired man hurriedly raises his hand. "When you're talking about innovating procedure, do you mean—"

"Quick!" Sadie's voice suddenly resounds in my ear,

making me jump. "Ask him on a date! He's leaving! You promised! Do it! Do-it-do-it-do-it—"

OK!!!!!! I scrawl, flinching. *JUST GIVE ME A SECOND.*

Sadie stalks to the other side of the room and watches me expectantly. After a while she starts making impatient *Come on!* gestures with her hands. Mr. American Frown has finished answering the sandy-haired guy and is pushing some papers into his briefcase.

I *can't* do this. It's ludicrous.

"Go on! *Go on!*" Sadie's voice blasts my eardrum again. *"Ask!"*

Blood is pulsating around my head. My legs are trembling under the table. Somehow I force myself to raise a hand.

"Excuse me?" I say in an embarrassed squeak.

Mr. American Frown turns and surveys me, looking puzzled. "I'm sorry, I don't think we've been introduced. You'll have to excuse me, I'm in a hurry—"

"I have a question."

Everyone around the table has swiveled to look at me. I can see a man whispering "Who's that?" to his neighbor.

"OK." He sighs. "One more quick question. What is it?"

"I . . . um . . . It's just . . . I wanted to ask . . ." My voice is jumpy and I clear my throat. "Would you like to go out with me?"

There's a stunned silence, apart from someone spluttering on their coffee. My face is boiling hot, but I hold steady. I can see a few astounded looks passing between the people at the table.

"Excuse me?" says the American man, looking bewildered.

"Like . . . on a date?" I risk a little smile.

Suddenly I'm aware of Sadie beside him. "Say *yes*!" she shrieks into his ear, so loudly that I want to flinch on his behalf. *"Say yes! Say yes!"*

To my astonishment, I can see the American man reacting. He's cocking his head as though he can hear some distant radio signal. Can he *hear* her?

"Young lady," says a gray-haired man curtly. "This really isn't the time or place—"

"I don't mean to interrupt," I say humbly. "I won't take up much time. I just need an answer, one way or the other." I turn to the American man again. "Would you like to go out with me?"

"Say yes! Say yes!" Sadie's yelling increases to an unbearable level.

This is unreal. The American man can definitely hear something. He shakes his head and takes a couple of steps away, but Sadie follows him, still yelling. His eyes are glazed and he looks like he's in a trance.

No one else in the room is moving or speaking. They all seem pinioned by shock; one woman has her hand clapped across her face as though she's watching a train wreck.

"Say yes!" Sadie's starting to sound hoarse as she screams. *"Right now! Say it! SAY YES!"*

It's almost comical, the sight of her yelling so hard and only getting the faintest reaction. But as I watch, I only feel pity. She looks so powerless, as though she's shouting behind a sheet of glass and the only one who can hear her properly is me. Sadie's world must be so frustrating, I find myself thinking. She can't touch anything, she can't communicate with anyone, it's obvious she's never going to get through to this guy—

"Yes." The American man nods desperately.

My pity dies away.

Yes?

There's a gasp all around the table and a hastily stifled giggle. Everyone immediately turns to gape at me, but I'm temporarily too dumbfounded to reply.

He said yes.

Does this mean . . . I actually have to go on a date with him?

"Great!" I try to gather my wits. "So . . . let's be in touch, shall we? My name's Lara Lington, by the way, here's my card. . . ." I scrabble in my bag.

"I'm Ed." The man still looks dazed. "Ed Harrison." He reaches into his inside pocket and produces his own business card.

"So . . . um . . . bye, then, Ed!" I pick up my bag and hurriedly beat a retreat, to the sound of a growing hubbub. I can hear someone saying, "Who the bloody hell was that?" and a woman saying in an urgent undertone, "You see? You just have to have the *guts*. You have to be *direct* with men. Stop the games. Lay it out there. If I'd known at her age what that girl knows . . ."

What I know?

I don't know anything except I need to get out of here.

EIGHT

$\mathcal{I}$'m still in a state of shock as Sadie catches up with me, halfway across the ground floor reception lobby. My mind keeps rerunning the scene in total disbelief. Sadie communicated with a man. He actually *heard* her. I'm not sure how much he heard—but obviously enough.

"Isn't he a peach?" she says dreamily. "I knew he'd say yes."

"What went on in there?" I mutter incredulously. "What's with the shouting? I thought you couldn't talk to anyone except me!"

"Talking's no good," she agrees. "But I've noticed that when I really let off a socking great scream right in someone's ear, most people seem to hear something faint. It's terribly hard work, though."

"Have you done this before? Have you spoken to anyone else?"

I know it's ridiculous, but I feel the tiniest bit jealous that she can get through to other people. Sadie is *my* ghost.

"Oh, I had a few words with the queen," she says airily. "Just for fun."

"Are you *serious*?"

"Maybe." She shoots me a wicked little smile. "It's

hell on the old vocal cords, though. I always have to give up after a while." She coughs and rubs her throat.

"I thought I was the only person you were haunting," I can't help saying childishly. "I thought I was special."

"You're the only person I can be with instantly," says Sadie after pondering a moment. "I just have to think of you, and I'm with you."

"Oh." Secretly, I feel quite pleased to hear this.

"So, where do you think he'll take us?" Sadie looks up, her eyes sparkling. "The Savoy? I *adore* the Savoy."

My attention is wrenched back to the present situation. She seriously envisages all three of us going on a date together? A weird, freaky, threesome-with-a-ghost date?

OK, Lara. Stay sane. That guy won't really claim a date. He'll tear up my card and blame the incident on his hangover/drug habit/stress levels and I'll never see him again. Feeling more confident, I stride toward the exit. That's enough craziness for one day. I have things to do.

As soon as I get back to the office, I put a call through to Jean, lean back in my swivel chair, and prepare to relish the moment.

"Jean Savill."

"Oh, hi, Jean," I say pleasantly. "It's Lara Lington here. I'm just calling about your no-dog policy again, which I totally understand and applaud. I can absolutely see why you'd wish to keep your workplace an animal-free zone. But I was just wondering why this rule doesn't extend to Jane Frenshew in room 1416?"

Ha!

I've never heard Jean so squirmy. At first she denies it altogether. Then she tries to say it's due to special circumstances and doesn't set any precedent. But it only takes one mention of lawyers and European rights for her to cave in. Shireen can bring Flash to work! It's going to be put in her contract tomorrow, and they're throwing in a dog basket! I put down the phone and dial Shireen's number. She's going to be so happy! Finally, this job is *fun*.

And it's even more fun when Shireen gasps incredulously over the phone.

"I couldn't imagine anyone at Sturgis Curtis taking the same trouble," she keeps saying. "This is the difference when you work with a smaller outfit."

"Boutique," I correct her. "We have the personal touch. Tell all your friends!"

"I will! I'm so impressed! How did you find out about the other dog, by the way?"

I hesitate briefly.

"Ways and means," I say finally.

"Well, you're brilliant!"

At last I put the phone down, glowing, and look up to see Kate gazing at me with avid curiosity.

"How *did* you find out about the other dog?" she says.

"Instincts." I shrug.

"Instincts?" echoes Sadie derisively, who has been wandering about the office throughout. "You didn't have any instincts! It was me! You should say, 'My marvelous great-aunt Sadie helped me and I'm extremely grateful.'"

"You know, Natalie would never have bothered tracking down a dog," says Kate suddenly. "Never. Not in a million years."

"Oh." My glow dims. Suddenly, looking at the whole thing through Natalie-type business eyes, I feel a little unprofessional. Maybe it *was* a bit ridiculous, to spend so much time and effort on one dog. "Well, I just wanted to save the situation; it seemed the best way—"

"No, you don't understand." Kate cuts me off, pink in the face. "I meant it in a good way."

I'm so taken aback, I don't know what to say. No one's ever compared me favorably to Natalie before.

"I'll go on a coffee run to celebrate!" Kate says brightly. "Do you want anything?"

"It's OK." I smile at her. "You don't have to do that."

"Actually . . ." Kate looks awkward. "I'm a bit ravenous. I haven't had a lunch break yet."

"Oh God!" I say, appalled. "Go! Have lunch! You'll starve!"

Kate leaps up, bashing her head on an open file drawer, and pulls her bag down off a high shelf. The minute she's closed the door behind her, Sadie comes over to my desk.

"So." She perches on the edge and regards me expectantly.

"What is it?"

"Are you going to ring him?"

"Who?"

"Him!" She leans right over my computer. *"Him!"*

"You mean Ed Whatsit? You want me to *ring* him?" I shoot her a pitying glance. "Do you have no idea how things work? If he wants to ring, he can ring." *Which he won't in a million years,* I silently add.

I delete a few emails and type a reply, then look up again. Sadie is sitting on top of a filing cabinet, staring fixedly at the phone. As she sees me looking, she jumps and quickly looks away.

"*Now* who's obsessing over a man?" I can't help a little dig.

"I'm not obsessing," she says haughtily.

"If you watch the phone, it doesn't ring. Don't you know anything?"

Sadie's eyes flash angrily at me, but she turns away and starts examining the blinds cord, as though she wants to analyze every fiber. Then she wanders over to the opposite window. Then she looks at the phone again.

I could really do without a lovelorn ghost trailing around my office when I'm trying to work.

"Why don't you go sightseeing?" I suggest. "You could look at the gherkin building, or go to Harrods. . . ."

"I've been to Harrods." She wrinkles her nose. "It looks very peculiar these days."

I'm about to suggest that she go for a long, long walk in Hyde Park, when my mobile trills. Like lightning, Sadie is by my side, watching eagerly as I check the display.

"Is it him? Is it him?"

"I don't know the number." I shrug. "Could be anyone."

"It's him!" She hugs herself. "Tell him we want to go to the Savoy for cocktails."

"Are you crazy? I'm not saying that!"

"This is my date, and I want to go to the Savoy," she says mulishly.

"Shut up or I won't answer!"

We glare at each other as the phone trills again, then Sadie takes a reluctant step backward, her cheeks pouchy.

"Hello?"

"Is this Lara?" It's a woman I don't recognize.

"It's not him, OK?" I hiss at Sadie. I make a shooing-away motion at her, then turn back to the phone.

"Yes, Lara speaking. Who's this?"

"It's Nina Martin. You left a message about a necklace? At the old folks' jumble sale?"

"Oh, yes!" I'm suddenly alert. "Did you buy one?"

"I bought two. Black pearls and a red one. Good condition. I can sell them both to you if you like; I was planning to put them on eBay—"

"No." I deflate. "They're not what I'm looking for. Thanks, anyway."

I take out the list and scribble off Nina Martin's name while Sadie watches critically.

"Why haven't you tried *all* the names?" she demands.

"I'll phone some more this evening. I have to work now," I add at her look. "Sorry, but I do."

Sadie heaves a huge sigh. "All this waiting is unbearable." She swishes over to my desk and stares at the phone. Then she swishes to the window, then back to the phone.

There's no way I can sit here all afternoon with her swishing and sighing. I'm going to have to be brutally honest.

"Look, Sadie." I wait until she turns. "About Ed. You should know the truth. He won't call."

"What do you mean, he won't call?" Sadie retorts. "Of course he will."

"He won't." I shake my head. "There's no way on earth he's going to call some loony girl who blagged her way into his meeting. He's going to throw my card away and forget all about it. Sorry."

Sadie is staring at me with reproach, as though I've deliberately set out to dash all her hopes.

"It's not my fault!" I say defensively. "I'm just trying to let you down lightly."

"He's going to call," she says with slow determination. "And we're going to go on a date."

"Fine. Whatever you think." I turn to my computer and start typing. When I glance up, she's gone, and I can't help breathing out in relief. Finally. Some space. Some silence!

I'm in the middle of typing a confirmation email to Jean about Flash when the phone rings. I pick it up absently and cradle the receiver under my chin. "Hello, Lara speaking."

"Hi there." An awkward-sounding male voice comes over the phone. "This is Ed Harrison."

I freeze. Ed Harrison?

"Um . . . hi!" I look wildly around the office for Sadie, but she's nowhere.

"So . . . I guess we're going on a date," says Ed stiffly.

"I . . . guess we are."

We sound like a pair of people who've won an outing in a raffle and don't know how to get out of it.

"There's a bar in St. Christopher's Place," he says. "The Crowe Bar. You want to have a drink there?"

I can read his mind instantly. He's suggesting a drink because that's about the quickest date you can have. He really doesn't want to do this. So why did he call? Is he so old-fashioned and polite that he felt he couldn't blow me off, even though for all he knows I could be a serial killer?

"Good idea," I say brightly.

"Saturday night, seven-thirty?"

"See you there."

As I put the phone down, I feel surreal. I'm actually going on a date with Mr. American Frown. And Sadie has no idea.

"Sadie." I look around. "Sa-die! Can you hear me? You won't believe it! He called!"

"I know," comes Sadie's voice from behind me, and I swivel around to see her sitting on the windowsill, looking totally unruffled.

"You missed it!" I say in excitement. "Your guy called! We're going on a—" I break off as it hits me. "Oh my God. *You* did this, didn't you? You went and shouted at him."

"Of course I did!" she says proudly. "It was simply *too* dreary waiting for him to call, so I decided to give him a little nudge." Her eyebrows lower disapprovingly. "You were right, by the way. He *had* thrown the card away. It was in his bin, all crumpled up. He wasn't planning to call you at all!"

She looks so outraged, I have to bite back a laugh.

"Welcome to twenty-first-century dating. So how did you change his mind?"

"It was terribly hard work!" Sadie looks affronted. "First I just told him to call you, but he absolutely ignored me. He kept turning away from me and typing more quickly. Then I got really close and told him if he didn't call you and fix a date at once, he'd be cursed with illness by the god Ahab."

"Who's the god Ahab?" I ask incredulously.

"He was in a penny novelette I once read." Sadie looks pleased with herself. "I said he'd lose the use of his limbs and be covered with grotesque warts. I could see him waver, but he was still trying to ignore me. So then I looked at his typewriter—"

"Computer?" I interject.

"Whatever it is," she says impatiently. "I told him it would break down and he would lose his job unless he called you." Her mouth curves into a reminiscent smile. "He moved quite quickly after that. Although, you know, even when he was picking up the card he kept clutching his head and saying to himself, 'Why am I calling this girl? Why am I doing this?' So I yelled in his ear, 'You *want* to call her! She's very pretty!'" Sadie tosses her hair back triumphantly. "And so he telephoned you. Aren't you impressed?"

I gaze back at her, speechless. She's blackmailed this guy into going on a date with me. She's messed with his mind. She's forced him into a romance that he had no intention of pursuing.

She is the only woman I've ever known who could make a man call. Ever.

OK, it took supernatural powers, but she did it.

"Great-Aunt Sadie," I say slowly, "you're brilliant."

NINE

Sometimes, when I can't get to sleep, I imagine all the rules I'd invent if I ever got to be in charge of the world. There are quite a few which involve ex-boyfriends, as it happens, and now I've got a new one:

Ex-boyfriends shall not be allowed to take another girl back to the special restaurant they used to go to with their previous girlfriend.

I still can't believe Josh is taking this girl to Bistro Martin. How can he? It's *our* place. We had our first date there, for God's sake. He's totally betraying all our memories. It's as if our whole relationship is an Etch A Sketch and he's deliberately shaking it clean and drawing a new picture, and forgetting all about the old, much better, and more interesting picture which used to be there.

Besides which, we've only just broken up. How can he be dating another girl after only six weeks? Doesn't he know *anything*? Rushing blindly into a new relationship is never the answer; in fact, it'll probably make him really unhappy. I could have told him that, if he'd asked me.

It's twelve-thirty on Saturday and I've been sitting here for twenty minutes. I know the restaurant so well, I've been able to plan things perfectly. I'm in the corner, tucked out of sight, wearing a baseball cap just to be on the safe side. The restaurant's one of those bustling brasseries with lots of tables and plants and hooks for coats, so I'm easily able to blend away in the background.

Josh is booked at one of the big wooden tables in the window—I peeked at the reservations list. I have a good view of it from my corner seat, so I'll be able to study this so-called Marie pretty carefully and watch their body language. Even better, I'll be able to listen to their conversation, because I've bugged the table.

This isn't a joke—I've genuinely bugged it. Three days ago I went online and bought a tiny remote microphone in a pack called My First Spy Kit. When it arrived, I realized it was designed for ten-year-old boys rather than adult ex-girlfriends, as it also came with a plastic Spy's Log Book and Cool Code Cracker.

But so what? I've tested it out and it works! It only has a range of twenty feet, but that's all I need. As soon as my waiter had taken my drink order, I made a pretext of needing the ladies' room. Casually, I sauntered past, pretended to drop something, and slapped the tiny sticky pad of the microphone on the underside of the table. The earpiece is hidden under my baseball cap. I just have to switch it on when I'm ready.

And, OK, I know you shouldn't spy on people. I know I'm doing a morally wrong thing. In fact, I had a big argument with Sadie about it. First she said I shouldn't come here at all. Then, when it was obvious she was going to lose that one, she said if I was *that* desperate to know what Josh was going to talk about, I should just sit near the table and eavesdrop. But what's the difference? If you're listening in, you're listening in, whether you're two feet or ten feet away.

The point is, when it comes to love there's a different set of morals. All's fair in love or war. It's for the greater good. Like those people at Bletchley, cracking German codes. That was an invasion of privacy, too, if you think about it. But they didn't care, did they?

I have an image of myself, happily married to Josh, sitting around at Sunday lunch and saying to my children, "You know, I very nearly *didn't* bug Daddy's table. And then none of you would be here!"

"I think he's coming now!" Sadie suddenly says beside me. I finally talked her into being my assistant, although all she's done so far is wander about the restaurant saying disparaging things about people's outfits.

I risk a tiny glance toward the door and feel a roller-coaster lurch. Oh God, oh God. Sadie's right—it's him. And her. They're together. Why are they together?

OK, don't freak out. Don't imagine them waking up in bed, all sleepy and sex-satisfied. There could be lots of other perfectly reasonable explanations. Maybe they met at the tube or something. I take a deep gulp of wine, then raise my eyes again. I don't know who to study first, Josh or her.

Her.

She's blond. Quite skinny, in orange pedal pushers and one of those crisp white sleeveless tops that women wear in ads for low-fat yogurt or toothpaste. The kind of top you can only wear if you're good at ironing, which just shows how tedious she must be. Her arms are tanned and there are streaks in her hair, as though she's been on holiday.

As I shift my gaze to Josh, I feel my stomach go all slithery. He's just . . . Josh. Same fair floppy hair, same goofy lopsided grin as he greets the maître-d', same faded jeans, same canvas sneakers (some cool Japanese label I've never quite got the hang of pronouncing), same shirt—

Hang on. I stare at him in disbelieving shock. That's the shirt I gave him for his birthday.

How can he be doing this? Does he have no heart? He's wearing *my* shirt in *our* place. And he's smiling at this girl as though no one exists but her. Now he's taking her arm and making some joke which I can't hear but makes her throw back her head and laugh with her toothpaste-ad white teeth.

"They look very well suited," says Sadie brightly in my ear.

"No, they don't," I mutter. "Be quiet."

The maître-d' is showing them to the window table. Keeping my head down, I reach into my pocket and switch on the remote control for the microphone.

The sound is faint and buzzy, but I can just about hear his voice.

". . . totally wasn't paying attention. 'Course, it turns out the bloody GPS has sent me to completely the wrong Notre Dame." He gives her a charming grin and she giggles.

I almost want to leap up from my table, I'm so livid. That's *our* anecdote! That happened to *us*! We ended up at the wrong Notre Dame in Paris and we never saw the real one. Has he forgotten he was with me? Is he just editing me out of his life?

"He looks very happy, don't you think?" observes Sadie.

"He's not happy!" I give her a venomous glare. "He's in total denial."

They're ordering a bottle of wine. Great. Now I have to watch them get all merry. I take a few olives and munch disconsolately. Sadie has slid into the seat opposite and is watching me with a trace of pity.

"I warned you, never be a trailer."

"I'm not being a trailer! I'm . . . trying to understand him." I swirl my wine around a few times. "We ended so suddenly. He just cut me off. I wanted to work at our relationship, you know? I wanted to talk things through. Like, *was* it the commitment thing? Or was there something else? But he wouldn't. He didn't give me a chance."

I glance over at Josh, who is smiling at Marie while the waiter uncorks a bottle. I could be watching our own first date. It was just the same, all smiles and amusing little stories and wine. Where did it go wrong? How did I end up sitting in a corner bugging him?

And then the solution hits me, with total clarity. I lean over toward Sadie with urgency.

"Go and ask him."

"Ask him what?" She makes a face.

"Where it went wrong! Ask Josh what was wrong with me! Get him to speak out loud, the way you did with Ed Harrison. Then I'll know!"

"I can't do that!" she objects at once.

"Yes, you can! Get inside his head! Make him talk! This is the only way I can get to him—" I break off as a waitress approaches the table, her notepad out. "Oh, hi. I'd love some . . . um . . . soup. Thanks."

As the waitress moves off, I gaze entreatingly at Sadie. "Please. I've come all this way. I've made all this effort."

There's a moment's silence—then Sadie rolls her eyes. "Very well."

She disappears, then a moment later reappears right by Josh's table. I watch, my heart galloping. I push my earpiece more firmly into my ear, ignoring the buzz, and listen to Marie's rippling laugh as she tells some story about horse riding. She's got a faint Irish brogue, which I didn't notice before. As I glance over, I see Josh topping up her glass of wine.

"Your childhood sounds amazing," he's saying. "You have to tell me more."

"What do you want to know?" She breaks off a piece of bread. But doesn't put it in her mouth, I notice.

"Everything." He smiles.

"Could take a while."

"I'm in no hurry." Josh's voice has deepened a smidgen. I'm watching in horror. They've got that whole eyes-meeting frissony thing going on. Any minute he'll take her hand, or even worse. What's Sadie *waiting* for?

"Well, I was born in Dublin." She smiles. "Third of three."

"Why did you break up with Lara?" Sadie's voice is so piercing through my earpiece, I nearly jump out of my chair.

Josh has heard her, I can tell. His hand has stopped halfway through pouring out fizzy water.

"My two brothers tormented me, all through my childhood." Marie is still speaking, obviously unaware of anything. "They were so evil. . . ."

"Why did you break up with Lara? What went wrong? Talk to Marie about it! Talk, Josh!"

". . . found frogs in my bed, in my satchel . . . once even in my cereal bowl!" Marie looks up at Josh, clearly expecting him to respond. But he's frozen like a statue, as Sadie yells in his ear, *"Say it, say it, say it!"*

"Josh?" Marie waves her hand in front of his face. "Did you hear a word I said?"

"Sorry!" He rubs his face. "I don't know what happened there. What were you saying?"

"Oh . . . nothing." She shrugs. "Just telling you about my brothers."

"Your brothers! Right!" With an obvious effort, he refocuses on her and smiles charmingly. "So, are they very protective of their little sister?"

"You'd better watch out!" She smiles back and takes a sip of wine. "How about you, any siblings?"

"Say why you split up with Lara! What was wrong with her?"

I can see Josh glaze over again. He looks as though he's trying to catch the distant echo of a nightingale across the valleys.

"Josh?" Marie leans forward. "Josh!"

"Sorry!" He comes to and shakes his head. "Sorry! It's weird. I was just thinking about my ex, Lara."

"Oh." Marie keeps smiling, exactly the same amount of smile, but I can see the muscles tense up a little in her jaw. "What about her?"

"I don't know." Josh screws up his face, looking perplexed. "I was just thinking what it was about her and me that went wrong."

"Relationships end." Marie sips her water. "Who knows why? These things happen."

"Yes." Josh still has a faraway look in his eyes, which isn't surprising, as Sadie is yelling like a siren in his ear. *"Say why it went wrong! Say it out loud!"*

"So." Marie changes the subject. "How was your week? I've had a hellish time with that client. Remember the one I was telling you about—"

"I suppose she was a bit intense," Josh blurts out.

"Who was?"

"Lara."

"Oh, really?" I can see Marie trying to feign interest.

"She used to read me out 'relationship issues' from some bullshit magazine and want to talk about how similar we were to some other random couple. For hours. That annoyed me. Why did she have to analyze everything? Why did she have to unpick every single row and conversation?"

He gulps at his wine and I stare at him across the restaurant, stricken. I never knew he felt that way.

"That does sound annoying." Marie nods sympathetically. "Anyway, how did that big meeting go? You said your boss had some announcement to make?"

"*What else?*" Sadie is shrieking at Josh, drowning out Marie. "*What else?*"

"She used to litter the bathroom with her creams and crap." Josh frowns distantly at the memory. "Every time I tried to shave I had to fight through this thicket of pots. It drove me mad."

"What a pain!" says Marie, overbrightly. "Anyway—"

"It was the little things. Like the way she used to sing in the shower. I mean, I don't mind singing, but the same song every bloody *day*? And she didn't want to open her mind. She's not interested in traveling, not interested in the same things as me. . . . Like, I once bought her this book of William Eggleston photography; I thought we could talk about it or whatever. But she just flipped through with zero interest—" Josh suddenly notices Marie, whose face has almost seized up with the effort of listening politely. "Shit. Marie. I'm sorry!" He rubs his face with both hands. "I don't know why Lara keeps popping into my head. Let's talk about something else."

"Yes, let's do that." Marie smiles stiffly. "I was going to tell you about my client, the really demanding one from Seattle? You remember?"

"Of course I remember!" He reaches for his wine— then seems to change his mind and picks up his glass of fizzy water instead.

"Soup? Excuse me, miss, didn't you order the soup? Excuse me?"

Suddenly I realize a waiter is standing by my table with a tray of soup and bread. I have no idea how long he's been trying to get my attention.

"Oh, right," I say, quickly turning to him. "Yes, thanks."

The waiter deposits my food and I pick up a spoon, but I can't eat. I'm too flabbergasted by everything Josh just said. How could he have felt all this and never mentioned it? If he was annoyed by my singing, then why didn't he say? And as for the photography book, I thought he'd bought it for himself! Not for me! How was I supposed to know it meant so much to him?

"Well!" Sadie bounces up to me and slides into the seat opposite. "*That* was interesting. Now you know where it all went wrong. I agree about the singing," she adds. "You are rather tuneless."

Doesn't she have an ounce of sympathy?

"Well, thanks." I keep my voice low and gaze morosely into my soup. "You know the worst thing? He never said any of this stuff to my face. None of it! I could have fixed it! I would have fixed it." I start crumbling a piece of bread into pieces. "If he'd just given me a chance—"

"Shall we go now?" She sounds bored.

"No! We haven't finished!" I take a deep breath. "Go and ask him what he liked about me."

"What he liked about you?" Sadie gives me a dubious look. "Are you sure there was anything?"

"Yes!" I hiss indignantly. "Of course there was! Go on!"

Sadie opens her mouth as though to speak—then shrugs and heads back across the restaurant. I push my earpiece in more firmly and dart a glance over at Josh. He's sipping his wine and skewering olives with a metal pick while Marie talks.

". . . three years is a long time." I hear her lilting voice over the buzz and crackle. "And, yes, it was hard to finish, but he wasn't right, and I've never regretted it or looked back. I guess what I'm trying to say is . . . relationships end, but you have to move forward." She gulps her wine. "You know what I mean?"

Josh is nodding automatically, but I can tell he isn't hearing a word. He has a bemused look on his face and keeps trying to edge his head away from Sadie, who's yelling, *What did you love about Lara? Say it! Say it!*

"I loved the way she had so much energy," he says in a desperate rush. "And she was quirky. She always had some cute necklace on, or a pencil stuffed into her hair or something. . . . And she really *appreciated* stuff. You know, some girls, you do things for them and they just take it as their due, but she never did. She's really sweet. Refreshing."

"Are we talking about your ex-girlfriend again, by any chance?" There's a steely edge to Marie's voice, which makes even me wince. Josh seems to come to.

"Shit! Marie. I don't know what's got into me. I don't know why I'm even thinking about her." He rubs his brow, looking so freaked out I almost feel sorry for him.

"If you ask me, you're still obsessed," Marie says tightly.

"What?" Josh gives a shocked burst of laughter. "I'm not obsessed! I'm not even interested in her anymore!"

"So why are you telling me how great she was?" I watch, agog, as Marie throws down her napkin, pushes back her chair, and stands up. "Call me when you're over her."

"I am over her!" Josh exclaims angrily. "Jesus Christ! This is fucking ridiculous. I hadn't *thought* about her until today." He pushes back his chair, trying to get Marie's full attention. "Listen to me, Marie. Lara and I had a relationship. It was fine, but it wasn't great. And then it finished. End of."

Marie is shaking her head.

"Which is why you bring her up in conversation every five minutes."

"I *don't*!" Josh almost yells in frustration, and a few people at nearby tables look up. "Not normally! I haven't talked about her or thought about her for weeks! I don't know what the fuck's wrong with me today!"

"You need to sort yourself out," Marie says, not unkindly. She picks up her bag. "See you, Josh."

As she moves swiftly between the tables and out of the restaurant, Josh sinks back into his seat, looking shell-shocked. He looks even more gorgeous when he's hassled than when he's happy. Somehow I suppress an urge to run over and fling my arms around him and tell him he never wanted to be with such an uptight, toothpaste-ad girl, anyway.

"Are you satisfied now?" Sadie returns to my side. "You've ruined the path of true love. I thought that was against your creed."

"That wasn't true love." I scowl at her.

"How do you know?"

"Because I know. Shut up."

We both watch in silence as Josh pays his bill, reaches for his jacket, and gets up to leave. His jaw is tight and his easy saunter has gone, and I feel a flash of guilt. But I force myself to quell it. I know I'm doing the right thing. Not just for me but for Josh. I can make it work between us, I *know* I can.

"Eat your lunch! Hurry up!" Sadie interrupts my reverie. "We need to go home now. You need to start getting ready."

"For what?" I look at her, confused.

"For our date!"

Oh God. That.

"It's nearly six hours away," I point out. "And we're only going for a drink. There's no rush."

"I used to take all day getting ready for parties." She shoots me an accusing look. "This is my date. You're representing me. You need to look divine."

"I'll look as divine as I can, OK?" I take a spoonful of soup.

"But you haven't even chosen a frock!" Sadie is hopping with impatience. "It's already two o'clock! We need to go home now. Now!"

For God's sake.

"Fine. Whatever." I push away my soup—it's gone cold, anyway. "Let's go."

All the way home, I'm deep in thought. Josh is vulnerable. He's confused. It's the perfect time for me to rekindle our love. But I have to *use* what I've learned. I have to change myself.

I keep obsessively tracking back over everything he said, trying to remember every detail. And every time I reach one particular phrase, I squirm and wince. *It was fine, but it wasn't great.*

It's all blindingly clear now. Our relationship wasn't great because he wasn't honest with me. He didn't tell me any of his little niggles. And they all built up in his head and that's why he chucked me.

But it doesn't matter—because now I know what the problems are, I can solve them! All of them! I've put together an action plan, and I'm going to start by tidying up my bathroom. As soon as we get back to my flat, I stride in, full of optimism, to find Sadie heading me off.

"What are you going to wear tonight?" she demands. "Show me."

"Later." I try to get past her.

"Not later! Now! Now!"

For God's sake.

"All right!" I head into my bedroom and wrench open the little curtain that hides my wardrobe. "What about . . . this." At random, I pull out a maxiskirt and my new limited-edition corset top from Topshop. "And some wedge sandals, maybe."

"*Stays?*" Sadie looks as though I'm brandishing a pig's corpse. "And a long skirt?"

"It's the maxi look, OK? It's really fashionable, actually. And these aren't stays, it's a corset top."

Sadie touches my corset top with a shudder. "My mother tried to make me wear stays to my aunt's wedding," she says. "I threw them on the fire, so she shut me in my room and told the servants not to let me out."

"Really?" I feel a spark of interest in spite of myself. "So you missed the wedding?"

"I climbed out the window, took the motor, drove to London, and had my hair shingled," she says proudly. "When my mother saw it, she went to bed for two days."

"Wow." I put the clothes down on the bed and look at Sadie properly. "You were a real rebel. Were you always doing things like that?"

"I did rather torture my parents. But they were so stifling. So *Victorian*. The whole house was like a museum." She shudders. "My father disapproved of the phonograph, the Charleston, cocktails . . . *everything*. He thought girls should spend their time arranging flowers and doing needlework. Like my sister, Virginia."

"You mean . . . Granny?" Now I'm fascinated to hear more. I only have hazy memories of Granny, as a gray-haired lady who liked gardening. I can't even imagine her as a girl. "What was she like?"

"Horribly virtuous." Sadie makes a face. "*She* wore stays. Even after the whole world had stopped wearing them, Virginia laced herself in and put her hair up and arranged the flowers in church every week. She was the dullest girl in Archbury. And then she married the dullest man in Archbury. My parents were overjoyed."

"What's Archbury?"

"Where we lived. A village in Hertfordshire."

This is ringing bells in my mind. *Archbury.* I know I've heard it—

"Hang on!" I say suddenly. "Archbury House. The house that burned down in the 1960s. Was that your house?"

It's all coming back to me now. Years ago Dad told me about the old family home, Archbury House, and even showed me a black-and-white photo dating from the 1800s. He said that he and Uncle Bill had spent summers there when they were little boys and then moved in when their grandparents died. It was a wonderful place, all old corridors and huge cellars and a great big grand staircase. But after the fire, the land was sold off and a development of new houses was built in its place.

"Yes. Virginia was living there with her family by then. In fact, she caused the fire. She left a candle alight." There's a moment's silence before Sadie adds with an acidic edge, "Not so perfect after all."

"We drove through the village once," I volunteer. "We saw the new houses. They looked OK."

Sadie doesn't seem to hear me. "I lost all my things," she says distantly. "All the things I was keeping there while I was abroad. All destroyed."

"That's awful," I say, feeling inadequate.

"What does it matter?" She suddenly seems to come to and gives me a brittle smile. "Who cares?" She whirls away, toward the wardrobe, and points imperiously. "Get out your clothes. I need to see them all."

"Whatever." I grab an armful of hangers and dump them on the bed. "So, tell me about your husband. What was he like?"

Sadie considers for a moment. "He wore a scarlet waistcoat at our wedding. Other than that, I remember very little about him."

"That's it? A waistcoat?"

"And he had a mustache," she adds.

"I don't get you." I throw another armful of clothes onto the bed. "How could you marry someone you didn't love?"

"Because it was my only way to escape," says Sadie, as though it's obvious. "I'd had the most terrible row with my parents. My father had stopped my allowance, the vicar called every second day, I was locked in my room every night—"

"What had you done?" I say, avid with curiosity. "Had you been arrested again?"

"It . . . doesn't matter," says Sadie after a slight pause. She turns away from my gaze and stares out of the window. "I had to leave. Marriage seemed as good a way as any. My parents had already found a suitable young man. And, believe me, they were hardly lining up in droves in those days."

"Oh, well, I know about that," I say, rolling my eyes in sympathy. "There are *no* single men in London. None. It's a well-known fact."

I look up to see Sadie gazing at me with a kind of blank incomprehension.

"We lost all ours in the war," she says.

"Oh. Of course." I swallow. "The war."

World War I. I hadn't quite put that together.

"The ones who survived weren't the same boys they'd been. They were wounded. Broken to bits. Or full of guilt because they'd survived . . ." A shadow passes across her face. "My older brother was killed, you know. Edwin. He was nineteen. My parents never really got over it."

I stare at her, appalled. I had a great-uncle Edwin who was killed in World War I? Why don't I *know* this stuff?

"What was he like?" I ask timidly. "Edwin?"

"He was . . . funny." Her mouth twists as though she wants to smile but can't let herself. "He made me laugh. He made my parents more bearable. He made *everything* more bearable."

The room is quiet, save for the tinny sound of the TV upstairs. Sadie's face is immobile, transfixed with memories or thoughts. She almost seems in a trance.

"But even if there weren't many men around," I venture, "did you have to settle? Did you have to marry some random guy? What about waiting for the right guy? What about love?"

"'What about love!'" she mimics me mockingly, snapping out of her reverie. "'What about love!' Goodness, you play a monotonous tune." She surveys the mound of clothes on the bed. "Lay them out so I can see properly. I'll choose your dress for this evening. And it *won't* be a ghastly long skirt to the ground."

Obviously the reminiscing is over.

"OK." I start spreading my clothes out on the bed. "You choose."

"And I'm in charge of your hairstyle and makeup," Sadie adds firmly. "I'm in charge of everything."

"Fine," I say patiently.

As I head back to the bathroom, my head is full of Sadie's stories. I've never been into family trees or history. But somehow this is all quite fascinating. Maybe I'll get Dad to dig out a few photos of the old family house. He'll love that.

I close the door and survey my pots of creams and cosmetics, all balanced on the counter around the basin. Hmm. Perhaps Josh had a point. Maybe I don't need apricot scrub and oatmeal scrub *and* sea salt scrub. I mean, how scrubbed should skin be, anyway?

Half an hour later I've got everything organized into rows and have assembled a whole carrier bag of ancient, half-empty pots to chuck out. Already my action plan is under way! If Josh saw this bathroom, he'd be so impressed! I almost feel like taking a picture of it and sending him a text. Feeling delighted with myself, I duck my head back into my bedroom, but Sadie's not there.

"Sadie?" I call, but there's no reply. I hope she's OK. It was obviously hard for her, remembering her brother. Maybe she needed a quiet moment alone.

I put the bag of pots next to the back door to deal with later and make myself a cup of tea. Next on my list is to find that photography book he was talking about. It must still be around here somewhere. Maybe under the sofa . . .

"I've found it!" Sadie's excited voice springing out of nowhere nearly makes me knock my head on the coffee table.

"Don't do that!" I sit up and reach for my cup of tea. "Listen, Sadie, I just want to say . . . are you OK? Do you want to talk? I know things can't have been easy—"

"You're right, it wasn't easy," she says crisply. "Your wardrobe is very deficient."

"I didn't mean clothes! I meant *feelings*." I give her an understanding look. "You've been through a lot, it must have affected you. . . ."

Sadie doesn't even hear me. Or, if she does, she pretends not to. "I've found you a frock," she announces. "Come and see! Hurry up!"

If she doesn't want to talk, she doesn't want to talk. I can't *make* her.

"Great. So what did you choose?" I get up and start heading toward my bedroom.

"Not there." Sadie darts in front of me. "We have to go out! It's in a shop!"

"A shop?" I stop and stare at her. "What do you mean, in a shop?"

"I was forced to go out." She lifts her chin defiantly. "There was nothing in your wardrobe. I've never seen such bedraggled clothes!"

"They're not bedraggled!"

"So I went out, and I found an *angel* of a dress! You simply have to buy it!"

"Where?" I'm trying to think where she could have gone. "Which shop? Did you go into central London?"

"I'll show you! Come on! Get your purse!"

I can't help feeling touched at the thought of Sadie wafting around H&M or wherever, trying to find an outfit for me.

"Well, OK," I say at last. "As long as it doesn't cost a zillion pounds." I reach for my bag and check I've got my keys. "Come on, then. Show me."

I'm expecting Sadie to lead me to the tube station and drag me to Oxford Circus or somewhere. But instead she veers around the corner and into a grid of backstreets I've never explored.

"Are you sure it's this way?" I hesitate, puzzled.

"Yes!" She tries to drag me forward. "Come on!"

We pass rows of houses and a little park and a college. There's nothing here that looks like a shop. I'm about to tell Sadie that she must have got her bearings wrong, when she turns a corner and makes a triumphant flourish.

"There!"

We're in front of a tiny parade of shops. There's a newsagent and a dry cleaner and, right at the end, a tiny shop with a wood-painted sign reading *Vintage Fashion Emporium*. There's a mannequin in the window wearing a long satin dress, gloves up to the elbow, a hat with a veil, and lots of brooches everywhere. Next to her is a pile of old hatboxes and a dressing table holding a large selection of enamel hairbrushes.

"This is by *far* the best shop you have in your area," says Sadie emphatically. "I've found everything we need. Come on!"

Before I can say anything, she's disappeared into the shop. I have no choice but to follow her. The door gives a little *ting* as I enter, and a middle-aged woman smiles at me from behind a tiny counter. She has straggly dyed hair in a vivid shade of yellow and is wearing what looks like an original seventies caftan in a wild green circular print, together with several amber necklaces strung around her neck.

"Hello!" She smiles pleasantly. "Welcome to the shop. I'm Norah. Have you shopped here before?"

"Hi." I nod back. "This is my first time."

"Were you interested in a particular garment or era?"

"I'll . . . just have a browse." I smile at her. "Thanks."

I can't see Sadie, so I start wandering around. I've never been into vintage clothes, but even I can tell there's some pretty amazing stuff here. A pink psychedelic sixties dress is displayed next to a beehive wig. There's a whole rack of original-looking boned corsets and petticoats. On a dressmaker's mannequin is a cream lace wedding dress with a veil and a tiny dried-flower bouquet. A glass case holds some white leather skating boots, all creased and weathered with use. There are collections of fans, handbags, old lipstick cases—

"Where are you?" Sadie's impatient voice pierces my eardrum. "Come here!"

She's beckoning from a rack toward the back. Feeling sudden misgivings, I head toward her.

"Sadie," I say in a low voice. "I agree this stuff is cool and everything. But I'm only going for a casual drink. You can't possibly think—"

"Look!" She gestures in triumph. "Perfect."

I'm never letting a ghost give me fashion advice again.

Sadie is pointing at a 1920s flapper's dress. A bronze silk flapper dress with a dropped waist, little beaded capped sleeves, and a matching cape. The store tag reads: *Original 1920s dress, made in Paris.*

"Isn't it darling?" She clasps her hands and whirls around, her eyes bright with enthusiasm. "My friend Bunty had one very similar, you know, only in silver."

"Sadie!" I find my voice. "I can't wear that on a date! Don't be stupid!"

"Of course you can! Try it on!" She's urging me with her skinny white arms. "You'll have to cut off all your hair, of course—"

"I'm not cutting off my hair!" I move away in horror. "And I'm not trying it on!"

"I've found you some matching shoes too." She flits eagerly to a rack and points at some little bronze-colored dancing slippers. "And some proper makeup." She whirls over to a glass counter and gestures at a Bakelite case next to a little sign reading: *Original 1920s makeup set. Very rare.*

"I had a set just like this." She's gazing at it fondly.

"This is the best lipstick that was ever made. I'll teach you how to do yours properly."

For God's sake.

"I know how to do my lipstick properly, thanks—"

"You have no idea," she cuts me off crisply. "But I'll teach you. And we'll marcel your hair. There are some irons for sale." She points at an old cardboard box inside which I can see some weird-looking ancient metal contraption. "You'll look *so* much better if you make an effort." Her head swivels around again. "If we could just find you some decent stockings—"

"Sadie, stop it!" I hiss. "You must be crazy! I'm not getting any of this stuff—"

"I still remember that delicious smell of getting ready for parties." She closes her eyes briefly as though transfixed. "Lipstick and singed hair—"

"Singed hair?" I squeak in horror. "You're not singeing my hair!"

"Don't fuss!" she says impatiently. "We only singed it *sometimes*."

"Are you getting on all right?" Norah appears, jangling amber, and I jump in surprise.

"Oh. Yes, thanks."

"Are you particularly interested in the 1920s?" She heads over to the glass case. "We've some marvelous original items here. All fresh in from a recent auction."

"Yes." I nod politely. "I was just looking at them."

"I'm not sure what this was for. . . ." She picks out a little jeweled pot mounted on a circular ring. "Strange little thing, isn't it? A locket, maybe?"

"A rouge ring," says Sadie, rolling her eyes. "Does no one have any idea about *anything* anymore?"

"I think it's a rouge ring," I can't help saying casually.

"Ah!" Norah looks impressed. "You're an expert! Maybe you know how to use these old marcel irons." She takes out the metal contraption and hefts it cautiously in her hand. "I believe there was quite a knack to it. Before my time, I'm afraid."

"It's easy," says Sadie scornfully into my ear. "I'll show you."

There's a *ting* from the door and two girls come in, oohing and aahing as they look around. "This place is wicked," I hear one of them saying.

"Excuse me." Norah smiles. "I'll let you keep browsing. If you'd like to try anything on, let me know."

"I will." I smile back at her. "Thanks."

"Tell her you want to try the bronze dress on!" Sadie shoos me forward. "Go on!"

"Stop it!" I hiss as the woman disappears. "I don't want to try it on!"

Sadie looks bemused. "But you have to try it. What if it doesn't fit?"

"I don't have to, because I'm not wearing it!" My frustration bubbles over. "Get real! This is the twenty-first century! I'm not using some ancient old lipstick and curling irons! I'm not wearing a flapper's dress on a date! It's just not happening!"

For a few moments Sadie seems too taken aback to reply.

"But . . . you promised." She fixes me with huge, wounded eyes. "You promised I could choose your dress."

"I thought you meant normal clothes!" I say in exasperation. "Twenty-first-century clothes! Not this." I pick up the dress and brandish it at her. "It's ridiculous! It's a costume!"

"But if you don't wear the dress I choose, then it might as well not be my date at all. It might as well be your date!" Sadie's voice starts rising; I can tell she's cranking up into a scream. "I might as well stay at home! Go out with him on your own!"

I sigh. "Look, Sadie—"

"He's *my* man! It's *my* date!" she cries passionately. "Mine! With my rules! This is my last chance to have some fun with a man, and you want to spoil it by wearing some frightful dreary outfit—"

"I don't want to *spoil* it—"

"You promised to do things my way! *You promised!*"

"Stop shouting at me!" I pull away, clutching my ear. "Jesus!"

"Is everything all right back here?" Norah appears again and eyes me suspiciously.

"Yes!" I try to compose myself. "I was just . . . er . . . on the phone."

"Ah." Her face clears. She nods toward the bronze silk flapper dress, still in my arms. "You want to try that on? Wonderful piece. Made in Paris. Have you seen the mother-of-pearl buttons? They're exquisite."

"I . . . um . . ."

"You promised!" Sadie's about three inches from me, her chin set, her eyes fiery. "You promised! It's my date! Mine! *Mine!*"

She's like a relentless fire-engine siren. I jerk my head away, trying to think straight as best I can. There's no way I can cope with a whole evening of Sadie yelling at me. My head will explode.

And let's face it. Ed Harrison thinks I'm a nutter anyway. What difference does it make if I turn up in a flapper dress?

Sadie's right. It's her evening. I might as well do it her way.

"All right!" I say at last, cutting across Sadie's insistent voice. "You've talked me around. I'll try on the dress."

TEN

*I*f anyone I know sees me, I will die. I will *die*.

As I get out of the taxi, I look quickly up and down the street. No one in sight, thank God. I have never looked so ludicrous in my life. This is what happens when you let a dead great-aunt take control of your looks.

I'm wearing the flapper dress from the shop, which I only just managed to zip up. Clearly they didn't go in for boobs in the twenties. My feet are squished into the dancing slippers. Six long bead necklaces are jangling around my neck. Circling my head is a black headband, beaded with jet, and sticking out of that is a feather.

A *feather*.

My hair has been tortured into a series of old-fashioned-looking waves and curls, which took about two hours to do with the marcel irons. When it was done, Sadie insisted I smother it in some weird pomade stuff that she also found in the vintage shop, and now it feels rock solid to the touch.

And as for my makeup: Did they honestly think this was a good look in the 1920s? My face is covered in pale powder, with a spot of rouge on each cheek. My eyes are heavily outlined in black kohl. My lids are smeared with a lurid green paste, which came out of the old Bakelite case. I still don't know exactly what's on my eyelashes: some weird lump of black goo which Sadie called "Cosmetique." She made me boil it up in a frying pan and then smear it all over my lashes.

I mean, hello, I *have* a new Lancôme mascara. It's waterproof, with flexible fibers and everything. But Sadie wasn't interested. She was too overexcited by all this stupid ancient makeup and telling me how she and Bunty used to get ready for parties together and pluck each other's eyebrows and take little swigs from their hip flasks.

"Let me see." Sadie appears beside me on the pavement and scans me. She's in a gold dress, with gloves up to her elbows. "You need to touch up your lipstick."

There's no point suggesting a nice subtle MAC lip gloss instead. With a sigh, I reach in my bag for the pot of red gunk and pat yet more color onto my exaggerated Cupid's bow.

Two girls pass by, nudging each other and giving me curious smiles. They obviously think I'm off to a costume party and am going for Most Over the Top outfit.

"You look divine!" Sadie hugs herself with excitement. "You just need a gasper." She starts looking up and down the street. "Where's a tobacconist? Oh, we should have bought you a darling little cigarette holder—"

"I don't smoke," I cut her off. "And you can't smoke in public places, anyway. It's the law."

"What a ridiculous law." She looks aggrieved. "How does one hold a cigarette party?"

"We don't hold cigarette parties! Smoking gives you cancer! It's *dangerous*!"

Sadie makes an impatient *tchuh* noise. "Come on, then!"

I begin to follow her up the street toward the *Crowe Bar* sign, barely able to walk in my vintage shoes. As I reach the door, I realize she's disappeared. Where's she gone?

"Sadie?" I turn around and scan the street. If she's left me in the lurch I will absolutely murder her—

"He's in there already!" She suddenly appears, looking even more hyper than before. "He's absolutely swoonsome."

My heart sinks. I was hoping he might have stood me up.

"How do I look?" Sadie's smoothing her hair down, and I feel a sudden pang of compassion for her. It can't be much fun, going on a date and being invisible.

"You look great," I say reassuringly. "If he could see you, he'd think you were really hot."

"Hot?" She looks confused.

"Sexy. Pretty. You're a hottie. It's what we say."

"Oh, good!" Her eyes travel nervously to the door and back. "Now, before we go in, remember this is *my* date."

"I know it's your date," I say patiently. "You've drummed it into me enough times—"

"What I mean is—be me." She fixes me with an urgent look. "Say whatever I tell you to say. Do whatever I tell you to do. Then I'll feel as though it's really me talking to him. Do you understand?"

"Don't worry! I get it. You feed me the lines and I'll say them. I promise."

"Go on, then!" She gestures at the entrance.

I push through the heavy frosted glass doors and find myself in a chic lobby with suede-paneled walls and low-level lighting. There's another set of double doors ahead, beyond which I can see the bar. As I pass through, I catch a glimpse of myself in a tinted mirror and feel a clench of dismay.

Somehow I feel a million times more ludicrous here than I did in my flat. My necklaces are jangling with every step. My feather is bobbing around in my head-dress. I look like a twenties-o-gram. And I'm standing in a minimalist bar full of cool people in understated Helmut Lang.

As I'm edging forward, all prickly with self-consciousness, I suddenly spot Ed. He's sitting about ten yards away, in a conventional trousers-and-jacket combo, drinking what looks like a conventional gin and tonic. He looks up, glances my way, then does a double take.

"You see?" says Sadie triumphantly. "He's trans-fixed by the sight of you!"

He's transfixed, all right. His jaw has fallen and his face has turned a pale green color.

Very slowly, as though forcing himself through nox-ious mud, he gets to his feet and approaches me. I can see the bar staff nudging one another as I walk through the bar, and from a nearby table comes a sudden gasp of hilarity.

"Smile at him!" Sadie is insisting loudly in my ear. "Walk toward him with a shimmy and say, 'Hello, Daddy-O!'"

Daddy-O?

It's not my date, I remind myself feverishly. It's Sadie's. I'm only acting a part.

"Hello, Daddy-O!" I say brightly as he draws near.

"Hi," he says faintly. "You look . . . " He moves his hands helplessly.

All around, the buzz of conversation has died to a halt. The whole bar is watching us. Great.

"Say some more!" Sadie is hopping around in excitement, clearly oblivious to the awkwardness. "Say, 'You look pretty dapper yourself, you old thing.' And twirl your necklace."

"You look pretty dapper yourself, you old thing!" I fix him with a rictus smile, swinging my beads around so hard that one of the necklaces catches me in the eye. Ow. That hurt.

"OK." Ed seems barely able to talk for embarrassment. "Well. Can I . . . get you a drink? A glass of champagne?"

"Ask for a swizzle stick!" instructs Sadie. "And smile! You haven't laughed once!"

"Could I have a swizzle stick?" I give a high-pitched giggle. "I simply adore swizzle sticks!"

"A swizzle stick?" Ed frowns. "Why?"

Fuck knows why. I dart a helpless look at Sadie.

"Say, 'To stir the bubbles out, darling!' " she hisses.

"To stir the bubbles out, darling!" I giggle brightly again, and twirl my necklaces for good measure.

Ed looks like he wants to sink into the floor. I don't blame him.

"Why don't you take a seat?" he says in a strained voice. "I'll bring over the drinks."

I head over to the table where he was sitting and pull up a suede upholstered chair.

"Sit like this," commands Sadie, adopting an affected pose with her hands on her knee, and I copy as best I can. "Open your eyes wider!" She looks restlessly around at all the clusters of people sitting in groups and standing at the bar. The hum of chatter has resumed, and there's a low throbbing of lounge-style music. "When does the band arrive? When will the dancing start?"

"There *isn't* any band," I mutter. "There *isn't* any dancing. It's not that kind of place."

"No dancing?" she says fretfully. "But there has to be dancing! Dancing is the whole point! Don't they have any snappier music? Don't they have anything with a bit of life?"

"I don't know," I say sarcastically. "Ask him." I jerk my head toward the barman, just as Ed appears before me with a glass of champagne and what looks like another gin and tonic. I should think it's a treble. He sits down opposite, puts down the drinks, then lifts his glass.

"Cheers."

"Chin chin!" I say with a dazzling smile, give my champagne a brisk stir with a plastic swizzle stick, and take a glug. I look up for Sadie's approval—but she's disappeared. I surreptitiously look around and spot her behind the bar, yelling something in the barman's ear.

Oh God. What havoc is she causing now?

"So . . . did you have far to come?"

My attention is wrenched away. Ed's talking to me. And there's no Sadie to feed me any lines. Great. I'm actually going to have to make conversation.

"Er . . . not too far. Kilburn."

"Ah. Kilburn." He nods as though I've said something really profound.

While I'm trying to think of something to say, I run my eyes over him. Nice charcoal jacket, I have to admit. He's taller than I remember, with a broader, firmer frame, in an expensive-looking shirt. A hint of five o'clock shadow; the same *V* of frown lines that he had in the office. For God's sake. It's the weekend, he's on a date, yet he looks as if he's at some really serious board meeting where everyone's about to be fired and lose all their bonuses.

I feel a flash of irritation. He could at least *try* to look like he's having a good time.

"So! Ed." I make a heroic effort and smile at him. "From your accent I'm guessing you're American?"

"That's right." He nods but doesn't volunteer any more.

"How long have you been over?"

"Five months."

"How do you like London?"

"Haven't seen much of it."

"Oh, you must!" I can't help my natural enthusiasm pouring out. "You should go to the London Eye, and Covent Garden, and then you should take a boat to Greenwich. . . ."

"Maybe." He gives me a tight smile and takes a slug of his drink. "I'm pretty busy at work."

That is the lamest thing I ever heard. How can you move to a city and not bother to get to know it? I *knew* I didn't like this guy. I glance up to see Sadie by my side, her arms folded sulkily.

"That barman is very stubborn," she says. "Go and tell him to change the music."

Is she *nuts*? Shooting her a discreet glare, I turn back to Ed and smile politely.

"So, Lara, what do you do?" Clearly he feels he's got to join in this conversation too.

"I'm a headhunter."

Immediately, Ed looks wary. "You're not with Sturgis Curtis, are you?"

"No, I have my own company, L&N Executive Recruitment."

"Good. I wouldn't have liked to offend you."

"What's wrong with Sturgis Curtis?" I can't resist asking.

"They're vultures from hell." He has such a look of horror on his face, I almost want to giggle. "They pester me every day. Do I want this job? Am I interested in that job? They use tricks to get past my secretary. . . . I mean, they're *good*." He shudders. "They even asked me to sit at their table at the *Business People* dinner."

"Oh, wow." I can't help sounding impressed. I've never been to the *Business People* dinner, but I've seen it written up in the magazine. It's always held at a big hotel in London, and it's pretty glam. "So . . . are you going?"

"I'm speaking at it."

He's *speaking*? Oh my God, he must be really important. I had no idea. I look up to raise an eyebrow at Sadie, but she's disappeared.

"Are you going?" he asks politely.

"Er . . . not this year." I try to imply this is just a temporary blip. "My firm wasn't quite able to make up a table this year."

Bearing in mind tables hold twelve people and cost five thousand pounds. And L&N Executive Recruitment has precisely two people and about minus five thousand pounds.

"Ah." He inclines his head.

"I'm sure we'll be there next year, though," I say quickly. "We'll probably make up two tables. You know, do it properly. We'll probably have expanded by then. . . ." I trail off. I don't know why I'm making any effort to impress this guy. He clearly isn't interested in anything I say.

As I swizzle my drink again, I realize the music has stopped. I turn to look at the barman, and he's standing by the CD player behind the bar, obviously experiencing a momentous struggle between his own will and the sound of Sadie shrieking something in his ear. What is she up to?

At last, with a visible capitulation, the barman takes a CD from its box and slides it into the machine. The next minute, some scratchy, old-fashioned Cole Porter–type band music fills the air. Sadie sweeps up behind Ed's chair, a beam of satisfaction on her face.

"At last! I *knew* that man would have something suitable in his drawer. Now ask Lara to dance!" she instructs Ed, and bends close to his ear. *"Ask her to dance!"*

Oh God. No way.

Resist her, I silently message Ed. *Don't listen. Be strong.* I'm sending him my strongest telepathic signals. But it's no good. As Sadie bellows in his ear, a pained, confused look is coming over Ed's face. He looks like someone who really, really doesn't want to vomit but is having no choice.

"Lara." He clears his throat and rubs his face. "Would you like to . . . dance?"

If I refuse him, Sadie will wreak her revenge on me, I know it. This is what she wanted; this is why we're all here. So she can dance with Ed.

"OK."

Hardly able to believe what I'm doing, I put down my glass and stand up. I follow Ed to a tiny patch of spare floor next to the bar stools, and he turns to face me. For a moment we both just stare at each other, paralyzed by the enormity of the situation.

This is a one hundred percent nondancing scenario. We're not on a dance floor. This isn't a club, it's a bar. No one else is dancing. The jazz band is still playing its scratchy music through the speakers, and some bloke is singing about his fancy shoes. There's no beat, there's no nothing. There's no way we can dance.

"Dance!" Sadie is flitting between us like quicksilver, a whirlwind of impatience. "Dance together! *Dance!*"

With a look of desperation in his eyes, Ed starts moving awkwardly from side to side, trying as best he can to follow the music. He looks so miserable, I start copying him, just to make him feel better. I've never seen less convincing dancing in my life.

Out of the corner of my eye I can see everyone turning to watch us. My dress is swishing backward and forward, and my necklaces are jangling. Ed's eyes are focused far ahead, as though he's having an out-of-body experience.

"Excuse me." A member of the bar staff, carrying a plate of dim sum, ducks between us.

Not only are we not on a dance floor, we're in the way of everyone. This is the most excruciating experience of my life.

"Dance properly!" I turn my head to see Sadie regarding me in horror. "That's not dancing!"

What does she expect us to do, the waltz?

"You look as though you're trudging through mud! This is how to dance."

She starts some twenties Charleston-type dance, all

flying legs and elbows and knees. Her face is beatific, and I can hear her humming along to the music. At least *someone's* having fun.

As I watch, she shimmies right up to Ed and places a slender hand on each of his shoulders. Now she's running a hand adoringly down his cheek.

"Isn't he blissful?" She runs both her hands down his chest, circling his waist and skimming down his back.

"Can you feel him?" I murmur incredulously, and Sadie flinches, as though I've caught her out.

"That's . . . not the point," she says defensively. "And it's none of your business."

OK, so she can't. Well, whatever rocks her boat, I suppose. But do I have to watch?

"Sadie!" I hiss as her hands travel even further down his body. "Get a room!"

"I'm sorry, what did you say?" With an obvious effort, Ed focuses on me. He's still dancing from side to side, totally oblivious to the fact that he has a twenty-three-year-old flapper running her hands voraciously all over his body.

"I said . . . let's stop." I avert my eyes from Sadie, who's trying to nibble his ear.

"No!" protests Sadie furiously. "More!"

"Great idea," says Ed at once, and starts back toward our chairs.

"Ed? Ed Harrison?" A blond woman interrupts his path. She's wearing beige trousers and a white shirt and an expression of incredulous glee. At the table behind her, I can see several other well-groomed business types watching avidly. "I thought that was you! Were you just . . . dancing?"

As Ed surveys all the faces at the table, it's obvious

his nightmare has just got about fifty times worse. I almost feel sorry for him.

"That's . . . that's right," he says at last, as though he can't quite believe it himself. "We were dancing." He seems to come to. "Lara, do you know Genevieve Bailey from DFT? Genevieve, Lara. Hello, Bill, Mike, Sarah . . ." He's nodding at all the people sitting round the table.

"Your dress is adorable." Genevieve flicks a condescending glance over my outfit. "Going for the twenties look, obviously."

"It's original." I nod.

"I have no doubt!"

I smile as best I can, but she's touched a nerve. I don't *want* to be dressed up like something out of a *Daily Mail* vintage-dolls collection series. Especially not in front of what's clearly a collection of high-profile businesspeople.

"I'll just touch up my makeup." I force another smile. "I'll be back in a minute."

In the ladies' room, I get out a tissue, wet it, and frantically scrub at my face. But nothing seems to be coming off.

"What are you doing?" Sadie appears behind me. "You'll ruin your face!"

"Just trying to tone down the color," I say between jerky rubs.

"Oh, that rouge won't come off," says Sadie airily. "It's indelible. Lasts for days. The lipstick too."

Indelible?

"Where did you learn to dance?" Sadie inserts herself between me and the mirror.

"I didn't. You don't learn to dance. You just pick it up."

"Well, it shows. You're terrible."

"Well, you're totally over the top," I retort, stung. "You looked like you wanted to jump his bones right there!"

"'Jump his bones.'" Sadie frowns. "What do you mean?"

"It means . . . You know." I stop awkwardly. I'm not sure bone-jumping is something I want to be discussing with my great-aunt.

"What?" Sadie says impatiently. "What does it mean?"

"You do it with someone else." I choose my words carefully. "It's like a pajama party. Except you take off your pajamas."

"Oh, that." Her face clicks with recognition. "You call it 'jumping his bones'?"

"Sometimes." I shrug.

"What an odd phrase. We used to call it sex."

"Oh," I say, discomfited. "Well. We do too—"

"Or barney-mugging," she adds.

Barney-mugging? And she has the nerve to call *jump his bones* an odd phrase?

"Well, whatever you call it." I take off one of my shoes and rub my sore toes. "You looked like you wanted to do it with him right there in the bar."

Sadie smirks and adjusts her headband, looking in the mirror. "You must admit he's handsome."

"On the outside, maybe," I say grudgingly. "But he doesn't have any personality."

"Yes, he does!" says Sadie, looking offended.

How would she know? It was me who had to make all the bloody conversation with him!

"No, he doesn't! He's lived in London for months, but he hasn't bothered to see anything!" I wince as I put my shoe back on. "What kind of narrow-minded person does that? What kind of person isn't interested in one of the greatest cities in the world?" My voice is rising with indignation. "He doesn't deserve to live here."

As a Londoner, I'm taking this quite personally. I look up to see what Sadie thinks, but her eyes are closed and she's humming. She's not even bloody listening to me.

"Do you think he'd like me?" She opens her eyes. "If he could see me. If he could dance with me."

Her face is so hopeful and glowing, all my outrage dies away. I'm being stupid. What does it matter what this guy is like? He's got nothing to do with me. This is Sadie's evening.

"Yes," I say as convincingly as I can. "I think he'd love you."

"I think so too." She looks satisfied. "Your headdress is crooked, did you realize?"

I tug at it and survey my reflection grumpily.

"I look so *ridiculous*."

"You look divine. You're the prettiest girl in the place. Apart from me," she adds airily.

"Do you know how stupid I feel?" I rub at my cheeks again. "No, of course not. All you care about is your date."

"I'll tell you something," says Sadie, watching me critically in the mirror. "You've got a film star's mouth. In my day, all the girls *died* to have a mouth like that. You could have been in the pictures."

"Yeah, right." I roll my eyes.

"*Look* at yourself, you ninny. You look like a film heroine!"

Reluctantly, I face the mirror again, trying to imagine

myself in flickery black and white, tied to a railway line while a piano bashes out some menacing tune. Actually . . . she's right. I do quite look the part.

"Oh, sir, please spare me!" I adopt a pose in front of the mirror, batting my eyelashes.

"Exactly! You'd have been a darling of the silver screen." Sadie meets my eyes, and I can't help grinning back. This has been the weirdest, stupidest date of my life, but somehow her mood is infectious.

As we head back out to the bar, I see that Ed is still chatting to Genevieve. She's leaning elegantly against a chair in a "casual" pose, which I instantly realize is designed to show off her tall, slim figure to Ed. I also instantly realize that he hasn't even noticed, which slightly endears him to me.

Sadie's noticed, though. She keeps crossly trying to elbow Genevieve out of the way, and yelling *"Move!"* in her ear—but Genevieve's ignoring her completely. She must be made of strong stuff.

"Lara!" Genevieve greets me with a fake smile. "I'm so sorry. I don't want to disrupt your evening *à deux* with Ed!"

"No worries." I give her an equally fake smile.

"Have you known each other long?" She gestures between Ed and me with an elegant, silk-cuffed wrist.

"Not long, no."

"So how did you two meet?"

I can't help a surreptitious glance at Ed. He looks so uneasy at the question that I want to giggle.

"It was in the office, wasn't it?" I say, to help him out.

"In the office. Yes." Ed nods in relief.

"Well!" Genevieve laughs—the kind of bright, trilling laugh you give when you're really quite an-

noyed about something. "Ed, you are secretive! I had
no idea you had a girlfriend!"

For a split second, Ed and I meet eyes. I can see he's
about as keen on that idea as I am.

"She's not my girlfriend," he says at once. "I mean,
that's not—"

"I'm not his girlfriend," I chime in hastily. "We're
just . . . it's kind of a one-off—"

"We're just having a drink," Ed supplies.

"We'll probably never see each other again."

"Probably not," Ed affirms. "Definitely not."

We're both nodding in total agreement. In fact, I
think we've bonded for the first time.

"I . . . see." Genevieve looks totally confused.

"Let me get you another drink, Lara." Ed gives me
the warmest smile he has all evening.

"No, I'll get them!" I beam back at him. There's
nothing like knowing you only have to spend ten more
minutes with someone to make you feel suddenly generous toward them.

"What do you mean?" A voice is shrieking behind
me, and as I turn I see Sadie heading toward me. Her
glow has disappeared; she's a whirl of fury. "It's not a
one-off! You made a promise!"

She's got a nerve. How about "Thank you for dressing up and looking like a fool, Lara"?

"I kept my promise!" I hiss out of the side of my
mouth as I approach the bar. "I've done my side of the
deal."

"No, you haven't!" She glares at me in outrage.
"You haven't even danced properly with him! You've
just shuffled around dismally."

"Too bad." I get out my phone and pretend to be
speaking into that. "You said you wanted a date, I've

given you one. The end. A glass of champagne and a G&T please," I add to the barman, and reach into my bag for some money. Sadie's silent, which probably means she's gearing up for a banshee moment. . . . But as I look up, she's gone. I swivel around and see her back beside Ed.

She's yelling in his ear. Oh God. What's she doing?

I pay for the drinks as quickly as I can and hurry back across the bar. Ed is staring into the middle distance, that glazed, transfixed look on his face again. Genevieve is in the middle of an anecdote about Antigua and doesn't even seem to have noticed Ed's faraway expression. Or maybe she thinks he's transfixed by admiration for her.

"And then I saw my bikini top!" She trills with laughter. "In the sea! I never lived that one down."

"Here you are, Ed," I say, and hand him his G&T.

"Oh. Thanks." He seems to come to.

"*Do it now!*" Sadie suddenly swoops forward and shrieks in his ear. "*Ask her NOW!*"

Ask me? Ask me what? This had better not be about another date, because it's not happening, no way, whatever Sadie wants—

"Lara." Ed focuses on me with what looks like some difficulty, his forehead furrowed more deeply than ever. "Would you like to be my guest at the *Business People* dinner?"

I do not *believe* it.

In shock, I swivel my eyes up to Sadie's—and she's looking at me with an expression of triumph, her arms folded across her chest.

"Don't say yes on my account," she says carelessly. "It's up to you. Entirely."

Ooh. She's *good*. She's a lot smarter than I thought.

I didn't even realize she was paying attention to the conversation.

This is impossible. There's no way I can turn down an invitation to the *Business People* dinner. It's such a huge event. It'll be stuffed full of important business types. . . . I'll be able to network . . . make contacts. . . . It's a massive opportunity. I can't say no. I just can't.

Damn her.

"Yes," I say at last, stiffly. "Thank you, Ed, that's very kind of you. I'd love to come."

"Good. That's great. I'll send you the details."

We both sound as though we're reading lines from cards. Genevieve is looking back and forth between our faces, bewildered.

"So . . . you *are* a couple," she says.

"No!" we reply in unison.

"No way," I add for emphasis. "Not at all. I mean . . . never. Not in a million years." I take a sip and glance over at Ed. Is it my imagination, or does he look just the tiniest bit offended?

I last about another twenty minutes, listening to Genevieve show off about every single holiday she's ever been on, practically. Then Ed glances at me, and my empty glass, and says, "Don't let me keep you."

Don't let me keep you. It's a good thing I'm not into this guy. If that isn't code for *I can't stand a moment more in your company,* I don't know what is.

"I'm sure you have dinner plans," he adds politely.

"Yes!" I say brightly. "I do, as it happens. Absolutely. Dinner plans." I do a pantomime sweep of my watch in front of my eyes. "Goodness, is that the time? I must run. My dinner companions will be waiting." I resist the temptation to add, "At Lyle Place, with champagne."

"Well, I have plans too." He nods. "So maybe we should . . ."

He made dinner plans. Of course he did. He probably has a whole other, superior date lined up.

"Yes, let's. It's been . . . fun."

We both stand up, make general parting gestures at the businesspeople, and head out of the bar onto the pavement.

"So." Ed hesitates. "Thanks for . . ." He makes as though to lean in for a peck on the cheek, then clearly decides against it and holds out his hand instead. "That was great. I'll let you know about the *Business People* dinner."

His face is so easy to read it's almost pitiful. He's already wondering how the hell he got himself into this one—but, having invited me in front of a crowd, he can hardly back out now.

"So . . . I'm going this way. . . ." he adds.

"I'm going the other way," I respond at once. "Thanks again. Bye!" I quickly turn on my heel and start striding down the street. What a fiasco.

"Why are you going home so early?" says Sadie crossly in my ear. "You should have suggested going to a nightclub!"

"I have dinner plans, remember?" I say pointedly. "And so does he." I stop dead on the pavement. I was in so much of a hurry to be off, I'm heading in totally the wrong direction. I turn around and look up the road, but there's no sign of Ed. He must have legged it as quickly as I did.

I'm feeling pretty starving, and a bit sorry for myself. I should have made real dinner plans, I think as I

head back up the road. I go into a Pret A Manger and
start perusing the sandwich bar. I'll get myself a wrap
and a carton of soup, *and* a chocolate brownie, I decide. Go all out.

I'm just reaching for a smoothie when a familiar
voice comes across the gentle buzz of customers.

"Pete. Hey, buddy. How's it going?"

Sadie and I lock eyes in startled recognition.

Ed?

Instinctively I shrink back, trying to hide behind a
rack of healthy crisps. My eyes scan the queues of people and land on an expensive overcoat. There he is.
Buying a sandwich and talking on the phone. *These* are
his so-called dinner plans?

"He didn't have plans at all!" I mutter. "He lied!"

"So did you."

"Yes, but . . ." I feel slightly outraged by this. I'm
not sure why.

"That's good. How's Mom?" Ed's voice is unmistakable over the hubbub.

I surreptitiously look around, trying to plan an escape route. But there are massive mirrors everywhere
in this shop. He's bound to spot me. I'll have to sit it
out here until he's gone.

"Tell her I read the letter from the lawyer. I don't
think they have a case. I'll send her an email later on
tonight." He listens for a moment. "Pete, it's no trouble; it'll take five minutes max. . . ." There's another,
longer silence. "I *am* having a good time. It's great.
It's . . ." He sighs, and when he speaks again he sounds
a little weary. "C'mon. It is what it is. You know that.
I had a weird evening."

My hand tightens around my smoothie in anticipation. Is he going to talk about me?

"I just wasted too much of my life with *the* most obnoxious woman in the world."

I can't help feeling a pang of hurt. I wasn't obnoxious! OK, so I'm dressed a bit differently—

"You may have met her. Genevieve Bailey? DFT? . . . No, it wasn't a date. I was with—" He hesitates. "It was a strange situation."

I'm so engrossed in trying to blend into the healthy-crisp stand, I've stopped watching Ed. But all of a sudden I'm aware that he's made his purchase and is striding out of Pret, holding a takeaway bag. He's heading past me. Right past me, feet away . . . please don't look. . . .

Shit.

As though he can hear my thoughts, he glances over to the right—and meets my eyes. He registers surprise but no embarrassment.

"Later, buddy," he says, and slides his phone shut. "Hi there."

"Oh. Hi!" I try to sound casually nonchalant, as though it was always the plan to be found lurking in Pret, clutching a wrap and a smoothie. "Fancy . . . um . . . seeing you here. My dinner plans . . . fell through." I clear my throat. "At the last minute. My friends called and canceled, so I thought I'd grab a bite to eat. . . . The wraps are great here. . . ."

Somehow I force myself to stop babbling. Why should I be embarrassed, anyway? Why isn't *he* embarrassed? He's been caught out as much as I have.

"So, I thought *you* had dinner arrangements," I say lightly, raising my eyebrows. "What happened to your plan? Was it canceled too? Or is it such a fancy dinner you're worried you won't get fed properly?" I glance at his takeaway bag with a little laugh, waiting for him to look discomfited.

He doesn't even flicker. "This *was* my plan. Buy some food and get some work done. I have to fly to Amsterdam first thing tomorrow for a conference. I'm giving a paper."

"Oh," I say, thrown.

His face is dead straight. I have a feeling he's telling the truth. Damn.

"Right," I say. "Well . . ."

There's an awkward pause, then Ed nods politely. "Have a good evening." He strides out of the Pret A Manger, and I watch him go, feeling wrong-footed.

Josh would never wrong-foot me. I *knew* I didn't like this guy.

"*Big Issue?*" A voice interrupts my thoughts.

"Oh." I focus on the skinny man in front of me. He's unshaven and wearing a woolen hat and an official *Big Issue* seller's badge. Feeling bad for all the times I've walked by because it's too much hassle, I decide to make amends. "I'll buy five copies," I say firmly. "Thanks very much."

"Cheers, love." The man nods at my vintage outfit. "Nice dress."

I hand over the money and take five magazines, then pick up my supper items and head to the checkout. I'm still trying to work out exactly the witty, snappy thing I should have said to Ed. I should have given a light-hearted laugh and said, "Next time you make dinner plans, Ed, remind me to—"

No, I should have said, "Really, Ed, when you said *dinner*—"

"What's the *Big Issue?*" Sadie's voice breaks me out

of my trance. I blink a few times, feeling suddenly annoyed with myself. Why am I wasting brain space on him? Who cares what he thinks?

"It's a street magazine," I explain. "The money goes to projects for the homeless. It's a really good cause."

I can see Sadie digesting this.

"I remember people living on the streets," she says, her eyes distant. "After the war. It seemed as though the country would never find its footing again."

"I'm sorry, sir, you can't sell that in here." I notice a girl in uniform escorting the *Big Issue* seller out of the sandwich shop. "We do appreciate the work you do, but it's company policy. . . ."

I watch the man through the glass door. He seems utterly resigned to being ejected, and after a moment I can see him offering copies to passersby, all of whom ignore him.

"Can I help you?" I realize a cashier is calling out to me, and I hurry forward to the till. My credit card has lodged itself right at the bottom of my bag, so I take a while paying and lose track of where Sadie is.

"What the—"

"Bloody hell! What's going on?"

Suddenly I become aware that all the cashiers are exclaiming and exchanging looks. Slowly, I turn around to see what they're looking at. I don't quite believe my eyes.

There's an exodus of customers from the shop. They're all piling out onto the pavement and accosting the *Big Issue* seller. I can see some holding several copies in their hands, others thrusting money at him.

There's one last customer remaining in the shop. Sadie is floating next to him, her face intense, her mouth to his ear. A moment later, with a startled look, he puts down the sushi box he's holding and hurries to join the throng outside, already pulling out his wallet. Sadie just stands back and watches, her arms folded in satisfaction. After a moment she glances at me, and I can't help giving her a huge beam.

"You rock, Sadie!" I mouth. The next moment she's right beside me, looking puzzled.

"Did you say I'm a *rock*?"

"You rock!" I pick up my bag and start walking. "It means . . . you're great. You did a really good thing." I gesture at the customers outside, all milling around the *Big Issue* seller. Passersby are now joining the crowd to see what's up, and the seller looks overwhelmed. We watch them for a moment, then turn and start heading down the street together, an easy silence between us.

"You rock too," says Sadie in a rush, and I look up in surprise.

"I'm sorry?"

"You did a good thing too. I know you didn't want to wear this dress tonight, but you did. For me." Her gaze is resolutely ahead. "So thank you."

"That's OK." I shrug and take a bite of chicken wrap. "It wasn't that bad in the end."

I'm not going to admit it to Sadie, because then she'd crow over me and be unbearable. But actually, this whole twenties look is kind of growing on me.

Kind of.

ELEVEN

Things are on the up! I feel it in my bones. Even this second date with Ed is a positive thing. One has to seize one's opportunities, like Uncle Bill said. And that's what this is all about. Going to the *Business People* dinner will be a great chance for me to meet loads of senior professionals, give out my card, and impress people. Natalie always said she had to be "out there" and keep her profile up. Well, now I'll be "out there" too.

"Kate!" I say as I enter the office on Monday morning. "I need all my business cards, and I need to buy one of those little holders, and I need all the back issues of *Business People*—" I break off in surprise. She's clutching the phone with one hand and circling the air wildly with the other. "What's wrong?"

"It's the police!" She claps her hand over the receiver. "They're on the phone. They want to come and see you."

"Oh, right."

A chunk of ice seems to descend nastily into my stomach. The police. I was hoping the police might just forget all about me.

I glance around to see if Sadie's here, but there's no sign of her. She was talking about some vintage shop in Chelsea at breakfast time, so maybe she's gone off there.

"Shall I put them through?" Kate is agog.

"Yes, why not?" I try to sound confident and unconcerned, like I'm someone who deals with police matters every day. Like Jane Tennison or someone. "Hello, Lara Lington speaking."

"Lara, it's DC Davies here." As soon as I hear her voice, I have a flashback to myself sitting in that room, telling her I'm a speed walker training for the Olympics, while she took notes, her face utterly impassive. What was I *thinking*?

"Hi! How are you?"

"I'm well, thanks, Lara." She's pleasant but brisk. "I'm in the area and was wondering if I could pop by your office for a chat. Are you free now?"

Oh God. A chat? I don't want to chat.

"Yes, I'm free." My voice has risen to a petrified squeak. "Look forward to it! See you then!"

I put the receiver down, hot around the face. Why is she following this up? Aren't the police always supposed to be chasing car fines and ignoring murders? Why couldn't they ignore *this* murder?

I look up to see Kate staring at me, her eyes like saucers. "What do the police want? Are we in trouble?"

"Oh, no," I say quickly. "Nothing to worry about. It's just about my aunt's murder."

"*Murder?*" Kate claps a hand over her mouth.

I keep forgetting how *murder* sounds when you just drop it into a sentence.

"Er . . . yes. So, anyway! What were you up to over the weekend?"

My distraction ruse doesn't work. Kate's boggled expression doesn't change; in fact, it becomes even more boggled.

"You never told me your aunt was murdered! The aunt whose funeral you went to?"

"Mmm-hmm." I nod.

"No wonder you were so upset! Oh, Lara, that's awful. How was she killed?"

Oh God. I really don't want to go into the details. But I'm not sure how else to get out of this conversation.

"Poison," I mumble at last.

"By who?"

"Well." I clear my throat. "They don't know."

"They don't *know*?" Kate sounds totally outraged. "Well, are they looking? Did they take fingerprints? God, the police are useless! They spend their whole time giving you parking tickets and then someone's actually murdered and they don't even care—"

"I think they're doing the best they can," I say hastily. "They're most likely giving me an update report. In fact, they've probably found the culprit."

Even as I'm speaking, the most horrific thought is hitting me. What if that's true?

What if DC Davies is coming here to tell me they've found the man with the scar and the plaited beard? What do I do then?

I have a sudden image of a gaunt, bearded man with wild eyes and a scar, locked up in a police cell, banging on the door, shouting, "You've made a mistake! I never knew the old lady!" while a young police officer watches through a two-way window, folding his arms in satisfaction and saying, "He'll crack soon enough."

For a moment I feel quite hollow with guilt. What have I started?

The buzzer goes, and Kate leaps up to answer it.

"Shall I make some tea?" she says when she's

pressed the buzzer. "Shall I stay or go? Do you want moral support?"

"No, you go." Trying to stay calm, I push my chair back, knock over a pile of post with my elbow, and scrape my hand picking it up. "I'll be fine."

It'll all be fine, I tell myself fervently. *It's no big deal.*

But I can't help it. As soon as I see DC Davies walking in the door, with her clumpy shoes and sensible trousers and air of authority, I can feel my calmness disintegrating into childlike panic.

"Have you found the murderer?" I blurt out anxiously. "Have you locked anyone up?"

"No," DC Davies says, giving me a strange look. "We haven't locked anyone up."

"Thank God." I subside in relief, then realize how that might sound. "I mean . . . why not? What are you doing all day?"

"I'll give you some privacy," says Kate, backing out, while simultaneously mouthing "Useless!" behind DC Davies's back.

"Have a seat." I gesture to a chair and retreat behind my desk, trying to regain a professional air. "So, how are things progressing?"

"Lara." DC Davies gives me a long, hard look. "We have conducted some preliminary inquiries, and we have found no evidence to suggest that your aunt was murdered. According to the doctor's report, she died of natural causes. Essentially, old age."

"Old *age*?" I adopt a shocked expression. "Well, that's just . . . ludicrous."

"Unless we can find any evidence to suggest otherwise, the case will be closed. Do you have any other evidence?"

"Um . . ." I pause as though considering the question

carefully from all sides. "Not what you'd call *evidence*. Not as such."

"What about this phone message you left?" She pulls out a piece of paper. "'The nurses didn't do it.'"

"Oh, that. Yes." I nod several times, playing for time. "I realized I'd got a tiny detail wrong in my statement. I just wanted to clarify things."

"And this 'man with a beard'? A man who didn't even appear in your original statement?"

The sarcasm in her voice is unmistakable.

"Absolutely." I cough. "Well, it suddenly came back to me. I remembered seeing him in the pub at the time and thinking he looked suspicious. . . ." I trail off, my face hot. DC Davies is looking at me like a teacher who's caught you cheating in the geography exam.

"Lara, I'm not sure you're aware of this," she says in calm, even tones. "But wasting police time is a criminal offense which can carry a penalty of imprisonment. If you have made a malicious accusation—"

"I wasn't being malicious!" I say in horror. "I was just . . ."

"What, exactly?"

Her eyes are fixed on mine. She isn't going to let me off the hook. Now I'm really scared.

"Look, I'm sorry," I say in total panic. "I didn't mean to waste your time. I just had this very strong instinct that my great-aunt was murdered. But maybe . . . thinking about it in the cold light of day . . . I got it wrong. Maybe she did die of old age. Please don't prosecute me," I add in a rush.

"We're not going to charge you this time." DC Davies lifts her eyebrows. "But consider this a warning."

"All right," I gulp. "Thank you."

"The case is closed. I'd like you to sign this form, confirming that we've had this talk."

She proffers a piece of paper with a printed paragraph which basically says *I, the undersigned, have had a telling-off and understood it and I won't pester the police again.* In so many words.

"OK." I nod humbly and scribble my signature. "So what will happen now with the . . . the . . ." I can hardly bring myself to say it. "What happens to my great-aunt?"

"The body will be handed back to the responsibility of the next of kin in due course," says DC Davies in a businesslike way. "Presumably they'll then arrange another funeral."

"And how soon will that be?"

"The paperwork might take a while." She zips up her bag. "Maybe two weeks, maybe a little longer."

Two *weeks*? I feel a jolt of horror. What if I can't find the necklace by then? Two weeks is nothing. I need more time. Sadie needs more time.

"Can that be . . . delayed at all?" I try to sound casual.

"Lara." DC Davies gives me a long look, then sighs. "I'm sure you were very fond of your great-aunt. I lost my gran last year; I know what it's like. But delaying her funeral and wasting everyone's time is not the answer." She pauses, then adds more gently, "You have to accept it. She's gone."

"She isn't!" I say before I can stop myself. "I mean . . . she needs more time."

"She was one hundred and five." DC Davies smiles kindly. "I think she had enough time, don't you?"

"But she—" I exhale in frustration. There's nothing I can say. "Well . . . thanks for all your help."

After DC Davies has left, I sit staring blankly at my computer until I hear Sadie's voice behind me.

"Why were the police here?"

I swivel around in alarm to see her sitting on top of a filing cabinet, dressed in a low-waisted cream dress and matching cream hat with blue-black feathers sweeping around to tickle her cheek. "I've been shopping! I've just found you the most divine little wrap. You must buy it." She adjusts her fur collar, then blinks at me. "Why were the police here?"

"Did you hear our conversation at all?" I ask casually.

"No. I told you, I've been shopping." She narrows her eyes. "Is something wrong?"

I gaze back at her, stricken. I can't tell her the truth. I can't tell her she has only two weeks left before they're going to . . . before . . .

"Nothing! Just a routine visit. They wanted to check a few details. I like your hat," I add, to distract her. "Go and find me a hat like that."

"You couldn't wear a hat like this," says Sadie complacently. "You don't have the cheekbones."

"Well, a hat that would suit me, then."

Sadie's eyes widen in surprise. "You promise to buy whatever I choose? And wear it?"

"Yes! Of course! Go on! Shop!"

As soon as she's disappeared, I yank open my desk drawer. I have to find Sadie's necklace. Now. I can't waste any more time. I pull out the list of names and rip off the back sheet.

"Kate," I say as she comes back into the office. "New job. We're trying to find a necklace. Long, glass beads with a dragonfly pendant. Any of these people might have bought it at a jumble sale at the Fairside Nursing Home. Can you ring this lot?"

There's a tiny flicker of surprise in her eyes, then she takes the list and nods without any questions, like some loyal army lieutenant. "Absolutely!"

I run my finger down past all the scribbled-out names and dial the next number. After a few rings a woman picks up.

"Hello?"

"Hi there! My name's Lara Lington, you don't know me. . . ."

It's two hours later before I finally put the phone down and look up wearily at Kate. "Any luck?"

"No." She sighs. "Sorry. How about you?"

"Nothing."

I slump back in my chair and rub my telephone-red cheeks. My adrenaline evaporated about an hour ago. As I neared the end of the list, it was turning to a heavy kind of disappointment. We've ruled out every single number. I don't have anywhere else to turn. What am I going to do now?

"Shall I go on a sandwich run?" says Kate tentatively.

"Oh. Yeah." I muster a smile. "Chicken and avocado please. Thanks so much."

"No problem!" She bites her lip anxiously. "I hope you find it."

As she leaves, I sink my head forward and rub my aching neck. I'll just have to go back to the nursing home and ask more questions. There have to be more avenues to explore. There *has* to be an answer. It just doesn't make sense. The necklace was there, around Sadie's neck, and now it's gone. . . .

A thought suddenly strikes me. That visitor she had, Charles Reece. I never followed him up. I might as well tick every box. Fishing for my mobile, I find the number for the nursing home and wearily dial.

"Hello, Fairside Nursing Home," answers a female voice.

"Hi! This is Lara Lington, Sadie Lancaster's great-niece."

"Oh, yes?"

"I was just wondering . . . can anyone tell me anything more about a visitor she had just before she died? A Charles Reece?"

"Just a moment."

As I'm waiting, I get out the sketch of the necklace and study it as though for clues. I've looked at this picture so many times, I could practically draw each bead by heart. The more I've got to know it, the more beautiful it seems. I can't bear it if Sadie never gets it back.

Maybe I should secretly have a copy made, I find myself thinking. An exact replica. I could get it distressed, tell Sadie it's the original, she might just fall for it—

"Hello?" A cheerful voice rouses me from my thoughts. "Lara? It's Sharon here, one of the nurses. I was with Sadie when Charles Reece visited; in fact, I signed him in. What do you want to know about him?"

I just want to know, has he got her necklace?

"Well . . . . what exactly happened during his visit?"

"He sat with her for a bit, then he left. That's it."

"In her room?"

"Oh, yes," she says at once. "Sadie didn't really leave her room much in those last weeks."

"Right. So . . . could he have taken a necklace from her?"

"Well, it's possible." She sounds doubtful.

It's possible. That's a start.

"Can you tell me what he was like? How old was he?"

"In his fifties or so, I'd say. Nice-looking chap."

This gets more and more intriguing. Who on earth is he? Sadie's boy toy?

"If he visits again or calls, could you let me know?" I scribble down *Charles Reece—50s* on my notepad. "And could you get his address?"

"I can try. Can't promise."

"Thanks." I sigh, feeling a bit dispirited. How am I ever going to track this guy down? "And there's nothing else you can tell me about him?" I add as a last-ditch attempt. "Nothing . . . distinctive? Nothing at all that you noticed?"

"Well." She laughs. "It's just funny, you being called Lington."

"How come?" I stare at the phone, puzzled.

"Ginny says you're not related to that Bill Lington off the coffee cups? Millionaire bloke?"

"Er . . . why do you ask?" I'm suddenly alert.

"Because that's exactly who he looked like! I said it at the time, to the girls. Even though he had dark glasses on and a scarf, you could see it. He was the spitting image of Bill Lington."

TWELVE

$\mathcal{I}$t makes no sense. None. It's crazy, whichever way you look at it.

Was "Charles Reece" really Uncle Bill? But why would he visit Sadie? Why would he use a fake name? And why wouldn't he mention it?

And as for the idea that he might have had anything to do with her necklace disappearing...I mean, hello? He's a multimillionaire. Why would he need some old necklace?

I feel like banging my head against the window, to make all the pieces fall into place. But since at this very minute I'm sitting in a plushy chauffeur-driven limo provided by Uncle Bill, I probably won't. Just to get this far has been a total hassle. I don't want to jeopardize things.

I've never phoned up Uncle Bill in my life, so at first I wasn't sure how to get in touch with him. (Obviously I couldn't ask Mum and Dad, or they'd want to know why I needed to see Uncle Bill and why had I been visiting Sadie's nursing home and what was I talking about, what necklace?) So I rang Lingtons head office, eventually persuaded someone that I was for real, got through to one of the assistants, and asked if I could make an appointment to see Uncle Bill.

It was as if I'd asked to see the president. Within the hour, about six assistants started sending me emails, coordinating a time, changing the time, changing the location, organizing a car, asking me to bring ID, telling me I couldn't overrun my slot, asking what Lingtons beverage I'd prefer in the car. . . .

All for a ten-minute meeting.

The car is pretty rock-star, I have to admit. It's got two rows of seats facing each other and a TV, and a chilled strawberry smoothie was waiting for me, just like I asked for, I'd be more grateful, except that Dad once said Uncle Bill always sends cars for people so that the minute he's had enough of them he can send them away again.

"William and Michael," Sadie pipes up thoughtfully from the seat opposite. "I left everything to those boys in my will."

"Oh, right." I nod. "Yes, I think I heard that."

"Well, I hope they were grateful. There must have been a fair amount."

"Loads!" I lie hastily, remembering a conversation I once heard between Mum and Dad. Apparently everything was swallowed up by the nursing-home fees, but Sadie wouldn't want to hear that. "And they were really thrilled."

"So they should be." She sits back in satisfaction. A moment later the car pulls off the road and approaches a pair of enormous gates. As the car stops by the gatehouse and a security guard approaches, Sadie peers past me at the mansion.

"Goodness." She looks at me uncertainly, as though someone must be playing a joke. "That's a rather large house. How on earth did he become so rich?"

"I told you," I say under my breath, as I give my passport to the driver. He hands it to the security guard, and they confer as though I'm some sort of terrorist.

"You said he ran coffee shops." Sadie wrinkles her nose.

"Yes. Thousands of them. All around the world. He's really famous."

There's a pause, then Sadie says, "I should have liked to be famous."

There's a trace of wistfulness in her voice, and I open my mouth to say automatically, "Maybe you will be one day!" Then, as the truth hits me, I close it again, feeling a bit sad. There isn't a "one day" for her anymore, is there?

By now the car is purring up the drive, and I can't help gazing out of the window like a child. I've only been to Uncle Bill's mansion a few times in my life, and I always forget how impressive and intimidating it is. It's a Georgian house with about fifteen bedrooms and a basement with two swimming pools in it. *Two.*

I'm not going to get nervous, I tell myself firmly. *It's just a house. He's just a person.*

But, oh *God*. Everything's so grand. There are lawns everywhere and fountains sprinkling, and gardeners snipping hedges. As we approach the entrance, a tall guy in a black suit and shades with a discreet earpiece is coming down the spotless white steps to greet me.

"Lara." He clasps my hand as though we're old friends. "I'm Damian. I work for Bill. He's looking forward to seeing you. I'll take you round to the office wing." As we start to crunch over the gravel, he adds lightly, "What exactly was it you wanted to talk to Bill about? Nobody seems very clear."

"It's . . . um . . . private. Sorry."

"No problem." He flashes a smile. "Great. Just approaching, Sarah," he says into his earpiece.

The side building is as impressive as the main house, just in a different style, all glass and modern art and a stainless-steel water feature. As if by clockwork, a girl comes out to greet us, also dressed immaculately in a black suit.

"Hi, Lara. Welcome. I'm Sarah."

"I'll leave you here, Lara." Damian flashes me his teeth again and crunches back over the gravel.

"So, it's an honor to meet Bill's niece!" says Sarah as she leads me into the building.

"Oh. Well . . . er, thanks."

"I don't know if Damian mentioned this." Sarah ushers me to a seat and sits down opposite me. "But I was wondering if you could tell me the subjects you'd like to discuss with Bill. It's something we ask all his visitors. So we can prep him, do any necessary research. . . . It makes life easier for everyone."

"Damian did ask. But it's kind of private, sorry."

Sarah's pleasant smile doesn't falter for an instant.

"If you could just indicate the broad areas? Give us an idea?"

"I don't really want to get into it." I can feel myself flushing. "I'm sorry. It's kind of a . . . family thing."

"Of course! That's fine. Excuse me a moment."

She moves away into a corner of the reception area, and I can see her muttering into her earpiece. Sadie glides over to Sarah for a minute or two, then appears back by my side. To my astonishment, she's cracking up with laughter.

"What is it?" I demand under my breath. "What was she saying?"

"She said she didn't think you looked violent but maybe they should call extra security anyway."

"*What?*" I can't help exclaiming, and Sarah immediately whips around to survey me.

"Sorry." I wave at her cheerily. "Just . . . er . . . sneezed. What else did she say?" I hiss as Sarah turns away again.

"Apparently you have a grudge against Bill? Something about a job he didn't give you?"

Grudge? Job? I stare at her baffled for a second—before the penny drops. The funeral. Of *course*.

"The last time Uncle Bill saw me, I was announcing a murder in the middle of a funeral. He must have told everyone I'm a total psychopath!"

"Isn't it a wheeze?" Sadie giggles.

"It's not funny!" I say crossly. "They probably all think I've come to assassinate him or something! You realize this is all *your* fault?" I hastily break off as Sarah approaches again.

"Hi, Lara!" Her voice is bright but tense. "So . . . one of Bill's team will sit in with you during the meeting. Just to take notes. Is that OK?"

"Look. Sarah." I try to sound as sane and calm as possible. "I'm not a nutter. I don't have a grudge against anyone. I don't need any notes taken. I just want to have a chat with my uncle, one to one. Five minutes. That's all I want."

There's silence for a moment. Sarah still has a vivid smile pasted on, but her eyes keep swiveling to the door and back again.

"OK, Lara," she says at last. "We'll do things your way."

As she sits down, I can see her touching her earpiece as though for reassurance.

"So . . . how's Aunt Trudy?" I say conversationally. "Is she here?"

"Trudy's at the house in France for a few days," Sarah says at once.

"How about Diamanté? Maybe we could have a quick coffee or something." I don't really want to have coffee with Diamanté, I only want to prove how friendly and normal I am.

"You want to see Diamanté?" Sarah's eyes have gone even more swivelly. "Now?"

"Just for a coffee, if she's around."

"I'll call her assistant." She leaps up, hurries away to the corner, and mutters in her earpiece, then almost immediately comes back to the seating area. "I'm afraid Diamanté's getting a manicure at the moment. She says maybe next time?"

Yeah, right. She never even put the call through. I'm feeling quite sorry for this Sarah, actually. She looks as nervous as if she's babysitting a lion. I have a wicked urge to yell "Hands up!" and see how quickly she throws herself to the floor.

"I love your bracelet," I say instead. "It's really unusual."

"Oh, yes." She extends her arm warily and shakes the two little silver disks on their chain. "Haven't you seen these yet? They're from the new Two Little Coins line. There's going to be a stand of products in each Lingtons coffee shop starting next January. I'm sure Bill will give you one. There's a pendant, too, and T-shirts . . . gift sets of two little coins in a treasure box. . . ."

"Sounds great," I say politely. "It must be doing well."

"Oh, Two Little Coins is huge," she assures me

earnestly. "Huge. It'll be as big a brand as Lingtons. You know it's going to be a Hollywood film?"

"Uh-huh." I nod. "Pierce Brosnan as Uncle Bill, I heard."

"And of course the reality show will be a big hit. It's such an empowering message. I mean, anyone can follow Bill's path." Sarah's eyes are shining, and she seems to have forgotten all about being scared of me. "Anyone can pick up two little coins and decide to change their future. And you can apply it to families, businesses, economies. . . . You know, lots of really senior politicians have called Bill since the book came out. They're, like, how can we apply your secret to our country?" She lowers her voice reverentially. "Including the President of the United States."

"The president phoned Uncle Bill?" I'm awed, in spite of myself.

"His people." She shrugs and shakes her bracelet out. "We all think Bill should get into politics himself. He has so much to offer the world. It's such a privilege to work for him."

She's totally signed up for the cult. I glance at Sadie, who has been yawning throughout Sarah's speech.

"I'm going to explore," she announces, and before I can say anything, she's disappeared.

"OK." Sarah's listening to her earpiece. "On our way. Bill's ready to see you, Lara."

She gets up and beckons me to follow. We make our way down a corridor lined with what look suspiciously like real Picassos, then pause in another, smaller reception area. I tug at my skirt and take a few deep breaths. It's ridiculous to feel nervous. I mean, this is my uncle. I have a right to see him. There's no need to feel anything except relaxed—

I can't help it. My legs are wobbling.

I think it's because the doors are so big. They're not like normal doors. They tower up to the ceiling, great blocks of pale polished wood that swing open silently every now and again as people come in and out.

"Is that Uncle Bill's office?" I nod at the door.

"That's the outer office." Sarah smiles. "You'll be seeing him in the inner office." She listens to her earpiece again, suddenly alert, then murmurs, "Bringing her in now."

She pushes open one of the tall doors and leads me through an airy, glass-walled office space with a couple of cool-looking guys at workstations, one of whom is wearing a Two Little Coins T-shirt. They both look up and smile politely but don't stop typing. We reach another set of giant doors and pause. Sarah glances at her watch—then, as though timing it to the second, knocks and pushes the door open.

It's a vast, light room with a vaulted ceiling and a glass sculpture on a podium and a sunken seating area. Six men in suits are getting up from chairs, as though finishing a meeting. And there, behind his massive desk, is Uncle Bill, looking lithe in a gray polo neck and jeans. He's more tanned than he was at the funeral, his hair as glossy black as ever, and he's cradling a Lingtons coffee mug in one hand.

"Thanks very much for your time, Bill," one of the men is saying fervently. "We appreciate it."

Uncle Bill doesn't even reply, just lifts a hand like the pope. As the men file out, three girls in black uniforms appear from nowhere and clear the table of coffee cups in about thirty seconds flat, while Sarah ushers me forward to a chair.

All of a sudden she looks nervous too.

"Your niece Lara," she murmurs to Uncle Bill. "She wants a one to one. Damian made the decision to give her five minutes, but we don't have any prep notes. We have Ted standing by." Sarah lowers her voice further. "I can call extra security—"

"Thanks, Sarah, we'll be fine." Uncle Bill cuts her off and turns his attention to me. "Lara. Have a seat."

As I sit down, I'm aware of Sarah moving away and the soft swoosh of the door closing behind me.

There's silence, apart from Uncle Bill tapping something into his BlackBerry. To pass the time, I look at the wall of pictures of Uncle Bill with famous people. Madonna. Nelson Mandela. The whole England football team.

"So, Lara." At last he looks up. "What can I do for you?"

"I . . . um . . ." I clear my throat. "I was . . ."

I had all sorts of punchy openers prepared. But now that I'm actually here, in the inner sanctum, they're all drying up on my lips. I feel paralyzed. This is Bill Lington we're talking about. Huge, jet-setting tycoon with a million important things to do, like telling the president how to run his country. Why would he go to an old people's home and take a necklace from an old lady? What have I been *thinking*?

"Lara?" He frowns questioningly.

Oh God. If I'm going to do this, I need to do it. It's like jumping off the diving board. Hold your nose, deep breath, go.

"I went to Aunt Sadie's nursing home last week," I say in a rush. "And apparently she had this visitor a few weeks ago who looked just like you, called Charles Reece, and it didn't make any sense to me, so I thought I'd come and ask you. . . ."

I trail off. Uncle Bill is looking at me with as much enthusiasm as if I'd whipped out a hula skirt and started dancing.

"Jesus Christ," he mutters. "Lara, are you still claiming Sadie was murdered? Is that what this is about? Because I *really* don't have time—" He reaches for the telephone.

"No, that's not it!" My face is boiling, but I force myself to persevere. "I don't really think she was murdered. I went there because . . . because I felt bad that no one had ever shown any interest in her. When she was alive, I mean. And there was another name in the visitors' book, and they said the guy looked exactly like you, and I was just . . . wondering. You know. Just wondering."

My heart is pounding in my ears as I finish.

Slowly, Uncle Bill replaces the telephone receiver and there's silence. For a few moments he looks as though he's weighing up exactly what to say.

"Well, it looks as though both of us had the same instincts," he says at last, leaning back in his chair. "You're right. I did go to see Sadie."

My jaw drops in astonishment.

Result! Total, instant result! I think I should become a private detective.

"But why did you use the name Charles Reece?"

"Lara." Uncle Bill gives a patient sigh. "I have a lot of fans out there. I'm a celebrity. There are a lot of things I do that I don't trumpet. Charity work, hospital visits . . ." He spreads his hands. "Charles Reece is the name I take when I want to stay anonymous. Can you imagine the fuss if it were known that Bill Lington had personally come to visit an old lady?" He meets my eyes with a friendly twinkle, and for a moment I can't help smiling back.

It kind of makes sense. Uncle Bill is such a rock star. Taking a pseudonym is the sort of thing he'd do.

"But why didn't you tell any of the family? At the service, you said you'd never visited Aunt Sadie."

"I know." Uncle Bill nods. "And I had my reasons for that. I didn't want to make the rest of the family feel in any way guilty or defensive about not having visited themselves. Especially your father. He can be . . . prickly."

Prickly? Dad's not prickly.

"Dad's fine," I say tightly.

"Oh, he's great," Bill says immediately. "An absolutely fantastic guy. But it can't be easy being Bill Lington's big brother. I feel for him."

Indignation surges through me. He's right. It's not easy being Bill Lington's big brother, because Bill Lington is such an arrogant *tosser*.

I should never have smiled at him. In fact, I wish there were a way to take smiles back.

"You don't need to feel sorry for Dad," I say as politely as I can. "He doesn't feel sorry for himself. He's done really well in life."

"You know, I've started using your dad as an example in my seminars." Uncle Bill adopts a musing tone. "Two boys. Same upbringing. Same education. The only difference between them was, one of them *wanted* it. One of them had the *dream*."

He sounds like he's rehearsing a speech for some promotional DVD. God, he's up himself. Who says everyone wants to be Bill Lington, anyway? Some people's dream would be *not* to have their face plastered across coffee cups all over the world.

"So, Lara." He focuses back on me. "It was a pleasure to see you; Sarah will show you out."

That's it? My audience is over? I haven't even *got* to the bit about the necklace yet.

"There's something else," I say hastily.

"Lara—"

"I'll be really quick, I promise! I just wondered, when you visited Aunt Sadie . . ."

"Yes?" I can see him trying to keep his patience. He glances at his watch and touches a key on his keyboard.

Oh God. How am I going to put this?

"Do you know anything about . . ." I'm stumbling over my words. "I mean, did you see . . . or possibly take, by accident . . . a necklace? A long necklace with glass beads and a dragonfly pendant?"

I'm expecting another patronizing sigh, a blank look, and a dismissive comment. I'm not expecting him to freeze. I'm not expecting his eyes to become suddenly sharp and wary.

As I stare back, I feel almost breathless with shock. He knows what I'm talking about. He *knows*.

The very next moment, the wariness has disappeared out of his eyes and he's back to empty politeness. I could almost think I imagined that other expression.

"A necklace?" He takes a sip of coffee and types something at his keyboard. "Do you mean something of Sadie's?"

The back of my neck is prickling all over. What's going on? I saw the recognition in his eyes, I know I did. Why is he pretending he doesn't know about it?

"Yes, it's an old piece I'm trying to track down." Some instinct tells me to act cool and unconcerned. "The nurses at the home said it had disappeared, so . . ." I watch Uncle Bill sharply for a reaction, but his bland mask is perfectly in place.

"Interesting. Why do you want it?" he asks lightly.

"Oh, no particular reason. I just saw a photo of Sadie wearing it at her hundred and fifth birthday and I thought it would be nice to find it."

"Fascinating." He pauses. "Can I see the photo?"

"I haven't got it on me, I'm afraid."

This conversation is so weird. It feels like a game of tennis, where we're both lobbing balls very gently into the air and resisting the urge to wallop a winner.

"Well, I'm afraid I don't know what you're talking about." Uncle Bill puts his mug down with an air of finality. "I'm pressed for time, so we'll have to leave it there."

He pushes back his chair but I don't move. He knows something about it. I'm sure he does. But what do I do? What options do I have?

"Lara?" He's standing by my chair, waiting. Reluctantly I get to my feet. As we approach the door, it opens as though by magic. We're greeted by Sarah, with Damian hovering behind, his BlackBerry out.

"All done?" he says.

"All done." Uncle Bill nods firmly. "Give my best to your dad, won't you, Lara? Good-bye."

Sarah puts a hand to my elbow and starts gently edging me out of the room. My chance is ebbing away. In desperation, I grip onto the door frame.

"It's a shame about the necklace, don't you think?" I look directly at Uncle Bill, trying to provoke a response. "What do you think happened to it?"

"Lara, I'd forget about the necklace," says Uncle Bill smoothly. "It was probably lost a long time ago. Damian, come in."

Damian hurries past me, and the two men head to the other side of the room. The door is already closing.

I stare after Uncle Bill, almost exploding with frustration.

What's going on? What *is* it with this necklace?

I need to speak to Sadie, right now. This minute. I swivel my head back and forth, but there's no sign of her. Typical. She's probably found some hunky gardener to lust after.

"Lara," says Sarah with a tense smile. "Could you please remove your fingers from the door frame? We can't close the door."

"All right!" I say, lifting up my hands. "Don't panic! I'm not going to stage a sit-in protest!"

Sarah's eyes jump in fear at the word *protest,* which she immediately covers with a fake little laugh. She should really give up working for Uncle Bill. She's way too nervous.

"Your car is waiting for you at the front. I'll take you there now."

Damn. If she escorts me out, there's no way I can sidle off or poke around any drawers or anything.

"A coffee for the ride?" asks Sarah as we pass through the lobby.

I quell an urge to say, "Yes, please, a Starbucks."

"No, thanks." I smile.

"Well, it's been so great to see you, Lara!" Her fake gushiness makes me wince. "Come back soon!"

Yeah, right. By which you mean "please never set foot in this place again, ever."

The limo driver opens the door, and I'm about to step in when Sadie appears right in front of me, blocking the way. Her hair is a little disheveled and she's breathing hard.

"I've found it!" she says dramatically.

"What?" I stop, foot halfway into the car.

"It's in the house! I saw it in a bedroom upstairs, on a dressing table! It's here! My necklace is here!"

I stare at her, gripped. I knew it, I *knew* it!

"You're absolutely sure it's yours?"

"Of course I'm sure!" Her voice rises shrilly and she starts gesturing at the house. "I could have picked it up! I *tried* to pick it up! Of course, I couldn't. . . ." She clicks her tongue in frustration.

"Lara, is there a problem?" Sarah is hurrying down the stairs again. "Is there something wrong with the car? Neville, is everything OK?" she snaps at the driver.

"Everything's fine!" he replies defensively, and jerks his head at me. "She just started talking to thin air."

"Would you like a different car, Lara?" I can see it's taking Sarah a supreme effort to keep up her pleasant manner. "Or to go to a different location? Neville can take you anywhere. Perhaps you'd like the use of him for the rest of the day?"

She really, *really* wants to get rid of me.

"This car's fine, thanks," I say brightly. "Get in the car," I mutter to Sadie out of the side of my mouth. "Can't talk here."

"I'm sorry?" Sarah frowns.

"Just . . . on the phone. Tiny earpiece." I tap my ear and quickly slide into the car.

The car door clunks and we glide away toward the gates. I check that the glass partition is closed, then flop back and look at Sadie.

"This is unbelievable! How did you find it?"

"I just went looking." She shrugs. "I looked in all the cupboards and the drawers and the safe—"

"You went in Uncle Bill's safe?" I'm agog. "Wow. What's in there?"

"Bits of paper and hideous jewels," says Sadie impatiently. "I was about to give up, when I walked past a dressing table and there it was."

I can't believe it. I'm popping with anger. Uncle Bill just sat in front of me and said he didn't know anything about any dragonfly necklace. He's a lying . . . *liar.* We have to make an action plan. As quickly as I can, I reach inside my bag for a notebook and pen.

"Something's going on," I say, writing *Action Plan* at the top of a page. "There has to be a reason he took it and a reason he's lying." I rub my brow in frustration. "But what? Why is it so important to him? Do you know anything else about it? Does it have some kind of history . . . or collectors' value—"

"Is this all you're going to do?" Sadie's voice explodes. "Talk, talk, drone, drone? We need to *get* it! You need to climb through the window and *get* it! At once!"

"Er . . ." I look up from my notebook.

"It'll be quite easy," Sadie adds confidently. "You can take off your shoes."

"Right."

I'm nodding. But truth be told, I don't feel *absolutely* prepared for this. Break in to Uncle Bill's house right now? Without making a plan?

"The only thing is," I venture after a moment, "he's got lots of security guards and alarms and stuff."

"So what?" Sadie's eyes narrow. "Are you frightened of a few alarms?"

"No!" I say at once. "Of course not."

"I bet you are!" she cries derisively. "I've never known such a ninny in all my life! You won't smoke because it's dangerous! You wear a safety belt in the motor because it's dangerous! You won't eat butter because it's dangerous!"

"I don't think butter's *dangerous*," I retort indignantly. "It's just, you know, olive oil spread has got better fats. . . ."

I trail off at the contemptuous look on Sadie's face.

"Are you going to climb in through the window and get my necklace?"

"Yes," I say, after only a split-second pause. "Of course I am."

"Well, come on, then! Stop the car!"

"Stop bossing me about!" I say resentfully. "I was just *about* to."

I lean forward and open the glass partition between us and the driver. "Excuse me? I'm feeling carsick. Could you let me out, please? I'll go home by tube. I'm not dissing your driving or anything," I add hastily, as I see him frowning into the rearview mirror. "You're great. Really . . . er . . . smooth action."

The car pulls over and the driver looks around dubiously. "I'm supposed to take you home to your door."

"Don't worry!" I say, clambering out. "Honestly, I just need some fresh air, thanks so much. . . ."

I'm already on the pavement. I bang the door shut and give the driver a little wave. He shoots me one last suspicious glance, then does a three-point turn and heads back toward Uncle Bill's house. As soon as he's out of sight, I start retracing my path, keeping unobtrusively to the side of the road. I round the corner, see Uncle Bill's gates ahead, and pause.

The gates are closed and they're massive. The security guard is there in his glass box. CCTV cameras are everywhere. You don't just march straight in to Uncle Bill's house. I need a strategy. I take a deep breath and approach the gates, looking as innocent as possible.

"Hi! It's me again, Lara Lington," I say into the pedestrian intercom. "I left my umbrella behind. Silly me!" After a moment, the guard opens the pedestrian gate for me and leans out of his window.

"I've spoken to Sarah. She doesn't know anything about an umbrella, but she's coming down."

"I'll meet her, save her the trouble!" I say brightly, and hurry past before he can protest. OK. I'm past one hurdle.

"Tell me the minute he looks away," I mutter to Sadie out of the side of my mouth. "Say 'Now.'"

"Now!" she says suddenly, and I dodge to the side of the path. I take a few steps across the grass, then drop down, roll behind a hedge, and come to a stop like someone in an action film.

My heart's thumping hard. I don't even care that I've run my tights. Through the hedge I can see Sarah crunching swiftly down the drive, a perturbed expression on her face.

"Where is she?" I hear her voice drifting up from the front gates.

" . . . saw her a moment ago . . ." The guard sounds baffled.

Ha!

Actually, not ha. They might start looking for me with Rottweilers in a minute.

"Where is it?" I whisper to Sadie. "Guide me. And keep a lookout!"

We start making our way over the lawn toward the house, dodging from hedge to water feature to prizewinning sculpture. I keep freezing as people walk down the drive. But so far no one's spotted me.

"There!" We turn the corner and Sadie nods at a set

of French doors on the second-floor level. They're ajar, and open onto a terrace with steps up to it from the garden. I won't need to clamber up the ivy after all. I'm almost disappointed.

"Keep guard!" I mutter to Sadie. I creep toward the steps, slip off my wedges, and run up them silently. Cautiously, I approach the ajar French doors—and catch my breath.

There it is.

It's lying on a dressing table, just inside the room. A long double row of beads in shimmering yellow glass, with the most exquisite carved dragonfly, inlaid with mother-of-pearl and studded with rhinestones. It's Sadie's necklace. Iridescent and magical, just as she described it, although it's longer than I imagined and a few of the beads are a little battered.

As I gaze at it, I feel overcome by emotion. After all this time. After all the hunting, the hoping; after secretly wondering if it even existed anymore . . . here it is. Only a few feet away from me. I could practically lean over and touch it without even entering the room.

"It's . . . stunning." I turn back to Sadie, my voice a little choked. "It's absolutely the most beautiful thing I've ever—"

"Get it!" She's whirling her arms in frustration, her beads jangling. "Stop talking! *Get it!*"

"OK, OK!"

I swing the French doors open, take a tentative step inside, and am just reaching toward the necklace, when I hear footsteps approaching the room. In what seems like a nanosecond, the door is thrown open. Shit. Someone's coming in.

In panic, I reverse onto the terrace and duck to one side.

"What are you doing?" demands Sadie from below. "Get the necklace!"

"Someone's in there! I'll wait 'til they've gone!"

In an instant, Sadie is up on the terrace and poking her head through the glass into the room.

"It's a maid." She glares at me. "You should have grabbed it!"

"I'll get it in a minute when she's gone! Don't stress! Just keep a lookout!"

I back right against the wall, praying that the maid or whoever she is doesn't decide to come out on the terrace for a breath of fresh air and madly thinking of excuses if she does.

Suddenly my heart jumps as the French doors start moving—but they're not opening. They close with a firm *clunk*. The next thing I hear is the *click* of a key being turned.

Oh no.

Oh no, oh no.

"She's locked you out!" Sadie darts into the room, then out again. "Now she's gone! You're stuck! You're stuck!"

I rattle the French doors, but they're well and firmly locked.

"You idiot!" Sadie is beside herself with fury. "You absolute fool! Why didn't you just grab it?"

"I was about to!" I retort defensively. "You should have gone to check if anyone was coming!"

"Well, what are we going to do?"

"I don't know! I don't *know*!"

There's silence as we face each other, panting slightly.

"I need to put my shoes on," I say at last. I head down the steps and slip on my wedges. Above, Sadie is still darting in and out of the room in frustration, as though she can't bear to relinquish her necklace. At last she gives up and joins me on the grass. For a few moments neither of us meets the other's eye.

"I'm sorry I wasn't quicker at grabbing it," I mumble at last.

"Well," says Sadie, clearly making a supreme effort. "I suppose it wasn't *completely* your fault."

"Let's go around the house. We may be able to slip in somewhere. Go inside and see if the coast is clear."

As Sadie disappears, I creep cautiously over the grass and start moving along the wall of the house. I'm making slow progress, because every time I pass a window I duck down and crawl on my stomach. Although that won't exactly help if one of the security guards comes along—

"There you are!" Sadie pops out of the wall beside me. "Guess what?"

"Jesus!" I clasp my chest. "What?"

"It's your uncle! I've been watching him! He's just been to his safe in his bedroom. He looked in it, but he couldn't find what he wanted. Then he banged it shut and started shouting for Diamanté. The girl. Odd name." She wrinkles her nose.

"My cousin." I nod. "Another of your great-nieces."

"She was in the kitchen. He said he needed a private word and sent all the staff away. *Then* he demanded, had she been going in his safe and taking things? Then he said an old necklace was missing and did she know anything about it?"

"Oh my God." I stare back at her. "Oh my God! What did she say?"

"She said no, but he didn't believe her."

"Maybe she's lying." My mind is working overtime. "Maybe that's her bedroom, where the necklace *was*."

"Exactly! So we have to get it now, before he realizes where it is and locks it away again. There's no one around. All the staff have got out of the way. We can go through the house."

I haven't got time to think about whether this is a good idea or not. My heart pumping, I follow Sadie to a side door and in through a laundry room as big as my whole flat. She beckons me through a pair of swing doors, down a passage, then holds up a hand as we reach the hall, her eyes widening warily. I can hear Uncle Bill shouting, his voice increasing in volume.

" . . . private safe . . . personal security . . . how *dare* you . . . code was for emergencies only . . ."

" . . . not bloody fair! You never let me have *anything*!"

It's Diamanté's voice, and it's getting closer. On instinct, I dart behind a chair and sink down, my knees trembling. The next moment she strides into the hall, wearing a strange asymmetrical pink miniskirt and a teeny-tiny T-shirt.

"I'll *buy* you a necklace." Uncle Bill comes striding in after her. "That's no problem. Tell me what you need, Damian will find it—"

"You always say that!" she shrieks at him. "You never listen! That necklace is perfect! I need it for my next Tutus and Pearls show! My whole new collection is based on butterflies and insects and stuff! I'm a *creative*, in case you hadn't realized—"

"If you're so creative, my love," says Uncle Bill with

a sarcastic edge, "why have I hired three designers to work on your dresses?"

For a moment I'm gobsmacked. Diamanté uses other designers? The next minute I can't believe I didn't work that one out before.

"They're . . . fucking . . . *assistants*!" she screams back. "It's *my* vision! And I need that necklace—"

"You're not using it, Diamanté." Uncle Bill's voice is ominous. "And you're never going in my safe again. You're going to give it back to me right now—"

"No, I'm not! And you can tell Damian to fuck off, he's a git." She runs up the stairs, closely followed by Sadie.

Uncle Bill looks so furious, it's as though he's not quite in possession of his faculties. He's breathing heavily and thrusting his hands through his hair as he gazes up the grand staircase. He looks so uncool and out of control, I almost want to giggle.

"Diamanté!" he shouts. "You come back here!"

"Fuck off!" comes a distant cry.

"Diamanté!" Uncle Bill starts to stride up the stairs himself. "That's it. I won't have this—"

"She's got it!" Sadie's voice is suddenly in my ear. "She's taken it! We need to catch her! You go round the back. I'll guard the front stairs."

With scrambling legs I get to my feet, run back down the passage, through the laundry room, and out onto the lawn. I sprint breathlessly around the house, not caring if anyone sees me—and stop dead in dismay.

Shit.

Diamanté is in a black, open-top Porsche, heading down the gravel at speed toward the front gates, which are hastily being opened by the security guard.

"Noooo!" I wail before I can stop myself.

As Diamanté pauses to exit, she flicks a V-sign back at the house and the next minute is out on the street. In her other hand I can just see Sadie's necklace, wrapped around her fingers, glinting in the sunshine.

THIRTEEN

There's only one possibility: They're not rhinestones, they're diamonds. The necklace is studded with rare antique diamonds and worth millions of pounds. It's *got* to be that. There's no other reason I can think of that Uncle Bill would be so interested in it.

I've Googled all sorts of websites on diamonds and jewelry, and it's amazing what people will pay for a 10.5-carat D-color diamond mined in 1920.

"How big was the biggest stone in the necklace?" I say yet again to Sadie. "About."

Sadie sighs noisily. "Half an inch or so?"

"Was it very sparkly? Did it look flawless at all? That could affect its value."

"You're terribly interested in the value of my necklace all of a sudden." Sadie gives me a resentful look. "I didn't think you were so mercenary."

"I'm not mercenary!" I say indignantly. "I'm just trying to work out why Uncle Bill was after it! He wouldn't waste his time unless it was valuable."

"What difference does it make if we can't lay our hands on it?"

"We *will* lay our hands on it."

I have a plan, and it's a pretty good one. I've been using all my detective skills in the few days since we got back from Uncle Bill's house. First of all, I found out about Diamanté's next Tutus and Pearls catwalk show. It's this Thursday at the Sanderstead Hotel, 6:30 p.m., private guest list. The only trouble was, I couldn't see Diamanté putting me on the private guest list in a million years, bearing in mind I'm not a photographer from *Hello!* or one of her celebrity chums or have four hundred quid to spend on a dress. So then came my master stroke. I emailed Sarah in a friendly way and said I'd really like to support Diamanté in her fashion venture and could I come and talk to Uncle Bill about it? Maybe I would just drop over to the house on spec, I suggested. Maybe tomorrow!!! And I added a few smiley faces for good measure.

Sarah immediately emailed back that Bill was a little busy right now and I *shouldn't* come tomorrow, but she could talk to Diamanté's personal assistant. And the next thing I knew, two tickets were biked to my door. Honestly, it's so easy to get what you want from people if they think you're a psycho.

The only downer is that the second and crucial part of my plan—talk to Diamanté and persuade her to give me the necklace straight after the show—has failed so far. Her assistant won't tell me where she is or give me her mobile phone number. She did allegedly pass on a message, but obviously I haven't heard anything. I mean, why would Diamanté bother to call her nonentity of a nonmillionaire cousin?

Sadie's tried going to Diamanté's office in Soho, to see if she can catch her and the necklace—but apparently Diamanté never sets foot there. It's staffed by assistants, and all the clothes are made by some company in Shoreditch. So that's no good.

There's only one thing for it. I'm going to have to go along to the show, wait until it's over, then grab

Diamanté and somehow talk her there and then into giving the necklace to me.

Or, you know. Pinch it.

With a sigh, I close down the jewelry website and swivel around to survey Sadie. Today she's wearing a silver dress which apparently she desperately wanted when she was twenty-one, but her mother wouldn't buy it for her. She's sitting on the sill of the open window, her feet dangling above the street below. The dress is backless except for two thin silver straps over her slender shoulders, and there's a rosette at the small of her back. Of all the ghost dresses she's worn, this is my favorite.

"The necklace would look amazing with that dress," I say impulsively.

Sadie nods but doesn't say anything. There's a low-slung, dispirited cast to her shoulders, which isn't exactly surprising. We were so near to it. We *saw* it. And then we lost it.

I watch her anxiously for a moment. I know Sadie hates "droning on about things." But maybe she'd feel better if she talked. Just a little bit.

"Tell me again—*why* is the necklace so special to you?"

For a while Sadie says nothing, and I wonder if she even heard the question.

"I told you," she says at last. "When I wore it, I felt beautiful. Like a goddess. Radiant." She leans against the window frame. "You must have something in your wardrobe that makes you feel like that."

"Er . . ." I hesitate.

I can't honestly say I've ever felt like a goddess. Or particularly radiant, come to that.

As if she can read my thoughts, Sadie turns and surveys my jeans dubiously. "Maybe you don't. You should try wearing something *beautiful* for a change."

"These are nice jeans!" I pat them defensively. "Maybe they're not beautiful, exactly—"

"They're blue." She's regained her spirit by now and shoots me a scathing look. "Blue! The ugliest color in the rainbow. I see the whole world, walking around with hideous blue legs. Why *blue*?"

"Because . . ." I shrug, nonplussed. "Dunno."

Kate has left the office early to go to the orthodondist, and all the phones are quiet. Maybe I'll leave too. It's nearly time, anyway. I glance at my watch and feel a shot of anticipation.

I adjust the pencil stuffed into my hair, stand up, and check over my outfit. Quirky printed T-shirt from Urban Outfitters. Cute little pendant of a frog. Jeans and ballet pumps. Not too much makeup. Perfect.

"So . . . I thought we could go for a walk, maybe," I say super-casually to Sadie. "It's such a nice day."

"A walk?" She peers at me. "What kind of walk?"

"Just . . . a walk!" Before she can say any more, I close down my computer, set the office answering machine, and grab my bag. Now that my plan is about to come to fruition, I'm quite excited.

It only takes twenty minutes to get to Farringdon, and as I hurry up the tube steps I glance at my watch—5:45. Perfect.

"What are we doing?" Sadie's suspicious voice follows me. "I thought you said we were going for a walk."

"We are. Kind of."

I half wish I'd ditched Sadie. The trouble is, I think

I might need her in reserve if things get tricky. I head to the corner of the main road and pause.

"What are you waiting for?"

"No one," I say, a little too defensively. "I'm not waiting for anyone. I'm just . . . hanging out. Watching the world go by." I lean casually against a pillar-box to prove my point, then hastily move away as a woman approaches to post a letter.

Sadie appears in front of me and scans my face, then suddenly inhales as she sees the book in my hand. "I know what you're doing! You're trailing! You're waiting for Josh! *Aren't* you?"

"I'm taking control of my life." I avoid her eye. "I'm showing him I've changed. When he sees me, he'll realize his mistake. You wait."

"This is a very bad idea. A very, very bad idea."

"It's not. Shut up." I check my reflection and apply more lip gloss, then blot it off.

I'm not going to listen to a word Sadie says. I'm totally psyched and ready to go. I feel empowered. All those times I tried to get inside Josh's head, all those times I tried to ask him what he really wanted out of our relationship, he kept batting me away. But now, finally, I know what he wants! I know how to make things work!

Ever since that lunch, I've totally transformed myself. I've kept the bathroom tidy. I've stopped singing in the shower. I've made a resolution never to mention anyone else's relationship, ever. I've even looked at that William Eggleston photography book, but I think it would seem a bit of a coincidence to be actually holding it. Which is why I'm clutching a book called *Los Alamos,* another collection by him. Josh is going to see me so differently. He's going to be amazed! Now I just have to bump into him accidentally-on-purpose as he leaves his office. Which is about two hundred yards away.

Keeping my eyes fixed on the entrance, I head toward a tiny alcove next to a shop where I have a good view of everybody as they head toward the tube station. A couple of Josh's colleagues hurry past, and I feel a clench of nerves in my stomach. He'll be here soon.

"Listen." I turn urgently to Sadie. "You might possibly have to help me out a bit."

"What do you mean, help you?" she says haughtily.

"Prompt Josh a bit. Tell him he likes me. Just to make sure."

"Why will he need telling?" she retorts. "You said he was going to realize his mistake when he saw you."

"He will," I say impatiently. "But he might not realize it *straightaway*. He might need . . . a nudge. A kick-start. Like old cars," I add in a moment of inspiration. "Like in your times. Remember? You wound the handle round and round and then suddenly the engine caught and off it went. You must have done that millions of times."

"To *motors*," she says. "Not men!"

"Same thing! Once he's up and running, everything will be fine, I know it. . . ." I catch my breath. Oh my God. There he is.

He's sauntering along, his iPod in his ears, carrying a bottle of water and a new, cool-looking laptop bag. My legs are suddenly trembling, but there's no time to lose. I take a step out from my hiding place, and then another and another, until I'm right in his path.

"Oh!" I try to adopt a tone of surprise. "Er . . . hi, Josh!"

"Lara." He rips out his earphones and gazes at me warily.

"I'd completely forgotten you work around here!" I plaster a bright smile on my face. "What a coincidence!"

"Ye-esss," he says slowly.

Honestly. He needn't look quite so suspicious.

"I was just thinking about you the other day," I continue hurriedly. "About that time we went to the wrong Notre Dame. D'you remember? When the GPS got it wrong? Wasn't it funny?"

I'm gabbling. Slow down.

"That's weird," says Josh after a pause. "I was thinking about that the other day too." His eyes alight on the book in my hand, and I can see the jolt of surprise. "Is that . . . *Los Alamos*?"

"Oh, yes," I say carelessly. "I was looking through this fantastic book called *Democratic Camera* the other day. The pictures were so amazing, I just *had* to go and buy this." I pat it fondly, then look up. "Hey, didn't you quite like William Eggleston too?" I wrinkle my brow innocently. "Or was that someone else?"

"I love William Eggleston," says Josh slowly. "It was me who gave you *Democratic Camera*."

"Oh, *that's* right." I slap my head. "I'd forgotten."

I can see bewilderment in his face. He's on the back foot. Time to press home my advantage.

"Josh, I've been meaning to say . . ." I give him a rueful smile. "I'm sorry for all those texts I sent you. I don't know what got into me."

"Well . . ." Josh coughs awkwardly.

"Will you let me buy you a quick drink? Just to make it up? No hard feelings?"

There's silence. I can almost see his thought processes. *It's a reasonable suggestion. It's a free drink. She looks sane enough.*

"OK." He puts his iPod away. "Why not?"

I shoot a triumphant look at Sadie, who is shaking her head and making deathlike finger-across-the-throat gestures. Well, I don't care what she thinks. I march Josh into a nearby pub, order a white wine for me and a beer for him, and find a table in the corner. We raise our glasses and sip, and I open some crisps.

"So." I smile at Josh and offer him the packet.

"So." He clears his throat, obviously feeling awkward. "How are things?"

"Josh." I lean my elbows on the table and look at him seriously. "You know what? Let's not *analyze* everything. God, I'm sick of people who analyze everything to death. I'm sick of unpicking conversations. Just live. Enjoy life. Don't think about it!"

Josh stares at me over his beer, looking totally confused. "But you used to love analyzing. You used to read that magazine *Analyze*."

"I've changed." I shrug simply. "I've changed in so many ways, Josh. I buy less makeup. My bathroom is totally empty. I was thinking I might like to travel. To Nepal maybe."

I'm sure I remember him mentioning Nepal, one of those times.

"You want to go traveling?" He seems taken aback. "But you never said—"

"It came to me recently," I say earnestly. "Why am I so unadventurous? There's so much out there to see. Mountains . . . cities . . . the temples of Kathmandu—"

"I'd love to see Kathmandu," he says, looking animated. "You know, I was thinking about going there next year."

"No!" I beam at him. "That's amazing!"

For the next ten minutes we talk about Nepal. At least, Josh talks about Nepal and I agree with everything he says, and the time just whizzes by. We both have color in our cheeks and are laughing as he glances at his watch. We look like a happy couple. I know, because I keep checking out our reflection in the mirror.

"I'd better shoot," Josh suddenly says, looking at his watch. "I've got a squash practice. It's been good to see you, Lara."

"Oh, right," I say, taken aback. "Great to see you too."

"Thanks for the drink." I watch in slight panic as he picks up his laptop case. This isn't how it's supposed to go.

"This was a good idea, Lara." He smiles, then bends to kiss my cheek. "No hard feelings. Let's stay in touch."

Stay in touch?

"Have another drink!" I try not to sound desperate. "Just a quick one!"

Josh considers for a moment, then looks at his watch again. "OK, a quick one. Same?" He heads toward the bar. The minute he's out of earshot I hiss, "Sadie!" and beckon her over from the bar stool where she's been sitting throughout, wedged between two businessmen with stripy-shirted guts.

"Tell him he loves me!"

"But he doesn't love you," says Sadie, as though explaining something very simple to someone very stupid.

"He does! He does, really! He's just scared to admit it, even to himself. But you saw us. We were getting on amazingly. If he only had a little nudge in the right di-

rection . . . please . . . please . . ." I gaze at her entreatingly. "After everything I've done for you . . . *please*."

Sadie gives an exasperated sigh. *"All right."*

A microsecond later she's at Josh's side, bellowing in
his ear, *"You still love Lara! You made a mistake! You
still love Lara!"*

I can see him stiffen and shake his head, trying to rid
himself of the noise. He brushes his ear a few times,
breathes heavily, and rubs his face. At last I see him
turn and survey me. He looks so dazed that if I wasn't
feeling so anxious I'd laugh.

"You still love Lara! You still love Lara!"

As Josh carries the drinks over and sits down next to
me, he seems transfixed. I shoot Sadie a grateful smile
and sip my wine, waiting for Josh to declare himself.
But he sits rigid, his eyes distant.

"Is there something on your mind, Josh?" I prompt
at last in a soft voice. "Because if there is, you can tell
me. I'm an old friend. You can trust me."

"Lara—" He stops.

I look desperately at Sadie for more help. He's
nearly there, he's *so* nearly there. . . .

"You love Lara! Don't fight it, Josh! You love her!"

Josh's brow is clearing. He's drawing breath. I think
he's going to—

"Lara."

"Yes, Josh?" I can hardly manage the words.

Go on, go on, go *on*. . . .

"I think maybe I made a mistake." Josh swallows
hard. "I think I still love you."

Even though I knew he was going to say it, there's a
huge, romantic swell in my heart, and tears start pricking my eyes.

"Well . . . I still love you, Josh," I say, my voice trembling. "I always did."

I'm not sure if he kisses me or I kiss him, but suddenly our arms are wrapped around each other, and we're devouring each other. (OK, I think I kissed him.) As we draw apart eventually, Josh looks even more dazed than before.

"Well," he says after a bit.

"Well." I lovingly mesh my fingers with his.

"Lara, I have this squash thing." He glances at his watch, looking uncomfortable. "I need to . . ."

"Don't worry," I say generously. "Go. We can talk later."

"OK." He nods. "I'll text you my new number."

"Great." I smile.

I won't bring up the fact that I think it was a total overreaction to change his mobile number just because of a few texts I sent him. We can talk about that another time. No hurry.

As he flips open his phone, I glance over his shoulder—and feel a jolt of sheer amazement. He's still got a photo of us on his screen. Him and me. Standing on a mountain in our skiwear at sunset. We're in silhouette, but I remember the moment vividly. We'd been skiing all day, and the sunset was spectacular. We asked this German guy to take a picture, and he spent about half an hour lecturing Josh about the settings on his phone. And Josh kept the photo! All this time!

"Nice picture," I say in a deadpan, casual way, nodding at it.

"Yeah." Josh's face softens as he gazes at it. "Makes me feel good whenever I look at it."

"Me too," I say breathlessly.

I knew it. I *knew* it. He does love me. He just needed

a nudge, he just needed a confidence boost, he just needed that inner voice to tell him it was OK.

My phone burbles with a text, and Josh's number pops up on my screen. I can't help a tiny sigh of satisfaction. I've got him back again. He's mine!

We head out of the pub, hands tightly clasped, and pause at the corner.

"I'll get a cab," says Josh. "Do you want to—"

I'm about to say, "Great! I'll share it with you!" But then the new Lara stops me. *Don't be too eager. Give him space.*

I shake my head. "No, thanks. I'm going the other way. Love you." I kiss his fingers, one by one.

"Love you." He nods. A cab stops, and Josh bends to kiss me again before getting in.

"Bye!" I wave as it pulls off, then turn away, hugging myself, zinging all over with triumph. We're back together! I'm back with Josh!

FOURTEEN

I can never resist telling people good news. I mean, why not brighten someone else's life too? So by the following morning I've texted all my friends that Josh and I are back together. And some of his friends, just because I happened to have their numbers programmed in my phone. And the guy at Dial-a-Pizza. (That was a mistake. He was pleased for me, though.)

"Oh my God, Lara!" Kate's voice bursts through the office door at the same time as she does. "You made up with Josh?"

"Oh, you got my text," I say nonchalantly. "Yeah, it's cool, isn't it?"

"It's amazing! I mean . . . it's incredible!"

She doesn't need to sound *quite* so surprised. But it's nice to have someone pleased for me. Sadie's such a downer on the whole thing. She hasn't said she's happy for me once, and every time I got a text back from one of my friends last night, she huffed. Even now she's gazing disapprovingly at me from her perch on top of the filing cabinet. But I don't care, because I've got my most important phone call of all to make, and I am *so* looking forward to it. I dial the number, lean back, and wait for Dad to pick up. (Answering the phone makes Mum anxious, because it might be kidnappers. Don't ask.)

"Michael Lington."

"Oh, hi, Dad, it's Lara," I say in the casual tone I've been practicing all morning. "I just thought I'd let you know that Josh and I are back together again."

"What?" says Dad after a pause.

"Yes, we bumped into each other yesterday," I say airily. "And he said he still loved me and he'd made a huge mistake."

There's another silence at the other end of the phone. Dad must be too gobsmacked to answer.

Ha. This is such a sweet moment! I want to relish it forever. After all those weeks of people telling me I was sad and deluded and should move on. They were *all wrong*.

"So it looks like I was right, doesn't it?" I can't resist adding. "I *said* we were meant to be together." I shoot Sadie a gloating look.

"Lara . . ." Dad doesn't sound as happy as I thought he would. In fact, he sounds pretty stressed, bearing in mind his younger daughter has found happiness in the arms of the man she loves. "Are you absolutely *sure* that you and Josh . . ." He hesitates. "Are you *sure* that's what he meant?"

Honestly. Does he think I've made it up or something?

"You can call him if you like! You can ask him! We bumped into each other, and we had a drink and talked about stuff, and he said he still loves me. And now we're back together. Just like you and Mum."

"Well." I can hear Dad breathing out. "That's quite . . . incredible. Wonderful news."

"I know." I can't help smiling complacently. "It just goes to show. Relationships are complicated things, and other people shouldn't barge in and think they know all about it."

"Indeed," he says faintly.

Poor Dad. I think I've practically given him a heart attack.

"Hey." I cast around for something to cheer him up. "Dad, I was thinking about our family history the other day. And I was wondering, have you got any pictures of Great-Aunt Sadie's house?"

"Sorry, darling?" Dad sounds like he's having trouble keeping up.

"The old family house that burned down. In Archbury. You showed me a photograph of it once. Have you still got it?"

"I think so." Dad's voice is wary. "Lara, you seem a bit obsessed by Great-Aunt Sadie."

"I'm not obsessed," I say resentfully. "All I'm doing is showing a little interest in my heritage. I thought you'd be *pleased*."

"I am pleased," says Dad quickly. "Of course I am. I'm just . . . surprised. You've never been interested in family history before."

This is a fair point. He brought out some old photo album last Christmas and I fell asleep while he was showing it to me. (In my defense, I *had* eaten quite a few liqueur chocolates.)

"Yes, well . . . people change, don't they? And I'm interested now. I mean, that photo's the only thing we've got left of the house, isn't it?"

"Not quite the only thing," says Dad. "You know, the oak desk in the hall came from that house."

"In our hall?" I stare at the phone in surprise. "I thought everything was lost in the fire."

"A very few things were salvaged." I can tell Dad's

relaxed a little. "They were put in a storage unit and left there for years. Nobody could face dealing with it. It was Bill who sorted it all out, after your grandfather died. He was at a loose end. I was doing my accountancy exams. Strange to imagine, but Bill was the idler in those days." Dad laughs, and I can hear him take a sip of coffee. "That was the year your mother and I got married. That oak desk was our first piece of furniture. It's a wonderful piece of original art nouveau."

"Wow."

I'm riveted by this story. I've walked past that desk about ten thousand times, but it's never once occurred to me to wonder where it came from. Maybe it was Sadie's own desk! Maybe it has all her secret papers in it! As I put the phone down, Kate is working industriously. I can't send her on yet another coffee run. But I'm desperate to tell Sadie what I just heard.

Hey, Sadie! I type in a new document. *Not everything was lost in the fire! There were some things in a storage unit! Guess what? We have a desk from your old house!*

Maybe it has a hidden drawer full of all her lost treasures, I'm thinking excitedly. And only Sadie knows how to open it. She'll tell me the secret code, and I'll gently tug it open and blow off the dust, and inside will be . . . something really cool. I gesticulate at her and point at my screen.

"I know that desk was saved," says Sadie, after reading my message. She sounds deeply unimpressed by the news. "I was sent a list of things at the time, in case I wanted to claim anything. Hideous crockery. Dull bits of pewter. Dreadful furniture. None of it interested me."

It's not dreadful furniture, I type, a little indignantly. *It's a wonderful piece of original art nouveau.*

I look up at Sadie, and she's sticking a finger down her throat. "It's minging," she says, and I can't help giggling.

Where did you learn that word? I type.

"Picked it up." Sadie gives an insouciant shrug.

So I told my dad about Josh, I type, and look at Sadie for a reaction. But she rolls her eyes and disappears.

Fine. *Be* like that. I don't care what she thinks, anyway. I lean back, take out my mobile, and flip to one of Josh's texts. I feel all warm and content, as though I just drank a cup of hot chocolate. I'm back with Josh, and all's right with the world.

Maybe I'll text Josh and tell him how pleased everyone is for us.

No. I don't want to hound him. I'll leave it half an hour or so.

Across the room, the phone rings, and I wonder if maybe it's him. But a moment later Kate says, "I'll put you on hold," and looks up anxiously. "Lara, it's Janet from Leonidas Sports. Shall I put her through?"

All the hot chocolate drains out of my stomach.

"Yes. OK, I'll speak to her. Just give me thirty seconds." I psych myself up, then lift the phone with my breeziest top-recruitment-consultant manner. "Hi, Janet! How are you? Did you get the short list all right?"

Kate emailed the short list to Janet last night. I should have known she'd call. I should have gone out for the day or pretended to have lost my voice.

"I hope you're as excited by it as I am," I add brightly.

"No, I'm not," Janet says in her usual hoarse,

peremptory tones. "Lara, I don't understand. Why's Clive Hoxton on the list?"

"Ah, Clive," I say, trying to sound confident, "What a man. What a talent."

OK, so here's the thing. I know my lunch with Clive didn't end brilliantly. But the truth is, he'd be perfect for the job. And I might be able to talk him around before the interview. So I put him on the list anyway, with *provisional* after his name in small letters.

"Clive's a really bright executive, Janet." I launch into my spiel. "He's experienced in marketing, very dynamic, ripe for a move—"

"I know all that." Janet cuts me off. "But I bumped into him at a reception last night. He said he'd made it clear he wasn't interested. In fact, he was shocked to learn he was on the short list."

Fuck.

"Really?" I summon tones of astonishment. "How . . . strange. How very strange. That's not the impression I got at all. As far as I was aware, we had a great meeting, he was enthusiastic—"

"He told me he walked out," says Janet flatly.

"He . . . left the meeting, obviously." I cough. "As we both did. You could say we *both* walked out—"

"He told me you were on the phone to another client throughout and he never wanted to do business with you again."

My face flushes red. Clive Hoxton is a mean sneak.

"Well." I clear my throat. "Janet, I'm baffled. All I can say is we must have had mixed messages—"

"What about this Nigel Rivers?" Janet has clearly moved on. "Is he the man with the dandruff? Applied to us once before?"

"It's a lot better these days," I say hastily. "I think he's using Head and Shoulders."

"You know our MD has strong views on personal hygiene?"

"I . . . er . . . was not aware of that, Janet. I'll make a note of it—"

"And what about this Gavin Mynard?"

"Very, very talented," I lie at once. "A very talented, creative guy who has been . . . overlooked. His résumé doesn't reflect his . . . wealth of experiences."

Janet sighs. "Lara . . ."

I stiffen with apprehension. Her tone is unmistakable. She's going to fire me right now. I can't let it happen, I can't, we'll be finished. . . .

"And, of course—I have another candidate!" I hear myself saying in a rush.

"Another candidate? You mean, not on the list?"

"Yes. Much better than any of the others! In fact, I'd say this candidate is definitely your person."

"Well, who is it?" says Janet suspiciously. "Why don't I have the details?"

"Because . . . I need to firm things up first." I'm crossing my fingers so hard they hurt. "It's all very confidential. This is a high-profile person we're talking about, Janet. Very senior, very experienced—believe me, I'm excited."

"I need a name!" she barks angrily. "I need a résumé! Lara, this is all highly unprofessional. Our in-house meeting is on Thursday. Can I speak to Natalie, please?"

"No!" I say in panic. "I mean . . . Thursday. Absolutely! You'll have all the information on Thursday. I promise. And all I can say is, you'll be bowled over by the caliber of this particular candidate. Janet, I must dash, great to talk." I put the phone down, my heart thumping.

Shit. *Shit*. What am I going to do now?

"Wow!" Kate looks up, eyes shining. "Lara, you're such a star. I knew you'd do it! Who's this amazing high-profile candidate?"

"There isn't one!" I say desperately. "We have to find one!"

"Right." Kate starts looking urgently around the office, as though a top-level marketing executive might be hiding in the filing cabinet. "Er . . . where?"

"I don't know!" I thrust my fingers through my hair. "There aren't any!"

There's a shrill electronic burble as my phone receives a text, and I grab it, hoping for one mad moment that it's a top marketing executive asking me if I have any jobs in sports retail going. Or maybe Josh, asking me to marry him. Or maybe Dad, saying he now realizes I was right all along and would like to apologize for ever having doubted me. Or even Diamanté, saying she doesn't need that old dragonfly necklace after all, should she send it around by courier?

But it's none of them. It's Natalie.

Hi babe! Am doing some yoga on the beach. It's so
mellow here. Have sent u a pic, look at the view.
Awesome, huh? Nataliexxxx
PS Everything OK in the office?

I feel like hurling it out of the window.

By seven o'clock my neck is aching and my eyes are red-rimmed. I've made a new, emergency long list of candidates, using old issues of *Business People,* the Internet, and a copy of *Marketing Week* I made Kate run out and buy. But none of them will even take my call—let alone talk about a job, let alone allow me to quickly slap them onto a short list. I have less than forty-eight hours. I'm going to have to invent a top marketing director. Or impersonate one.

On the plus side, they had a half-price offer on pinot grigio at Oddbins.

The minute I get home, I turn on the TV and start glugging down the wine at speed. By the time *EastEnders* starts, I've got through half a bottle, the room is swinging from side to side, and my work troubles are receding nicely.

After all. I mean. All that really matters is love, isn't it?

You have to get things in perspective. In proportion. Love is the thing. Not work. Not marketing directors. Not scary conversations with Janet Grady. I just need to cling on to that and I'll be OK.

I'm cradling my phone in my lap, and every so often I turn on my texts to read them again. I've been texting Josh all day, just to keep my spirits up. And he's sent two texts back! Quite short ones, but even so. He's at some dreary work conference in Milton Keynes and he said he can't wait to be back home.

Which obviously means he can't wait to see me!

I'm debating whether to send him another light, friendly text, asking him what he's doing, when I glance up and notice Sadie sitting on the fireplace in a pale gray chiffony dress.

"Oh, hi," I say. "Where did you get to?"

"At the cinema. I watched two films." She shoots me an accusing look. "You know, it gets very lonely during the day. You're so preoccupied with your work."

She'd be preoccupied if she had Janet Grady on her tail.

"Well, I'm very sorry I have to earn a living," I reply, a little sarcastically. "I'm sorry I'm not a lady of leisure and can't watch movies all day—"

"Have you got the necklace yet?" she says, right over me. "Have you done anything more about it?"

"No, Sadie," I say tetchily. "I haven't. I've had a few other problems today, as it happens." I wait for her to ask what those problems are, but she just gives a distant shrug. Isn't she even going to ask me what happened? Isn't she going to offer me any sympathy? Some guardian angel she is.

"Josh has been texting me; isn't that great?" I add, to annoy her.

She gives me a baleful look. "It's not great. The whole thing is absolutely false."

She glares at me and I glare back. Obviously, neither of us is in a brilliant mood tonight.

"It's *not* false. It's real. You saw him kiss me; you heard what he said."

"He's a puppet," says Sadie dismissively. "He said whatever I told him to say. I could have told him to make love to a tree and he would have done. I've never known anyone so weak-willed! I barely had to whisper at him and he jumped."

She's so arrogant. Who does she think she is, God?

"That's rubbish," I say coldly. "OK, I know you nudged him a bit. But he would never say he loved me unless there was a basis of truth. He was obviously expressing what he really feels, deep down."

Sadie gives a sarcastic laugh. "'What he really feels

deep down.' Darling, you're too amusing. He doesn't *have* any feelings for you."

"He does!" I spit. "Of course he does! He had my picture on his phone, didn't he? He'd been carrying it around all this time! That's love."

"It's not love. Don't be ridiculous." Sadie seems so sure of herself, I feel a swell of absolute fury.

"Well, you've never even *been* in love! So what would you know about it? Josh is a real man, with real feelings and real love, something you know *nothing* about. And you can think what you like, but I really believe I can make things work, I really believe Josh has deep feelings for me—"

"It's not enough to believe!" Sadie's voice is suddenly passionate, almost savage. "Don't you see that, you stupid girl? You could spend your whole life hoping and believing! If a love affair is one-sided, then it's only ever a question, never an answer. You can't live your life waiting for an answer."

She flushes and swivels away.

There's a sharp silence, except for two EastEnders laying into each other on-screen. My mouth has dropped open in astonishment, and I notice I'm about to tip wine all over the sofa. I right my hand and take a gulp. Bloody hell. What was that outburst all about?

I thought Sadie didn't care about love. I thought she only cared about having fun and tally-ho and the sizzle. But just then she sounded as if . . .

"Is that what happened to you, Sadie?" I say tentatively to her back. "Did you spend your whole life waiting for an answer?"

Instantly, she disappears. No warning, no "see you later." She just vanishes.

She *can't* do this to me. I have to know more.

There's got to be a story here. I switch off the TV and call loudly into thin air. All my annoyance has evaporated; I'm consumed by curiosity instead.

"Sadie! Tell me! It's good to talk about things!" The room is silent, but somehow I'm sure she's still there. "Come on," I say, wheedling. "I've told you everything about me. And I'm your great-niece. You can trust me. I won't tell anyone."

Still nothing.

"Whatever." I shrug. "Thought you had more guts than that."

"I do have guts." Sadie appears in front of me, looking furious.

"So tell me." I fold my arms.

Sadie's face is motionless, but I can see her eyes flickering to me and away again.

"There's nothing to tell," she says finally, her voice low. "It's simply that I *do* know what it's like to think you're in love. I know what it's like to squander all your hours and all your tears and all your heart on something which turns out to be . . . nothing. Don't waste your life. That's all."

That's all? Is she kidding? She *can't* leave it there! There was a something. What was the something?

"What happened? Did you have a love affair? Was there some guy when you were living abroad? Sadie, tell me!"

For a moment Sadie looks as though she's still not going to answer, or else disappear again. Then she sighs, turns away, and walks toward the mantelpiece.

"It was a long time ago. Before I went abroad. Before I was married. There was . . . a man."

"The big row with your parents!" I suddenly put two and two together. "Was that because of him?"

Sadie tilts her head forward about a millimeter in assent. I should have *known* it was a man. I try to picture her with a boyfriend. Some dapper twenties guy in a boater, maybe. With one of those old-fashioned mustaches.

"Did your parents catch you together or something? Were you . . . barney-mugging?"

"No!" She bursts into laughter.

"So what happened? Tell me! Please!"

I still can't quite get over the fact that Sadie's been in love. After giving me such a hard time about Josh. After pretending she didn't care about anything.

"They found sketches." Her laughter dies away and she hugs her skinny chest. "He was a painter. He liked to paint me. My parents were scandalized."

"What's wrong with him painting you?" I say, puzzled. "They should have been pleased! I mean, it's a compliment, an artist wanting to—"

"Naked."

"Naked?"

I'm gobsmacked. And kind of impressed. I would never pose naked for a painting. Not in a million years! Not unless the painter could do some kind of airbrushing.

Brushing, maybe. Whatever artists do.

"I had a drape over me. But, even so, my parents . . ." Sadie presses her lips together. "That was a dramatic day, the day they found the sketches."

My hand is clapped over my mouth. I know I shouldn't laugh, I know it's not really funny, but I can't help it.

"So they saw you—your—"

"They became absolutely hysterical." She gives a tiny snort, almost a laugh. "It was funny—but it was dreadful too. His parents were as angry as mine. He was supposed to be going into law." She shakes her head. "He would never have made a lawyer. He was a great big shambles of a man. He painted all night, and drank wine, and smoked gaspers back to back, stubbed them out on his palette. . . . We both did. I used to spend all night with him at his studio. In his parents' shed. I used to call him Vincent, after van Gogh. He called me Mabel." She gives another tiny snort.

"*Mabel?*" I wrinkle my nose.

"There was a maid at his house called Mabel. I told him I thought it was the ugliest name I'd ever heard and they should make her change it. So he instantly started calling *me* Mabel. Cruel beast that he was."

Her tone is half jokey, but there's a strange flickering in her eyes. I can't tell if she wants to remember all this or not.

"Did you . . ." I begin—then chicken out before I can finish the question. I wanted to ask, "Did you really love him?" But Sadie's lost in her own thoughts, anyway.

"I used to creep out of the house when everyone was asleep, climb down the ivy. . . ." She trails away, her eyes distant. Suddenly she looks really sad. "When we were discovered, everything changed. He was sent to France, to some uncle, to 'get it all out of his system.' As if anyone could ever stop him painting."

"What was his name?"

"His name was Stephen Nettleton." Sadie breathes out heavily. "I haven't said that name aloud for . . . seventy years. At least."

Seventy *years*?

"So what happened? After that?"

"We were never in touch with each other, ever again," says Sadie matter-of-factly.

"Why not?" I say in horror. "Didn't you write to him?"

"Oh, I wrote." She gives a brittle smile that makes me wince. "I sent letter after letter to France. But I never heard from him. My parents said I was a naïve little simpleton. They said he'd used me for what he could get. I wouldn't believe them at first, hated them for saying it. But then . . ." She looks up, her chin set, as though defying me to pity her. "I was like you. 'He does love me, he really does!'" She puts on a mocking, high-pitched voice. "'He'll write! He'll come back for me. He *loves* me!' Do you know how it felt when I finally came to my senses?"

There's a taut silence.

"So . . . what did you do?" I hardly dare speak.

"Got married, of course." I can see the flash of defiance. "Stephen's father conducted the service. He was our vicar. Stephen must have known, but he didn't even send a card."

She lapses into silence, and I sit there, my thoughts teeming. She got married to Waistcoat Guy out of revenge. It's obvious. It's awful. No wonder it didn't last.

I'm totally deflated. I wish I hadn't pressed Sadie so hard now. I didn't want to stir up all these painful memories. I just thought she'd have some fun, juicy anecdote and I could find out what sex was like in the 1920s.

"Didn't you ever think about following Stephen to France?" I can't help asking.

"I had my pride." She gives me a pointed look, and I feel like retorting, "Well, at least I got my guy back!"

"Did you keep any of the sketches?" I'm desperately casting around for an upside.

"I hid them." She nods. "There was a big painting too. He smuggled it to me, just before he left for France, and I hid it in the cellar. My parents had no idea. But then, of course, the house was burned and I lost it."

"Oh God." I sag in disappointment. "What a shame."

"Not really. I didn't care. Why should I care?"

I watch her for a minute pleating her skirt, over and over, obsessively, her eyes busy with memories.

"Maybe he never got your letters," I say hopefully.

"Oh, I'm sure he did." There's an edge to her voice. "I know they went into the post. I had to smuggle them out of the house and into the postbox myself."

I can't bear this. Smuggling letters, for God's sake. *Why* didn't they have mobile phones in the 1920s? Think how many misunderstandings in the world could have been avoided. Archduke Ferdinand could have texted his people—*I think a weirdo's following me*—and he wouldn't have got assassinated. World War I wouldn't have happened. And Sadie could have called her man; they could have talked it through. . . .

"Is he still alive now?" I'm gripped by irrational hope. "We could track him down! We could Google him, we could go to France, I bet we'd find him—"

"He died young." Sadie cuts me off, her voice remote. "Twelve years after he left England. They brought home his remains and had a funeral in the village. I was living abroad by then. I wasn't invited, anyway. And I wouldn't have gone."

I'm so horrified, I can't reply. Not only did he leave

her, he *died*. This is a rubbish story with a terrible ending, and I wish I'd never asked.

Sadie's face is drawn as she gazes out of the window. Her skin seems paler than ever, and there are shadows under her eyes. In her silver-gray dress she looks like a vulnerable little wisp. I feel tears spring to my eyes. She loved this artist. It's obvious. Underneath all the bravado and the back chat, she really loved him. All her life, probably.

How could he not have loved her back? Bastard. If he were alive now I'd go and find him and beat him up. Even if he was some quavery million-year-old man with twenty grandchildren.

"It's so sad." I rub my nose. "It's just so sad."

"It's not sad," she retorts at once, her old flippant air returning. "It's the way things are. There are other men, there are other countries, there are other lives to live. But that's why I know." She suddenly rounds on me. "I *know*, and you have to believe me."

"Know what?" I'm not following her at all. "Believe what?"

"You'll never work things out with your chap. Your Josh."

"Why?" I glare back at her defensively. Trust her to bring Josh into it.

"Because you can want and want and want." She turns away, hugging her knees. I can see the bony line of her spine through her dress. "But if he doesn't want you back . . . you might as well wish the sky were red."

FIFTEEN

$\mathcal{I}$'m not panicking. Even though it's Wednesday and I still don't have a solution and Janet Grady is on the warpath.

I'm kind of beyond panic. I'm in an altered state. Like a yogi.

I've been dodging calls from Janet all day. Kate's told her I'm in the loo, at lunch, *trapped* in the loo, and then at last I heard her saying desperately, "I can't disturb her, I really can't disturb her. . . . Janet, I don't know who the candidate is. . . . Janet, please don't threaten me. . . ."

She put the phone down, shaking. Apparently Janet's in a vicious mood. I think she's become a bit obsessed by this short list. So am I. Résumés are swimming in front of my eyes, and the phone feels like it's welded to my ear.

Yesterday I had a flash of inspiration. At least, it felt like inspiration. Maybe it was just desperation. Tonya! She's tough and hard and ironlike and all those scary qualities. She'd be a total match for Janet Grady.

So I called up and casually asked if she'd thought about returning to work, now the twins had turned two. Had she thought about moving into marketing, maybe? In sportswear, perhaps? Tonya was quite senior at Shell before she had the boys. I bet her résumé looks really impressive.

"But I'm on a career break," she objected. "Magda! NOT those fish fingers. Look in the bottom drawer of the freezer—"

"You've had enough of a break, surely. A woman with your talents—you must be *dying* to get back to work."

"Not really."

"But your brain will go soggy!"

"It won't go soggy!" She sounded affronted. "You know, I do Suzuki music every week with the boys. It's stimulating for both children and parents, and I've met some other great mums there."

"You're telling me you'd rather do Suzuki music and drink cappuccinos than be a top marketing director." I tried to inject an incredulous note, even though I would a *million* times rather be doing Suzuki music and drinking cappuccinos right now than dealing with all this.

"Yes," she said flatly. "I would. Why are you approaching me, anyway, Lara?" Suddenly her voice was more alert. "What's going on? Have you got a problem? Because you can always talk to me about it, you know, if things are going wrong. . . ."

Oh God. Not the fake-o sympathy.

"Nothing's going wrong! Just trying to do my big sister a favor." I left it a moment or two before adding casually, "So, those mums you've met at Suzuki music. None of them used to be a top marketing director, did they?"

You'd think out of eight formerly professional mothers there'd have been *one* marketing director with retail experience who wanted to return to work at once. You'd think.

Anyway. So much for that bright idea. In fact, so much for *all* my ideas. The only possibility I've found is a guy in Birmingham who might move if Leonidas Sports pays for his helicopter commute every week. Which is never going to happen in a million years. I'm doomed. All in all, you'd think now would not be the best time to be glammed up and going to a party.

Nevertheless, here I am in a taxi, glammed up and going to a party.

"We're here! Park Lane!" Sadie peers out of the window. "Pay the driver! Let's go!"

Bright flashes from cameras are filling our taxi, and I can hear the hubbub of people greeting one another. I see a group of about ten people in evening dress arriving on the red carpet leading up to the Spencer Hotel, where the *Business People* dinner is taking place. According to the *Financial Times*, four hundred of the top business talents in London are going to be gathered here tonight.

As one of those talents, I was all set to cancel, for many, many reasons:

1. I'm back with Josh now and shouldn't be attending dinners with other men.
2. I'm too stressed out by work.
3. I mean, really stressed out.
4. Janet Grady might be here and yell at me.
5. Clive Hoxton, ditto.
   Not to mention:
6. Have to talk to Mr. American Frown all night.

But then it hit me. Four hundred businesspeople, all together in one room. Some of them have got to be top-level marketing executives. And some of them have got to want a new job. Surely.

So this is my last-ditch plan. I'm going to find a candidate for Leonidas Sports tonight, at the dinner.

I double-check that my evening bag is well stocked with business cards and glance at my reflection in the window. Needless to say, Sadie took charge of my outfit again. I'm in a black sequined vintage dress with fringed sleeves and beaded Egyptian-style medallions at the shoulders. Over this I'm wearing a cloak. My eyes are heavily kohled, I have a long gold snake bracelet, and even a pair of original stockings, just like Sadie used to wear, apparently. And on my head is a close-fitting diamanté mesh cap, which Sadie found at some antique market.

Tonight I feel a lot more confident, though. For a start, everyone else will be dressed up too. And even though I protested about the cap, I secretly think I look quite cool. I look kind of glam and retro.

Sadie's dolled up too, in a fringed dress, all turquoise and green, with a peacock feather shawl. She's wearing about ten necklaces, and on her head is the most ludicrous headdress, with a diamanté waterfall cascading past her ear. She keeps flipping her evening bag open and shut and seems in a manic mood. In fact, she's been manic ever since she told me that story about her old dead lover. I've tried to ask her more about it, but no dice. She just glides away or vanishes or changes the subject. So I've given up.

"Let's go!" Her legs are twitching. "I can't wait to start dancing!"

For God's sake. She's obsessed. And if she thinks I'm dancing with Ed in the middle of the bar for a second time, she needs to think again.

"Sadie, listen," I say firmly. "It's a business dinner. There won't be any dancing. I'm here to work."

"We'll find some," she says confidently. "You can always find dancing."

Yeah. Whatever.

As I get out, people in evening dress are everywhere, shaking hands confidently and laughing and posing for the cameras. Several of them I recognize from *Business People* photo spreads. For a moment I feel all twingey with nerves. But then I glance at Sadie and raise my chin, just like she does. So what if they're important? I'm as good as they are. I'm a partner in my own company. Even if it consists of two people and a dodgy coffee machine.

"Hi. Lara." Ed's voice greets me from behind, and I turn. There he is, looking as square-cut and handsome as I might have expected. His dinner jacket fits him perfectly; his dark hair is brushed back perfectly.

Josh never wears a standard DJ. He always wears something offbeat, like a Nehru jacket over jeans. But then, Josh is really cool.

"Hi." I take Ed's hand before he gets any idea of kissing me. Not that I think he would. He's looking my outfit up and down with a quizzical expression.

"You look very . . . twenties."

Well spotted, Einstein. "Yes, well." I shrug. "I like twenties clothes."

"No kidding," he says, deadpan.

"You look delicious!" says Sadie joyfully to Ed. She flings herself at him, wraps both arms around his chest, and nuzzles his neck.

Urgh. Is she going to do that all night?

We're approaching a small group of photographers, and at a signal from a lady with an earpiece, Ed stops with a slight roll of his eyes. "Sorry. I have to do this, I'm afraid."

"Shit!" I say in panic as the camera flashes blind me. "What do I do?"

"Stand a little side-on," he murmurs reassuringly. "Chin up and smile. Don't worry, it's natural to freak out. I did media training for this stuff. The first time, I was so stiff I looked like a Thunderbird puppet."

I can't help smiling. Actually, he does look a bit like a Thunderbird, with his square jaw and dark brows.

"I know what you're thinking," he says, as the flashes keep coming. "I look like a Thunderbird anyway. It's OK. I can take the truth."

"I wasn't thinking that!" I say unconvincingly. We move on to another group of photographers. "How come you know about *Thunderbirds,* anyway?"

"Are you kidding? I saw it when I was a kid. I was obsessed. I wanted to be Scott Tracy."

"I wanted to be Lady Penelope." I glance up at him. "So you're interested in *one* piece of British culture, at least."

I'm not sure if a children's TV show counts as "culture," but I can't resist making my point. Ed looks surprised and draws breath as though to answer—but before he can, the earpiece lady comes to escort us onward, and the moment's gone.

As we head into the hotel, I'm looking around, trying to suss out all the people, trying to see if there's anyone I could approach about the Leonidas Sports job. I have to circulate quickly, before everyone sits down to eat.

Meanwhile, Sadie has been glued to Ed's side, stroking his hair and rubbing her face against his and running her hand over his chest. As we come to a halt in front of a reception table, she suddenly dips down and pokes her head into his dinner jacket pocket. I'm so disconcerted, I jump.

"Sadie!" I mutter furiously behind Ed's back. "What are you doing?"

"Having a look at his things!" she says, standing up. "There wasn't anything very interesting, just some papers and a pack of cards. I wonder what's in his trouser pockets ... hmm ..." Her eyes focus on his crotch, and a gleam appears.

"Sadie!" I hiss in horror. "No!"

"Mr. Harrison!" A woman in a chic navy cocktail dress has swooped down on Ed. "I'm Sonia Taylor, head of PR at Dewhurst Publishing. We're so looking forward to your speech."

"Pleased to be here." Ed nods. "May I introduce Lara Lington, my ..." He looks at me dubiously, as though searching for the word. "Date."

"Hello, Lara." Sonia turns to me with a warm smile. "What line are you in?"

Oh wow. The head of PR at Dewhurst Publishing.

"Hi, Sonia." I shake her hand in my most professional manner. "I'm in recruitment; do let me give you my card—*No!*" An involuntary cry leaves my lips.

Sadie has bent down and plunged her face into Ed's trouser pocket.

"Are you all right?" Sonia Taylor looks concerned.

"I'm fine!" My eyes are darting all around, anywhere but at the sight in front of me. "Fine. Really, really fine ..."

"That's good." Sonia gives me a slightly strange look. "I'll just find your name badges."

Sadie's head reappears briefly, then plunges back in again. What's she *doing* in there?

"Lara, is something wrong?" Ed turns to me with a puzzled frown.

"Um . . . no!" I manage. "It's all good, all good. . . ."

"Goodness!" Sadie's head suddenly reappears. "I got a good view there."

I clap a hand over my mouth. Ed eyes me suspiciously.

"Sorry," I manage. "Just . . . coughing."

"Here we are!" Sonia turns back from the table and hands us each a badge. "Ed, can I steal you for a moment to run through the order of events?" She smiles stiffly, then leads Ed away.

At once, I pull out my phone as camouflage, then wheel around to Sadie.

"Don't do that again! You put me off! I didn't know where to look!"

Sadie raises her eyebrows wickedly. "Just wanted to satisfy my curiosity."

I'm not even going to *ask* what that means.

"Well, don't! That woman Sonia thinks I'm a complete flake now. She didn't even take my business card."

"So what?" Sadie gives an insouciant shrug. "Who cares what she thinks?"

It's as if a switch flips inside me. Doesn't she realize how desperate I am? Hasn't she noticed me and Kate working thirteen-hour days?

"I care!" I round on her furiously and she shrinks back. "Sadie, why d'you think I'm here? I'm trying to build up my business! I'm trying to meet important people!" I gesture around at the milling hall. "I've got to find a candidate for Leonidas Sports by tomorrow! If I don't do something soon, we'll go bust. We practically *are* bust. I've been totally stressed out and you don't even care. You haven't even noticed." My voice is suddenly shaking a bit, which must be because of all the double-shot lattes I've drunk today. "Anyway. Whatever. Do what you like. Just stay away from me."

"Lara—" Sadie starts to speak, but I stride away from her toward the double doors to the main banqueting room. Ed and Sonia are on the podium, and I can see her explaining the microphone to him. Around me, tables are filling up with dynamic-looking men and women. I can hear snatches of conversation about markets and retail sectors and TV campaigns.

This is my big chance. *Come on, Lara.* Plucking up all my courage, I take a glass of champagne from a passing waiter, then approach a group of business types, all laughing merrily away about something.

"Hi!" I plunge in brightly. "I'm Lara Lington, L&N Executive Recruitment. Let me give you my card!"

"Hello," says a friendly-looking man with red hair. He makes introductions around the group, and I hand cards to everyone. From their name badges, it seems they all work for software companies.

"So, does anyone here work in marketing?" I ask casually. All eyes turn to a blond-haired man.

"Guilty." He smiles.

"Would you like a new job?" I blurt out. "It's at a sports-equipment company—great benefits, a really fab opportunity!"

There's silence. I can't breathe for hope. Then everyone bursts into laughter.

"I like your style," says the red-haired guy, and turns to his neighbor. "Can I interest you in an Asian software subsidiary, only ten years on the clock?"

"One careful owner," quips another guy, and there's more laughter.

They think I'm joking. Of course they do.

I hastily join in the laughter too. But inside, I feel like a total moron. I'm never going to find a candidate. This was a ridiculous idea. After a little while I excuse myself and move away, to find Ed approaching me across the floor.

"How's it going? Sorry to abandon you."

"No worries. I was . . . you know. Networking."

"We're at table one." He leads me toward the stage and I feel a flicker of pride, in spite of my low mood. Table 1 at the *Business People* dinner!

"Lara, I have a question," says Ed as we walk. "Please don't take this the wrong way."

"I'm sure I won't," I say. "Fire ahead."

"I just want to get something straight. You don't want to be my girlfriend. Is that right?"

"That's right." I nod. "And you don't want to be my boyfriend."

"No," he says, emphatically shaking his head. "Uh-uh." We've arrived at the table by now. Ed folds his arms and surveys me as though mystified. "So what are we doing here together?"

"Er . . . well. Good question."

I'm not sure how to answer. The truth is, there is no sane reason.

"Friends?" I suggest at last.

"Friends," he echoes doubtfully. "I guess we could be friends."

He pulls out my chair and I sit down. By every place is a program with *Guest Speaker: Ed Harrison* written across the bottom.

"Are you nervous?"

Ed's eyes flicker, then he gives me a tiny smile. "If I were I wouldn't say."

I flick to the back of the program and feel a little kick when I find my own name in the list. *Lara Lington, L&N Executive Recruitment.*

"You don't strike me as a typical headhunter," says Ed, following my gaze.

"Really?" I'm not quite sure how to react. Is that a good thing or a bad thing?

"You don't seem obsessed with money, for a start."

"I'd like to make more money," I say honestly. "Lots more. But I suppose that isn't the main point for me. I've always seen headhunting as a bit like—" I break off, embarrassed, and take a sip of wine.

I once told my headhunting theory to Natalie, and she said I was crazy and to shut up about it.

"What?"

"Well. Like matchmaking. Matching the perfect person with the perfect job."

Ed looks amused. "That's a different way of looking at it. I'm not sure most people around here would say they were having a love affair with their jobs." He gestures around the crowded room.

"Maybe they would if it was the right job, though," I say eagerly. "If you could just match people up with exactly what they want . . ."

"And you'd be Cupid."

"You're laughing at me."

"I'm not." He shakes his head firmly. "I like it as a theory. How does it work in practice?"

I sigh. There's something about Ed that makes me lower my guard. Maybe it's because I honestly don't care what he thinks of me.

"Not great. In fact, right now, pretty shit."

"That bad, huh?"

"Even worse." I take another drink of my wine, then look up to see Ed watching me quizzically.

"You're in a partnership, right?"

"Yes."

"So . . . how did you decide who to go into partnership with?" he says lightly. "How did that all happen?"

"Natalie?" I shrug. "Because she's my best friend and I've known her forever and she's a very talented top headhunter. She used to work for Price Bedford Associates, you know. They're huge."

"I know." He seems to think for a moment. "Out of interest, who told you she was a very talented top headhunter?"

I stare at him, feeling slightly wrong-footed. "No one had to *tell* me. She just *is*. I mean . . ." I meet his skeptical gaze. "What?"

"It's none of my business. But when you and I first . . ." Again he hesitates, as though searching for the word. "Met."

"Yes." I nod impatiently.

"I did a little asking around. Nobody had even heard of you."

"Great." I take a slug of champagne. "There you go."

"But I have a contact at Price Bedford, and he told me a little about Natalie. Interesting."

I feel a sudden foreboding at his expression. "Oh, really?" I say defensively. "Because I bet they were pissed off to lose her. So whatever he said—"

Ed lifts his hands. "I don't want to get into this. It's your partnership, your friend, your choices."

OK. Now I have a bad feeling.

"Tell me." I put my glass down, all my bravado gone. "Please, Ed. Tell me. What did he say?"

"Well," Ed shrugs. "The story went that she lured a number of high-profile people onto a list for some anonymous 'blue-chip job' that didn't exist. Then she tried to offer them up to some less-than-blue-chip client and claim this was the job she'd meant all along. The shit hit the fan, big-time. The senior partner at her firm had to step in, calm things down. That's why she was fired." Ed hesitates. "But you knew this, right?"

I stare at him, speechless. Natalie was fired? She was *fired*?

She told me she'd decided to quit Price Bedford because she was undervalued and she could make far more money working for herself.

"Is she here tonight?" He's looking around the room. "Will I meet her?"

"No." I eventually manage to find my voice. "She's . . . not around at the moment."

I can't tell him she's left me in the lurch to run the company all by myself. I can't admit that it's even worse than he thinks. Blood is ebbing in and out of my face as I try to process all this.

She never told me she'd been fired. Never. I can still remember her first pitching the idea of our company to me, over champagne at some fancy bar. She told me everyone in the industry was dying to set up with her, but she wanted to link up with someone she really trusted. An old friend. Someone she could have *fun* with. She painted such an amazing picture and dropped so many big names, I was bowled over. I quit my job the next week and took out all my savings. I'm such a gullible . . . *idiot.* I feel tears trembling on the brink of my lashes and quickly take a gulp of champagne.

"Lara?" Sadie's shrill voice comes in my ear. "Lara, come quick! I need to talk to you."

I really don't feel like talking to Sadie. But nor can I keep sitting here with Ed looking at me with so much concern. I think he's guessed this is all a total shock to me.

"I'll be back in a second!" I say overbrightly, and push my chair back. I head across the crowded room, trying to ignore Sadie, who's pursuing me, jabbering in my ear.

"I'm very sorry," she's saying. "I thought about it and you're right, I was selfish and thoughtless. So I decided to help you, and I have! I've found you a candidate! A wonderful, perfect candidate!"

Her words interrupt my painful, circular thought pattern.

"What?" I turn. "What did you say?"

"You may think I'm not interested in your work, but I am," she announces. "You need a trophy, and I've found you one. Aren't I clever?"

"What are you talking about?"

"I've been listening in on everyone's conversations!" she says proudly. "I was starting to think it was hopeless, but then I heard a woman called Clare whispering to her friend in a corner. She's not happy. It's the power games, you know." Sadie opens her eyes at me impressively. "Things are getting so bad at her place, she's thinking of quitting."

"Right. So the point is—"

"She's a head of marketing, of course!" Sadie says triumphantly. "It was on her badge. I knew that's what you wanted, a head of marketing. She won an award last month, you know. But her new 'chief exec' didn't even congratulate her. He's a total pig," she adds confidingly. "That's why she wants to leave."

I swallow several times, trying to stay calm. A marketing head who wants to move jobs. An award-winning marketing head who wants to move jobs. Oh God. I would die and go to heaven.

"Sadie . . . is this for real?"

"Of course! She's over there!" Sadie gestures at the other side of the room.

"Is she into sports? Exercise?"

"Brawny calves," says Sadie. "I noticed them at once."

I hurry to a nearby board and look through the list of guests. Clare . . . Clare . . .

"Clare Fortescue, marketing director of Shepherd Homes?" I feel a jab of excitement. "She was on my new long list! I wanted to talk to her, but I couldn't get through!"

"Well, she's here! Come on, I'll show her to you!"

My heart is thumping as I cross the crowded room, searching all the faces for someone looking like a Clare.

"There!" Sadie is pointing at a woman with glasses in a royal blue dress. She has cropped dark hair, a mole on her nose, and is on the short side. I probably wouldn't even have spotted her if Sadie hadn't pointed her out to me.

"Hi!" I walk up to her and take a deep breath. "Clare Fortescue?"

"Yes?" she says briskly.

"May I have a quick word?"

"Well . . . OK." Looking a bit puzzled, Clare Fortescue allows me to draw her away from the group she's in.

"Hi." I give her a nervous smile. "My name's Lara, and I'm a recruitment consultant. I've been meaning to make contact with you. Your reputation has spread, you know."

"Really?" She looks suspicious.

"Of course! In fact . . . I must congratulate you on your recent award!"

"Oh." A pink tinge comes to Clare Fortescue's ears. "Thanks very much."

"I'm recruiting for a marketing director position right now"—I lower my voice discreetly—"and I just wanted to mention it. It's a really exciting sportswear company with massive potential, and I think you'd be perfect. You'd be my number-one pick." I pause, then add lightly, "But, of course, you may be very happy where you are right now. . . ."

There's silence. I can't tell what's going on behind Clare Fortescue's glasses. My whole body is so tense, I can't even breathe.

"Actually . . . I have been thinking about a move," she says at last, so quietly I can barely hear. "I might very well be interested. But it would have to be the right situation." She gives me a bulletlike look. "I'm not compromising myself. I have standards."

Somehow I manage not to whoop. She's interested *and* she's tough!

"Great!" I smile. "Maybe I can call you in the morning. Or if you had a few minutes to spare right now?" I try not to sound desperate. "We could have a chat? Just quickly?"

Please . . . please . . . please please please . . .

Ten minutes later I walk back to the table, giddy with joy. She's going to send me her résumé tomorrow. She used to play right wing in hockey! She's a perfect match!

Sadie seems even more thrilled than I am as we head back to the table.

"I knew it!" she keeps saying "I knew she'd be right!"

"You're a star," I say joyfully. "We're a team. High-five!"

"High what?" Sadie looks perplexed.

"High-five! Don't you know what a high-five is? Hold up your hand. . . ."

OK. It turns out high-fiving a ghost is a mistake. That woman in red thought I was trying to hit her. Hastily, I resume walking. I arrive at the table and beam at Ed. "I'm back!"

"So you are." He gives me a quizzical look. "How's it going?"

"Brilliantly, since you ask."

"Brilliantly!" echoes Sadie, and jumps into his lap. I reach for my champagne glass. Suddenly I'm in the mood for a party.

SIXTEEN

Tonight is turning out to be one of the best evenings of my life. The dinner is delicious. Ed's speech goes down fantastically. Afterward, people keep coming over to congratulate him, and he introduces me to everyone. I've given out all my business cards and set up two meetings for next week, and Clare Fortescue's friend has just come over to ask discreetly if there's anything I can do for *her*.

I'm euphoric. Finally I feel like I'm getting myself on the map!

The only slight pain is Sadie, who's got bored by business talk and has started on about dancing again. She's been out exploring, and according to her there's some tiny nightclub down the street which is perfect and we *have* to go there immediately.

"No!" I mutter, as she pesters me yet again. "Shh! The magician's doing another trick!"

As we all sip our coffee, a magician is doing the rounds of the tables. He's just pushed a bottle of wine through the table, which was quite amazing. Now he's asking Ed to choose a shape on a card and saying he'll mind read it.

"OK," says Ed, choosing a card. I glance over his shoulder, and it shows a squiggle shape. It was between the squiggle, a square, a triangle, a circle, or a flower.

"Focus on the shape and nothing else." The magician, who is wearing a jeweled jacket, fake tan, and eyeliner, fixes his gaze firmly on Ed. "Let The Great Firenzo use his mysterious powers and read your mind."

The magician's name is The Great Firenzo. He's mentioned this fact about ninety-five times; plus, all his props have *The Great Firenzo* written on them in big swirly red writing.

There's a hush around the table. The Great Firenzo takes both hands up to his head, as though in a trance.

"I am communing with your mind," he says, his voice low and mysterious. "The message is coming in. You have chosen . . . this shape!" With a flourish, he produces a card which exactly matches Ed's.

"Correct." Ed nods and shows his card to the table.

"Amazing!" gasps a blond woman opposite.

"Pretty impressive." Ed is turning his own card over, examining it. "There's no way he could have seen what I picked."

"It's the power of the mind," intones the magician, swiftly collecting the card from Ed. "It's the power of . . . The Great Firenzo!"

"Do it to me!" begs the blond woman excitedly. "Read my mind!"

"Very well." The Great Firenzo turns to face her. "But beware. When you open your mind to me, I can read all your secrets. Every deepest, darkest one." His eyes flash and she giggles.

She totally fancies The Great Firenzo, it's obvious. She's probably beaming her deepest, darkest secrets at him right now.

"I find the ladies' minds are often easier to . . . *penetrate*." The Great Firenzo raises an eyebrow suggestively. "They are weaker, softer . . . but more delightful within." He grins toothily at the blond woman, who gives an embarrassed laugh.

Ugh. He's revolting. I glance at Ed, who has an expression of distaste on his face.

We all watch as the blond woman picks a card, studies it for a moment, then says decidedly, "I've chosen."

"It's the triangle," says Sadie, with interest. She's bobbing behind the back of the blond woman, looking down at the card. "I thought she'd choose the flower."

"Relax." The Great Firenzo is focusing intently on the blond woman. "Years of study in the East have made me attuned to the thought waves of the human mind. Only The Great Firenzo can penetrate the brain to such a degree. Do not resist, sweet lady. Let Firenzo probe your thoughts. I promise . . ." He gives the toothy smile again. "I'll be gentle."

Eeuuww. He thinks he's so hot, but he's a total sleazeball. *And* sexist.

"Only The Great Firenzo has such powers," he says dramatically, looking around the table at us all. "Only The Great Firenzo can achieve such a feat. Only The Great Firenzo can—"

"Actually, I can too," I say brightly. I'll show *him* who's got a weaker mind.

"What?" The Great Firenzo shoots me a look of dislike.

"I can commune with the mind too. I know what card she chose."

"Please, young lady." The Great Firenzo gives me a savage smile. "Do not interrupt the work of The Great Firenzo."

"I'm just saying." I shrug. "I know what it is."

"No, you don't," says the blond woman, a little aggressively. "Don't be ridiculous. You're spoiling it for everyone. Has she had too much to drink?" She turns to Ed.

What a nerve.

"I do know!" I say indignantly. "I'll draw it if you like. Does anyone have a pen?" A nearby man holds out a pen, and I start drawing on my napkin.

"Lara," says Ed in a low voice. "What exactly are you doing?"

"Magic," I say confidently. I finish my triangle and thrust the napkin at the blond woman. "Is that right?"

The blond woman's jaw drops. She looks incredulously at me, then down at the napkin again.

"She's right." She turns her card over and there's a gasp around the table. "How did you do that?"

"I told you, I can do magic. I, too, have mysterious powers granted to me from the East. They call me The Great Lara." I catch Sadie's eye and she smirks.

"Are you a member of the Magic Circle?" The Great Firenzo looks livid. "Because our protocol states—"

"I'm not in any circle," I say in a pleasant tone. "But my mind's pretty strong, I think you'll find. For a lady."

The Great Firenzo looks totally put out and starts gathering his props.

I glance over at Ed, who raises his dark eyebrows. "Very impressive. How d'you do that?"

"Magic." I shrug innocently. "I told you."

"The Great Lara, huh?"

"Yes. That's what my disciples call me. But you can call me Greatie for short."

"Greatie." His mouth is twitching, and I see a smile pop out at one corner. A real, genuine smile.

"Oh my God!" I point at him in triumph. "You smiled! Mr. American Frown actually smiled!"

Oops. Maybe I *have* had too much to drink. I didn't mean to call him Mr. American Frown out loud. For an instant Ed looks a bit taken aback—then he shrugs, as deadpan as ever.

"Must have been a mistake. I'll speak to someone about it. Won't happen again."

"Well, good. Because you could do your face an injury, just *smiling* like that."

Ed doesn't reply, and for a moment I wonder whether I've gone too far. He does seem quite sweet. I don't want to offend him.

Suddenly I hear a pompous-looking guy in a white tuxedo holding forth to his friend. "It's simply a balance of probabilities, nothing more. Any one of us could work out the likelihood of picking the triangle, with a bit of practice—"

"No, you couldn't!" I interrupt him indignantly. "OK, I'll do another trick. Write down anything. Anything. Like, a shape, a name, a number. I'll read your mind and tell you what you wrote."

"Very well." The man gives a little raised-eyebrows smile around the table, as though to say, "I'll indulge her," and takes a pen out of his pocket. "I'll use my napkin."

He lowers his napkin onto his lap so it's completely out of view. I glance meaningfully at Sadie, who immediately hovers behind his back and leans forward to watch.

"He's writing down . . . *Season of mists and mellow fruitfulness*." She makes a face. "Dreadful handwriting."

"All right." The pompous man looks up. "Tell me what shape I've drawn."

Oh, very sneaky.

I smile sweetly back and lift my hands toward him, just like The Great Firenzo did.

"The Great Lara will now read your mind. A shape, you say. Hmm . . . What shape could it be? Circle . . . square . . . I'm getting a square. . . ."

The pompous man is exchanging smug smiles with the guy next to him. He thinks he's so clever.

"Open your mind, sir!" I shake my head reproachfully at him. "Get rid of those thoughts saying *I'm better than everyone at this table!* They're blocking me!"

The man's face has turned red.

"Really—" he begins.

"I have it." I cut him off firmly. "I have read your mind, and you did not draw a shape. No one can fool The Great Lara. On your napkin is written . . ." I pause, wishing I had a drum roll. "*Season of mists and mellow fruitfulness.* Show the table your napkin, please."

Ha! The pompous man looks like he swallowed a fish. Slowly, he holds up the napkin, and there's a massive gasp, followed by applause.

"Fucking hell," says his neighbor bluntly. "How did you do that?" He appeals to the table. "There's no way she could have known that."

"It's a trick," the pompous man is saying, but he's sounding less convinced.

"Do it again! Do it to someone else!" A man opposite is beckoning to the next table. "Hey, Neil, you have to see this. What's your name again?"

"Lara," I say proudly. "Lara Lington."

"Where did you train?" The Great Firenzo is by my side, breathing heavily as he murmurs in my ear. "Who taught you that?"

"No one," I say. "I told you, I have special powers.

Female powers," I can't help adding. "Which means they're especially strong."

"Fine," he snaps. "Forget it. I'm speaking to the union about you."

"Lara, let's go." Sadie has appeared on my other side and is stroking Ed's chest with her hand. "I want to dance. Come on!"

"Just do a few more tricks," I mutter under my breath as guests start gathering around the table to watch. "Look at all these people! I can talk to them, give out my cards, make a few contacts—"

"I don't care about your contacts!" She pouts. "I want to shake my booty!"

"A couple more." I speak sidelong under camouflage of my wineglass. "Then we'll go. Promise."

But I'm in such demand that before I know it, nearly an hour has whizzed by. Everyone wants to have their mind read. Everyone in the room knows my name! The Great Firenzo has packed up and gone. I feel a bit bad about him, but then, he shouldn't have been so obnoxious, should he?

Several tables have been pushed aside, chairs have been dragged forward, and an audience has assembled. By now I've refined my act so that I go off into a little side room, and the person writes down whatever it is and shows the whole audience. Then I come back in and guess. So far I've had names, dates, Bible verses, and a drawing of Homer Simpson. (Sadie described it to me. Luckily I got it.)

"And now." I look impressively around the little crowd. "The Great Lara will perform a yet more astounding feat. I will read . . . five minds at once!"

There's a satisfying gasp and spatter of applause.

"Me!" A girl rushes forward. "Me!"

"And me!" Another girl is scrambling over the chairs.

"Sit on that chair." I gesture with a flourish. "The Great Lara will now retire and then return to read your mind!"

There's a round of applause and a few cheers, and I beam modestly. I head off into the side room and take a swig of water. My face is glowing and I'm totally wired. This is fantastic! We should do it full-time!

"All right," I say as soon as the door closes. "We'll do them in order; it should be quite easy—" I break off in surprise. Sadie has planted herself right in front of me.

"When are we going to leave?" she demands. "I want to dance. This is *my* date."

"I know." I'm redoing my lip gloss quickly. "And we will."

"When?"

"Sadie, come on. This is so much fun. Everyone's having a brilliant time. You can dance anytime!"

"I can't dance anytime!" Her voice rises in fury. "Who's being selfish now? I *want to go! Now!*"

"We will! I promise. One more trick—"

"No! I've had enough of helping you! You're on your own."

"Sa—" I stop dead as she disappears before my eyes. "Sadie, don't joke." I wheel around, but there's no answer or sight of her. "OK, very funny. Come back."

Great. She's in a huff.

"Sadie." I adopt a humbler tone. "I'm sorry. I can understand you're annoyed. Please come back and let's talk about it."

There's no response. The little room is dead. I look around, feeling a bit more alarmed.

She can't have gone.

I mean, she can't have just *left* me.

I jump as there's a knock at the door and Ed comes in. Ed's turned into my unofficial assistant. He's been marshaling the requests and handing out pens and paper.

"Five minds at once, huh?" he says as he enters.

"Oh." I hastily plaster on a smile. "Er . . . yes! Why not?"

"There's quite a crowd out there. All the people who were in the bar have come in to watch. Standing room only." He gestures at the door. "Ready?"

"No!" Instinctively I back away. "I mean, I might take a moment first. I need to get my head straight. Have a breather."

"I'm not surprised. Must take a lot of concentration." Ed leans against the door frame and surveys me for a moment. "I've been watching you as hard as I can, but I still can't figure it out. However you do it . . . it's awesome."

"Oh. Er . . . thanks."

"See you out there." The door closes behind Ed, and I wheel around.

"Sadie," I call desperately. "Sadie! *Sadie!*"

OK. I'm in trouble.

The door opens and I give a small squeak of fright. Ed looks in again, a bit puzzled.

"I forgot—do you want a drink from the bar?"

"No." I smile weakly. "Thanks."

"Everything OK?"

"Yes! Of course. I'm just . . . focusing my powers. Getting into the zone."

"Sure." He nods understandingly. "I'll leave you be." The door closes again.

Fuck. What am I going to do? In a minute they'll start demanding I come out. They'll expect me to mind read. They'll expect me to do magic. My chest is tight with fear.

There's only one option: I have to escape. I look desperately around the little room, which is obviously used to store spare banquet furniture. No window. There's a fire escape door in the far corner, but it's blocked by a massive stack of gold chairs about ten feet high. I try to pull the chairs aside, but they're too heavy. Fine. I'll climb over them.

Determinedly, I put one foot on a chair and haul myself up. Then another. The gold lacquer is a bit slippery, but I'm managing. It's like a ladder. A wonky, rickety ladder.

The only trouble is, the higher I get, the more the chairs are swaying. By the time I'm about eight feet up, the stack of chairs is teetering at quite a scary angle. It's like the Leaning Tower of Gold Chairs, with me crouching in terror near the top.

If I took just one more huge step, I'd be over the summit and I could quickly scramble down the other side to the fire exit. But every time I move my foot, the stack wobbles so much I withdraw it in fright. I try shifting to the side—but the stack lurches even more. I clutch another chair desperately, not daring to look down. The whole thing feels like it's going to fall, and the ground seems a really long way away.

I take a deep breath. I can't stay here frozen forever. There's nothing for it. I have to be brave and go over the top. I take a massive step up, placing my foot on a chair about three from the top. But as I shift my weight, the stack leans back so far I can't help screaming.

"Lara!" The door bursts open and Ed appears. "What the hell—"

"Heeelp!" The whole stack of chairs is collapsing. I *knew* I should never have moved—

"Jesus Christ!" Ed rushes forward as I tumble down. He doesn't exactly catch me in his arms so much as break my fall with his head.

"Ow!"

"Oof!" I crash to the floor. Ed grabs my hand and helps me to my feet, then rubs his chest with a wince. I think I kicked it by mistake on the way down.

"Sorry."

"What are you doing?" He stares at me incredulously. "Is something wrong?"

I shoot an agonized glance at the door to the banquet room. Following my gaze, he goes and shuts it. "What's up?" he says more gently.

"I can't do magic," I mumble, staring at my feet.

"What?"

"I can't do magic!" I look up in desperation.

Ed eyes me uncertainly. "But . . . you did it."

"I know. But I can't do it anymore."

Ed surveys me silently for a few seconds, his eyes flickering as they meet mine. He looks deadly grave, as if some massive worldwide company is facing collapse and he's working out a master plan to save it.

At the same time, he quite looks like he wants to laugh.

"You're saying your mysterious Eastern mind-reading powers have deserted you," he says at last.

"Yes," I say in a small voice.

"Any idea why?"

"No." I scuff my toe, not wanting to look at him.

"Well. Just go out there and tell everybody."

"I can't!" I wail in horror. "Everyone will think I'm a flake. I've been The Great Lara. I can't just go and say, 'Sorry, I can't do it anymore.'"

"Sure you can."

"No." I shake my head firmly. "No way. I have to go. I have to escape."

I start heading toward the fire exit again, but Ed grabs my arm.

"No escaping," he says firmly. "No running away. Turn the situation around. You can do it. C'mon."

"But how?" I say hopelessly.

"Play with them. Make it an entertainment. So you can't read their thoughts—you can make them laugh. And then we leave, right away, and you're still The Great Lara in everyone's mind." His gaze bores firmly into mine. "If you run away now, you really will be The Great Flake."

He's right. I don't want him to be right, but he is.

"OK," I say at last. "I'll do it."

"D'you need some more time?"

"No. I've had enough time. I just want to get it over with. And then we go?"

"Then we go. Deal." A tiny grin pops through again. "Good luck."

"Thanks." *That's two smiles,* I want to add. (But don't.)

Ed strides through the door and I follow him, somehow managing to hold my head high. There's a buzz of chatter, which dies down as I appear, and turns to a roar of applause. I can hear wolf whistles from the back, and someone's even videoing me on their phone. I've been out so long, they obviously think I've been building up to some amazing finale.

The five victims are sitting on chairs, each holding a piece of paper and a pen. I smile at them, then look at the crowd.

"Ladies and gentlemen, forgive my leave of absence. I have been opening my mind to a number of thought waves tonight. And quite frankly . . . I'm shocked at what I've discovered. Shocked! You." I wheel around to the first girl, who's holding her piece of paper close to her chest. "Obviously I know what you've *drawn*." I make a brushing-aside gesture, as though what she's drawn is neither here nor there. "But far more interesting is the fact that there's a man in your office who you think is rather delicious. Don't deny it!"

The girl flushes, and her reply is drowned by a roar of laughter. "It's Blakey!" someone yells, and there's more laughter.

"You, sir!" I turn to a cropped-haired guy. "They say most men think about sex once every thirty seconds, but with you it's far, *far* more frequent than that." There are gales of laughter, and I hastily turn to the next man. "Whereas you, sir, think about *money* every thirty seconds."

The man bursts into laughter. "She *is* a bloody mind reader!" he calls out.

"Your thoughts were unfortunately too steeped in alcohol for me to make out." I smile kindly at the portly guy sitting on the fourth chair. "And as for you . . ." I pause as I face the girl on the fifth chair. "I suggest you never, ever tell your mother what you were just thinking." I raise my eyebrows teasingly, but she doesn't rise.

"What?" She frowns. "What are you talking about?"

Shit.

"You know." I force myself to hold my smile steady. "*You* know . . ."

"No." She shakes her head stolidly. "I've got no idea what you're on about."

The audience's chatter has died away. Faces are turned to us with interest.

"Do I have to spell it out?" My smile is becoming forced. "Those . . . thoughts? Those particular thoughts you were just having . . ." I'm nearing the end of my rope here. "Just now . . ."

Suddenly her face snaps in horror. "Oh God. That. You're right."

Somehow I manage not to expire with relief.

"The Great Lara is always right!" I make an elaborate bow. "Farewell, and see you all again."

I head quickly through the applauding audience toward Ed.

"I got your bag," he murmurs above the clapping. "One more bow, then we're out."

I don't breathe until we're safely out on the street. The air is clear and there's a warmish breeze. The hotel doorman is surrounded by groups of people waiting for taxis, but I don't want to risk anyone from the dinner catching up with me, so I hastily walk down onto the pavement.

"Well done, Greatie," says Ed as we fall into step.

"Thanks."

"Shame about the magic powers." He's looking at me inquiringly, but I pretend not to notice.

"Yes, well." I shrug casually. "They come, they go,

that's the mystery of the East. Now, if we walk this way"—I squint at a street sign—"we should be able to pick up a taxi."

"I'm in your hands," says Ed. "I don't know this area."

This not-knowing-London is really starting to annoy me.

"Is there any area you *do* know?"

"I know my route to work." Ed shrugs. "I know the park opposite my building. I know the way to Whole Foods."

OK, I've had it. How dare he come to this great city and show zero interest in it?

"Don't you think that's really narrow-minded and arrogant?" I stop dead. "Don't you think if you come and live in a city you should respect it enough to get to know it? London is one of the most fascinating, historic, amazing cities in the world! And bloody Whole Foods! That's an American shop! Couldn't you try Waitrose?" My voice rises. "I mean, why did you take a job here if you weren't interested in the place? What were you planning to do?"

"I was planning to explore it with my fiancée," Ed says calmly.

His answer slightly takes the wind out of my sails.

Fiancée. What fiancée?

"Until she broke up with me, a week before we were supposed to come," Ed continues conversationally. "She asked her company to transfer her London placement to someone else. So, you see, I had a dilemma. Come to England, stay focused, and do the best I could, or stay in Boston, knowing I'd see her almost every day. She worked in the same building as me." He pauses a second before adding, "And her lover."

"Oh." I stare at him in dismay. "I'm sorry. I . . . didn't realize."

"No problem."

His face is so impassive, it almost seems like he doesn't care—but I'm getting to understand his dead-pan style. He does care, of course he does. Suddenly his frown is making more sense. And that closed-up expression. And that weary voice he had in the restaurant. God, what a bitch his fiancée must be. I can see her now. Big white American teeth and swingy hair and killer heels. I bet he bought her a massive ring. I bet she's kept it.

"That must have been horrible," I say feebly as we start walking again.

"I had the guidebooks." He's gazing resolutely ahead. "I had the itineraries. I had a million projects planned. Stratford-upon Avon . . . Scotland . . . Oxford . . . But they were all planned with Corinne. Kind of takes the fun out of it."

A vision comes to me of a pile of guidebooks, all scribbled and annotated with their exciting plans. And then shut away. I feel so sorry for him, I think I should probably shut up now and stop giving him a hard time. But some stronger instinct makes me push on.

"So you just go your route to work and back again every day," I say. "You never look left or right. You go to Whole Foods and the park and back again and that's it."

"Works for me."

"How long have you been over here again?"

"Five months."

"Five months?" I echo in horror. "No. You can't exist like that. You can't lead your life in tunnel vision. You have to open your eyes and look around. You have to move on."

"Move on," he echoes, in mock-amazed tones. "Wow. Right. Not a phrase anyone's said to me much."

OK, so obviously I'm not the only one who's given him a pep talk. Well, too bad.

"I'll be gone in two more months," he adds curtly. "It hardly matters whether I get to know London or not—"

"So, what, you're just treading water, just existing, waiting until you feel better? Well, you never will! Not unless you *do* something about it!" All my frustration with him pours out in a stream. "Look at you, doing memos for other people, and emails for your mum, and solving everyone else's problems because you don't want to think about your own! Sorry, I overheard you in Pret A Manger," I add sheepishly as Ed's head jerks up. "If you're going to live in a place, doesn't matter how long, you need to *engage* with it. Otherwise you're not really living. You're just functioning. I bet you haven't even unpacked properly, have you?"

"As it *happens* . . ." He pauses for a few steps. "My housekeeper unpacked for me."

"There you go." I shrug, and we walk on a little more in silence, our footsteps almost in time. "People break up," I say at last. "It's just the way things are. And you can't dwell on what might have been. You have to look at what is."

As I'm saying the words, I have a weird flash of déjà vu. I think Dad said something to me like this once about Josh. In fact, he might even have used those exact words.

But that was different. I mean, obviously it's an entirely different scenario. Josh and I weren't planning a trip, were we? Or to move cities. And now we're back together again. Totally different.

"Life is like an escalator," I add wisely.

When Dad says that to me, I get all annoyed because he just doesn't understand. But somehow it's different when *I'm* giving advice.

"An escalator," echoes Ed. "Thought it was a box of chocolates."

"No, definitely an escalator. You see, it carries you on regardless." I mime an escalator. "And you might as well enjoy the view and seize every opportunity while you're passing. Otherwise it'll be too late. That's what my dad told me when I broke up with this . . . this guy."

Ed walks on a few paces. "And did you take his advice?"

"Er . . . well . . ." I brush my hair back, avoiding his eye. "Kind of."

Ed stops and looks at me gravely. "Did you 'move on'? Did you find it easy? Because I sure as hell haven't."

I clear my throat, playing for time. What I did isn't really the point here, surely?

"You know, there are lots of definitions of 'move on.'" I try to maintain my wise tone. "Many different variations. Everyone has to move on in their own way."

I'm not sure I want to get into this conversation, actually. Maybe now is the moment to find a cab.

"Taxi!" I wave my hand at a passing cab, but it sails past, even though its light is on. I *hate* when they do that.

"Let me." Ed approaches the curb, and I take out my mobile phone. There's a pretty good minicab company that I use. Maybe they could come and pick us up. I retreat into a doorway, dial the number, and wait on hold, before I eventually discover that all the cabs are out tonight and it'll be a half-hour wait.

"No good." I come out of the doorway to see Ed standing stock-still on the pavement. He's not even trying to hail a cab. "No luck?" I say in surprise.

"Lara." He turns to me. His face is confused and his eyes are a little glassy. Has he been taking drugs or something? "I think we should go dancing."

"What?" I peer at him, perplexed.

"I think we should go dancing." He nods. "It would be a perfect way to round off the evening. It just came to me out of the blue."

I don't believe it. *Sadie*.

I whirl around on the pavement, searching the darkness, and suddenly spot her, floating by a lamppost.

"You!" I exclaim furiously, but Ed doesn't even seem to notice.

"There's a nightclub near here," he's saying. "Come on. Let's have a quick dance. It's a great idea. I should have thought of it before."

"How do you know there's a nightclub here?" I retort. "You don't know London!"

"Yeah, right." He nods, looking a bit flummoxed himself. "But I'm pretty sure there's a nightclub down that street." He gestures. "Down there, third left. We should go check it out."

"I'd love to," I say sweetly. "But I must just make a call. There's a conversation I need to have." I direct the words meaningfully at Sadie. "If I don't have this conversation, I *won't be able to dance*."

Sulkily, Sadie descends to the pavement, and I pretend to punch a number into my phone. I'm so angry with her, I almost don't know where to start.

"How could you just leave me like that?" I spit in an undertone. "I was completely lost!"

"No, you weren't! You did very well. I was watching."

"You were *there*?"

"I felt rather bad," says Sadie, looking distantly over my shoulder. "I came back to see if you were all right."

"Well, thanks a lot," I say sarcastically. "You really helped. And now what's all this?" I gesture at Ed.

"I want to dance!" she says with defiance. "I had to take extreme measures."

"What have you done to him? He looks shell-shocked!"

"I made some . . . threats," she says evasively.

"Threats?"

"Don't look at me like that!" She suddenly rounds on me. "I wouldn't need to if you weren't so selfish. I know your career's important, but I want to go dancing! Proper dancing! You *know* I do. That's why we're here. It's supposed to be my evening. But you take over and I don't get a look in! It's not fair!"

She sounds almost tearful. And suddenly I feel bad. It *was* supposed to be her evening, and I did kind of hijack it.

"OK. You're right. Come on, let's go dancing."

"Wonderful! We'll have such a good time. This way . . ." Her spirits restored, Sadie directs me through some tiny Mayfair streets I've never been down before. "Nearly there . . . Here!"

It's a tiny place called the Flashlight Dance Club. I've never heard of it. Two bouncers are standing outside, looking half asleep, and they let us in, no question.

We descend a set of dim wooden steps and find ourselves in a large room carpeted in red, with chandeliers, a dance floor, a bar, and two guys in leather trousers sitting morosely at the bar. A DJ on a tiny stage is playing some JLo track. No one's dancing.

Is this the best Sadie could find?

"Listen, Sadie," I mutter as Ed goes up to the neon-lit bar. "There are better clubs than this. If you really want to dance, we should go somewhere a bit more happening—"

"Hello?" A voice interrupts me. I turn to see a slim, high-cheeked woman in her fifties, wearing a black top and gauze skirt over leggings. Her faded red hair is up in a knot, her eyeliner is crooked, and she looks anxious. "Are you here for the Charleston lesson?"

Charleston lesson?

"I'm so sorry," the woman continues. "I suddenly remembered we had an arrangement." She stifles a yawn. "Lara, is it? You're certainly wearing the right clothes!"

"Excuse me." I smile, haul out my phone, and turn to Sadie.

"What have you done?" I mutter. "Who's this?"

"You need lessons," Sadie says unrepentantly. "This is the teacher. She lives in a little room upstairs. Normally the lessons are during the day."

I stare at Sadie incredulously. "Did you wake her up?"

"I must have forgotten to put the appointment in my diary," the woman is saying as I turn back. "It's not like me—thank goodness I remembered! Out of the blue, it came to me that you would be waiting here."

"Yes!" I shoot daggers at Sadie. "Amazing, the powers of the human brain."

"Here's your drink." Ed arrives by my side. "Who's this?"

"I'm your dance instructor, Gaynor." She holds out her hand and Ed takes it, looking bewildered. "Have you always been interested in the Charleston?"

"The Charleston?" Ed looks mystified.

I feel a bit hysterical. The truth is, Sadie always gets her way. She wants us to dance the Charleston. We're going to dance the Charleston. I owe it to her. And it might as well be here and now.

"So!" I smile winningly at Ed. "Ready?"

The thing about the Charleston is, it's more energetic than you realize. And it's really complicated. And you have to be really coordinated. After an hour, my arms and legs are aching. It's relentless. It's worse than my Legs Bums and Tums class. It's like running a marathon.

"And forward and back . . ." the dance instructor is chanting. "And swivel those feet . . ."

I can't swivel my feet anymore. They're going to fall off. I keep confusing right and left and bashing Ed in the ear by mistake.

"Charleston . . . Charleston . . ." The music is tripping along, filling the club with its peppy beat. The two leather-trousered guys at the bar have been watching in a silent stupor since we started the lesson. Apparently dance lessons are quite common here in the evenings. But everyone wants to learn salsa, according to Gaynor. She hasn't given a Charleston lesson for about fifteen years. I think she's quite chuffed we're here.

"And step and kick . . . wave your arms . . . very good!"

I'm waving my hands so hard I'm losing sensation in them. The fringes on my dress are swishing back and forth. Ed is doggedly crossing his hands back and forth over his knees. He shoots me a quick grin as I look at him, but I can tell he's concentrating too hard to talk. He's quite deft with his feet, actually. I'm impressed.

I glance over at Sadie, who's dancing in bliss. She's amazing. *So* much better than the teacher. Her legs are twinkling back and forth, she knows a zillion different steps, and she never seems to get out of breath.

Well. She doesn't have any breath, let's face it.

"Charleston . . . Charleston . . ."

Sadie catches my eyes, grins, and throws back her head in rapture. I guess it's been a long time since she's sparkled on the dance floor. I should have done this before. I feel really mean now. We'll do Charleston dancing every night from now on, I resolve. We'll do all her favorite twenties things.

The only trouble is, I've got a stitch. Panting, I head to the side of the dance floor. What I need to do is to get Ed to dance with Sadie. The two of them alone. Somehow. Then I really will have made her evening.

"OK?" Ed has followed me off.

"Yes. Fine." I mop my brow with a napkin. "It's hard work!"

"You've done very well!" Gaynor comes over to us and, in a sudden show of emotion, clasps our hands in turn. "You're very promising, the pair of you! I think you could go far! Shall I see you again next week?"

"Er . . . maybe." I don't quite dare look at Ed. "I'll call you, shall I?"

"I'll leave the music on," she says enthusiastically. "You can practice!"

As she goes, hurrying across the floor with dancer steps, I nudge Ed.

"Hey, I want to watch you. Go and dance on your own for a bit."

"Are you crazy?"

"Go on! Please! You can do that one–two thing with your arms. I want to see how you do it. Please . . ."

Rolling his eyes good-humoredly, Ed heads out on the floor.

"Sadie!" I hiss, and gesture at Ed. "Quick! Your partner's waiting!"

Her eyes widen as she realizes what I mean. In half a second she's out there, facing him, her eyes lit up joyfully.

"Yes, I'd love to dance," I hear her saying. "Thank you so much!"

As Ed starts swinging his legs back and forth, she synchronizes with him perfectly. She looks so happy. She looks so right. Her hands are on his shoulders, her bracelets are glittering under the lights, her headdress is bobbing, the music is fizzing along, it's like watching an old film—

"That's enough," says Ed suddenly with a laugh. "I need a partner." And to my dismay, he barges right through Sadie, toward me.

I can see the shock on Sadie's face. As she watches him leave the floor, she looks devastated. I wince, wishing so hard he could see her, that he knew. . . .

"I'm sorry," I mouth at Sadie as Ed drags me onto the floor. "I'm really sorry."

We dance awhile longer, then head back to the table. I can't help feeling exhilarated after all that effort, and Ed seems in pretty good spirits too.

"Ed, do you believe in guardian angels?" I say on impulse. "Or ghosts? Or spirits?"

"No. None of the above. Why?"

I lean forward confidentially. "What if I told you that there's a guardian angel in this very room who fancies the pants off you?"

Ed gives me a long look. "Is 'guardian angel' a euphemism for 'male prostitute'?"

"No!" I splutter with laughter. "Forget it."

"I've had a good time." He drains his glass and smiles at me. A full-on, proper smile. Crinkled eyes, uncreased brow, everything! I almost want to shout "Geronimo! We got there!"

"So have I."

"I didn't expect to end the evening like this." He looks around the little club. "But it's . . . great!"

"Different." I nod.

He rips open a bag of peanuts and offers it to me, and I watch him as he crunches them hungrily. Even though he's looking relaxed, the frown lines are still faintly etched on his brow.

Well, no wonder. He's had a lot to frown about. I can't help feeling a rush of pity for him as I think about it. Losing his fiancée. Coming to work in a strange city. Just getting through life, week after week, without enjoying it. It was probably really good for him to come dancing. It was probably the most fun he's had in months.

"Ed," I say on impulse. "Let me take you sightseeing. You should see London. It's criminal that you haven't. I'll show you around. At the weekend sometime?"

"I'd like that." He seems genuinely touched. "Thanks."

"No problem! Let's email." We smile at each other, and I drain my sidecar with a slight shudder. (Sadie made me order it. Totally revolting.)

Ed glances at his watch. "So, are you ready to go?"

I glance over at the dance floor. Sadie's still going strong, flinging her arms and legs around with no sign of flagging. No wonder all the girls in the twenties were so skinny.

"Let's go." I nod. Sadie can catch up with us when she's ready.

We head out into the Mayfair night. The street lanterns are on, mist is rising from the pavements, and nobody's about. We head to the corner and after a few minutes flag down a couple of cabs. I'm starting to shiver, in my skimpy dress and threadbare cloak. Ed ushers me into the first taxi, then pauses, holding the door open.

"Thanks, Lara," he says in that formal preppy way he has. I'm actually starting to find it quite endearing. "I had a good time. It was . . . quite a night."

"Wasn't it!" I adjust my diamanté cap, which has fallen lopsided with all the dancing, and Ed's mouth twitches with amusement.

"So, should I wear my spats for sightseeing?"

"Definitely." I smile. "And a top hat."

Ed laughs. I think it's the first time I've ever heard him laugh. "Good night, twenties girl."

"Good night." I close the door and the taxi roars off.

SEVENTEEN

Next morning I feel a bit dazed. Charleston music is ringing in my ears and I keep having flashbacks to being The Great Lara. The whole thing feels like a dream.

Except it's not a dream, because Clare Fortescue's résumé is already in my in-box when I arrive at work. Result!

Kate's eyes are like saucers as I print out the email. "Who on earth's this?" she says, poring over the résumé. "Look, she's got an MBA! She's won a prize!"

"I know," I say nonchalantly. "She's a top, award-winning marketing director. We networked last night. She's going on the Leonidas Sports short list."

"And does she *know* she's going on the short list?" says Kate in excitement.

"Yes!" I snap, flushing slightly. "Of course she does."

By ten o'clock the list has been finalized and sent off to Janet Grady. I flop back in my chair and grin at Kate, who's staring intently at her computer screen.

"I've found a picture of you!" she says. "From the dinner last night. *Lara Lington and Ed Harrison arrive at the* Business People *dinner.*" She hesitates, looking puzzled. "Who's he? I thought you were back with Josh."

"Oh, I am," I say at once. "Ed is just . . . a business contact."

"Oh, right." Kate is gazing at her computer screen, a little dreamily. "He's quite good-looking, isn't he? I mean, Josh is too," she amends hastily. "In a different way."

Honestly, she has no taste. Josh is a million times better-looking than Ed. Which reminds me, I haven't heard from him for a while. I'd better call, just in case his phone has gone wrong and he's been sending texts and wondering why I haven't been answering.

I wait until Kate has gone to the bathroom so I have a little privacy, then dial his office.

"Josh Barrett."

"It's me," I say lovingly. "How was the trip?"

"Oh, hi. It was great."

"Missed you!"

There's a pause. I'm pretty sure Josh says something in response, but I can't quite hear.

"I was wondering if your phone was going wrong?" I add. "Because I haven't received any texts from you since yesterday morning. Are mine getting through OK?"

There's another indistinct mumble. What's wrong with this line?

"Josh?" I tap the receiver.

"Hi." His voice suddenly breaks through more clearly. "Yeah. I'll look into it."

"So, shall I come over tonight?"

"You can't go tonight!" Sadie appears out of nowhere. "It's the fashion show! We're getting the necklace!"

"I know," I mutter, putting my hand over the

receiver. "*Afterward*. I have a thing first," I continue to
Josh. "But I could come around ten?"

"Great." Josh sounds distracted. "Thing is, I've got
a work bash tonight."

More work? He's turning into a workaholic.

"OK," I say understandingly. "Well, how about
lunch tomorrow? And we can take it from there."

"Sure," he says after a pause. "Great."

"Love you," I say tenderly. "Can't wait to see you."

There's silence.

"Josh?"

"Er . . . yeah. Me too. Bye, Lara."

I put down the phone and sit back. I feel a bit dissatisfied, but I don't know why. Everything's fine. Everything's good. So why does it feel like there's something
missing?

I want to call Josh back and say, "Is everything OK,
do you want to talk?" But I mustn't. He'll think I'm obsessing, which I'm *not*; I'm just thinking. People are allowed to think, aren't they?

Anyway. Whatever. Move on.

Briskly, I log on to my computer and find an email
waiting in my in-box from Ed. Wow, that was quick
off the mark.

Hi, twenties girl. Great evening last night. Re: your
corporate travel insurance. Might want to look at
this link. I've heard they're good. Ed

I click on it and find a site offering reduced insurance rates for small companies. That's just like him: I
mention a problem once, and he instantly finds a solution. Feeling touched, I click Reply and briskly type an
email:

Thanks, twenties guy. I appreciate it. Hope you're
dusting off your London guide. PS: have you
demonstrated the Charleston to your staff yet?

Immediately an answer pops back.

Is this your idea of blackmail?

I giggle and start browsing online to find a picture of
a dancing couple to send him.

"What's funny?" says Sadie.

"Nothing." I close down the window. I won't tell
Sadie I'm emailing Ed. She's so possessive, she might
take it the wrong way. Or, even worse, start dictating
endless emails full of stupid twenties slang.

She starts reading the *Grazia* that's lying open on my
desk and after a few moments orders me: "Turn." This
is her new habit. It's quite annoying, in fact. I've become her page-turning slave.

"Hey, Lara!" Kate comes rushing into the office.
"You've got a special delivery!"

She hands me a bright pink envelope printed with
butterflies and ladybugs, with *Tutus and Pearls* embla-
zoned across the top. I rip it open, to find a note from
Diamanté's assistant.

*Diamanté thought you might like this. We look for-
ward to seeing you later!*

It's a printed sheet with details about the fashion
show, together with a laminated card on a chain, reading *VIP Backstage Pass.* Wow. I've never been a VIP
before. I've never even been an IP.

I turn the card over in my fingers, thinking ahead to
this evening. Finally we'll get the necklace! After all
this time. And then—

My thoughts stop abruptly. Then . . . what? Sadie said she couldn't rest until she got her necklace. That's why she's haunting me. That's why she's here. So when she gets it, what will happen? She can't . . .

I mean, she won't just . . .

She wouldn't just . . . *go*?

I stare at her, suddenly feeling a bit weird. This whole time, I've only been focused on getting the necklace. I've lost sight of what might happen *beyond* the necklace.

"Turn," says Sadie impatiently, her eyes avidly fixed on an article about Katie Holmes. "Turn!"

In any case, I'm resolved: I'm not letting Sadie down this time. The minute I see this bloody necklace, I'm grabbing it. Even if it's around someone's neck. Even if I have to rugby-tackle them to the floor. I approach the Sanderstead Hotel feeling all hyped up. My feet are springy and my hands are ready to snatch.

"Keep your eyes peeled," I mutter to Sadie as we walk through the bare white lobby. Ahead of us, two skinny girls in miniskirts and heels are heading toward a pair of double doors decorated with swags of pink silk and butterfly helium balloons. That must be it.

Nearing the room, I see a babble of well-dressed girls milling around, knocking back glasses of champagne while music thuds gently. There's a catwalk running through the center of the room, with a net of silver balloons strung above it, and rows of silk-swagged chairs.

I wait patiently as the girls ahead of me are ticked off, then I step forward to a blond girl in a pink prom dress. She's holding a clipboard and gives me a chilly smile. "Can I help you?"

"Yes." I nod. "I'm here for the fashion show."

She scans my top-to-toe black outfit dubiously. (Pencil trousers, camisole, little cropped jacket. I chose it especially because all fashionistas wear black, don't they?) "Are you on the list?"

"Yes." I reach for my invitation. "I'm Diamanté's cousin."

"Oh, her cousin." Her smile becomes even more frozen. "Lovely."

"In fact, I need to talk to her before the show; do you know where she is?"

"I'm afraid Diamanté's tied up—" the girl begins smoothly.

"It's urgent. I really, really do need to see her. I've got this, by the way." I brandish my VIP backstage pass at her. "I could just go hunting. But if you could locate her it would help. . . ."

"OK," the girl says after a pause. She reaches for her teeny jewel-encrusted phone and dials a number. "Some cousin wants to see Diamanté; is she around?" She adds in a barely concealed murmur, "No. Never saw her before. Well, if you say so . . ." She puts her phone away. "Diamanté says she'll meet you backstage. Through there?" She points down the corridor to another door.

"Go ahead!" I instruct Sadie in a whisper. "See if you can find the necklace backstage! It must be easy to spot!" I follow a guy with a crate of Moët down the carpeted corridor and am flashing my VIP backstage pass at a bouncer when Sadie reappears.

"Easy to spot?" she says, her voice trembling. "You must be joking! We're never going to find it! *Never!*"

"What do you mean?" I say anxiously as I walk in. "What are you—"

Oh no. Oh bloody hell.

I'm standing in a large area filled with mirrors and chairs and hair dryers blasting and the chatter of makeup artists and about thirty models. They're all tall and skinny, slouching on their chairs or milling around talking on their mobile phones. They're all wearing skimpy diaphanous dresses. And they're all wearing at least twenty necklaces piled high around their necks. Chains, pearls, pendants . . . Everywhere I look there are necklaces. It's a necklace haystack.

I'm exchanging horrified looks with Sadie when I hear a drawling voice.

"Lara! You came!"

I wheel around to see Diamanté teetering toward me. She's wearing a tiny skirt covered in love hearts, a skinny vest, a studded silver belt, and patent stiletto shoe boots. She's holding two glasses of champagne, and she offers one to me.

"Hi, Diamanté. Congratulations! Thanks so much for inviting me. This is amazing!" I gesture around the room, then take a deep breath. The important thing is not to seem too desperate or needy. "So, anyway." I aim for a light, casual tone. "I have this huge favor to ask you. You know that dragonfly necklace that your father was after? The old one with the glass beads?"

Diamanté blinks at me in surprise. "How d'you know about that?"

"Er . . . long story. Anyway, it was originally Great-Aunt Sadie's, and my mum always loved it and I wanted to surprise her with it." My fingers are crossed tightly behind my back. "So, maybe after the show I could . . . er . . . have it? Possibly? If you didn't need it anymore?"

Diamanté stares back at me for a few moments, her

blond hair streaming down her back and her eyes glazed.

"My dad's a fuckhead," she says at last, with emphasis.

I stare at her uncertainly until the penny finally drops. Oh, great. This is all I need. She's pissed. She's probably been drinking champagne all day.

"He's a fucking . . . fuckhead." She swigs her champagne.

"Yes," I say quickly. "He is. And that's why you need to give the necklace to me. *To me*," I repeat, very loudly and clearly.

Diamanté's swaying on her shoe boots, and I grab her arm to steady her.

"The dragonfly necklace," I say. "Do-you-know-where-it-is?"

Diamanté turns her face to survey me a minute, leaning so close I can smell champagne and cigarettes and Altoids on her breath.

"Hey, Lara, why aren't we friends? I mean, you're cool." She frowns slightly, then amends, "Not cool, but . . . you know. Sound. Why don't we hang out?"

Because you mostly hang out in your massive villa in Ibiza and I mostly hang out in the wrong end of Kilburn? Maybe?

"Er . . . I dunno. We should. It'd be great."

"We should get hair extensions together!" she says, as though seized by inspiration. "I go to this great place. They do your nails too. It's, like, totally organic and environmental."

Environmental hair extensions?

"Absolutely." I nod as convincingly as I can. "Let's definitely do that. Hair extensions. Great."

"I know what you think of me, Lara." Her eyes

suddenly focus with a kind of drunken sharpness. "Don't think I don't know."

"What?" I'm taken aback. "I don't think anything."

"You think I sponge off my dad. Because he paid for all this. Whatever. Be honest."

"No!" I say awkwardly. "I don't think that! I just think . . . you know . . ."

"I'm a spoiled little cow?" She takes a gulp of champagne. "Go on. Tell me."

My mind flips back and forth. Diamanté's never asked me for my opinion before, on anything. Should I be honest?

"I just think that . . ." I hesitate, then plunge in. "Maybe if you waited a few years and did all this on your own, learned the craft and worked your way up, you'd feel even better about yourself."

Diamanté nods slowly, as though my words are getting through to her.

"Yeah," she says at last. "Yeah. I could do that, I suppose. 'Cept it would be really *hard*."

"Er . . . well, that's kind of the point—"

"And then I'd have an obnoxious *fuckhead* of a dad who thinks he's bloody God and makes us all be in his stupid documentary . . . and nothing in return! What's in it for me?" She spreads her skinny tanned arms wide. "What?"

OK. I'm not getting into this debate.

"I'm sure you're right," I say hastily. "So, about the dragonfly necklace—"

"You know, my dad found out you were coming today." Diamanté doesn't even hear me. "He called me up. He was, like, what's she doing on the list? Take her off. I was like, fuck you! This is my fucking first cousin or whatever."

My heart misses a beat.

"Your dad . . . didn't want me here?" I lick my dry lips. "Did he say why?"

"I said to him, who cares if she's a bit of a psycho?" Diamanté talks right through me. "Be more fucking *tolerant*. Then, you know, *he* was on about that necklace." She opens her eyes wide. "He offered me all these substitutes. I was like, don't patronize me with fucking *Tiffany*. I'm a designer, OK? I have a *vision*."

The blood is beating hard in my ears. Uncle Bill is still after Sadie's necklace. I don't understand why. All I know is, I need to get hold of it.

"Diamanté." I grab her shoulders. "Please listen. This necklace is really, really important to me. To my mum. I totally appreciate your vision as a designer and everything—but after the show, can I have it?"

For a moment Diamanté looks so blank, I think I'm going to have to explain the whole thing again. Then she puts an arm around my neck and squeezes hard.

"'Course you can, babe. Soon as the show's over, 's'yours."

"Great." I try not to give away how relieved I am. "Great! That's great! So where is it right now? Could I . . . see it?"

The minute I clap eyes on this thing, I'm grabbing it and running. I'm not taking any more chances.

"Sure! Lyds?" Diamanté calls to a girl in a stripy top. "D'you know where that dragonfly necklace is?"

"What, babe?" Lyds comes over, holding a mobile phone.

"The vintage necklace with the cute dragonfly. D'you know where it is?"

"It has yellow glass beads in a double row," I chime in urgently. "Dragonfly pendant, falls to about here . . ."

Two models walk past, their necks piled high with necklaces, and I squint desperately at them.

Lyds is shrugging easily. "Don't remember. It'll be on one of the girls somewhere."

It'll be in the haystack somewhere. I look around the room hopelessly. Models are everywhere. Necklaces are everywhere.

"I'll look for it myself," I say. "If you don't mind—"

"No! The show's about to start!" Diamanté starts pushing me toward the door. "Lyds, take her in. Put her in the front row. That'll show Dad."

"But—"

It's too late. I've been ushered out.

As the doors swing shut, I'm hopping with frustration. It's in there. Somewhere in that room, Sadie's necklace is hanging around a model's neck. But which bloody one?

"I can't find it anywhere." Sadie suddenly appears beside me. To my horror, she seems almost in tears. "I've looked at every single girl. I've looked at all the necklaces. It's nowhere."

"It has to be!" I mutter as we head back down the corridor. "Sadie, listen. I'm sure it's on one of the models. We'll look really carefully at each one as they go past, and we'll find it. I promise."

I'm being as upbeat and convincing as I can, but inside . . . I'm not so sure. I'm not sure at all.

Thank God I'm in the front row. As the show starts, the crowd is six deep, and everyone's so tall and skinny there's no way I would have got a view from further back. Music starts thudding and lights start flashing around the room, and there's a whoop from what must be a group of Diamanté's friends.

"Go, Diamanté!" one of them yells.

To my slight horror, clouds of dry ice start to appear on the catwalk. How am I going to spot any models through that? Let alone any necklaces. Around me, people are coughing. "Diamanté, we can't bloody see!" yells some girl. "Turn it off!"

At last the fog starts to clear. Pink spotlights flash onto the catwalk and a Scissor Sisters track starts thumping through the speakers. I'm leaning forward, alert for the first model, ready to concentrate as hard as I can, when I glimpse something out of the corner of my eye.

Opposite me on the other side of the catwalk, taking his seat in the front row, is Uncle Bill. He's dressed in a dark suit and open-necked shirt and accompanied by Damian, together with another assistant. As I stare in horror, he looks up and catches my eye.

My stomach lurches. I feel frozen.

After a minute he lifts a hand calmly in greeting. Numbly, I do the same. Then the music increases in volume and suddenly the first model is on the catwalk, wearing a white slip dress printed with spiderwebs and doing that sashay-model walk, all hip bones and cheekbones and skinny arms. I stare desperately at the necklaces jangling around her neck, but she whizzes past so quickly, it's almost impossible to get a good view.

I glance over at Uncle Bill and feel a prickle of horror. He's scanning the necklaces too.

"This is useless!" Sadie appears from nowhere and leaps up onto the catwalk. She goes right up to the model and peers intently at the jumble of chains and beads and charms around her neck. "I can't see it! I told you, it's not there!"

The next model appears, and in a flash she's examining that girl's necklaces too.

"Not here either."

"Super collection," a girl next to me exclaims. "Don't you think?"

"Er . . . yes," I say distractedly. "Great." I can't look at anything except the necklaces. My vision is a blur of beads and gilt and paste jewels. I'm feeling a growing foreboding, a sense of failure—

Oh my God.

Oh my God oh my God! There it is! Right in front of me. Wound around a model's ankle. My heart is hammering as I stare breathlessly at the pale-yellow beads, casually twined into an anklet. An *anklet*. No wonder Sadie couldn't find it. As the model sashays nearer, the necklace is about two feet away from me on the catwalk. Less than that. I could lean over and grab it. This is absolutely unbearable. . . .

Sadie suddenly follows my gaze and gasps.

"My necklace!" She zooms up to the oblivious model and yells, "That's mine! It's mine!"

The moment that model is off the catwalk I'm going after her and I'm getting it. I don't care what it takes. I glance at Uncle Bill—and to my horror his eyes are glued on Sadie's necklace too.

The model is sashaying back now. She'll be off the catwalk in a minute. I glance across, squinting as a spotlight catches me right in the eye, and see Uncle Bill getting to his feet and his people clearing a way for him.

Shit. *Shit.*

I leap to my feet, too, and start making my way out, muttering apologies as I tread on people's feet. At least I have an advantage: I'm on the side of the catwalk nearer the doors. Not daring to look back, I fling myself through the double doors and sprint up the corridor to the backstage area, flashing my pass at the bouncer guy on the door.

The backstage area is mayhem. A woman in jeans is barking instructions and pushing models onto the stage. Girls are ripping clothes off, having clothes put on, having their hair dried, having their lips touched up. . . .

I look around in breathless panic. I've already lost sight of my model. Where the hell is she? I start moving between all the hair stations, dodging rails of clothes, trying to catch a glimpse of her—when suddenly I become aware of a row at the door.

"This is Bill Lington, OK?" It's Damian, and he's obviously losing it. "*Bill Lington.* Just because he doesn't have a backstage pass—"

"No backstage pass, no entry," I can hear the bouncer saying implacably. "Rules of the boss."

"He *is* the fucking boss," snaps Damian. "He paid for all this, you moron."

"What you call me?" The bouncer sounds ominous, and I can't help smiling—but my smile dies away as Sadie materializes, her eyes dark and desperate.

"Quick! Come!"

I start to move, but Sadie vanishes. A moment later she reappears, looking wretched.

"She's gone!" she gulps, hardly able to get the words out. "That model girl has taken my necklace. She was hailing a taxi and I dashed back to get you, but I knew you'd be too slow. And when I returned to the street . . . she'd gone!"

"A *taxi*?" I stare at her in horror. "But . . . but—"

"We've lost it again." Sadie seems beside herself. "We've lost it!"

"But Diamanté promised." I swivel my head frantically, looking for Diamanté. "She promised I could have it!"

I'm hollow with dismay. I can't believe I've let it slip away again. I should have grabbed it, I should have been quicker, I should have been cleverer. . . .

Massive cheers and whoops are coming from the main hall. The show must have finished. A moment later, models stream into the backstage area, followed by a pink-faced Diamanté.

"Fucking fantastic!" she yells at everyone. "You all rock! I love you all! Now let's party!"

I struggle through the melee toward her, wincing as stilettos puncture my feet and shrieky voices pierce my eardrum.

"Diamanté!" I call over the hubbub. "The necklace! The girl wearing it has gone!"

Diamanté looks vague. "Which girl?"

Jesus Christ. How many drugs is she on?

"She's called Flora," Sadie says urgently in my ear.

"Flora! I need Flora, but apparently she's gone!"

"Oh, Flora." Diamanté's brow clears. "Yeah, she's gone to Paris for a ball. On her dad's PJ. Private jet," she explains, at my blank look. "I said she could wear her dress."

"But she's taken the necklace too!" I'm trying really hard not to scream. "Diamanté, please. Call her. Call her now. Tell her I'll meet her. I'll go to Paris, whatever it takes. I *need* to get hold of this necklace."

Diamanté gapes at me for a moment, then raises her eyes to heaven.

"My dad's right about you," she says. "You're nuts. But I quite like that." She gets out her phone and speed-dials a number.

"Hey, Flora! Babe, you were awesome! So are you on the plane yet? OK, listen. Remember that dragonfly necklace you had on?"

"Anklet," I interject urgently. "She was wearing it as an anklet."

"The anklet thing?" says Diamanté. "Yeah, that one. My crazy cousin really wants it. She's gonna come to Paris to get it. Where's the ball? Can she meet you?" She listens for a while, lighting a cigarette and dragging on it. "Oh, right. Yeah. Totally . . . Of course . . ." At last she looks up, blowing out a cloud of smoke. "Flora doesn't know where the ball is. It's, like, some friend of her mum's holding it? She says she wants to wear the necklace 'cause it totally suits her dress, but then she'll FedEx it to you."

"Tomorrow morning? First thing?"

"No, after the ball, yeah?" says Diamanté, as though I'm very slow and stupid. "I dunno what day exactly, but as soon as she's done with it she'll send it. She promised. Isn't that perfect?" She beams and lifts her hand to give me a high-five.

I stare back at her in disbelief. *Perfect?*

The necklace was two feet away from me. It was within my reach. It was promised to me. And now it's on its way to Paris and I don't know when I'll get it back. How can this in any way be perfect? I feel like having a total meltdown.

But I don't dare. There's only the thinnest, most fragile chain linking me to the necklace now, and the strongest link in it is Diamanté. If I piss her off I'll lose it forever.

"Perfect!" I force myself to smile back and high-five Diamanté. I take the phone and dictate my address to Flora, spelling out every single word twice.

Now all I can do is cross all my fingers. And my toes. And wait.

EIGHTEEN

We'll get the necklace back. I have to believe it. I *do* believe it.

But, still, both Sadie and I have been on edge since last night. Sadie snapped when I stood on her toe this morning (through her toe, more accurately), and I told her off for criticizing my makeup. The truth is, I feel like I've failed her. The necklace has been within my reach twice. And each time I've let it get away. Anxiety is gnawing inside me, making me uptight and defensive.

This morning I woke up wondering if I should just get on a train to Paris. But how would I ever track Flora down? Where would I start? I feel totally powerless.

Neither of us is chatting much this morning; in fact, Sadie has been silent for a while. As I finish typing my emails at work, I watch her staring out the window, her back rigid. She's never said so, but it must be lonely for her, wafting around the world with only me to talk to.

Sighing, I shut down my computer, wondering where the necklace is right this minute. In Paris somewhere. Around that girl Flora's neck, maybe. Or in an open bag, carelessly left on an open-top-car seat.

My stomach feels all stabby and nauseous again. I

have to stop this or I'll turn into Mum. I can't keep obsessing about what might happen or what might go wrong. The necklace will come back. I have to believe it. Meanwhile, I have a life to lead. I have a boyfriend to meet for lunch.

I push back my chair, shrug on my jacket, and grab my bag.

"See you later," I say toward both Kate and Sadie, and head out of the office hurriedly before either can reply. I don't want any company. I'm feeling a bit jittery about seeing Josh again, to be honest. I mean, it's not like I have any *doubts* or anything. Nothing like that. I suppose I'm just . . . apprehensive.

What I'm really not in the mood for is Sadie suddenly appearing beside me as I'm nearly at the tube station.

"Where are you going?" she demands.

"Nowhere." I hurry on, trying to ignore her. "Leave me alone."

"You're meeting Josh, aren't you?"

"If you knew, then why did you bother asking?" I say childishly. "Excuse me. . . ." I swing around a corner, trying to shake her off. But she won't be shaken.

"As your guardian angel, I insist that you see sense," she says crisply. "Josh is not in love with you, and if you think for a moment he is, you're even more self-deceiving than I thought."

"You said you weren't my guardian angel," I say over my shoulder. "So butt out, old lady."

"Don't call me old!" she says in outrage. "And I'm not going to let you throw yourself away on some lily-livered, weak-willed puppet."

"He's not a puppet," I snap, then run down the tube

steps. I can hear the train coming, so I swipe my Oyster card, dash onto the platform, and make it onto the tube just in time.

"You don't even love him." Sadie's voice follows me. "Not really."

This is the final outrage. I'm so incensed I swivel to face her, whipping out my phone. "Of course I do! Why do you think I've been so miserable? Why would I want him back if I didn't love him?"

"To prove to everyone that you're right." She folds her arms.

This one takes me by surprise. In fact, it takes me a moment to gather my thoughts.

"That's just . . . rubbish! That shows how little you know! It's got nothing to do with that! I love Josh, and he loves me. . . ." I trail off as I feel the attention of all the travelers in the carriage turning toward me.

I stump to a corner seat, pursued by Sadie. As she draws breath to launch into another speech, I take out my iPod and put it on. A moment later her voice is drowned out.

Perfect! I should have thought of this a long time ago.

I suggested to Josh that we meet at Bistro Martin, just to exorcise all memories of that stupid Marie. As I hand in my coat I see him, already sitting at the table, and feel a whoosh of relief, mixed with vindication.

"You see?" I can't help muttering to Sadie. "He's early. *Now* tell me he doesn't care for me."

"He doesn't know his own mind." She shakes her head dismissively. "He's like a ventriloquist's dummy. I told him what to say. I told him what to think."

She's such a bighead.

"Look, you," I say angrily. "You're not as powerful as you think you are, OK? Josh is pretty strong-minded, if you want to know."

"Darling, I could make him dance on the table and sing 'Baa Baa, Black Sheep' if I wanted to!" she replies scornfully. "Maybe I will! Then you'll see sense!"

There's no point arguing with her. Deliberately, I barge right through her and head to Josh's table, ignoring her squeals of protest. Josh is pushing his chair back and the light is catching his hair, and his eyes are as soft and blue as ever. As I reach him, something bubbles up in my stomach. Happiness, maybe. Or love. Or triumph. Like, a mixture.

I reach up for a hug and his lips meet mine, and all I can think is *Yessss!* After a minute he moves to sit down, but I pull him back into another passionate kiss. I'll show Sadie who's in love.

At last he really does pull away, and we sit down. I lift the glass of white wine Josh has already ordered for me.

"So," I say, a bit breathless. "Here we are."

"Here we are." Josh nods.

"Here's to us! Isn't it wonderful, being back together again? At our favorite restaurant? I'll always associate this restaurant with you," I add a bit pointedly. "No one else. I never could."

Josh has the grace to look a bit uncomfortable. "How's work?" he asks quickly.

"Fine." I sigh. "Actually, to be honest . . . not that fine. Natalie's gone off to Goa and left me all alone to run the company. It's been a bit of a nightmare."

"Really?" Josh says. "That's bad." He picks up the menu and starts reading as though the subject's closed, and I feel a tiny pinprick of frustration. I was expecting more of a response. Although, now I remember, Josh never does respond to stuff much. He's so easygoing. It's what I love about him, I quickly remind myself: his lovely laid-back nature. He never stresses. He never overreacts. He never gets ratty. His approach to life is: *Just get along.* Which is so *sane.*

"We should go to Goa one day!" I change the subject, and Josh's brow clears.

"Definitely. It's supposed to be great. You know, I'm really into the idea of taking some time off. Like six months or so."

"We could do it together!" I say joyfully. "We could both give up our jobs, we could travel around, start off in Mumbai—"

"Don't start *planning* it all," he says in suddenly tetchy tones. "Don't hem me in. Jesus!"

I stare at him in shock. "Josh?"

"Sorry." He looks taken aback by himself too. "Sorry."

"Is something wrong?"

"No. At least . . ." He rubs his head roughly with both hands, then looks up, confused. "I know this is great, you and me being back together. I know I'm the one who wanted it. But sometimes I have this flash of . . . what the fuck are we *doing?*"

"You see?" Sadie's crowing voice above the table makes me jump. She's hovering above us like an avenging angel.

Focus. Don't look up. Pretend she's just a big lamp shade.

"I . . . I think that's pretty normal," I say, determinedly gazing at Josh. "We've both got to adjust; it'll take time."

"It's not normal!" Sadie cries impatiently. "He doesn't really want to be here! I told you, he's a puppet! I can make him say or do anything! *You want to marry Lara one day!*" says Sadie loudly into Josh's ear. *"Tell her!"*

Josh's look of confusion deepens.

"Although I do think . . . one day . . . maybe you and I should . . . get married."

"On a beach!"

"On a beach," he repeats obediently.

"And have six children!"

"I'd like loads of kids too," he says bashfully. "Four . . . or five . . . or even six. What do you think?"

I dart Sadie a look of hatred. She's spoiling everything with her stupid party trick.

"Hold that thought, Josh," I say as pleasantly as I can. "I just need to go to the loo."

I have never moved so quickly as I do across that restaurant. In the ladies', I bang the door shut and glower at Sadie.

"What are you doing?"

"Proving a point. He has no mind of his own."

"He does!" I say furiously. "And, anyway, just because you're prompting him to say these things, it doesn't prove he doesn't love me. He probably *does* want to get married to me, deep down! *And* have lots of kids!"

"You think so," Sadie says scoffingly.

"Yes! You couldn't make him say anything he didn't genuinely believe on some level."

"You think?" Sadie's head jerks up, and her eyes glitter at me for a moment. "Very well. Challenge accepted." She zooms toward the door.

"What challenge?" I say in horror. "I didn't challenge you!"

I hurry back into the restaurant—but Sadie streaks ahead of me. I can see her yelling in Josh's ear. I can see his eyes glazing over. I can't get to the table because I'm stuck behind a waiter with about five plates. What the hell is she *doing* to him?

All of a sudden Sadie appears beside me again. Her lips are pressed together as though she's trying not to laugh.

"What have you done?" I snap.

"You'll see. And then you'll believe me." She looks so gleeful, I feel like throttling her.

"Leave me *alone*!" I mutter. "Just go *away*!"

"Very well!" she says, with an insouciant toss of her chin. "I'll go! But you'll still see I'm right!"

She vanishes and I approach the table nervously. Josh looks up with that faraway, punch-drunk expression, and my heart sinks. Sadie obviously got through to him, big-time. What's she been saying?

"So!" I begin brightly. "Have you decided what to eat yet?"

Josh doesn't even seem to hear. It's as though he's in a trance.

"Josh!" I snap my fingers. "Josh, wake up!"

"Sorry. I was miles away. Lara, I've been thinking." He leans forward and gazes at me with great intensity. "I think I should become an inventor."

"An *inventor*?" I gape at him.

"And I should move to Switzerland." Josh is nodding seriously. "It's just come to me, out of nowhere. This amazing . . . insight. I have to change my life. At once."

I will murder her.

"Josh . . ." I try to keep calm. "You don't want to move to Switzerland. You don't want to be an inventor. You work in advertising."

"No, no." His eyes are shining as if he's a pilgrim who's seen the Blessed Virgin. "You don't understand. I've been on the wrong path. It's all falling into place. I want to go to Geneva and retrain in astrophysics."

"You're not a scientist!" My voice is shrill. "How can you be an astrophysicist?"

"But maybe I was *meant* to study science," he says fervently. "Didn't you ever hear a voice inside your head, telling you to change your life? Telling you that you're on the wrong path?"

"Yes, but you don't listen to the voice!" I lose all semblance of composure. "You ignore the voice! You say, 'That's a stupid voice!'"

"How can you say that?" Josh looks taken aback. "Lara, you have to *listen* to yourself. You're the one who always told me that."

"But I didn't mean—"

"I was just sitting here, minding my own business, when the inspiration came to me." He's overflowing with enthusiasm. "Like an epiphany. Like a realization. Like when I realized I should be back with you. It's exactly the same."

His words are like a splinter of ice in my heart. For a few moments I can't bring myself to speak.

"Is it . . . exactly the same?" I say at last.

"Well, of course." Josh peers at me uncomprehendingly. "Lara, don't get upset." He reaches across the table. "Come with me to Geneva. We'll start a new life.

And do you want to know the other idea I've just had, out of the blue?" His face glows with happiness as he draws breath. "I want to open a zoo. What do you think?"

I want to cry. I think I might cry.

"Josh—"

"No, hear me out." He slaps a hand on the table. "We start an animal charity. Endangered species. We hire experts, get some funding. . . ."

Tears are welling up in my eyes as he talks. *OK*, I'm saying savagely to Sadie in my mind. *I get it. I GET it.*

"Josh." I cut him right off. "Why did you want to get back together with me?"

There's silence. Josh still has that trancey look in his eyes.

"I don't remember." His brow creases in a frown. "Something just told me it was the right thing to do. This voice in my head. It told me I still loved you."

"But *after* you heard the voice." I try not to sound too desperate. "Did it seem like all your old feelings for me were kicking in? Like an old car after you turn the handle round and round and it's sputtering and then suddenly the engine comes to life. Did anything come to life?"

Josh looks as though I've asked him a trick question. "Well, it was like I heard this voice in my head—"

"*Forget the voice!*" I practically scream at him. "Was there anything else?"

Josh frowns irritably. "What else would there be?"

"The photo of us!" I'm scrabbling desperately. "On your phone. You must have kept that for a reason."

"Oh. That." Josh's face softens, exactly the same way I saw it soften before when he looked at the two of us on that mountain. "I love that picture." He gets his phone out and looks at it. "My favorite view in all the world."

His favorite view.

"I see," I say at last. My throat is aching from trying not to cry. I think, finally, I do see.

For a while I can't say a word. I'm just circling the rim of my wineglass around and around with my finger, unable to look up. I was so convinced. I was so sure that once he was back with me he'd realize. We'd click. It would be fantastic, like it was before.

But maybe I've been thinking about a different Josh all this time. There was real-life Josh and there was Josh-in-my-head. And they were almost, *almost* exactly the same, except for one tiny detail.

One loved me and the other one didn't.

I lift my head and look at him now as though for the first time. At his handsome face; his T-shirt with some obscure band logo, the silver bracelet he always wears around his wrist. He's still the same person. There's nothing wrong with him. It's just . . . I'm not the violin to his bow.

"Have you ever been to Geneva?" Josh is saying, and my thoughts are wrenched back to the present.

For God's sake. Geneva. A zoo. How did Sadie *think* of all this stuff? She's totally screwed with his mind. She's so irresponsible.

Thank God she's stuck to meddling with my love life, I think grimly. Thank God she hasn't gone around trying to influence any world leaders or anything. She would have caused global meltdown.

"Josh, listen," I say at last. "I don't think you should move to Geneva. Or train as an astrophysicist.

Or open a zoo. Or . . ." I swallow hard, psyching myself up to say it. "Or . . . be with me."

"What?"

"I think this is all a mistake." I gesture at the table. "And . . . it's my fault. I'm sorry for pestering you all this time, Josh. I should have let you get on with your life. I won't bother you again."

Josh looks poleaxed. But then, he's looked fairly poleaxed throughout most of the conversation.

"Are you . . . sure?" he says feebly.

"Totally." As the waiter approaches the table, I close the menu I'm holding. "We're not going to eat anything after all. Just the bill, please."

As I walk back to the office from the tube, I feel almost numb. I turned Josh down. *I* told *him* we weren't right together. I can't quite process the enormity of what just happened.

I know I did the right thing. I know Josh doesn't love me. I know Josh-in-my-head was a fantasy. And I know I'll come to terms with it. But it's hard to accept. Especially when I could have had him so easily. So *easily*.

"So!" Sadie's voice jolts me out of my reverie. She's obviously been waiting for me. "Did I prove a point? Don't tell me, it's all over between you."

"Geneva?" I say coldly. "Astrophysics?"

Sadie bursts into giggles. "Too funny!"

She thinks it's all just entertainment. I *hate* her.

"So what happened?" She's bobbing around, her face lit up with glee. "Did he say he wanted to open a zoo?"

She wants to hear that she was completely right and it's all over and it was all down to her super-skills, doesn't she? Well, I'm not going to give her the satisfaction. I'm not going to have her exulting over me. Even if she *was* completely right and it *is* all over and it *was* all down to her super-skills.

"Zoo?" I adopt a perplexed expression. "No, Josh never mentioned any zoo. Should he have?"

"Oh." Sadie stops bobbing.

"He mentioned Geneva briefly, but then he realized that was a ridiculous idea. Then he said he'd been hearing this really annoying, whiny voice in his head recently." I shrug. "He said he was sorry if he hadn't been making much sense. But the most important thing was, he wanted to be with me. And then we agreed to take things slowly and sensibly." I stride on, avoiding her eyes.

"You mean . . . you're still seeing each other?" Sadie sounds astounded.

"Of course we are," I say, as though surprised she's even asking. "You know, it takes more than a ghost with a loud voice to break up a real relationship."

Sadie looks utterly flummoxed.

"You can't be serious." She finds her voice. "You *can't* be."

"Well, I am," I shoot back, as my phone buzzes with a text. I glance down, and it's from Ed.

Hey. R u still on for sightseeing on Sunday? E

"That was from Josh." I smile lovingly at my phone. "We're meeting up on Sunday."

"To get married and have six children?" says Sadie sarcastically. But she sounds on the defensive.

"You know, Sadie," I give her a patronizing smile, "you may be able to sway people's heads. But you can't sway their hearts."

Ha. Take that, ghostie.

Sadie glowers at me, and I can tell she can't think of a reply. She looks so disconcerted, I almost feel cheered up. I swing around the corner and into the door of our building.

"There's a girl in your office, by the way," says Sadie, following me. "I don't like the look of her one little bit."

"Girl? What girl?" I hurry up the stairs, wondering if Shireen has come by. I push open the door, stride in—and stop dead with shock.

It's Natalie.

What the hell is Natalie doing here?

She's right there in front of me. Sitting in *my* chair. Talking on *my* phone. She's looking deeply tanned and wearing a white shirt with a navy pencil skirt, and laughing throatily at something. As she sees me, she demonstrates no surprise, just gives me a wink.

"Well, thanks, Janet. I'm glad you appreciate the work," she says in her confident, drawling way. "You're right—Clare Fortescue has hidden her light under a bushel. Hugely talented. Perfect for you. I was determined to woo her. . . . No, thank *you*. That's my job, Janet, that's why you pay me my commission. . . ." She gives that deep, throaty laugh again.

I shoot a shocked glance over at Kate, who gives me a helpless shrug.

"We'll be in touch." Natalie's still talking. "Yeah, I'll talk to Lara. She obviously has a few things to learn, but . . . Well, yes, I did have to pick up the

pieces, but she's a promising girl. Don't write her off."
She winks at me again. "OK, thanks, Janet. We'll do
lunch. Take care now." As I stare in disbelief, Natalie
puts down the phone, swivels around, and smiles at me
lazily. "So. How's tricks?"

NINETEEN

It's Sunday morning, and I'm still seething. At myself. How could I be so *lame*?

On Friday I was so shocked that somehow I let Natalie take charge of the situation. I didn't confront her. I didn't make any of my points. They were all buzzing around my head like trapped flies.

I know *now* all the things I should have said to her. I should have said, "You can't just come back and act like nothing's happened." And: "How about an apology for leaving us in the lurch?" And: "Don't you dare take credit for finding Clare Fortescue; that was all down to me!"

And maybe even: "So you were fired from your last job, huh? When were you planning to tell me that?"

But I didn't say any of those things. I just gasped and said feebly, "Natalie! Wow! How come you're—What—"

And she launched into a long story about how the guy in Goa turned out to be a two-timing asshole, and there's only so much downtime you can have before you go crazy, and she'd decided to surprise me, and wasn't I relieved?

"Natalie," I began, "it's been really stressy with you gone—"

"Welcome to big business." She winked at me. "Stress comes with the territory."

"But you just disappeared! We didn't have any warning! We had to pick up all the pieces—"

"Lara." She held out a hand, as though to say, *Calm down.* "I know. It was tough. But it's OK. Whatever fuckups happened while I was gone, I'm here to put them right. Hello, Graham?" She turned to the phone. "Natalie Masser here."

And she carried on all afternoon, moving seamlessly from phone call to phone call, so I couldn't get a word in. As she left for the evening, she was gabbing on her mobile and just gave Kate and me a casual wave.

So that's it. She's back. She's acting like she's the boss and she did nothing wrong and we should all be really grateful to her for coming back.

If she winks at me one more time, I will *throttle* her.

Miserably, I wrench my hair into a ponytail. I'm barely making any effort today. Sightseeing does *not* require a flapper dress. And Sadie still thinks I'm going out with Josh, so she's not bossing me around for once.

I eye Sadie surreptitiously as I do my blusher. I feel a bit bad, lying to her. But then, she shouldn't have been so obnoxious.

"I don't want you coming along," I warn her for the millionth time. "Don't even think about it."

"I wouldn't *dream* of coming along!" she retorts, affronted. "You think I want to trail along beside you and the ventriloquist's dummy? I'm going to watch television. There's a Fred Astaire special today. Edna and I will have a lovely day together."

"Good. Well, give her my love," I say sarcastically.

Sadie's found an old woman called Edna who lives a

few streets away and does nothing but watch black-and-white films. She goes there most days now, sits on the sofa beside Edna, and watches a movie. She says the only problem comes when Edna gets phone calls and talks through the movie—so now she's taken to yelling, "*Shut up! Finish your phone call!*" right in Edna's ear. Whereupon Edna gets all flustered and sometimes even thrusts the phone down mid-sentence.

Poor Edna.

I finish doing my blusher and stare at my reflection. Black skinny jeans, silver ballet pumps, a T-shirt, and a leather jacket. Normal, 2009-style makeup. Ed probably won't recognize me. I should stick a feather in my hair just so he knows it's me.

The thought makes me snort with laughter, and Sadie glances at me suspiciously.

"What's funny?" She looks me up and down. "Are you going out like that? I've never *seen* such a dull ensemble. Josh will take one look at you and expire of boredom. If you don't expire of boredom first."

Oh, haha. But maybe she has a point. Maybe I've dressed down *too* much.

I find myself reaching for one of my twenties vintage necklaces and looping it around my neck. The silver and jet beads fall down in rows and click together as I move, and at once I feel a bit more interesting. More glamorous.

I line my lips again in a darker color, giving them a bit more of a twenties shape. Then I pick up a vintage silver leather clutch and survey myself again.

"Much better!" says Sadie. "And what about a darling little cloche?"

"No, thanks." I roll my eyes.

"If it were me, I'd wear a hat," she persists.

"Well, I don't want to look like you." I throw back my hair and smile at myself. "I want to look like me."

I suggested to Ed that we start off our tour at the Tower of London, and as I come out of the tube station into the crisp air, I feel immediately cheered. Never mind about Natalie. Never mind about Josh. Never mind about the necklace. Look at all this. It's fantastic! Ancient stone battlements, towering against the blue sky as they have done for centuries. Beefeaters wandering about in their red and navy costumes, like something out of a fairy tale. This is the kind of place that makes you feel proud to be a born-and-bred Londoner. How could Ed not even have bothered to come here? It's, like, one of the wonders of the world!

Come to think of it, I'm not sure I've ever actually visited the Tower of London myself. I mean, gone in or anything. But that's different. I live here. I don't have to.

"Lara! Over here!"

Ed's already in the queue for tickets. He's wearing jeans and a gray T-shirt. He hasn't shaved, either, which is interesting. I had him down as someone who'd look smart even at the weekend. As I draw near, he looks me up and down with a little smile.

"So you do sometimes wear clothes from the twenty-first century."

"Very occasionally." I grin back.

"I was convinced you were going to turn up in another twenties dress. In fact, I found an accessory for myself. Just to keep you company." He reaches in his pocket and produces a small rectangular case made of battered silver. He springs it open and I see a deck of playing cards.

"Cool!" I say, impressed. "Where did you get this?"

"Bid for it on eBay." He shrugs. "I always carry a deck of cards. It's 1925," he adds, showing me a tiny hallmark.

I can't help feeling touched that he went to that effort.

"I love it." I look up as we arrive at the head of the queue. "Two adults, please. This is on me," I add firmly as Ed makes to get out his wallet. "I'm the host."

I buy the tickets and a book called *Historic London* and lead Ed to a spot in front of the tower.

"So, this building you see before you is the Tower of London," I begin in a knowledgeable, tour-leader tone. "One of our most important and ancient monuments. One of many, many wonderful sights. It's criminal to come to London and not find out more about our amazing heritage." I look at Ed severely. "It's really narrow-minded, plus you don't have anything like it in America."

"You're right." He looks suitably chastened as he surveys the tower. "This is spectacular."

"Isn't it great?" I say proudly.

There are some times when being English is really the best, and big-historic-castle time is one of them.

"When was it built?" asks Ed.

"Um . . ." I look around for a handy sign. There isn't one. Damn. There should be a sign. I can't exactly look it up in the guidebook. Not with him watching me expectantly.

"It was in the . . ." I turn casually away and mumble something indistinct. ". . . teenth century."

"Which century?"

"It dates from . . ." I clear my throat. "Tudor. Er . . . Stuart times."

"Do you mean Norman?" suggests Ed politely.

"Oh. Yes, that's what I meant." I dart him a suspicious look. How did he know that? Has he been boning up?

"So, we go in this way." I lead Ed confidently toward a likely-looking rampart, but he pulls me back.

"Actually, I think the entrance is this way, by the river."

For God's sake. He's obviously one of these men who have to take control. He probably never asks for directions either.

"Listen, Ed," I say kindly. "You're American. You've never been here before. Who's more likely to know the way in, me or you?"

At that moment, a passing Beefeater stops and gives us a friendly beam. I smile back, ready to ask him the best way in, but he addresses Ed cheerily.

"Morning, Mr. Harrison. How are you? Back again already?"

What?

What just happened? Ed knows the Beefeaters? How does Ed know the Beefeaters?

I'm speechless as Ed shakes the hand of the Beefeater and says, "Good to see you, Jacob. Meet Lara."

"Er . . . hello," I manage feebly.

What's going to happen next? Will the queen arrive and ask us in for tea?

"OK," I splutter as soon as the Beefeater has continued on his way. "What's going on?"

Ed takes one look at my face and bursts into laughter.

"Tell me!" I demand, and he lifts his hands apologetically.

"I'll come clean. I was here Friday. It was a work team-building day out. We were able to talk to some of the Beefeaters. It was fascinating." He pauses, then adds, his mouth twitching, "That's how I know the tower was begun in 1078. By William the Conqueror. And the entrance is this way."

"You could have told me!" I glare at him.

"I'm sorry. You seemed so into the idea, and I thought it would be cool to go around with you. But we can go someplace else. You must have seen this a million times. Let's rethink." He takes the *Historic London* guidebook and starts consulting the index.

I'm flipping the tickets back and forth in my hands, watching a group of schoolkids take pictures of one another, feeling torn. Obviously he's right. He saw the tower on Friday so why on earth would we go around it again?

On the other hand, we've bought the tickets now. And it looks amazing. And I want to see it.

"We could head straight down to St. Paul's." Ed is peering at the tube map. "It shouldn't take too long—"

"I want to see the Crown jewels," I say in a small voice.

"What?" He raises his head.

"I want to see the Crown jewels. Now we're here."

"You mean . . . you've never seen them?" Ed stares incredulously at me. "*You've* never seen the Crown jewels?"

"I live in London!" I say, nettled at his expression. "It's different! I can see them anytime I want, when the occasion arises. It's just that . . . the occasion has never arisen."

"Isn't that a bit narrow-minded of you, Lara?" I can tell Ed's loving this. "Aren't you interested in the heritage of your great city? Don't you think it's criminal to ignore these unique historic monuments—"

"Shut up!" I can feel my cheeks turning red.

Ed relents. "Come on. Let me show you your own country's fine Crown jewels. They're great. I know the whole deal. You realize that the oldest pieces date from the Restoration?"

"Really?"

"Oh, yes." He starts guiding me through the crowd. "The Imperial State Crown contains an enormous diamond cut from the famous Cullinan Diamond, the largest diamond ever mined."

"Wow," I say politely. Obviously Ed memorized the entire Crown jewels lecture yesterday.

"Uh-huh." He nods. "At least, that's what the world thought until 1997. When it was discovered to be a fake."

"*Really?*" I stop dead. "It's *fake*?"

Ed's mouth twitches. "Just checking you're listening."

We see the jewels and we see the ravens and we see the White Tower and the Bloody Tower. In fact, all the towers. Ed insists on holding the guidebook and reading out facts, all the way around. Some of them are true and some of them are bullshit and some . . . I'm not sure. He has this totally straight face with just a tiny gleam in his eye, and you honestly can't tell.

As we finish our Yeoman Warder's tour, my head is spinning with visions of traitors and torture, and I feel I don't need to hear anything else about When Executions Go Horribly Wrong, ever again. We wander through the Medieval Palace, past two guys in medieval costume doing medieval writing (I guess), and find ourselves in a room with tiny castle windows and a massive fireplace.

"OK, clever clogs. Tell me about that cupboard." I point randomly at a small, nondescript door set in the wall. "Did Walter Raleigh grow potatoes in there or something?"

"Let's see." Ed consults the guidebook. "Ah, yes. This is where the Seventh Duke of Marmaduke kept his wigs. An interesting historical figure, he beheaded many of his wives. Others he cryogenically froze. He also invented the medieval version of the popcorn maker. Or ye poppecorn, as it was known."

"Oh, really?" I adopt a serious tone.

"You'll obviously have learned about the poppecorn craze of 1583." Ed squints at the guidebook. "Apparently Shakespeare very nearly called *Much Ado About Nothing, Much Ado About Ye Poppecorn*."

We're both gazing intently at the tiny oak door, and after a moment an elderly couple in waterproof jackets joins us.

"It's a wig cupboard," says Ed to the woman, whose face lights up with interest. "The wigmaster was compelled to live in the cupboard along with his wigs."

"Really?" The elderly woman's face falls. "How terrible!"

"Not really," says Ed gravely. "Because the wigmaster was very small." He starts to demonstrate with his hands. "Very, very tiny. The word *wig* is derived from the phrase *small man in a cupboard*, you know."

"Really?" The poor woman looks bewildered, and I nudge Ed hard in the ribs.

"Have a good tour," he says charmingly, and we move on.

"You have an evil streak!" I say as soon as we're out of earshot. Ed thinks about this for a moment, then gives me a disarming grin.

"Maybe I do. When I'm hungry. You want some lunch? Or should we see the Royal Fusiliers Museum?"

I hesitate thoughtfully, as though weighing these two options. I mean, no one could be more interested in their heritage than me. But the thing with any sight-seeing is, after a while it turns into sight-trudging, and all the heritage turns into a blur of winding stone steps and battlements and stories about severed heads stuffed on pikes.

"We could do lunch," I say casually. "If you've had enough for now."

Ed's eyes glint. I have this disconcerting feeling he knows exactly what I'm thinking.

"I have a very short attention span," he says, deadpan. "Being American. So maybe we should eat."

We head to a café serving things like "Georgian onion soup" and "wild boar casserole." Ed insists on paying since I bought the tickets, and we find a table in the corner by the window.

"So, what else do you want to see in London?" I say enthusiastically. "What else was on your list?"

Ed flinches, and I suddenly wish I hadn't put it like that. His sightseeing list must be a sore point.

"Sorry," I say awkwardly. "I didn't mean to remind you—"

"No! It's fine." He considers his forkful for a moment, as though debating whether to eat it. "You know what? You were right, what you said the other day. Shit happens, and you have to get on with life. I like your dad's thing about the escalator, I've thought about that since we talked. Onward and upward." He puts the fork in his mouth.

"Really?" I can't help feeling touched. I'll have to tell Dad.

"Mmm-hmm." He chews for a moment, then eyes me questioningly. "So . . . you said you had a breakup too. When was that?"

Yesterday. Less than twenty-four hours ago. Even thinking about it makes me want to close my eyes and moan.

"It was . . . a while ago." I shrug. "He was called Josh."

"And what happened? If you don't mind me asking?"

"No, of course not. It was . . . I just realized . . . we weren't—" I break off, with a heavy sigh, and look up. "Have you ever felt really, *really* stupid?"

"Never." Ed shakes his head. "Although I have on occasion felt really, really, *really* stupid."

I can't help a little smile. Talking to Ed puts everything into perspective a bit. I'm not the only person in the world to feel like a fool. And at least Josh didn't two-time me. At least I didn't end up marooned all alone in a strange city.

"Hey, let's do something that wasn't on your list," I say on impulse. "Let's see some sight that was never in the plan. *Is* there anything?"

Ed breaks off a piece of bread, mulling.

"Corinne didn't want to go on the London Eye," he says at last. "She's scared of heights and she thought it was kinda dumb."

I *knew* I didn't like this woman. How can anyone think the London Eye is dumb?

"London Eye it is," I say firmly. "And then maybe Ye Olde Starbucks? It's a traditional English custom, very quaint."

I wait for Ed to laugh, but he just gives me an appraising look as he eats his bread.

"Starbucks. Interesting. You don't go to Lingtons Coffee?"

Oh, right. So he's worked it out.

"Sometimes. Depends." I shrug defensively. "So . . . you know I'm related."

"I told you, I asked around about you."

His face is impassive. He hasn't done what people usually do when they find out about Uncle Bill, which is say, "Oh, wow, that's amazing, what's he like in real life?"

Ed's in big business, it occurs to me. He must have come across Uncle Bill in some way or another.

"What do you think of my uncle?" I say lightly.

"Lingtons Coffee is a successful organization," he replies. "Very profitable. Very efficient."

He's avoiding the question. "What about Bill?" I persist. "Have you ever come across him?"

"Yes. I have." He swallows his wine. "And I think Two Little Coins is manipulative bullshit. Sorry."

I've never heard anyone be so rude about Uncle Bill, not to my face. It's kind of refreshing.

"Don't be sorry," I say at once. "Say what you think. Tell me."

"What I think is . . . your uncle is the one in the million. And I'm sure a lot of different factors went into his success. But that's not the message he's selling. He's selling the message 'It's easy! Come be a millionaire like me!' " Ed sounds curt, almost angry. "The only people who go to those seminars will be self-deluding fantasists, and the only person who'll make any money is your uncle. He's exploiting a lot of sad, desperate people. Just an opinion."

The instant he says all this, I know it's true. I saw the people at the Two Little Coins seminar. Some of them had traveled miles. Some of them *did* look desperate. And it's not like the seminar cost nothing.

"I went to one of his day seminars once," I admit. "Just to see what it was all about."

"Oh, really. And did you instantly make your fortune?"

"Of course I did! Didn't you spot my limo earlier?"

"Oh, that was yours. I assumed you'd use your helicopter."

We're both grinning by now. I can't believe I called Ed Mr. American Frown. He doesn't frown *that* often. And when he does, he's usually thinking of something funny to say. He pours me some more wine and I lean back, relishing the view of the tower, and the warm glow that the wine is giving me, and the prospect of the rest of the day ahead.

"So, why do you carry cards with you?" I say, deciding it's my turn to start. "Do you play patience the whole time or something?"

"Poker. If I can find anyone to play with. You'd be great at poker," he adds.

"I'd be terrible!" I contradict him. "I'm crap at gambling, and—" I stop as Ed shakes his head.

"Poker's not about gambling. It's about being able to read people. Your Eastern mind-reading powers would come in handy."

"Oh, right." I blush. "Well . . . my powers seem to have abandoned me."

Ed raises an eyebrow. "You're not hustling me here, Miss Lington?"

"No!" I laugh. "They really have! I'm a total novice."

"OK, then." He takes out the pack of cards and shuffles it expertly. "All you need to know is, do the other players have good cards or bad? Simple as that. So you look at your opponents' faces. And you ask yourself, *Is something going on?* And that's the game."

" 'Is something going on?' " I repeat. "And how can you tell?"

Ed deals himself three cards and glances at them. Then he gazes at me. "Good or bad?"

Oh God. I have no idea. His face is dead straight. I survey his smooth forehead, the tiny lines around his eyes, the hint of weekend stubble—searching for clues. There's a glint in his eye, but that could mean anything.

"Dunno," I say helplessly. "I'll go with . . . good?"

Ed looks amused. "Those Eastern powers really did desert you. They're terrible." He shows me three low cards. "Now your turn." He shuffles the pack again, deals out three cards and watches me pick them up.

I've got the three of clubs, the four of hearts, and the ace of spades. I study them, then look up with my most inscrutable expression.

"Relax," says Ed. "Don't laugh."

Of course, now he's said that, I can feel my mouth twitching.

"You have a terrible poker face," says Ed. "You know that?"

"You're putting me off!" I wriggle my mouth around a bit, getting rid of the laugh. "OK, then, what have I got?"

Ed's dark brown eyes lock on mine. We're both silent and still, gazing at each other. After a few seconds I feel a weird flip in my stomach. This feels ... strange. Too intimate. Like he can see more of me than he should. Pretending to cough, I break the spell and turn away. I take a gulp of wine and look back to see Ed sipping his wine too.

"You have one high card, probably an ace," he says matter-of-factly. "And two low ones."

"No!" I put the cards down. "How do you know?"

"Your eyes popped out of your face when you saw the ace." Ed sounds amused. "It was totally obvious. Like, 'Oh wow! A high one!' Then you looked right and left as though you might have given yourself away. Then you put your hand over the high one and gave me a dirty look." He's starting to laugh now. "Remind me not to give you any state secrets to keep anytime soon."

I can't believe it. I thought I was being really inscrutable.

"But, seriously." Ed begins shuffling the cards again. "Your mind-reading trick. It's all based on analyzing behavioral traits, isn't it?"

"Er ... that's right," I say cautiously.

"That can't have just deserted you. Either you know that stuff or you don't. So what's going on, Lara? What's the story?"

He leans forward intently, as though waiting for an answer. I feel a bit thrown. I'm not used to this kind of focused attention. If he were Josh, I'd have been able to fob him off easily. Josh always took everything at face value. He'd have said, "Right, babe," and I could have moved the subject on quickly and he never would have questioned it or thought about it again. . . .

Because Josh was never really that interested in me.

It hits me like a drench of cold water. A final, mortifying insight that instantly has the feel and ring of truth to it. All the time we were together, Josh never challenged me, never gave me a hard time, barely even remembered the fine details of my life. I thought he was just easygoing and laid-back. I loved him for it. I saw it as a plus. But now I understand better. The truth is, he was laid-back because he didn't really care. Not about me. Not enough, anyway.

I feel like I'm finally stepping out of some trance. I was so busy chasing after him, so desperate, so sure of myself, I never looked closely enough at what I was chasing. I never stopped to ask if he really was the answer. I've been such an *idiot*.

I look up to see Ed's dark, intelligent eyes still keenly scanning me. And in spite of myself I feel a sudden weird exhilaration that he, someone I barely know, wants to find out more about me. I can see it in his face: He's not asking for the sake of it. He genuinely wants to know the truth.

Only I can't tell him. Obviously.

"It's . . . quite tricky to explain. Quite complicated." I drain my glass, stuff a last bite of cake into my mouth, and beam distractingly at Ed. "Come on. Let's go to the London Eye."

As we arrive at the South Bank, it's buzzing with Sunday afternoon tourists, buskers, secondhand-book stalls, and lots of those living statues, which always slightly freak me out. The London Eye is creeping around like a massive Ferris wheel, and I can see people in each transparent pod, peering down at us. I'm quite excited, actually. I've only been in the London Eye once before, and that was at a work do with lots of obnoxious drunk people.

A jazz band is playing an old twenties tune to a crowd of onlookers, and as we pass I can't help meeting Ed's eye. He does a couple of Charleston steps and I twirl my beads at him.

"Very good!" says a bearded guy in a hat, approaching us with a bucket for donations. "Are you interested in jazz?"

"Kind of," I say as I root in my bag for some money.

"We're interested in the 1920s," says Ed firmly, and winks at me. "Only the twenties, right, Lara?"

"We're holding an open-air jazz event in Jubilee Gardens next week," says the guy eagerly. "You want tickets? Ten percent off if you buy them now."

"Sure," says Ed, after glancing at me. "Why not?"

He hands the guy some money, takes two tickets, and we walk on.

"So," says Ed after a bit. "We could go to this jazz thing . . . together. If you wanted to."

"Er . . . right. Cool. I'd like that."

He gives me one of the tickets, and a little awkwardly I put it in my bag. For a while I walk on silently, trying to work out what just happened. Is he asking me on a date? Or is this just an extension of the sightseeing? Or . . . what? What are we doing?

I reckon Ed must be thinking something along the same lines, because as we join the queue for the Eye, he suddenly looks at me with a kind of quizzical expression.

"Hey, Lara. Tell me something."

"Er . . . OK." I'm instantly nervous. He's going to ask about me being psychic again.

"Why'd you burst into that conference room?" His forehead crinkles humorously. "Why did you ask me on a date?"

A million times worse. What am I supposed to say?

"That's . . . a good question. And . . . and I have one for you," I parry. "Why did you come? You could have turned me down!"

"I know." Ed looks mystified. "You want to know the truth? It's almost a blur. I can't decipher my own thought processes. A strange girl arrives in the office. Next moment I'm on a date with her." He turns to me with renewed focus. "C'mon. You must have had a reason. Had you seen me around the place or something?"

There's an edge of hope to his voice. Like he's hoping to hear something that will make his day better. I feel a sudden, horrible pang of guilt. He has no idea he's just being used.

"It was . . . a dare with a friend." I stare over his shoulder. "I don't know why I did it."

"Right." His voice is as relaxed as before. "So I was a random dare. Doesn't sound so good to the grandkids. I'll tell them you were sent to me by aliens. Right after I tell them about the Duke of Marmaduke's wigs."

I know he's joking. I know this is all banter. But as I glance up I can see it in his face. I can see the warmth. He's falling for me. No, scratch that, he *thinks* he's falling for me. But it's all fake. It's all wrong. It's another puppet show. He's been manipulated by Sadie as much as Josh was. None of this is real, none of it means anything.

I feel suddenly, ridiculously upset. This is all Sadie's fault. She creates trouble wherever she goes. Ed is a really, really nice guy and he's been screwed up enough already, and she's messed with him and it's not fair.

"Ed." I swallow.

"Yes?"

Oh God. What do I say? *You haven't been dating me, you've been dating a ghost, she's been influencing your mind, she's like LSD without the upside. . . .*

"You might think you like me. But . . . you don't."

"I do." He laughs. "I really like you."

"You don't." I'm struggling here. "You're not thinking for yourself. I mean . . . this isn't real."

"Feels pretty real to me."

"I know it does. But . . . you don't understand—" I break off, feeling helpless. There's silence for a moment—then, Ed's face abruptly changes.

"Oh. I see."

"You do?" I say doubtfully.

"Lara, you don't have to soften me with an excuse." His smile turns wry. "If you've had enough, just say. I can cope with an afternoon on my own. It's been fun and I appreciate the time you've taken, thanks very much—"

"No!" I say in dismay. "Stop it! I'm not trying to bail out! I'm having a really good time today. And I want to go on the London Eye."

Ed's eyes scan my face, up and down, left and right, as though they're lie detectors.

"Well, so do I," he says at last.

"Well . . . good."

We're so engrossed in our conversation, we haven't noticed the gap growing in the queue ahead of us.

"Get on with it!" A guy behind suddenly prods me. "You're on!"

"Oh!" I wake up. "Quick, we're on!" I grab Ed's hand and we run forward toward the big oval pod. It's inching its way along the platform, and people are stepping on, amid giggles and shrieks. I step on, still hand in hand with Ed, and we beam at each other, all the awkwardness gone.

"OK, Mr. Harrison." I revert to my tour-operator voice. "*Now* you're going to see London."

It's brilliant. I mean, it just is *brilliant*.

We've been right up to the top and seen the whole city stretching out below us, like the A–Z map come to life. We've peered down at the little people scurrying around like ants, getting into ant cars and ant buses. I've knowledgeably pointed out St. Paul's, and Buckingham Palace, and Big Ben. Now I've taken charge of the *Historic London* guidebook. It doesn't have a section on the London Eye, but I'm reading out facts from it anyway, which I'm making up.

"The pod is made of transparent titanium melted down from eyeglasses," I inform Ed. "If plunged underwater, each pod will automatically convert to a fully operational submarine."

"I would expect no less." He nods, gazing out of the glass.

"Each pod could survive underwater for thirteen hours. . . ." I trail off. I can tell he isn't really listening. "Ed?"

He turns around to face me, his back against the glass wall of the pod. Behind him, the panoramic view of London is shifting slowly, infinitesimally upward. While we've been up, the sunshine has disappeared, and solid gray clouds are gathering overhead.

"You want to know something, Lara?" He glances around to check no one is listening, but everyone else in the pod has piled to the other side, watching a police boat on the Thames.

"Maybe," I say warily. "Not if it's a really important secret and I'm not supposed to give it away."

Ed's face flickers with a smile. "You asked me why I agreed to go on that first date with you."

"Oh. That. Well, it doesn't matter," I say hurriedly. "Don't feel you have to tell me—"

"No. I want to tell you.. It was . . . freaky." He pauses. "I felt as though something inside my head was *telling* me to say yes. The more I resisted, the louder it shouted. Does that make any sense?"

"No," I say hastily. "None. I've no idea. Maybe it was . . . God."

"Maybe." He gives a short laugh. "I could be the new Moses." He hesitates. "Point is, I've never felt such a strong impulse, or voice, or whatever it was. Kinda blew me away." He takes a step forward, his voice lower. "And whatever instinct it was—whatever deep place it came from—it was right. Spending time with you is the best thing I could have done. I feel like I've woken up from a dream, or limbo . . . and I want to thank you."

"There's no need!" I say at once. "It was my pleasure. Anytime."

"I hope so." His tone is oblique, and I feel a bit flustered under his gaze.

"So . . . um . . . you want to hear more from the guidebook?" I riffle through the pages.

"Sure."

"The pod is . . . um." I can't concentrate on what I'm saying. My heart has started beating more quickly. Everything seems heightened. I'm aware of every movement I'm making.

"The wheel travels . . . it goes around. . . ." I'm making no sense. I close the book and meet Ed's gaze head-on, trying to match his deadpan expression, trying to appear as if nothing's concerning me at all.

Except quite a lot of things are concerning me. The heat rushing to my face. The hairs prickling at the back of my neck. The way Ed's eyes are boring into mine, like they want to get straight to the point. They're giving me twinges.

Truth is, he's giving me twinges all over the place.

I don't know how I ever thought he wasn't good-looking. I think I must have been a bit blind.

"Is something going on?" says Ed softly.

"I . . . I don't know." I can barely speak. "Is something going on?"

He puts a hand up to my chin and cups it for a moment, as though surveying the terrain. Then he leans forward and pulls my face gently up to his with both hands and kisses me. His mouth is warm and sweet and his stubble is grazing my skin but he doesn't seem to care and . . . oh God. *Yes, please.* All my twinges have turned into singing, dancing urges. As he wraps his arms around me and pulls me tighter to him, two thoughts are jostling in my brain.

He's so different from Josh.

He's so *good.*

I'm not having many other thoughts right now. At least you couldn't really call them thoughts so much as ravening desires.

At last Ed pulls away, his hands still cradling the back of my neck.

"You know . . . that wasn't the plan for today," he says. "Just in case you were wondering."

"Wasn't my plan either," I say breathlessly. "Not at all."

He kissed me again, and I close my eyes, exploring his mouth with mine, inhaling the scent of him, wondering how much longer this London Eye ride has to go. As though reading my mind, Ed releases me.

"Maybe we should look at the view one more time," he says with a small laugh. "Before we land."

"I suppose we should." I give him a reluctant smile. "We've paid for it, after all."

Arm in arm, we turn to face the transparent wall of the pod. And I scream in fright.

Hovering outside the pod, looking in with searing, laserlike eyes, is Sadie.

She saw us. She saw us kissing.

Shit. Oh . . . shit. My heart is thumping like a rabbit's. As I quiver in terror, she advances through the transparent wall, her nostrils flared, her eyes flashing, making me back away on stumbling legs as if I really have seen a terrifying ghost.

"Lara?" Ed is staring at me in shock. "Lara, what's wrong?"

"How *could* you?" Sadie's shriek of betrayal makes me clap my hands to my ears. "*How could you?*"

"I . . . I didn't . . . it wasn't . . ." I gulp, but the words won't come out properly. I want to tell her I didn't plan all this, that it's not as bad as she might think—

"*I saw you!*"

She gives a huge, racking sob, wheels around, and disappears.

"Sadie!" I rush forward and clutch at the transparent wall of the pod, peering out, trying to glimpse her in the clouds or in the rushing water of the Thames or among the nearing crowds of people on the ground.

"Lara! Jesus! What happened?" Ed looks totally freaked out. I suddenly notice that all the other people in the pod have stopped staring out at the view and are goggling at me.

"Nothing!" I manage. "Sorry. I just . . . I was . . ." As he puts his arm around me, I flinch. "Ed, I'm sorry . . . I can't . . ."

After a pause Ed takes his arm away. "Sure."

We've reached the ground now. Shooting anxious glances at me, Ed ushers me off the pod and onto solid ground.

"So." His tone is cheerful, but I can tell he's perturbed. As well he might be. "What's up?"

"I can't explain," I say miserably. I'm desperately scanning the horizon, searching for any sight of Sadie.

"Would a Ye Olde Starbucks help? Lara?"

"Sorry." I stop looking around and focus on Ed's concerned face. "Ed, I'm so sorry. I can't do . . . this. It's been a lovely day, but . . ."

"But . . . it didn't go according to plan?" he says slowly.

"No. It's not that!" I rub my face. "It's . . . it's complicated. I need to sort myself out."

I look up at him, willing him to understand. Or half understand. Or at least not think I'm a flake.

"No problem." He nods. "I get it. Things aren't always clear-cut." He hesitates, then touches my arm briefly. "Let's leave it here, then. It's been a great day. Thanks, Lara. You've been very generous with your time."

He's retreated into his formal gentlemanly style. All the warmth and joking between us has ebbed away. It's like we're two distant acquaintances. He's protecting himself, I suddenly realize with a pang. He's going back into his tunnel.

"Ed, I'd love to see you again sometime," I say desperately. "Once things are . . . sorted out."

"I'd like that." I can tell he doesn't believe me for a minute. "Let me call you a taxi." As he looks up and down the road, I can see his frown returning, like little lines of disappointment.

"No. I'll just stay here a bit and wander about, get my head straight." I muster a smile. "Thanks. For everything."

He gives me a farewell wave, like a salute, then heads off into the crowd. I stare after him, feeling crushed. I like him. I really, really like him. And now he feels hurt. And so do I. And so does Sadie. What a mess.

"So this is what you do behind my back!" Sadie's voice in my ear makes me jump and clasp my chest. Has she been waiting there all this time? "You lying snake. You backstabber. I came here to see how you were getting on with Josh. With *Josh*!"

She whirls around in front of me, looking so incandescent, I find myself backing away.

"I'm sorry," I stutter, clutching my phone to my ear as camouflage. "I'm sorry I lied to you. I didn't want to admit Josh and I broke up. But I'm not a backstabber! I didn't mean for Ed and me to kiss, I didn't mean any of this, I didn't plan it—"

"I don't care whether you planned it or not!" she shrieks. "Keep your hands off him!"

"Sadie, I'm really sorry—"

"I found him! I danced with him! He's mine! Mine! *Mine!*"

She's so self-righteous, and so livid, and she's not even listening to what I'm saying. And suddenly, from underneath all my guilt I feel a surge of resentment.

"How can he be yours?" I hear myself yelling. "You're dead! Haven't you realized that yet? You're *dead*! He doesn't even know you exist!"

"Yes, he does!" She brings her face close to mine, a murderous look in her eye. "He can hear me!"

"So what? It's not like he'll ever meet you, is it? You're a ghost! A *ghost*!" All my misery at the situation is bursting out in a vent of anger. "Talk about self-deluded! Talk about not facing up to the truth, Sadie! You keep telling me to move on! How about *you* move on?"

Even as I'm uttering the words, I'm realizing how they sound, how they might be misinterpreted. And I'm wishing beyond anything I could take them back. A tremor of shock passes across Sadie's face. She looks as though I've slapped her.

She can't think I meant . . .

Oh God.

"Sadie, I wasn't . . . I didn't . . ." My words are all jumbled up in my mouth. I don't even quite know what I want to say. Sadie looks hollow-eyed. She's gazing out at the river as though she's not even aware of me anymore.

"You're right," she says at last. All the spirit has gone out of her voice. "You're right. I'm dead."

"No you're not!" I say in distress. "I mean . . . OK, maybe you are. But—"

"I'm dead. It's over. You don't want me. He doesn't want me. What's the point?"

She starts walking away toward Waterloo Bridge and disappears from view. Racked with guilt, I hurry

after her and up the steps. She's already halfway along
the bridge, and I run to catch up. She's standing still,
staring out toward St. Paul's Cathedral, a willowy figure in the grayness, and gives no sign of realizing I'm
there.

"Sadie, it's not over!" My voice is almost lost in the
wind. "Nothing's over! I wasn't thinking, I was just
angry at you, I was talking rubbish—"

"No. You're right." She speaks fast, without turning
her head. "I'm as self-deceiving as you. I thought I
could have some last fun in this world. I thought I
could have a friendship. Make a difference."

"You have made a difference!" I say in dismay.
"Please don't talk like this. Look, come home, we'll
put on some music, have a good time—"

"Don't patronize me!" She turns her head and I can
see her trembling. "I know what you really think. You
don't care about me, no one cares about me, some
meaningless old person—"

"Sadie, stop it, that's not true—"

"*I heard you at the funeral!*" Sadie suddenly erupts
passionately, and I feel a cold horror. She *heard* us?

"I heard you at the funeral," she repeats, regaining
her dignity. "I heard all the family talking together.
Nobody wanted to be there. Nobody mourned me. I
was just a 'million-year-old nobody.'"

I feel queasy with shame as I remember what everyone said. We were so callous and horrible. All of us.

Sadie's chin is taut and she's gazing fixedly over my
shoulder. "Your cousin put it exactly right. I didn't
achieve anything in my life, I left no mark, I wasn't
anything special. I don't know why I bothered living,
really!" She gives a brittle laugh.

"Sadie . . . please don't." I swallow.

"I didn't have love," she continues, inexorably, "or a career. I didn't leave behind children or achievements or anything to speak of. The only man I ever loved . . . forgot about me." There's a sudden shake in her voice. "I lived for one hundred and five years, but I didn't leave a trace. Not one. I didn't mean anything to anybody. And I still don't."

"Yes, you do. Of course you do," I say desperately. "Sadie, please—"

"I've been a fool, clinging on. I'm in your way." With dismay, I see that her eyes are glimmering with tears.

"No!" I grasp at her arm, even though I know it's useless. I'm almost crying myself. "Sadie, *I* care about you. And I'm going to make it up to you. We'll dance the Charleston again, and we'll have some fun, and I'm going to get your necklace for you if it kills me—"

"I don't care about the necklace anymore." Her voice wobbles. "Why should I? It was all nothing. My life was all for nothing."

To my horror, she disappears over the side of Waterloo Bridge.

"Sadie!" I yell. "Sadie, come back. Sa-die!" I'm peering desperately down at the murky, swirling water, tears streaming down my cheeks. "It wasn't for nothing! Sadie, please, can you hear me?"

"Oh my *God*!" A girl beside me in a checked coat gasps. "Someone's jumped in the river! *Help!*"

"No, they haven't!" I lift my head, but she's not listening; she's beckoning her friends. Before I can gather my wits, people are crowding around the parapet and gazing down at the water.

"Someone's jumped!" I can hear people saying. "Call the police!"

"No, they *haven't*!" I say, but I'm drowned out. A boy in a denim jacket is already filming the water with his mobile phone. A man to my right is peeling off his jacket as though preparing to dive in, while his girlfriend watches admiringly.

"No!" I grab at his jacket. "Stop!"

"Someone's got to do the right thing," says the man, in a hero-like voice, glancing at his girlfriend.

For God's sake.

"No one's jumped!" I shout, waving my arms. "There's been a mistake! Everything's fine! No one's jumped; repeat, no one's jumped!"

The man stops, halfway through taking off his shoes. The boy with the mobile phone swivels and starts filming me instead.

"Then who were you talking to?" The girl in the checked coat gives me an accusing look, as though suspecting me of lying. "You were shouting at the water and crying! You gave us all a fright! Who were you talking to?"

"I was talking to a ghost," I say shortly. I turn away before she can reply, and push my way through the crowd, ignoring the exclamations and grumbling comments.

She'll come back, I tell myself. When she's calmed down and forgiven me. She'll come back.

TWENTY

But next morning the flat is still and silent. Normally Sadie appears as I'm making a cup of tea, perching on the work surface, making rude comments about my pajamas and telling me I don't know how to make tea properly.

Today there's nothing. I fish my tea bag out of my cup and look around the kitchen.

"Sadie? Sadie, are you there?"

There's no reply. The air feels dead and empty.

As I get ready for work, it's weirdly quiet without Sadie's constant babble. In the end I turn the radio on for company. And, on the plus side, at least there's no one bossing me around. At least I can do my makeup *my* way today. Defiantly, I put on a frilled top I know she hates. Then, feeling a bit bad, I add another coat of mascara. Just in case, somehow, she's watching.

Before I leave, I can't help looking around one last time.

"Sadie? Are you there? I'm going to work now, so if you want to talk or anything, just come to the office. . . ."

Holding my tea, I go around the whole flat, calling out, but there's no response. God knows where she is or what she's doing, or what she's feeling—I feel a fresh spasm of guilt as I remember her hollow face. If I'd only *known* she heard us talking at the funeral—

Anyway. There's nothing I can do about it now. If she wants me, she knows where to find me.

I get to work just after nine thirty to find Natalie already at her desk, flicking her hair back as she talks on the phone. "Yeah. That's what I said to him, babe." She winks at me and taps her watch. "In a bit late, aren't you Lara? Got into bad habits when I was away? Anyway, babe . . ." She swivels back again.

Bad habits? *Me?*

I'm instantly seething. Who does she think she is? She's the one who buggered off to India. She's the one who behaved unprofessionally. And now she's treating me like the dim work-experience girl.

"Natalie," I say as she puts the phone down. "I need to talk to you."

"And I need to talk to *you*." Natalie's eyes gleam at me. "Ed Harrison, eh?"

"What?" I say, confused.

"Ed Harrison," she repeats impatiently. "You've kept him a bit quiet, haven't you?"

"What do you mean?" Faint alarm bells are ringing. "How do you know about Ed?"

"*Business People*!" Natalie turns a magazine toward me, open at the picture of Ed and me. "Good-looking chap."

"I'm not . . . it's a business thing," I say hurriedly, looking up.

"Oh, I know, Kate told me. You're back with Josh, whatever. . . ." Natalie gives a mock-yawn to show just how interesting my love life is to her. "That's my point. This Ed Harrison is a nice juicy bit of talent. Do you have a plan?"

"Plan?"

"For placing him!" Natalie leans forward and

speaks with elaborate patience. "We're a headhunting firm, Lara. We place people in jobs. That's what we *do*. That's how we make *money*."

"Oh!" I try to hide my horror. "No. No. You don't understand. He's not that kind of contact. He doesn't want a new job."

"He *thinks* he doesn't," Natalie corrects me.

"No, really, forget it. He hates headhunters."

"He *thinks* he does."

"He's not interested."

"Yet." Natalie winks, and I feel like hitting her.

"Stop it! He's not!"

"Everyone has their price. When I dangle the right salary in front of him, believe me, the story will change."

"It won't! Not everything's about money, you know."

Natalie bursts into mocking laughter.

"What's happened while I've been away? Have we turned into the bloody Mother Teresa Agency? We need to earn *commission*, Lara. We need to make a *profit*."

"I know," I snap. "That's what I was doing while you were lying on the beach in Goa, remember?"

"Ooh!" Natalie tosses back her head and laughs. "Miaou!"

She's not remotely shamefaced. She hasn't once apologized, for anything. How could I have thought she was my best friend? I feel like I don't even know her.

"Just leave Ed alone," I say fiercely. "He doesn't want a new job. I'm serious. He won't talk to you, anyway—"

"He already did." She leans back, looking supremely pleased with herself.

"What?"

"I called him this morning. That's the difference between you and me: I don't hang around. I get the job done."

"But he doesn't take calls from headhunters," I say, bewildered. "How did you—"

"Oh, I didn't give my name at first," says Natalie gaily. "Just said I was a friend of yours and you'd asked me to call. We had quite a little chat, as it happens. He didn't seem to know anything about Josh, but I gave him the full picture." She raises her eyebrows. "Interesting. Keeping the boyfriend from him for a reason, were you?"

I feel a rising dismay.

"What—what exactly did you say about Josh?"

"Ooh, Lara!" Natalie looks delighted at my discomfiture. "Were you planning on a little intrigue with him? Have I ruined things for you?" She puts a hand over her mouth. "Sorry!"

"Shut up!" I yell, finally losing it. "Shut *up*!"

I have to talk to Ed. Now. Grabbing my mobile, I hurry out of the office, bumping into Kate on the way. She's carrying a coffee tray and widens her eyes as she sees me.

"Lara! Are you OK?"

"*Natalie*," I say shortly, and she winces.

"I think she's worse with a tan," she whispers, and I can't help a reluctant smile. "Are you coming in?"

"In a minute. I have to make a call. It's kind of . . . private." I head down the stairs and out onto the street, speed-dialing Ed's number. God knows what Natalie said to him. God knows what he thinks of me now.

"Ed Harrison's office." A woman's voice answers.

"Hi." I try not to sound as apprehensive as I feel. "It's Lara Lington here. Could I possibly speak to Ed?"

As I'm put on hold, my mind can't help traveling back to yesterday. I can remember exactly how his arms felt around me. How his skin felt against mine. The smell of him, the taste of him . . . And then that awful way he retreated into his shell. It makes me flinch just remembering.

"Hi, Lara. What can I do for you?" His voice comes on the line. Formal and businesslike. Not one shred of warmth. My heart sinks slightly, but I try to sound upbeat and pleasant.

"Ed, I gather my colleague Natalie rang you this morning. I'm so sorry. It won't happen again. And I also wanted to say . . ." I hesitate awkwardly. "I'm really sorry about how yesterday ended."

And I don't have a boyfriend, I want to add. *And I wish we could rewind and go up on the London Eye and you'd kiss me again. And this time I wouldn't pull away, whatever happened, however many ghosts yelled at me.*

"Lara, please don't apologize." Ed sounds remote. "I should have realized you had more . . . commercial concerns, shall we say. That's why you were trying to let me down. I appreciate that little blast of honesty, at any rate."

I feel a sudden iciness in my spine. Is that what he thinks? That I was just after him for business?

"Ed, no," I say quickly. "It wasn't like that. I really enjoyed our day together. I know things went a bit weird, but there were . . . complicating factors. I can't explain—"

"Please don't patronize me," Ed interrupts evenly. "You and your colleague clearly cooked up a little plan. I don't particularly appreciate your methods, but I suppose you have to be applauded for perseverance."

"It's not true!" I say in horror. "Ed, you can't believe anything Natalie says. You *know* she's unreliable. You can't believe we cooked up a plan, it's a ludicrous idea!"

"Believe me," he says shortly, "after the small amount of research I did on Natalie, I'd believe her capable of any plan, however devious or dumb-assed. Whether you're simply naïve or as bad as she is, I don't know—"

"You've got it all wrong!" I say desperately.

"Jesus, Lara!" Ed sounds at the end of his tether. "Don't push it. I know you have a boyfriend. I know you and Josh got back together, probably never even broke up. The whole thing was a sting, and don't fucking insult me by carrying on with the charade. I should've realized the instant you showed up in my office. Maybe you did your research and found out about Corinne and me. Figured you could get to me that way. God knows what you people are capable of. Nothing would surprise me."

His voice is so harsh, so hostile, I flinch.

"I wouldn't do that! I would never do that, never!" My voice trembles. "Ed, what we had was real. We danced . . . we had such fun. . . . You can't think it was all fake— "

"And you don't have a boyfriend, I suppose." He sounds like a barrister in court.

"No! Of course not—I mean yes," I correct myself. "I did, but I split up with him on Friday—"

"On Friday!" Ed gives a humorless laugh which makes me wince. "How convenient. Lara, I don't have time for this."

"Ed, please." My eyes are welling up. "You have to believe me—"

"Bye, Lara."

The phone goes dead. I stand for a moment, motionless, little darts of pain shooting around my body. There's no point calling back. There's no point trying to explain. He'll never believe me. He thinks I'm a cynical user—or, at best, naïve and weak. And there's nothing I can do.

No. I'm wrong. There is something I can do.

I fiercely brush at my eyes and turn on my heel. As I arrive upstairs, Natalie's on the phone, filing her nails and uproariously laughing at something. Without pausing, I head for her desk, reach over and cut the line.

"What the fuck?" Natalie spins around. "I was on the phone!"

"Well, now you're not," I say evenly. "And you're going to listen to me. I've had enough. You can't behave like this."

"What?" She laughs.

"You swan off to Goa. You expect us to pick up the pieces. It's arrogant and unfair."

"Hear, hear!" chimes in Kate, then claps a hand to her mouth as we both swivel to look at her.

"Then you come back and take credit for a client who I found! Well, I'm not going to put up with it! I'm not going to be used anymore! In fact . . . I can't work with you anymore!"

I wasn't actually planning to say that last bit. But now I've said it, I realize I mean it. I can't work with her. I can't even spend time with her. She's toxic.

"Lara. Babe. You're stressed out." Natalie rolls her eyes humorously. "Why don't you take the day off—"

"I don't need the day off!" I explode. "I need you to be honest! You lied about being fired from your last job!"

"I was *not* fired." An ugly scowl appears on Natalie's face. "It was a mutual decision. They were total assholes, anyway; they never appreciated me properly—" She suddenly seems to realize how she's sounding. "Lara, come on. You and me, we're going to make a great team."

"We're not!" I shake my head. "Natalie, I don't think like you! I don't work like you! I want to put people into great jobs, not treat them like bits of meat. It's *not* all about salary!" Feeling fired up, I grab her stupid *Salary, salary, salary* Post-it off the wall and try to rip it up, except it keeps sticking to my fingers so in the end I just crumple it. "It's about the package, the person, the company—the whole picture. Matching people. Making it right for everyone. And if it's not about that, it *should* be."

I'm still half hoping that I might get through to her somehow. But her incredulous expression doesn't alter one iota.

"Matching people!" She bursts into derisive laughter. "News flash, Lara: This isn't a lonely hearts bureau!"

She's never going to understand me. And I'm never going to understand her.

"I want to break up our partnership," I say, my jaw set. "It was a mistake. I'll speak to the lawyer."

"Whatever." She stands, folding her arms, and leans back proprietorially against her desk. "But you're not poaching any of my clients; it's in our agreement. So don't get any bright ideas about ripping me off."

"Wouldn't dream of it," I say tightly.

"Go on, then." Natalie shrugs. "Clear your desk. Do whatever you've got to do."

I glance over at Kate. She's watching us, utterly aghast.

"Sorry," I mouth. In response, she gets out her phone and starts texting something. A moment later, my phone bleeps and I pull it out.

I don't blame u. If u start a company can I come? Kx

I text back.

Of course. But I don't know what I'm going to do yet.
Thanks, Kate. L xx

Natalie has sat back down at her desk and is ostentatiously typing at her computer as if I don't exist.

I feel a bit light-headed as I stand there in the middle of the office. What have I just done? This morning I had a business and a future. Now I don't. I'll never get all my money back off Natalie. What will I tell Mum and Dad?

No. Don't think about that now.

My throat is tight as I pick up a cardboard box from the corner, empty the computer paper out of it, and start packing my stuff. My hole punch. My pen holder.

"But if you think you can set up on your own and do what I do, you're wrong." Natalie suddenly lashes out, swiveling on her chair. "You don't have any contacts. You don't have any expertise. All your airy-fairy 'I want to give people great jobs' and 'Look at the whole picture.' That's not going to run a business. And don't expect me to give you a job when you're starving in the street."

"Maybe Lara isn't going to stay in recruitment!" To my astonishment, Kate chimes in from across the room. "Maybe she's going to do something else altogether! She has other talents, you know." She nods at me excitedly, and I peer back in slight confusion. I do?

"Like what?" says Natalie scathingly.

"Like mind reading!" Kate brandishes *Business People*. "Lara, you've kept so quiet about this! There's a whole piece about you at the back on the gossip page! *Lara Lington entertained crowds for an hour with her spectacular mind-reading feats. Organizers have been inundated with requests for Ms. Lington to entertain at corporate events. 'I've never seen anything like it,' said John Crawley, chairman of Medway plc. 'Lara Lington should have her own TV show.'*"

"Mind reading?" Natalie looks gobsmacked.

"It's . . . something I've been working on." I shrug.

"It says here you read five minds at once!" Kate is bubbling over. "Lara, you should go on *Britain's Got Talent*! You've got a real gift!"

"Since when could you mind read?" Natalie's eyes narrow suspiciously.

"That would be telling. And, yes, maybe I *will* do a few corporate events," I add defiantly. "Start a little business up. So I probably won't be starving in the street, thanks very much, Natalie."

"Read my mind, then, if you've got such a gift." Natalie thrusts her chin out challengingly. "Go on."

"No, thanks," I say sweetly. "I'd rather not pick up anything nasty."

There's a snuffling noise from Kate. For the first time today, Natalie looks discomfited. I pick up my box before she can think of anything else to say and head over to Kate to give her a hug.

"Bye, Kate. Thanks for everything. You're a star."

"Lara, good luck." She squeezes me back tightly and whispers, "I'll miss you," in my ear.

"Bye, Natalie," I add shortly as I head to the door. I push it open and walk along the corridor to the lift, press the button, and heft the box in my arms. I feel a bit numb. What am I going to do now?

"Sadie?" I say out of habit. But there's no reply. Of course there isn't.

The lift in our building is slow and ancient, and I'm just starting to hear its dim, cranking sound when there are footsteps behind me. I turn to see Kate approaching, looking breathless.

"Lara, I wanted to catch you before you left," she says urgently. "Do you need an assistant?"

Oh God, she's so sweet. She's like the girl in *Jerry Maguire*. She wants to come with me and bring the goldfish. If we had one.

"Er . . . well, I don't know whether I'm setting up another company yet, or what, but I'll definitely let you know—"

"No, for your *mind reading,*" she interrupts. "Do you need an assistant to help you with your tricks? Because I'd love to do it. I can wear a costume. And I can juggle!"

"Juggle?" I can't help echoing.

"Yes! With beanbags! I could be your warm-up act!"

She looks so excited, I can't bear to crush her hopes. I can't bear to say, "I can't really mind read; none of this is real."

I'm so weary of no one else understanding. I wish I could sit down with just *one person* and say, "You know, the truth is, there's this ghost. . . ."

"Kate, I'm not sure that'll work out." I try to think of how to let her down lightly. "The truth is . . . I already have an assistant."

"Oh, really?" Kate's eager face deflates. "But they didn't mention any assistant in the article. They said you did it all on your own."

"She was kind of . . . backstage. She didn't really want to be seen."

"Who is she?"

"She's . . . a relation," I say at last.

Kate's face falls still further. "Oh, right. Well, I suppose you probably work well together if you're related."

"We've got to understand each other pretty well." I nod, biting my lip. "I mean, we've had a zillion arguments along the way. But, you know. We've spent a lot of time together. We've been through quite a lot. We're . . . friends."

I feel a pang in my chest even as I'm saying it. Maybe we were friends. I don't know what we are now. And all of a sudden I feel heavy despair. Look at me. I've messed everything up with Sadie, with Ed, with Josh, I don't have a business anymore, my parents are going to freak out, I've spent all my spare money on bloody flapper dresses—

"Well, if she ever doesn't want to do it anymore . . . " Kate's face brightens. "Or if *she* wants an assistant?"

"I don't know what our plans are. I just . . . it's all been a bit . . ." I feel my eyes sting. Kate's face is so sympathetic and open, and I've been feeling so tense, the words start slipping out. "The thing is . . . we had a row. And she disappeared. I haven't seen her or heard from her since."

"You're joking!" says Kate in dismay. "What was the row about?"

"Lots of things," I say miserably. "I suppose mostly about . . . a man."

"And do you know if she's . . ." Kate hesitates. "I mean . . . is she OK?"

"I don't know. I don't know what's happened to her. She could be anywhere. I mean, normally we're talking to each other all day long. But now . . . total silence." With no warning, a tear rolls down my cheek.

"Oh, Lara!" says Kate, looking almost as upset as I feel. "And all this with Natalie too. Can Josh help?" She suddenly lights up. "Does he know her? He's so supportive—"

"I'm not with Josh anymore!" I give a sudden sob. "We split up!"

"You split *up*?" Kate gasps. "Oh God, I had no idea! You must be so stressed out!"

"It hasn't been my best week, to be honest." I wipe my eyes. "Or my best day. Or my best hour."

"You did the right thing, though, leaving Natalie." Kate lowers her voice fervently. "And you know what? Everyone will want to do business with you. They love you. And they hate Natalie."

"Thanks." I try to smile. The lift arrives, and Kate holds the doors open for me while I lug my box in and balance it on the rail.

"Is there anywhere you could look for your relation?" Kate surveys me anxiously. "Is there any way you could track her down?"

"Dunno." I shrug despondently. "I mean, she knows where I am, she knows how to get hold of me—"

"Maybe she wants you to make the first move, though?" Kate says tentatively. "You know, if she's feeling hurt, maybe she's waiting for *you* to get hold of *her*. It's just an idea. . . ." she calls as the doors begin to close. "I don't want to interfere. . . ."

The lift starts inching creakily downward, and I stare at the grotty carpet-wall, suddenly transfixed. Kate's a genius. She's got it in one. Sadie's so proud, she'd never make the first move. She'll be waiting somewhere; waiting for me to come and apologize and make up. But where?

After what seems like hours, the lift arrives at the ground floor, but I don't move, even though this box is starting to weigh my arms down. I've left my job. I have no idea what my future is. My life feels as if it's just been through the shredder, on *extra-fine, totally destroy* mode.

But I refuse to wallow. Or cry. Or drone on about it. I can almost hear Sadie's voice in my ear. *Darling, when things go wrong in life, you lift your chin, put on a ravishing smile, mix yourself a little cocktail. . . .*

"Tally-ho!" I say to my reflection in the grimy mirror, just as Sanjeev, who works on the ground floor, walks into the lift.

"Sorry?" he says.

I summon the most ravishing smile I can. (At least, I hope it's ravishing, as opposed to deranged-looking.) "I'm leaving. Bye, Sanjeev. Nice knowing you."

"Oh," he says in surprise. "Well, good luck. What are you doing next?"

I don't even pause to think.

"I'll be doing a bit of ghost-hunting," I say.

"Ghost-hunting?" He looks confused. "Is that like . . . headhunting?"

"Kind of." I smile again and head out of the lift.

TWENTY-ONE

Where is she? Where the bloody fuck *is* she?

This is getting beyond a joke. I've spent three days searching. I've been to every vintage shop I can think of and hissed "Sadie?" through the racks of clothes. I've knocked on the doors of all the flats in this building and called out "I'm looking for my friend Sadie!" loud enough for her to hear. I've been to the Flashlight Dance Club and peered among the dancers on the dance floor. But there was no sight of her.

Yesterday I went to Edna's house and made up a story about my cat being lost, which resulted in both of us going around the house, calling, "Sadie? Puss puss puss?" But there was no answer. Edna was very sweet, and she's promised to get in touch if she sees a stray tabby around the place. But that doesn't exactly help me.

Looking for lost ghosts is a total pain, it turns out. No one can see them. No one can hear them. You can't pin a photo to a tree with *Missing: Ghost*. You can't ask anyone, "Have you seen my friend the ghost, looks like a flapper, shrieky voice, ring any bells?"

Now I'm standing in the British Film Institute. There's an old black-and-white movie playing and I'm at the back, scanning the dark rows of heads. But it's no good. How am I supposed to see anything in this pitch blackness?

I start creeping down the aisle, crouching down, looking right and left along the dimly lit profiles.

"Sadie?" I hiss, as discreetly as I can.

"Shh!" says someone.

"Sadie, are you there?" I whisper as I reach the next row. "Sadie?"

"Shut up!"

Oh God. This will never work. There's only one thing for it. Plucking up all my courage, I stand up straight, take a deep breath, and call out at the top of my voice.

"Sadie! It's Lara here!"

"Shhhh!"

"If you're here, please let me know! I know you're upset and I'm sorry and I want to be friends and—"

"Shut up! Who is that? Be *quiet*!" There's a wave of head-turning and angry exclamations along the rows. But no answering call from Sadie.

"Excuse me?" An usher has come up. "I'm going to have to ask you to leave."

"OK. I'm sorry. I'll go." I follow the usher back up the aisle toward the exit, then suddenly turn around for one last shot. "Sadie? Sa-die!"

"Please be quiet!" exclaims the usher furiously. "This is a cinema!"

I'm desperately peering into the blackness, but there's no sight of her pale skinny arms, no beads clicking, no feathers bobbing among the heads.

The usher escorts me right out of the BFI, issuing me with stern warnings and lectures all the way, then leaves me alone on the sidewalk, feeling like a dog who's been kicked out of a house.

Deflated, I start trudging along, shrugging my jacket on. I'll have a coffee and regroup. Although, to be honest, I'm nearly out of ideas. As I head toward the river, there's the London Eye, towering into the sky, still making its way around jauntily, like nothing ever happened. Glumly, I turn my head away. I don't want to see the London Eye. I don't want to be reminded of that day. Trust me to have a painful, embarrassing moment on the most prominent sight in London. Why couldn't I have chosen a small out-of-the-way spot which I could then avoid?

I head into a café, order a double-strength cappuccino, and slump into a chair. It's starting to get me down, all this searching. The adrenaline that powered me to begin with is fading away. What if I never find her?

But I can't let myself think like that. I have to keep going. Partly because I refuse to admit defeat. Partly because the longer Sadie's gone, the more worried I am about her. And partly because, if I'm honest, I'm clinging on to this. While I'm searching for Sadie, it feels as if the rest of my life is on hold. I don't have to think about the where-does-my-career-go-now thing. Or the what-do-I-tell-my-parents thing. Or the how-could-I-have-been-so-stupid-about-Josh thing.

Or even the Ed thing. Which still upsets me whenever I let myself think about it. So . . . I just won't. I'll focus on Sadie, my Holy Grail. I know it's ridiculous, but I feel like if I can just track her down, everything else might fall into place.

Briskly, I unfold my list of *Find Sadie* ideas, but most of them are crossed out. The cinema was the most promising. The only other entries are *Try other dancing clubs?* and *Nursing home?*

I consider the nursing home for a moment as I sip my coffee. Sadie wouldn't go back there, surely. She hated it. She couldn't even face going in. Why would she be there now?

But it's worth a try.

I almost put on a disguise before I arrive at the Fairside Home, I'm so nervous. I mean, here I am, the girl who accused the staff of murder, pitching up on the doorstep.

Did they know it was me? I keep wondering in trepidation. Did the police tell them, "It was Lara Lington who besmirched your good name"? Because, if so, I'm dead meat. They'll surround me in a nurse mob and kick me with their white clumpy shoes. The old people will bash me with their walkers. And I'll deserve it.

But as Ginny opens the door, she shows no sign of knowing I'm the false-accusation-maker. Her face creases into a warm smile, and of course I feel guiltier than ever.

"Lara! What a surprise! Can I help you with that?"

I'm slightly laden down with cardboard cartons and a massive flower arrangement, which is starting to slip out of my arms.

"Oh, thanks," I say gratefully, handing her one. "It's got boxes of chocolate in it for you all."

"Goodness!"

"And these flowers are for the staff too. . . ." I follow her into the beeswax-scented hall and put the arrangement on the table. "I wanted to say thank you to everyone for looking after my great-aunt Sadie so well."

And not murdering her. The thought never crossed my mind.

"How lovely! Everybody will be very touched!"

"Well," I say awkwardly. "On behalf of the family, we're all very grateful and feel bad that we didn't visit my great-aunt . . . more often."

Ever.

As Ginny unpacks the chocolates, exclaiming in delight, I surreptitiously sidle toward the stairs and look up them.

"Sadie?" I hiss under my breath. "Are you here?" I scan the upstairs landing, but there's no sign.

"And what's this?" Ginny is looking at the other cardboard carton. "More chocolates?"

"No. Actually that's some CDs and DVDs. For the other residents."

I open it and pull out the CDs. *Charleston Tunes. The Best of Fred Astaire. 1920s–1940s—The Collection.*

"I just thought sometimes they might like to listen to the tunes they danced to when they were young," I say tentatively. "Especially the really old residents? It might cheer them up."

"Lara, how incredibly thoughtful! We'll put one on straightaway!" She heads into the dayroom, which is full of elderly people sitting in chairs and on sofas, with a daytime talk show blaring out of the television. I follow, looking all around the white heads for any sign of Sadie.

"Sadie?" I hiss, looking around. "Sadie, are you here?"

There's no reply. I should have known this was a ridiculous idea. I should leave.

"There we are!" Ginny straightens up from the CD player. "It should come on in a minute." She zaps the TV off and we both stand motionless, waiting for the music. And then it starts. A scratchy 1920s recording of a jaunty, jazzy tune. It's a bit faint, and after a moment Ginny increases the volume to full blast.

On the other side of the room, an old man sitting under a tartan blanket with a tank of oxygen next to him turns his head. I can see the light of recognition coming on in faces around the room. Somebody starts humming along in a quavery voice. One woman even begins tapping her hand, her whole self lit up with pleasure.

"They love it!" says Ginny to me. "What a good idea! Shame we've never thought of it before!"

I feel a sudden lump in my throat as I watch. They're all Sadie inside, aren't they? They're all in their twenties inside. All that white hair and wrinkled skin is just cladding. The old man with the oxygen tank was probably once a dashing heartthrob. That woman with distant rheumy eyes was once a mischievous young girl who played pranks on her friends. They were all young, with love affairs and friends and parties and an endless life ahead of them.

And as I'm standing there, the weirdest thing happens. It's as if I can *see* them, the way they were. I can see their young, vibrant selves, rising up out of their bodies, shaking off the oldness, starting to dance with each other to the music. They're all dancing the Charleston, kicking up their heels skittishly, their hair dark and strong, their limbs lithe again, and they're laughing, clutching each other's hands, throwing back their heads, reveling in it—

I blink. The vision has gone. I'm looking at a room full of motionless old people.

I glance sharply at Ginny. But she's just standing there, smiling pleasantly and humming along to the CD, out of tune.

The music is still playing away, echoing through the rest of the home. Sadie can't be here. She would have heard the music and come to see what was going on. The trail's gone cold yet again.

"I know what I meant to ask you!" Ginny suddenly turns to me. "Did you ever find that necklace of Sadie's? The one you were looking for?"

The necklace. Somehow, with Sadie gone, that all seems a million miles away now.

"No, I never did." I try to smile. "This girl in Paris was supposed to be sending it to me, but . . . I'm still hoping."

"Oh well, fingers crossed!" says Ginny.

"Fingers crossed." I nod. "Anyway, I'd better go. I just wanted to say hi."

"Well, it's lovely to see you. I'll show you out."

As we make our way through the hall, my head is still full of the vision I saw of all the old people dancing, young and happy again. I can't shake it.

"Ginny," I say on impulse as she opens the big front door. "You must have seen a lot of old people . . . passing on."

"Yes, I have," she says, matter-of-factly. "That's the peril of the job."

"Do you believe in . . ." I cough, feeling embarrassed. "In the afterlife? Do you believe in spirits coming back and that kind of thing?"

My mobile phone rings shrilly in my pocket before Ginny can answer, and she nods at it.

"Please, do get that."

I haul it out—and see Dad's number on the ID display.

Oh God. Why is Dad calling? He'll have heard about me leaving my job somehow. He'll be all stressy and asking what my plans are. And I can't even dodge the call, with Ginny watching.

"Hi, Dad," I say hurriedly. "I'm just in the middle of something, can I put you on hold a minute?" I jab at the phone and look up at Ginny again.

"So what you're asking is, do I believe in ghosts?" she says with a smile.

"Er . . . yes. I suppose I am."

"Truthfully? No, I don't. I think it's all in the head, Lara. I think it's what people *want* to believe. But I can understand what a comfort it must be to those who have lost loved ones."

"Right." I nod, digesting this. "Well . . . bye. And thanks."

The door closes and I'm halfway down the path before I remember Dad, still waiting patiently on the line. I grab my phone and press Talk.

"Hey, Dad! Sorry about that."

"Not at all, darling! I'm sorry to disturb you at work."

Work? So he *doesn't* know.

"Oh, right!" I say quickly, crossing my fingers. "Work. Yes. Absolutely. Work! Where else would I be?" I give a shrill laugh. "Although, as it happens, I'm not in the office right now. . . ."

"Ah. Well, this may be ideal timing, then." Dad hesitates. "I know this may sound odd. But I've got something I need to talk to you about and it's rather important. Could we meet?"

TWENTY-TWO

This is weird. I'm really not sure what's going on.

We've agreed to meet at Lingtons in Oxford Street, because it's central and we both know it. And also because whenever we arrange to meet up, Dad suggests Lingtons. He's unfailingly loyal to Uncle Bill, plus he has a Lingtons Gold VIP Card, which gets you free coffee and food, anywhere, anytime. (I don't. I only have Friends and Family, fifty percent off. Not that I'm complaining.)

As I arrive at the familiar chocolate-brown-and-white frontage, I'm quite apprehensive. Maybe Dad's got some really bad news to break. Like Mum's ill. Or *he's* ill.

And even if he hasn't, what am I going to say about my bust-up with Natalie? How will he react when he realizes his flake of a daughter has invested loads of money in a business only to walk out on it? Just the thought of seeing his face crumple in disappointment—yet again—makes me wince. He'll be devastated. I can't tell him. Not yet. Not until I have a plan of action.

I push open the door and inhale the familiar scent of coffee, cinnamon, and baking croissants. The plushy brown velvet chairs and gleaming wooden tables are the same as in every other Lingtons around the world.

Uncle Bill is beaming down from a massive poster behind the counter. Lingtons mugs, coffeepots, and grinders are arranged on a display shelf, all in the trademark chocolate brown and white. (No one else is allowed to use that shade of chocolate brown, apparently. It belongs to Uncle Bill.)

"Lara!" Dad waves from the head of the queue. "Just in time! What do you want?"

Oh. He looks quite cheerful. Maybe he's not ill.

"Hi." I give him a hug. "I'll have a caramel Lingtoncino and a tuna melt."

You can't ask for a cappuccino in Lingtons. It has to be a Lingtoncino.

Dad orders the coffees and food, then proffers his Gold VIP Card.

"What's this?" says the guy behind the till, looking dubious. "I've never seen one of these before."

"Try scanning it," says Dad politely.

"Wow." The guy's eyes widen as something bleeps on the till screen. He looks up at Dad, a bit awestruck. "That'll be . . . free."

"I always feel a bit guilty using that card," confesses Dad, as we collect our coffees and make our way to a table. "I'm doing poor Bill out of his rightful income."

Poor Bill? I feel a tiny wrench in my heart. Dad is so good. He thinks about everyone except himself.

"I think he can probably afford it." I glance wryly at Uncle Bill's face printed on my coffee mug.

"Probably." Dad smiles and glances at my jeans. "You're dressed very casually, Lara! Is this the new dress-down approach at your office?"

Shit. I never even thought about what I was wearing.

"Actually . . . I've been at a seminar," I hurriedly

improvise. "They requested casual clothes. It was role play, that kind of thing."

"Wonderful!" says Dad, so encouragingly that my cheeks flame with guilt. He unwraps a sugar and pours it into his coffee, then stirs it.

"Lara. I want to ask you a question."

"Absolutely." I nod earnestly.

"How is your business going? Really?"

Oh God. Of all the zillions of questions he could have asked.

"Well . . . you know. It's . . . it's good." My voice has shot up two notches. "All good! We've got some great clients, and we've recently done some work with Macrosant, and Natalie's back now—"

"Back?" echoes Dad with interest. "Has she been away?"

The thing about lying to your parents is, you have to keep track of which lies you've told.

"She popped away for a little bit." I force myself to smile. "No big deal."

"But you feel you made the right decision?" Dad looks as if this really matters to him. "You're enjoying it?"

"Yes," I say miserably. "I'm enjoying it."

"You feel the business has a good future?"

"Yes. Really good." I stare at the table. The thing about lying to your parents is, sometimes you really wish you hadn't. Sometimes you just want to dissolve into tears and wail, "Dad, it's all gone wrooooong! What shall I doooooo?"

"So . . . what did you want to talk to me about?" I say, to get off the subject.

"No matter." Dad gives me an affectionate look. "You've answered my question already. Your business is going well. It's fulfilling you. That's all I needed to hear."

"What do you mean?" I stare at him, confused. Dad shakes his head, smiling.

"There was an opportunity I wanted to talk to you about. But I don't want to disrupt your new business. I don't want to throw a spanner in the works. You're doing what you love and doing it well. You don't need a job offer."

Job offer?

My heart is suddenly beating fast. But I mustn't give away my excitement.

"Why don't you tell me about it, anyway?" I try to sound casual. "Just in case."

"Darling." Dad laughs. "You don't have to be polite."

"I'm not being polite," I say quickly. "I want to know."

"I wouldn't insult you. Darling, I'm so proud of what you've achieved," says Dad lovingly. "This would mean you'd have to give it all up. It wouldn't be worth it."

"Maybe it would! Just tell me!" Shit. I sound too desperate. I quickly adjust my expression to one of mild interest. "I mean, why not just fill me in? It can't do any harm."

"Well. Maybe you're right." Dad takes a sip of coffee, then looks at me directly. "Bill called me yesterday. Quite a surprise."

"Uncle Bill?" I say, taken aback.

"He said you'd been to see him at his house recently?"

"Oh." I clear my throat. "Yes, I did pop round for a chat. I was going to tell you. . . ."

Not.

"Well, he was impressed. What did he describe you as, now?" Dad gives that crooked little smile he gets when he's amused. "Oh, yes; 'tenacious.' Anyway, the upshot is . . . this."

He takes an envelope out of his pocket and slides it across the table. Disbelievingly, I open it. It's a letter on Lingtons headed paper. It's offering me a full-time job in the Lingtons human-resources department. It's offering me a salary of six figures.

I feel a bit faint. I look up, to see Dad's face glowing. Despite his cool demeanor, he's obviously really chuffed.

"Bill read it out over the phone before he biked it over. Quite something, isn't it?"

"I don't understand." I rub my brow, feeling confused. "Why did he send the letter to you? Why not straight to me?"

"Bill thought it would be a nice touch."

"Oh. Right."

"Smile, darling!" Dad laughs. "Whether you take it up or not, it's a huge compliment!"

"Right," I say again. But I can't smile. Something's wrong.

"It's a wonderful tribute to you," Dad is saying. "I mean, Bill doesn't owe us anything. He's done this purely through appreciation of your talent and the goodness of his heart."

OK, that's what's wrong: Dad's nailed it. I don't believe in Uncle Bill's appreciation of my talent. Nor in the goodness of his heart.

I drop my gaze down to the letter again, to the six-figure sum printed in black and white. Suspicions are creeping over me like spiders.

He's trying to buy me off.

OK, maybe that's putting it too strongly. But he's trying to get me on side. I've got under Uncle Bill's skin. Ever since I mentioned Sadie's necklace. I saw it in his eyes instantly: A shock. A wariness.

And now, out of the blue, a job offer.

"But I don't want this to sway you," Dad is saying. "Mum and I are both so proud of you, Lara, and if you want to carry on with your business, we'll be one hundred percent behind you. The choice is absolutely up to you. No pressure either way."

He's saying all the right things. But I can see the hope flickering in Dad's eyes, even if he's trying to hide it. He'd love me to have a stable job at a massive multinational firm. And not just any massive multinational firm, the *family* massive multinational firm.

And Uncle Bill knows that. Why else has he sent this letter via Dad? He's trying to manipulate both of us.

"I think Uncle Bill feels rather bad that he turned you down flat at the funeral," Dad continues. "He was very impressed at your persistence. And so am I! I had no idea you were planning to go and ask him again!"

"But I didn't even mention a job! I went to ask him about—" I stop hopelessly. I can't mention the necklace. I can't mention Sadie. This is all impossible.

"To be honest . . ." Dad lowers his voice, leaning across the little table. "I think Bill's been having a few problems with Diamanté. He regrets having brought her up so . . . lavishly. We had quite a heart-to-heart, and do you know what he said?" Dad's face suffuses with pleasure. "He said he sees you as the kind of self-starting young person who should be a role model for Diamanté."

He doesn't really think that! I want to cry out. *You*

don't know what's going on! He just wants me to stop chasing the necklace!

I bury my head in my hands despairingly. It's such a preposterous story. It all sounds so unlikely. And now the necklace is gone and Sadie's gone and I don't know what to think . . . or do. . . .

"Lara!" exclaims Dad. "Darling! Are you all right?"

"I'm . . . fine." I raise my head. "Sorry. It's all just a bit . . . overwhelming."

"This is my fault," says Dad, his smile fading. "I've thrown you. I should never have mentioned it, your business is doing so well—"

Oh God. I can't let this charade go on any longer.

"Dad." I cut him off. "The business isn't going well."

"I'm sorry?"

"It's not doing at all well. I lied. I didn't want to tell you." I'm crushing a sugar wrapper between my fingers, unable to meet his eye. "But the truth is . . . it's a disaster. Natalie left me in the lurch and we had a big row and I walked out on her. And . . . and I've split up with Josh again. For good." I swallow, forcing myself to say it. "I've finally realized how wrong I got everything with him. He didn't love me. I just really, really wanted him to."

"I see." Dad sounds a bit shocked. "Goodness." There's silence as he takes this all in. "Well . . . perhaps this offer has come at just the right time," he says at last.

"Maybe," I mumble, still staring at the table.

"What's wrong?" asks Dad gently. "Darling, why are you resisting this? You *wanted* to work for Uncle Bill."

"I know. But it's . . . complicated."

"Lara, can I give you a piece of advice?" Dad waits until I look up. "Don't be so hard on yourself. Relax. Maybe it's not as complicated as you think."

I look at Dad, at his straight face, his honest eyes. If I told him the truth, he wouldn't believe any of it. He'd think I'm a paranoid delusional or taking drugs. Or both.

"Did Uncle Bill mention a necklace at all?" I can't help saying.

"A necklace?" Dad looks puzzled. "No. What necklace?"

"I . . . it's nothing." I sigh. I take a sip of Lingtoncino and look up to see that Dad is watching me. He smiles, but I can tell he's troubled.

"Darling, you have a wonderful opportunity here." He gestures at the letter. "A chance for you to get your life back on track. Maybe you should just take it. Don't overthink it. Don't look for problems that don't exist. Just take your chance."

He doesn't understand. How could he? Sadie isn't a problem that doesn't exist. She *does* exist. She's real. She's a person, and she's my friend, and she needs me—

Then where is she? says a sharp voice in my head, like a knife thumping into a block. *If she exists, where is she?*

I start in shock. Where did that voice come from? I can't be doubting—I can't be thinking—

I feel a sudden feathery panic. Of course Sadie's real. Of course she is. Don't be ridiculous. Stop thinking like this.

But now Ginny's voice is running through my head again. *I think it's all in the head, Lara. It's what people want to believe.*

No. No way. I mean . . . *No.*

Feeling giddy, I take a gulp of Lingtoncino and look around the coffee shop, trying to anchor myself to reality. Lingtons is real. Dad is real. The job offer is real. And Sadie is real. I know she is. I mean, I saw her. I heard her. We talked together. We *danced* together, for God's sake.

And, anyway, how could I possibly have invented her? How would I have known anything about her? How would I have known about the necklace? I never even met her!

"Dad." I look at him abruptly. "We never visited Great-Aunt Sadie, did we? Except that time when I was a baby."

"Actually, that's not quite true." Dad shoots me a cautious look. "Mum and I were talking about it after the funeral. We remembered that we once took you to see her when you were six."

"Six." I swallow. "Was she . . . wearing a necklace?"

"She might have been." Dad shrugs.

I met Great-Aunt Sadie at the age of six. I could have seen the necklace. I could have remembered . . . without realizing that I remembered.

My thoughts are in free fall. I'm hollow and chilly inside. I feel as though everything's turning on its head. For the first time I'm seeing a new possible reality.

I could have made this whole story up in my head. It's what I wanted. I felt so guilty we never knew her that I invented her in my subconscious. I mean, when I first saw her that's what I thought she was. A hallucination.

"Lara?" Dad peers at me. "Are you OK, darling?"

I try to smile back at him, but I'm too preoccupied. There are two voices arguing in my head, right across each other. The first is crying out, *Sadie's real, you know she is! She's out there! She's your friend and she's hurt and you have to find her!* The second is calmly intoning, *She doesn't exist. She never did. You've wasted enough time. Get your life back.*

I'm breathing hard, trying to let my thoughts balance out, let my instincts settle. But I don't know what to think. I don't trust myself anymore. Maybe I really am crazy. . . .

"Dad, do you think I'm mad?" I blurt out in desperation. "Seriously. Should I see someone?"

Dad bursts into laughter. "No! Darling, of course not!" He puts his coffee cup down and leans forward. "I think your emotions run high and sometimes your imagination too. You get that from your mother. And sometimes you let them get the better of you. But you're not mad. No madder than Mum, anyway."

"Right." I swallow. "Right."

That's not much consolation, to be honest.

With fumbling fingers, I pick up Uncle Bill's letter and read it through again. If I look at it in a completely different way, there's nothing sinister. There's nothing wrong. He's just a rich guy trying to help out his niece. I could take the job. I'd be Lara Lington of Lingtons Coffee. I'd have a great future in front of me, salary, car, prospects. Everyone would be happy. Everything would be easy. My memories of Sadie would melt away. My life would feel normal.

It would be so, *so* easy.

"You haven't been home for a while," Dad says kindly. "Why not come and spend the weekend? Mum would love to see you."

"Yes," I say after a pause. "I'd like that. I haven't been back for ages."

"It'll restore your spirits." Dad gives me his endearing little crooked smile. "If your life's at a juncture and you need to think about things, there's nowhere better than home. However old you are."

" 'There's no place like home.' " I raise half a smile.

"Dorothy had a point. Now eat up." He gestures at my tuna melt. But I'm only half listening.

Home. The word has riveted me. I never thought of that.

She could have gone home.

Home to where her old house used to be. After all, it's the place of her earliest memories. It's where she had her big love affair. She refused ever to go back during her lifetime—but what if she's softened? What if she's right there, right now?

I'm stirring my Lingtoncino around and around obsessively. I know the sane, sensible move would be to blank out all thoughts about her. Accept Uncle Bill's job and buy a bottle of champagne to celebrate with Mum and Dad. I know this.

But . . . I just can't. Deep down, I can't believe she's not real. I've come so far, I've tried so hard to find her. I have to give it one last go.

And if she's not there I'll take the job and give up. For good.

"So." Dad wipes his mouth with a chocolate-brown napkin. "You look happier, darling." He jerks his head toward the letter. "Have you decided which way you want to go?"

"Yes." I nod firmly. "I need to go to St. Pancras station."

TWENTY-THREE

OK. This is the very, very last place I'm looking. This is her last chance. And I hope she appreciates the effort I've made.

It took me an hour from St. Pancras to St. Albans and another twenty minutes in a taxi to Archbury. And now here I am, standing in a little village square, with a pub and a bus stop and a weird modern-looking church. I suppose it would be quite picturesque if lorries didn't keep rumbling by at a million miles an hour and three teenage boys weren't having a brawl under the bus shelter. I thought it was supposed to be quiet in the country.

I edge away before one of the boys pulls out a gun or something and head over to the green. There's a board with a map of the village, and I quickly locate Archbury Close. That's what they turned Archbury House into after it burned down. If Sadie really has gone home, that's where she'll be.

After a few minutes' walk, I can see the gates ahead: wrought iron with *Archbury Close* written in swirly iron writing. There are six little red-brick houses, each with a tiny drive and garage. It's hard to imagine that once upon a time there was just one big beautiful house sitting in its own gardens.

Feeling conspicuous, I enter through a small side

gate and start to wander around, peering in through the windows, crunching on the little patches of gravel, and murmuring, "Sadie?"

I should have asked Sadie more about her home life. Maybe she had a favorite tree or something. Or some favorite corner of the garden, which is now someone's utility room.

There doesn't seem to be anyone around, so after a bit I raise my voice a little. "Sadie? Are you here? Sadie?"

"Excuse me!" I jump in shock as someone pokes me in the back. I turn to see a gray-haired woman in a flowered shirt, tan slacks, and rubbery-looking shoes peering at me suspiciously.

"I'm Sadie. What do you want?"

"Er . . ."

"Are you here about the drainage?" she adds.

"Um . . . no." I find my voice. "I was after a different Sadie."

"Which Sadie?" Her eyes narrow. "I'm the only Sadie in this close. Sadie Williams. Number four."

"Right. The Sadie I want is . . . actually . . . a dog," I improvise. "She ran away and I was looking for her. But I expect she's run off somewhere else. Sorry to bother you. . . ."

I start to walk off, but Sadie Williams grabs my shoulder with surprisingly strong fingers.

"You let a dog loose in the close? What did you want to do that for? We have a dog-free policy here, you know."

"Well . . . sorry. I didn't know. Anyway, I'm sure she's run off somewhere else—" I try to wriggle free.

"She's probably prowling around in the bushes, waiting to strike!" Sadie Williams is glowering furiously at me. "Dogs are dangerous beasts, you know. We've got kiddies living here. You people are irresponsible!"

"I'm not irresponsible!" I retort indignantly before I can stop myself. "She's a perfectly friendly dog. I wouldn't let a dangerous dog loose!"

"All dogs are savage."

"No, they're not!"

Lara, stop it. You're talking about an imaginary dog.

"And, anyway." I finally wrench myself free from the woman's grasp. "I'm sure she's not here, because she would have come when I called. She's very obedient. In fact . . . she's a prizewinner at Crufts," I add for good measure. "So I'd better go and find her."

Before Sadie Williams can grab me again, I start walking swiftly toward the gates. There's no way Sadie's here. She would have come out to watch the entertainment.

"What breed is she, then?" calls Sadie Williams tetchily. "What are we looking for?"

Oh God. I just can't help myself.

"Pit bull," I call back over my shoulder. "But, like I say, she's very friendly."

Without looking back, I hurry out of the gates, back along the road, and toward the village square. So much for that bright idea. What a waste of time.

I head to the bench on the green and sink down and take out a Twix, my gaze fixed ahead. Coming here was stupid. I'll eat this, then call a taxi and head back to London. I'm not even going to think about Sadie anymore. Let alone look for her. I've used up enough of my life already. I mean, why should I think about her? I bet she isn't thinking about me.

I finish my Twix and tell myself to dial the taxi number. It's time to go. It's time to put all this out of my mind and start on a new, sane, ghost-free life.

Except . . .

Oh *God*. I keep having flashes back to Sadie's stricken face on Waterloo Bridge. I keep hearing her voice. *You don't care about me. . . . No one cares*.

If I give up after only three days, am I proving her right?

I feel a sudden surge of frustration—at her, at myself, at the whole situation. Crossly, I scrunch up my Twix wrapper and chuck it into a bin. I mean, what am I supposed to do? I've looked and looked and looked. If she would just *come* when I called her . . . if she would just *listen* and not be so stubborn. . . .

Hang on. A new thought strikes me, out of the blue. I'm psychic, aren't I? Maybe I should *use* my psychic powers. I should summon her from the underworld. Or Harrods. Or wherever she is.

OK. This is my last try. I really, really mean it.

I stand up and approach the little pond on the green. I'm sure ponds are spiritual places. More spiritual than benches, anyway. There's a mossy stone fountain in the middle, and I can just picture Sadie dancing in it, splashing and shrieking, all those years and years ago, with some policeman trying to drag her out.

"Spirits." I extend my arms cautiously. There's a rippling in the water, but that could just be the wind.

I have no idea how to do this. I'll make it up as I go along.

"It is I, Lara," I intone in a low sepulchral voice. "Friend to the spirits. Or, at least, one spirit," I amend quickly.

I don't want Henry the Eighth appearing.

"I seek . . . Sadie Lancaster," I say momentously.

There's silence, except for a duck quacking on the pond. Maybe *seek* isn't powerful enough.

"I hereby summon Sadie Lancaster," I intone, more commandingly. "From the depths of the spirit world, I call her. I, Lara Lington, the psychic one. Hear my voice. Hear my summons. Spirits, I entreat thee." I start to wave my arms around impressively. "If thou knowest Sadie, send her to me. Send her to me now."

Nothing. Not a voice, not a glimpse, not a shadow.

"Fine!" I say, dropping my arms down. "*Don't* be summoned." I aim my words into the air, in case she's listening. "I don't care. I've got better things to do all day than stand here talking to the spirit world. So there."

I stump back to the bench, pick up my bag and grab my mobile phone. I dial the taxi firm that brought me here and ask for a taxi straightaway.

Enough is enough. I'm out of here.

The taxi guy tells me the cab driver will meet me in front of the church in ten minutes, so I head over to it, wondering if they might have a coffee machine in the lobby or anything. The whole place is locked up, though. I head back out and am just reaching for my phone again to check my texts, when something catches my eye. It's a sign on a gate: *The Old Vicarage.*

The Old Vicarage. I suppose that would have been where the vicar lived in the old days. Which means . . . it would have been where Stephen Nettleton lived. He was the son of the vicar, wasn't he?

Curiously, I peer over the wooden gate. It's a big old gray house with a gravel drive and some cars parked at the side. There are some people going in the front door, a group of about six. The family living here must be at home.

The garden's overgrown, with rhododendrons and trees and a path leading round the side of the house. I can just glimpse an old shed in the distance and wonder if that's where Stephen did his painting. I can just imagine Sadie creeping along that path, her shoes in one hand, her eyes shining in the moonlight.

It's quite an atmospheric place, with its old stone wall and long grass and shady patches in the garden. Nothing modern seems to have been introduced. It's still got the feel of history to it. I wonder—

No. Stop it. I'm giving up. I'm not looking anymore. But maybe—

No. She wouldn't be here. No way. She's got too much dignity. She said it herself—she'd never be a trailer. Never in a million years would she hang around an old boyfriend's house. Especially the old boyfriend who broke her heart and never even wrote to her. It's a stupid idea—

Already my hand is unlatching the gate.

This is the very, very, *very* last place I'm looking.

I crunch over the gravel, trying to think of an excuse to be here. Not a lost dog. Maybe I'm studying old vicarages? Maybe I'm an architecture student. Yes. I'm doing a thesis on "religious buildings and the families who live in them." At Birkbeck.

No. Harvard.

I approach the entrance and am raising my hand to ring the old bell when I notice the front door is unlatched. Maybe I can sidle in without anyone noticing. I cautiously push the door open and find myself in a hall with paneled walls and old parquet. To my surprise, a woman with a mousy bob and a Fair Isle jumper is standing behind a table covered with books and leaflets.

"Hello." She smiles as though she's not at all surprised to see me. "Are you here for the tour?"

The tour?

Even better! I can wander around and I don't even have to invent a story. I had no idea vicarages were charging for tours these days, but I suppose it makes sense.

"Er . . . yes, please. How much?"

"That'll be five pounds."

Five whole *pounds*? Just to see a vicarage? Bloody hell.

"Here's a guide." She hands me a leaflet, but I don't look at it. I'm not exactly interested in the house. I walk swiftly away from the woman, into a sitting room filled with old-fashioned sofas and rugs, and look all around.

"Sadie?" I hiss. "Sadie, are you here?"

"This would have been where Malory spent his evenings." The woman's voice makes me jump. I didn't realize she'd followed me.

"Oh, right." I have no idea what she's talking about. "Lovely. I'll just go through here. . . ." I head into an adjacent dining room, which looks like a stage set for a period drama. "Sadie?"

"This was the family dining room, of course. . . ."

For God's sake. People should be able to take tours of vicarages without being followed. I head over to the window and look out at the garden, where the family I saw before is wandering around. There's not a whisper of Sadie.

This was a stupid idea. She's not here. Why would she hang around the house of the guy who broke her heart, anyway? I turn around to leave and almost bump into the woman, standing behind me.

"I take it you're an admirer of his work?" She smiles.

Work? Whose work?

"Er . . . yes," I say hastily. "Of course. A great admirer. Very great." For the first time I glance down at the leaflet in my hand. The title reads: *Welcome to the House of Cecil Malory,* and underneath is a landscape painting of some cliffs.

Cecil Malory. He's a famous artist, isn't he? I mean, not like Picasso, but I've definitely heard of him. For the first time I feel a spark of interest.

"So is this where Cecil Malory once lived or something?" I ask.

"Of course." She looks taken aback by the question. "That's the reason for the house being restored as a museum. He lived here 'til 1927."

Until 1927? Now I'm genuinely interested. If he was living here in 1927, Sadie would have known him, surely. They would have hung out together.

"Was he a friend of the vicar's son? A guy called Stephen Nettleton?"

"Dear . . ." The woman eyes me, apparently perplexed at the question. "Surely you know that Stephen Nettleton *was* Cecil Malory. He never used his family name for his work."

Stephen was Cecil Malory?

Stephen . . . is *Cecil Malory?*

I'm too gobsmacked to speak.

"He later changed his name by deed poll," she continues. "As a protest against his parents, it's thought. After his move to France . . ."

I'm only half listening. My mind is in turmoil. Stephen became a famous painter. This makes no sense. Sadie never told me he was a famous painter. She would have boasted unbearably about it. Didn't she *know*?

"... and never reconciled before his tragically young death." The woman ends on a solemn note, then smiles. "Perhaps you would like to see the bedrooms?"

"No. I mean ... Sorry." I rub my forehead. "I'm a bit ... confused. Steph—I mean Cecil Malory—was a friend of my great-aunt, you see. She lived in this village. She knew him. But I don't think she ever realized he became famous."

"Ah." The woman nods knowledgeably. "Well, of course, he wasn't during his lifetime. It wasn't until long after his death that interest began in his paintings, first in France and then in his homeland. Since he died so young, there is of course a limited body of work, which is why his paintings became so prized and valuable. In the 1980s they shot up in value. That's when his name really became known widely."

The 1980s. Sadie had her stroke in 1981. She went into care. No one told her anything. She had no idea what was going on in the outside world.

I look up from my reverie to see the woman giving me another odd look. I bet she's wishing she could give me my five quid back and get rid of me.

"Er ... Sorry. I'm just thinking. Did he work in a shed in the garden?"

"Yes." The woman's face lights up. "If you're interested, we do sell a number of books on Malory. ..." She hurries out and returns holding a slim hardback. "Details about his early life are a little sketchy, as many village records were lost during the war, and by the time the research was being done, many of his contemporaries had passed away. However, there are some lovely accounts of his time in France, when his land-scape drawing really took off." She hands me the book, which has a painting of the sea on the front.

"Thanks." I take it from her and start flipping through. Almost at once I come across a black-and-white photograph of a man painting on a cliff, captioned *A rare image of Cecil Malory at work*. I can instantly see why he and Sadie would have been lovers. He's tall and dark and powerful-looking, with dark eyes and an ancient tattered shirt.

Bastard.

He probably thought he was a genius. He probably thought he was too good for a normal relationship. Even though he's long dead, I'm fighting an urge to yell at him. How could he treat Sadie so badly? How could he go off to France and forget about her?

"He was a towering talent." The woman is following my gaze. "His early death was one of the tragedies of the twentieth century."

"Yeah, well, maybe he deserved it." I give her a baleful look. "Maybe he should have been nicer to his girlfriend. Did you think of *that*?"

The woman looks totally confused. She opens her mouth and closes it again.

I flip on, past pictures of the sea and more cliffs and a line drawing of a hen . . . and then I suddenly freeze. An eye is looking out of the book at me. It's a blown-up detail from a painting. Just one eye, with long, long lashes and a teasing glint.

I know that eye.

"Excuse me." I can barely get the words out. "What's this?" I'm jabbing at the book. "Who's this? Where does this come from?"

"Dear . . ." I can see the woman trying to keep her

patience. "You *must* know that, surely. That's a detail from one of his most famous paintings. We have a version in the library if you'd like to have a look—"

"Yes." I'm already moving. "I would. Please. Show me."

She leads me down a creaking corridor, through to a dim, carpeted room. There are bookshelves on every wall, old leather chairs, and a large painting hanging over the fireplace.

"There we are," she says fondly. "Our pride and joy."

I can't reply. My throat's too tight. I stand motionless, clutching the book, just staring.

There she is. Gazing out of the ornate gilt frame, looking as though she owns the world, is Sadie.

I've never seen her as radiant as she looks in this picture. I've never seen her so relaxed. So happy. So beautiful. Her eyes are massive, dark, luminous with love.

She's reclining on a chaise, naked except for a gauze fabric draped over her shoulder and hips, which only partially obscures the view. Her shingled hair exposes the length of her elegant neck. She's wearing glittering earrings. And around her neck, falling down between her pale, gauzy breasts, twined around her fingers, tumbling in a shimmering pool of beads, is the dragonfly necklace.

I can suddenly hear her voice again in my ears. *I was happy when I wore it . . . I felt beautiful. Like a goddess.*

It all makes sense. This is why she wanted the necklace. This is what it means to her. At that time in her life, she was happy. Never mind what happened before or after. Never mind that her heart got broken. At that precise moment, everything was perfect.

"It's . . . amazing." I wipe a tear from my eye.

"Isn't she wonderful?" The woman gives me a pleased look. Obviously I'm finally behaving as proper art-lovers are supposed to. "The detail and brushwork are just exquisite. Every bead in the necklace is a tiny masterpiece. It's painted with such love." She regards the portrait affectionately. "And all the more special, of course, because it's the only one."

"What do you mean?" I say, confused. "Cecil Malory painted lots of pictures, didn't he?"

"Indeed. But he never painted any other portraits. He refused to, his whole life. He was asked plenty of times in France as his reputation grew locally, but he would always reply, *'J'ai peint celui que j'ai voulu peindre.'*" The woman leaves a poetic pause. "*I have painted the one I wanted to paint.*"

I stare at her, dumbfounded, my head sparking as I take this all in. He only ever painted Sadie? His whole life? He'd painted the one he wanted to paint?

"And in this bead . . ." The woman moves toward the painting with a knowing smile. "Right in this bead here there's a little surprise. A little secret, if you like." She beckons me forward. "Can you see it?"

I try to focus obediently on the bead. It just looks like a bead.

"It's almost impossible, except under a magnifying glass . . . here." She produces a piece of matte paper. Printed on it is the bead from the painting, enlarged massively. As I peer at it, to my astonishment I find I'm looking at a face. A man's face.

"Is that . . ." I look up.

"Malory." She nods in delight. "His own reflection in the necklace. He put himself into the painting. The most miniature hidden portrait. It was discovered only ten years ago. Like a little secret message."

"May I see?"

With shaking hands, I take the paper from her and stare at him. There he is. In the painting. In the necklace. Part of her. He never painted another portrait. He'd painted the one he wanted to paint.

He did love Sadie. He did. I know it.

I look up at the painting, tears blurring my eyes again. The woman's right. He painted her with love. You can see it in every brushstroke.

"It's . . . amazing." I swallow. "Are there . . . um . . . any more books about him?" I'm desperate to get this woman out of the room. I wait until her footsteps have disappeared down the passage, then tilt my head up.

"Sadie!" I call desperately. "Sadie, can you hear me? I've found the painting! It's beautiful. *You're* beautiful. You're in a museum! And you know what? Stephen didn't paint anyone but you. Never, his whole life. You were the only one. He put himself in your necklace. He loved you. Sadie, I know he loved you. I *so* wish you could see this—"

I break off breathlessly, but the room is silent and dead. She's not hearing me, wherever she is. As I hear footsteps, I quickly turn and plaster on a smile. The woman hands me a pile of books.

"This is all our available stock. Are you an art-history student or simply interested in Malory?"

"I'm just interested in this one painting," I say frankly. "And I was wondering. Do you . . . or the experts . . . have any idea who this is? What's the painting called?"

"It's called *Girl with a Necklace*. And, of course,

many people are interested in the identity of the sitter." The woman launches into what's clearly a well-rehearsed speech. "Some research has been done, but unfortunately, to date, no one has been able to identify her beyond what is believed to be her first name." She pauses, then adds fondly, "Mabel."

"*Mabel?*" I stare at her in horror. "She wasn't called Mabel!"

"Dear!" The woman gives me a reproving smile. "I know to modern ears it may seem a little quaint, but, believe me, Mabel was a common name of the time. And on the back of the painting there's an inscription. Malory himself wrote, *My Mabel.*"

For God's sake.

"It was a nickname! It was their private *joke*! Her name was Sadie, OK? Sadie Lancaster. I'll write it down. And I know it was her because . . ." I hesitate momentously. "This is my great-aunt."

I'm expecting a gasp or something, but the woman just gives me a dubious look.

"Goodness, dear. That's quite a claim. What makes you think she's your great-aunt?"

"I don't think she is, I *know* she is. She lived here in Archbury. She knew Steph—I mean Cecil Malory. They were lovers. It's definitely her."

"Do you have any evidence? Do you have a photograph of her in her youth? Any archives?"

"Well . . . no," I say, a little frustrated. "But I know it's her, beyond a doubt. And I'll prove it somehow. And you should put a sign up saying her name and *stop* calling her Mabel—" I pause mid-track as something new and startling occurs to me. "Hang on a minute. This is Sadie's painting! He gave it to her! She lost it for years, but it's still hers. Or, I suppose, Dad's and Uncle Bill's now. How did you get it? What's it doing here?"

"I'm sorry?" The woman sounds bewildered, and I give an impatient sigh.

"This painting belonged to my great-aunt. But it was lost, years and years ago. The family house burned down and she thought the painting was destroyed. So how did it end up hanging on this wall?" I can't help sounding accusing, and she recoils.

"I'm afraid I have no idea. I've worked here for ten years and it's certainly been here all that time."

"Right." I assume a businesslike air. "Well, can I please talk to the director of this museum or whoever's in charge of this painting? At once?"

The woman gives me a wary, puzzled look. "Dear . . . you do realize this is only a reproduction, don't you?"

"What?" I feel wrong-footed. "What do you mean?"

"The original is four times the size and, dare I say it, even more splendid."

"But . . ." I look at the painting in confusion. It looks pretty real to me. "So, where's the original? Locked up in a safe or something?"

"No, dear," she says patiently. "It's hanging in the London Portrait Gallery."

TWENTY-FOUR

It's massive. It's radiant. It's a million times better than the one in the house.

I've been sitting in front of Sadie's portrait in the London Portrait Gallery for about two hours. I can't drag myself away. She's gazing out at the gallery, her brow clear, her eyes a velvety dark green, like the most beautiful goddess you've ever seen. Cecil Malory's use of light on her skin is unmatched in its artistry. I know, because I heard an art teacher telling her class half an hour ago. Then they all went up to see if they could spot the little miniature portrait in the necklace.

I must have seen a hundred people coming and looking at her. Sighing with pleasure. Smiling at one another. Or just sitting down and gazing.

"Isn't she lovely?" A dark-haired woman in a mac smiles at me and sits down beside me on the bench. "This is my favorite portrait in the whole gallery."

"Me too." I nod.

"I wonder what she's thinking?" the woman muses.

"I think she's in love." I look yet again at Sadie's glowing eyes, the flush in her cheek. "And I think she's really, really happy."

"You're probably right."

For a moment we're both quiet, just drinking her in.

"She does you good, doesn't she?" says the woman.

"I often come and look at her in my lunchtimes. Just to cheer myself up. I've got a poster of her at home too. My daughter bought it for me. But you can't beat the real thing, can you?"

There's a sudden lump in my throat, but I manage to smile back. "No. You can't beat the real thing."

As I'm speaking, a Japanese family approaches the painting. I can see the mother pointing out the necklace to her daughter. They both sigh happily, then adopt identical poses, arms folded, heads tilted, and just gaze at her.

Sadie's adored by all these people. Tens, hundreds, thousands. And she has no idea.

I've called for her until I'm hoarse, over and over, out the window, up and down the street. But she doesn't hear. Or she doesn't want to hear. Abruptly, I stand up and consult my watch; I have to go, anyway. It's five o'clock. Time for my appointment with Malcolm Gledhill, the collections manager.

I make my way back to the foyer, give my name to the receptionist, and wait among a swarming crowd of French schoolchildren until a voice from behind says, "Miss Lington?" I turn to see a man in a purple shirt, with chestnut beard and tufts of hair growing out of his ears, beaming at me with twinkly eyes. He looks like Father Christmas before he grew old, and I can't help warming to him instantly.

"Hi. Yes, I'm Lara Lington."

"Malcolm Gledhill. Come this way." He leads me through a hidden door behind the reception desk, up some stairs, and into a corner office overlooking the Thames. Postcards and reproductions of paintings are everywhere, stuck up on the walls and propped against books and adorning his massive computer.

"So." He hands me a cup of tea and sits down. "You're here to see me about *Girl with a Necklace*?" He eyes me warily. "I wasn't sure from your message quite what the issue was. But it's clearly . . . pressing?"

OK, perhaps my message was a bit extreme. I didn't want to have to tell the whole story to some nameless receptionist, so I simply said it was to do with *Girl with a Necklace* and a matter of life and death, state urgency, and national security.

Well. In the art world, it probably is all those things.

"It is quite pressing." I nod. "And the first thing I want to say is, she wasn't just 'a girl.' She was my great-aunt. Look."

I reach into my bag and produce my photograph of Sadie at the nursing home, wearing the necklace.

"Look at the necklace," I add, as I hand it over.

I knew I liked this Malcolm Gledhill guy. He reacts in a totally satisfactory manner. His eyes bulge. His cheeks turn pink with excitement. He looks up sharply at me, then back at the photo. He peers at the necklace around Sadie's neck. Then he gives a harrumphing cough as though he's concerned he's given too much away.

"Are you saying," he says at last, "that this lady here is the 'Mabel' in the painting?"

I really have to knock this Mabel thing on the head.

"She wasn't called Mabel. She hated the name Mabel. She was called Sadie. Sadie Lancaster. She lived in Archbury and she was Stephen Nettleton's lover. She was the reason he was sent to France."

There's silence, apart from Malcolm Gledhill breathing out, his cheeks two deflating balloons of air.

"Do you have any evidence that this is the case?" he says at last. "Any documents? Any old photographs?"

"She's wearing the necklace, isn't she?" I feel a flicker of frustration. "She kept it all her life. How much more evidence do you need?"

"Does the necklace still exist?" His eyes bulge again. "Do you have it? Is she still alive?" As this new thought occurs to him, his eyes nearly pop out of his head. "Because that would really be—"

"She's just died, I'm afraid." I cut him off before he can get too excited. "And I don't have the necklace. But I'm trying to track it down."

"Well." Malcolm Gledhill takes out a paisley handkerchief and wipes his perspiring brow. "Clearly, in a case like this, much careful inquiry and research is required before we can come to any definitive conclusion—"

"It's her," I say firmly.

"So I'll refer you, if I may, to our research team. They will look at your claim very carefully, study all the evidence available."

He needs to play the official game properly. I can understand that.

"I'd love to talk to them," I say politely. "And I know they'll agree with me. It's her."

I suddenly spot a postcard of *Girl with a Necklace* stuck on his computer with Blu-Tack. I take it down and lay it beside the photo of Sadie from the nursing home. For a moment we both look silently at the two images. Two radiant, proud eyes in one picture; two hooded, ancient eyes in the other. And the necklace glimmering, a constant talisman, linking the two.

"When did your great-aunt die?" says Malcolm Gledhill at last, his voice soft.

"A few weeks ago. But she lived in a nursing home since the 1980s, and she didn't know much about the outside world. She never knew Stephen Nettleton became famous. She never knew that *she* was famous. She thought she was a nobody. And that's why I want the world to know her name."

Malcolm Gledhill nods. "Well, if the research team comes to the conclusion that she was the sitter in the portrait . . . then, believe me, the world *will* know her name. Our marketing team did some research recently, and it turns out *Girl with a Necklace* is the most popular portrait in the gallery. They want to expand her profile. We consider her an exceedingly valuable asset."

"Really?" I flush with pride. "She'd have loved to know that."

"May I call in a colleague to see this photograph?" His eyes brighten. "He has a special interest in Malory, and I know he will be extremely interested in your claim—"

"Wait." I hold up a hand. "Before you call in anyone else, there's another issue I need to talk to you about. In private. I want to know how you got the painting in the first place. It belonged to Sadie. It was hers. How did you get it?"

Malcolm Gledhill stiffens very slightly.

"I thought this matter might arise at some stage," he says. "Following your phone call, I went and retrieved the file, and I've looked up the details of the acquisition." He opens a file, which has been sitting on the desk all this while, and unfolds an old piece of paper. "The painting was sold to us in the 1980s."

Sold? How could it have been sold?

"But it was lost after a fire. No one knew where it was. Who on earth sold it to you?"

"I'm afraid . . ." Malcolm Gledhill pauses. "I'm

afraid the vendor asked at the time that all details of the acquisition should be kept confidential."

"Confidential?" I stare at him in outrage. "But the painting was Sadie's. Stephen gave it to her. Whoever got hold of it didn't have the right to sell it. You should check these things!"

"We do check these things," says Malcolm Gledhill, a little defensively. "All the provenance was deemed to be correct at the time. The gallery went to all reasonable lengths to determine that the painting was the vendor's to sell. Indeed, a letter was signed in which the vendor made all the correct assurances. I have it here."

His eyes keep dropping down to the paper in his hand. He must be looking at the name of whoever sold it. This is totally maddening.

"Well, whatever that person said to you, they were *lying*." I glare at him. "And you know what? I'm a taxpayer, and I fund you lot. In fact, in a way, I *own* you lot. And I hereby demand to know who sold it to you. At once."

"I'm afraid you're mistaken," says Malcolm Gledhill mildly. "We are not a publicly owned gallery, and you don't own us. Believe me, I would like to clear this matter up as much as you would. But I am bound by our confidentiality agreement. I'm afraid my hands are tied."

"What if I come back with police and lawyers?" I plant my hands on my hips. "What if I report the painting as stolen goods and force you to reveal the name?"

Malcolm Gledhill raises his tufty eyebrows high. "Obviously, if there was a police inquiry, we would comply fully."

"Well, fine. There will be. I have friends in the

police, you know," I add darkly. "DI James. He'll be very interested to hear about all this. That painting belonged to Sadie, and now it belongs to my dad and his brother. And we're not just going to sit around and do nothing."

I feel all fired up. I'm going to get to the bottom of this. Paintings don't just turn up out of the blue.

"I can understand your concerns." Malcolm Gledhill hesitates. "Believe me, the gallery takes the issue of rightful ownership extremely seriously."

He won't meet my eye. His gaze keeps flicking to the paper in his hand. The name's on there. I know it. I could hurl myself across the desk, wrestle him to the ground, and—

No.

"Well, thank you for your time," I say formally. "I'll be in touch again."

"Of course." Malcolm Gledhill is closing up the file again. "Before you go, if I might just call in my colleague Jeremy Mustoe? I'm sure he'd be very interested to meet you and to see the photograph of your great-aunt. . . ."

A few moments later, a skinny man with fraying cuffs and a prominent Adam's apple is in the room, poring over the photograph of Sadie and saying, "Remarkable," over and over under his breath.

"It's been extremely hard to discover anything about this painting," Jeremy Mustoe says, looking up at last. "There are so few contemporary records or photographs, and by the time researchers returned to the village, it was generations later and no one could remember anything. And, of course, it had been assumed that the sitter was indeed named Mabel." He wrinkles his brow. "I think one thesis was published in

the early 1990s suggesting that a servant of the Nettleton house was Malory's sitter, and that his parents disapproved of their liaison for class reasons, which led to
him being sent to France. . . ."

I want to laugh. Someone basically made up a completely wrong story and called it "research"?

"There was a Mabel," I explain patiently. "But she
wasn't the sitter. Stephen called Sadie 'Mabel' to wind
her up. They were lovers," I add. "That's why he was
sent to France."

"Indeed." Jeremy Mustoe looks up and focuses on
me with renewed interest. "So . . . would your great-
aunt also be the 'Mabel' in the letters?"

"The letters!" exclaims Malcolm Gledhill. "Of
course! I'd forgotten about those. It's such a long time
since I've looked at them—"

"Letters?" I look from face to face. "What letters?"

"We have in our archive a bundle of old letters written by Malory," explains Jeremy Mustoe. "One of the
very few sets of documents salvaged after his death. It's
not clear if all of them were sent, but one has clearly
been posted and returned. Unfortunately the address
was scribbled out in blue-black ink, and despite the
very best modern technology, we've been unable to—"

"I'm sorry to interrupt." I cut him off, trying to hide
my agitation. "But . . . could I see them?"

An hour later I walk out of the gallery, my mind
whirling. When I close my eyes all I can see is that
faded, loopy script on tiny sheets of writing paper.

I didn't read all his letters. They felt too private, and
I only had a few minutes to look at them, anyway. But
I read enough to know. He loved her. Even after he'd

gone to France. Even after he heard that she'd got married to someone else.

Sadie spent all her life waiting for the answer to a question. And now I know he did too. And even though the affair happened more than eighty years ago, even though Stephen is dead and Sadie is dead and there's nothing anyone can do about it, I'm still seething with misery as I stride along the pavement. It was all so unfair. It was all so wrong. They should have been together. Someone obviously intercepted his letters before they got to Sadie. Probably those evil Victorian parents of hers.

So she sat there with no idea of the truth. Thinking she'd been used. Too proud to go after him and find out for herself. She accepted the proposal of Waistcoat Guy as some stupid gesture of revenge. Maybe she was hoping Stephen would appear at the church. Even as she was getting ready for the wedding, she must have hoped, surely. And he let her down.

I can't bear it. I want to go back in time and put it all right. If only Sadie hadn't married Waistcoat Guy. If only Stephen hadn't gone to France. If only her parents had never caught them. If only—

No. Stop with the if-onlys. There's no point. He's long dead. She's dead. The story's over.

There's a stream of people walking past me on their way to Waterloo station, but I don't feel ready to go back to my little flat yet. I need some fresh air. I need a bit of perspective. I push my way past a group of tourists and head up to Waterloo Bridge. The last time I was here, the clouds were low and gray. Sadie was standing on the barricade. I was yelling desperately into the wind.

But this evening is warm and balmy. The Thames is blue, with only the tiniest white ruffles. A pleasure boat is cruising slowly along, and a couple of people are waving up at the London Eye.

I stop at the same place as before and gaze out toward Big Ben. But I'm not seeing anything properly. My mind feels lodged in the past. I keep seeing Stephen's dated, scratchy writing. I keep hearing his old-fashioned phrases. I keep picturing him, sitting on a clifftop in France, writing to Sadie. I even keep hearing snatches of Charleston music, as though a twenties band is playing. . . .

Hang on a minute.

A twenties band *is* playing.

I suddenly focus on the scene below me. A few hundred meters away in Jubilee Gardens, people are gathered on the big square of grass. A bandstand has been put up. A band is playing a jazzy dance number. People are dancing. Of course. It's the jazz festival. The one they were leafleting about when I came here with Ed. The one I still have a ticket for, folded up in my purse.

For a moment I just stand there on the bridge, watching the scene. The band is playing the Charleston. Girls in twenties costumes are dancing on the stage, fringes and beads flashing back and forth. I can see bright eyes and twinkling feet and bobbing feathers. And suddenly, among the crowd, I see . . . I think I glimpse . . .

No.

For a moment I'm transfixed. Then, without allowing my brain to think what it's trying to think, without letting a single hope flicker to life, I turn and start walking calmly along the bridge, down the steps. Somehow I force myself not to rush or run. I just move steadily toward the sound of the music, breathing hard, my hands clenched tight.

There's a banner strung over the bandstand, silver balloons are gathered in bunches, and a trumpeter in a shiny waistcoat is on his feet, playing a tricky solo. All around, people are gathered, watching the Charleston dancers onstage, and on a wooden dance-floor laid on the grass, people are dancing themselves—some in jeans and some in so-called 1920s costumes. Everyone's smiling admiringly and pointing at the costumes, but to me, they look rubbish. Even the flapper girls onstage. They're just imitations, with fake feathers and plastic pearls and modern shoes and twenty-first-century makeup. They look nothing like the real thing. Nothing like a proper twenties girl. Nothing like—

And I stop dead, my heart in my throat. I was right.

She's up by the bandstand, dancing her heart out. She's in a pale yellow dress, with a matching band around her dark hair. She looks more wraithlike than ever. Her head is thrown back and her eyes are closed in concentration, and she looks as though she's shutting out the world. People are dancing through her, trampling on her feet and elbowing her, but she doesn't even seem to notice.

God knows what she's been doing, these last few days.

As I watch, she disappears behind two laughing girls in denim jackets, and I feel a dart of panic. I can't lose her again. Not after all this.

"Sadie!" I start pushing my way through the crowd. "Sa-die! It's me, Lara!"

I catch a glimpse of her again, her eyes opened wide. She's looking all around. She heard me.

"Sadie! Over here!" I'm waving frantically, and a few people turn to see who I'm yelling at.

Suddenly she sees me, and her whole body goes motionless. Her expression is unfathomable and, as I near her, I feel a sudden apprehension. Somehow my perspective on Sadie has changed over the past few days. She's not just a girl. She's not even just my guardian angel, if she ever was that. She's a part of art history. She's famous. And she doesn't even know it.

"Sadie—" I break off helplessly. I don't know where to start. "I'm so sorry. I've been looking everywhere for you—"

"Well, you can't have looked very hard!" She's busy scanning the band and appears totally unmoved by my appearance. In spite of myself, I feel a familiar indignation rising.

"I did! I've spent days searching, if you want to know! Calling, shouting, looking—you have no idea what I went through!"

"Actually, I do. I saw you being thrown out of that cinema." She smirks. "It was very funny."

"You were *there*?" I stare at her. "So how come you didn't answer?"

"I was still upset." Her chin tightens proudly. "I didn't see why I should."

Typical. I should have realized she would have borne a grudge against me for days.

"Well, I went all over the place. And I had quite a voyage of discovery. I need to tell you about it." I'm trying to find a way of edging tactfully into the subject of Archbury and Stephen and the painting, but all of a sudden Sadie lifts her head and says, with a tiny grudging shrug:

"I missed you."

I'm so taken aback I'm thrown off my stride. I feel a sudden prickle in my nose and rub it awkwardly.

"Well . . . me too. I missed you too." Instinctively, I

put my arms out to give her a hug—then realize how pointless that is and drop my hands down again. "Sadie, listen. There's something I've got to tell you."

"And there's something I've got to tell you!" she cuts in with satisfaction. "I knew you'd come tonight. I was waiting for you."

Honestly. She really does think she's an all-powerful deity.

"You can't have known," I say patiently. "Even *I* didn't know I was going to come. I just happened to be in the area, I heard the music, I wandered over—"

"I did know," she insists. "And if you didn't appear, I was going to find you and make you come. And do you know the reason?" Her eyes have started to glitter, and she's peering this way and that through the crowd.

"Sadie." I try to fix her eyes. "Please. Listen to me. I've got something really, really important to tell you. We need to go somewhere quiet, you need to listen, it'll be a shock—"

"Well, I've got something really important to show you!" She's not even listening to me properly. "There!" She suddenly points in triumph. "Over there! Look!"

I follow her gaze, squinting as I try to make out what she's talking about . . . and my heart drops in dismay.

Ed.

He's standing at the side of the dance floor. He's holding a plastic glass of something, watching the band, and occasionally stumping from side to side to the music as though out of a sense of duty. He looks so unenthusiastic, I would almost want to laugh, if I didn't also want to shrivel up and hide in a little box somewhere.

"Sadie . . ." I clutch my head. "What have you done?"

"Go and talk to him!" She motions me briskly.

"No," I say in horror. "Don't be stupid!"

"Go on!"

"I can't talk to him. He hates me." I quickly swivel away and hide behind a group of dancers before Ed can catch sight of me. Just seeing him is bringing back all kinds of memories I would rather forget. "Why did you make him come here, anyway?" I mutter at Sadie. "What exactly are you trying to achieve?"

"I felt guilty." She gives me an accusing gaze, as though this is all my fault. "I don't like feeling guilty. So I decided to do something about it."

"You went and yelled at him." I shake my head in disbelief.

This is all I need. She obviously frog-marched him here under total duress. He was probably planning a nice quiet evening in and now he finds himself standing at some stupid jazz festival, amid a load of dancing couples, all on his own. He's probably having the worst evening of his life. And now she expects me to *talk* to him.

"I thought he was yours, anyway. I thought I ruined everything. What happened to all that?"

Sadie flinches slightly but holds her head high. I can see her looking at Ed through the crowd. There's a brief, soft longing in her eyes, then she turns away.

"Not my type after all," she says crisply. "He's far too . . . alive. And so are you. So you're well matched. Off you go! Ask him to dance." She tries to push me toward Ed again.

"Sadie." I shake my head. "I really appreciate you making the effort. But I can't just make things up with him out of the blue. It's not the right place, it's not the right time. Now, can we go somewhere and talk?"

"Of course it's the right time and place!" retorts Sadie, affronted. "That's why he's here! That's why you're here!"

"It's not why I'm here!" I'm starting to lose it. I wish I could take her by the shoulders and shake her. "Sadie, don't you understand? I need to talk to you! There are things I need to tell you! And you have to focus. You have to listen. Forget about Ed and me. This is about you! And Stephen! And your past! I've found out what happened! I've found the painting!"

Too late, I realize that the jazz band has come to a halt. Everyone's stopped dancing and a guy up onstage is making a speech. At least, he's trying to make a speech, but the entire crowd has turned to look at me, yelling like a lunatic into empty space.

"Sorry." I swallow. "I . . . didn't mean to interrupt. Please, carry on." Hardly daring to, I swivel my gaze to where Ed is standing, hoping desperately that he's already got bored and gone home. But no such luck. He's standing there staring at me, along with everyone else.

I want to shrivel up even more. My skin starts to prickle with mortification as he makes his way across the dance floor toward me. He isn't smiling. Did he hear me mentioning his name?

"You found the painting?" Sadie's voice is only a whisper and her eyes seem suddenly hollow as she stares at me. "You found Stephen's painting?"

"Yes," I mutter, a hand in front of my mouth. "You have to see it, it's amazing—"

"Lara." Ed has reached me. At the sight of him I have a flashback to the London Eye, and all sorts of crawling feelings come over me again.

"Oh. Um, hi," I manage, my chest tight.

"Where is it?" Sadie tries to tug at my arm. "Where is it?"

Ed looks as uncomfortable as I feel. His hands are jammed in his pockets, and his frown is back in place as deep as it ever was. "So you came." He meets my eyes briefly, then looks away. "I wasn't sure if you would."

"Um . . . well . . ." I clear my throat. "I just thought . . . you know . . ."

I'm trying to be coherent, but it's almost impossible with Sadie bobbing around to get my attention.

"What did you find out?" Now she's right in front of me, her voice high-pitched and urgent. It's as though she's suddenly woken up and realized I might have something of genuine importance for her. "Tell me!"

"I will tell you. Just wait." I'm trying to talk subtly, out of the side of my mouth, but Ed is too sharp. He picks up everything.

"Tell me what?" he says, his eyes scanning my face intently.

"Um . . ."

"Tell me!" demands Sadie.

OK. I cannot cope with this. Both Sadie and Ed are standing in front of me, with expectant faces. My eyes are darting madly from one to the other. Any minute Ed is going to decide I really am a lunatic, and go.

"Lara?" Ed takes a step toward me. "Are you OK?"

"Yes. I mean, no. I mean . . ." I take a breath. "I wanted to tell you that I'm sorry I left our date in such a rush. I'm sorry you thought I was setting you up for a job. But I wasn't. I really wasn't. And I really hope you believe me—"

"Stop talking to him!" interrupts Sadie in a burst of

fury, but I don't move a muscle. Ed's dark, serious gaze is on mine and I can't tear my eyes away.

"I do believe you," he says. "And I need to apologize too. I overreacted. I didn't give you a chance. Afterward I regretted it. I realized I'd thrown away something . . . a friendship . . . that was . . ."

"What?" I manage.

"Good." There's a questioning look in his face. "I think we had something good. Didn't we?"

This is the moment to nod and say yes. But I can't leave it at that. I don't want a good friendship. I want that feeling back, when he wrapped his arms around me and kissed me. I want him. That's the truth.

"You want me just to be your . . . friend?" I force myself to say the words, and instantly I can see something change in Ed's face.

"Stop it! Talk to me!" Sadie whirls over to Ed and screeches in his ear. "*Stop talking to Lara! Go away!*" For a moment he gets that distant look in his eye, and I can tell he's heard her. But he doesn't move. His eyes just crinkle into a warm, tender smile.

"You want the truth? I think you're my guardian angel."

"What?" I try to laugh, but it doesn't quite come out right.

"Do you know what it's like to have someone crash into your life with no warning?" Ed shakes his head reminiscently. "When you landed in my office, I was, like, *Who the fuck is this?* But you shook me up. You brought me back to life at a time when I was in limbo. You were just what I needed." He hesitates, then adds, "You're just what I need." His voice is lower and darker; there's something in his look which is making me tingle all over.

"Well, I need you too." My voice is constricted. "So we're even."

"No, you don't need me." He smiles ruefully. "You're doing just fine."

"OK." I hesitate. "Maybe I don't need you. But . . . I want you."

For a moment neither of us speaks. His eyes are locked on mine. My heart is thumping so hard, I'm sure he can hear it.

"*Go away, Ed!*" Sadie suddenly screeches in Ed's ear. "*Do this later!*"

I can see Ed flinch at the sound of her, and I feel a familiar foreboding. If Sadie messes this up for me, I will, I will . . .

"*Leave!*" Sadie is shrieking incessantly at him. "*Tell her you'll call later! Go away! Go home!*"

I'm aching with anger at her. *Stop!* I want to yell. *Leave him alone!* But I'm powerless. I just have to watch the light come on in Ed's eyes as he hears her and registers what she's saying. It's like Josh all over again. She's ruined everything again.

"You know, sometimes you hear a voice in your head," Ed says, as though the thought has just occurred to him. "Like . . . an instinct."

"I know you do," I say miserably. "You hear a voice and it has a message and it's telling you to go away. I understand."

"It's telling me the opposite." Ed moves forward and firmly takes hold of my shoulders. "It's telling me not to let you go. It's telling me you're the best thing that's happened to me and I better not fuck this one up."

And before I can even take a breath, he leans down and kisses me. His arms wrap around me, strong and secure and resolute.

I'm in a state of total disbelief. He's not walking away. He's not listening to Sadie. Whatever voice is in his head . . . it's not hers.

At last he draws away and smiles down at me, pushing a strand of hair gently off my face. I smile back, breathless, resisting the temptation to pull him down straightaway for another snog.

"Would you like to dance, twenties girl?" he says.

I want to dance. I want to do more than dance. I want to spend all evening and all night with him.

I shoot a surreptitious glance at Sadie. She's moved away a few feet and is studying her shoes, her shoulders hunched over, her hands twisted together in a complicated knot. She looks up and shrugs, with a tiny sad smile of defeat.

"Dance with him," she says. "It's all right. I'll wait."

She's waited years and years and years to find out the truth about Stephen. And now she's willing to wait even longer, just so I can dance with Ed.

There's a tugging in my heart. If I could, I'd throw my arms around her.

"No." I shake my head firmly. "It's your turn. Ed . . ." I turn to him with a deep breath. "I have to tell you about my great-aunt. She died recently."

"Oh. OK. Sure. I didn't know." He looks puzzled. "You want to talk over dinner?"

"No. I need to talk about it right now." I drag him to the edge of the dance floor, away from the band. "It's really important. Her name was Sadie, and she was in love with this guy Stephen in the 1920s. And she thought he was a bastard who used her and forgot about her. But he loved her. I know he did. Even after he went to France, he loved her."

My words are spilling out in an urgent stream. I'm looking directly at Sadie. I have to get my message across. She has to believe me.

"How do you know?" Her chin is as haughty as ever, but her voice has a giveaway tremble. "What are you talking about?"

"I know because he wrote letters to her from France." I speak across Ed to Sadie. "And because he put himself in the necklace. And because he never painted another portrait, his whole life. People begged him to, but he would always say, '*J'ai peint celui que j'ai voulu peindre.*' 'I have painted the one I wanted to paint.' And when you see the painting, you realize why. Because why would he ever want to paint anyone else after Sadie?" My throat is suddenly thick. "She was the most beautiful thing you ever saw. She was radiant. And she was wearing this necklace. . . . When you see the necklace in the painting, it all makes sense. He loved her. Even if she lived her whole life without knowing it. Even if she lived to one hundred and five without ever getting an answer." I brush away a tear from my cheek.

Ed looks lost for words. Which is hardly a surprise. One minute we're snogging. The next I'm downloading some random torrent of family history on him.

"Where did you see the painting? Where is it?" Sadie takes a step toward me, quivering all over, her face pale. "It was lost. It was burned."

"So, did you know your great-aunt well?" Ed is saying simultaneously.

"I didn't know her when she was alive. But after she died I went down to Archbury, where she used to live. He's famous." I turn again to Sadie. "Stephen's famous."

"Famous?" Sadie looks bewildered.

"There's a whole museum dedicated to him. He's called Cecil Malory. He was discovered long after his death. And the portrait is famous too. And it was saved and it's in a gallery and everyone loves it . . . and you have to see it. You have to see it."

"Now." Sadie's voice is so quiet, I can barely hear her. "Please. Now."

"Sounds awesome," says Ed politely. "We'll have to go see it someday. We could take in some galleries, do lunch—"

"No. Now." I take his hand. "Right now." I glance at Sadie. "Come on."

We sit on the leather bench, the three of us, in a silent row. Sadie next to me. Me next to Ed. Sadie hasn't spoken since she came into the gallery. When she first saw the portrait, I thought she might faint. She flickered silently and just stared, and then at last exhaled as though she'd been holding her breath for an hour.

"Amazing eyes," says Ed at length. He keeps shooting me wary looks, as though he's not sure how to deal with this situation.

"Amazing." I nod, but I can't concentrate on him. "Are you OK?" I give Sadie a worried glance. "I know this has been a real shock for you."

"I'm good." Ed sounds puzzled. "Thanks for asking."

"I'm all right." Sadie gives me a wan smile. Then she resumes gazing at the painting. She's already been up close to it, to see the portrait of Stephen hidden in her necklace, and her face was briefly so contorted with love and sorrow that I had to turn away and give her a moment of privacy.

"They've done some research at the gallery," I say to Ed. "She's the most popular painting here. They're going to launch a range of products with her picture on them. Like posters and coffee mugs. She's going to be famous!"

"Coffee mugs." Sadie tosses her head. "How terribly vulgar." But I can see a sudden glimmer of pride in her eyes. "What else will I be on?"

"And tea towels, jigsaw puzzles . . ." I say as though informing Ed. "You name it. If she was ever worried about not making any mark on this world . . ." I leave my words trailing in the air.

"Quite the famous relative you have." Ed raises his eyebrows. "Your family must be very proud."

"Not really," I say after a pause. "But they will be."

"Mabel." Ed is consulting the guidebook which he insisted on buying at the entrance. "It says here: *The sitter is thought to be called Mabel.*"

"That's what they thought." I nod. "Because the painting says *My Mabel* on the back."

"*Mabel?*" Sadie swivels around, looking so horrified I can't help snorting with laughter.

"I told them it was a joke between her and Cecil Malory," I hastily explain. "It was her nickname, but everyone thought it was real."

"Do I *look* like a Mabel?"

A movement attracts my attention and I look up. To my surprise, Malcolm Gledhill is entering the gallery. As he sees me, he gives a sheepish smile and shifts his briefcase from one hand to another.

"Oh, Miss Lington. Hello. After our conversation today, I just thought I'd come and have another look at her."

"Me too." I nod. "I'd like to introduce . . ." Abruptly

I realize I'm about to introduce Sadie to him. "Ed." I quickly switch my hand to the other direction. "This is Ed Harrison. Malcolm Gledhill. He's in charge of the collection."

Malcolm joins the three of us on the bench, and for a moment we all just look at the painting.

"So you've had the painting in the gallery since 1982," says Ed, still reading the guidebook. "Why did the family get rid of it? Strange move."

"Good question," says Sadie, suddenly waking up. "It belonged to me. Nobody should have been allowed to sell it."

"Good question," I echo firmly. "It belonged to Sadie. Nobody should have been allowed to sell it."

"And what I want to know is, who *did* sell it?" she adds.

"Who *did* sell it?" I echo.

"Who *did* sell it?" repeats Ed.

Malcolm Gledhill shifts uncomfortably on the bench.

"As I said today, Miss Lington, it was a confidential arrangement. Until such time as a formal legal claim is made, the gallery is unable to—"

"OK, OK," I cut him off. "I get it, you can't tell me. But I'm going to find out. That painting belonged to my family. We deserve to know."

"So, let me get this straight." Ed is finally showing a real interest in the story. "Someone *stole* the painting?"

"Dunno." I shrug. "It was missing for years, and then I found it here. All I know is, it was sold to the gallery in the 1980s, but I don't know who sold it."

"Do you know?" Ed turns to Malcolm Gledhill.

"I . . . do." He nods reluctantly.

"Well, can't you tell her?"

"Not . . . well . . . no."

"Is this some official secret?" demands Ed. "Does it involve weapons of mass destruction? Is national security at stake?"

"Not so to speak." Malcolm looks more flustered than ever. "But there was a confidentiality clause in the agreement—"

"OK." Ed snaps into his business-consultant, taking-command-of-the-situation mode. "I'll have an attorney on this in the morning. This is ridiculous."

"Absolutely ridiculous," I chime in, bolstered by Ed's bullish attitude. "And we won't stand for it. Are you aware my uncle is Bill Lington? I know he will use every resource to fight this . . . ridiculous confidentiality. It's *our painting*."

Malcolm Gledhill looks utterly beleaguered.

"The agreement clearly states . . ." he manages at last, then trails off. I can see his eyes constantly flicking toward his briefcase.

"Is the file in there?" I say, in sudden inspiration.

"As it happens, it is," says Malcolm Gledhill guardedly. "I'm taking the papers home to study. Copies, of course."

"So you could show the agreement to us," says Ed, lowering his voice. "We won't snitch."

"I could not show you anything!" Malcolm Gledhill nearly falls off the bench in horror. "That, as I keep repeating, is confidential information."

"Of course it is." I adopt a soothing voice. "We understand that. But maybe you could do me a small favor and check the date of acquisition? That's not confidential, is it?"

Ed gives me a questioning glance, but I pretend I haven't noticed. Another plan has occurred to me. One which Ed won't understand.

"It was June 1982, as I remember," says Malcolm Gledhill.

"But the exact date? Could you just have a quick look at the agreement?" I open my eyes innocently at him. "Please? It could be very helpful."

Malcolm Gledhill gives me a suspicious look but obviously can't think of any reason to refuse. He bends down, clicks open his briefcase, and draws out a file of papers.

I catch Sadie's eye and jerk my head surreptitiously at Malcolm Gledhill.

"What?" she says.

For God's sake. And she calls *me* slow.

I jerk my head again at Malcolm Gledhill, who is now smoothing out a sheet of paper.

"What?" she repeats impatiently. "What are you trying to say?"

"Here we are." He puts on a pair of reading glasses. "Let me find the date. . . ."

My neck's going to crick if I jerk my head any more. I honestly think I'm going to die of frustration in a minute. There's the information we want. Right there. Open for anyone to read who happens to be of a ghostly invisible nature. And still Sadie is peering at me uncomprehendingly.

"Look!" I mutter, out of the corner of my mouth. "Look at it! *Look at it!*"

"Oh!" Her face snaps in sudden understanding. A nanosecond later she's standing behind Malcolm Gledhill, peering over his shoulder.

"Look at what?" says Ed, sounding puzzled, but I barely hear him. I'm avidly watching Sadie as she reads, frowns, gives a small gasp—then looks up.

"William Lington. He sold it for five hundred thousand pounds."

"William Lington?" I stare back at her stupidly. "You mean . . . Uncle Bill?"

The effect of my words on Malcolm Gledhill is extreme and immediate. He starts violently, clutches the letter to his chest, turns white, turns pink, looks at the letter, then clasps it close again. "What—what did you say?"

I'm having a hard time digesting this myself.

"William Lington sold the painting to the gallery." I try to sound firm, but my voice is coming out faint. "That's the name on the agreement."

"You are fucking kidding." Ed's eyes gleam. "Your own uncle?"

"For half a million pounds."

Malcolm Gledhill looks like he wants to burst into tears. "I don't know how you got that information." He appeals to Ed. "You will be a witness to the fact I did not reveal any information to Miss Lington."

"So she's right?" says Ed, raising his eyebrows. This only seems to panic Malcolm Gledhill more.

"I can't say whether or not—whether—" He breaks off and wipes his brow. "At no stage was the agreement out of my sight, at no stage did I let it into her view—"

"You didn't have to," says Ed reassuringly. "She's psychic."

My mind is going around in circles as I try to get over my shock and think this all through. Uncle Bill had the painting. Uncle Bill sold the painting. Dad's voice keeps running through my mind: *. . . put in a storage unit and left there for years. Nobody could* *face dealing with it. It was Bill who sorted it all out. . . . Strange to imagine, but Bill was the idler in those days.*

It's all obvious. He must have found the painting all those years ago, realized it was valuable, and sold it to the London Portrait Gallery in a secret agreement.

"Are you OK?" Ed touches my arm. "Lara?"

But I can't move. Now my mind is moving in bigger circles. Wilder circles. I'm putting two and two together. I'm putting eight and eight together. And I'm making a hundred million.

Bill set up Lingtons Coffee in 1982.

The same year he secretly made half a million from selling Sadie's painting.

And now, finally, *finally* . . . it's all falling into place. It's all making sense. He had £500,000 that no one knew about, £500,000 that he's never mentioned. Not in any interview. Not in any seminar. Not in any book.

I feel light-headed. The enormity of this is only slowly sinking in. The whole thing is a lie. The whole world thinks he's a business genius who started with two little coins. Half a million notes, more like.

And he covered it up so no one would know. He must have realized the painting was of Sadie as soon as he saw it. He must have realized it belonged to her. But he let the world believe it was some servant called Mabel. He probably fed them that story himself. That way, no one would come knocking on any Lington's door, asking about the beautiful girl in the painting.

"Lara?" Ed's waving a hand in front of my face. "Speak to me. What is it?"

"The year 1982." I look up in a daze. "Sound familiar? That's when Uncle Bill started up Lingtons Coffee. You know? With his famous 'Two Little Coins.' " I do quote marks with my fingers. "Or was there, in fact, half a million pounds which started him off? Which he somehow forgot to mention because it wasn't his in the first place?"

There's silence. I can see the pieces falling into place in Ed's mind.

"Jesus Christ," he says at last, and looks up at me. "This is huge. Huge."

"I know." I swallow. "Huge."

"So the whole Two Little Coins story, the seminars, the book, the DVD, the movie . . ."

"All complete bullshit."

"If I were Pierce Brosnan, I'd be calling my agent right about now." Ed raises his eyebrows comically.

I'd want to laugh, too, if I didn't want to cry. If I wasn't so sad and furious and sick at what Uncle Bill did.

That was Sadie's painting. It was hers to sell or keep. He took it and he used it and he never breathed a word. How dare he? How *dare* he?

With sickening clarity, I can see a parallel universe in which someone else, someone decent like my dad, had found the painting and done the right thing. I can see Sadie sitting in her nursing home, wearing her necklace, looking at her beautiful painting throughout her old age, until the very last light faded from her eyes.

Or maybe she would have sold it. But it would have been hers to sell. It would have been *her* glory. I can see her brought out of her nursing home and shown the painting hanging in the London Portrait Gallery. I can see the joy that would have given her. And I can even see her sitting in her chair, having Stephen's letters read aloud to her by some kind archivist.

Uncle Bill robbed her of years and years of possible happiness. And I'll never forgive him.

"She should have known." I can't contain my anger anymore. "Sadie should have known she was hanging up here. She went to her death with no idea. And that was wrong. It was wrong."

I glance over at Sadie, who has wandered away from the conversation as though she's not interested. She shrugs, as though to brush away all my angst and fury.

"Darling, don't drone on about it. *Too* dull. At least I've found it now. At least it wasn't destroyed. And at least I don't look as *fat* as I remember," she adds with sudden animation. "My arms look rather wonderful, don't they? I always did have good arms."

"Too twiggy for my taste," I can't help shooting back.

"At least they're not *pillows*."

Sadie meets my eyes and we exchange wary smiles. Her bravado doesn't fool me. She's pale and flickery, and I can tell this discovery has thrown her. But her chin is up, high and proud as ever.

Malcolm Gledhill is still looking deeply uncomfortable. "If we'd realized she was still alive, if anyone had told us—"

"You couldn't have known," I say, my anger abated a little. "We didn't even know it was her ourselves."

Because Uncle Bill didn't say a word. Because he covered the whole thing up with an anonymous deal. No wonder he wanted the necklace. It was the only thing left linking Sadie to her portrait. It was the only thing which might uncover his massive con trick. This painting must have been a time bomb for him, ticking away quietly all these years. And now, finally, it's gone off. *Boom.* I don't know how yet, but I'm going to avenge Sadie. Big-time.

All four of us have silently, gradually, turned to face the painting again. It's almost impossible to sit in this gallery and *not* end up staring at it.

"I told you that she's the most popular painting in the gallery," says Malcolm Gledhill presently. "I spoke to the marketing department today, and they're making her the face of the gallery. She'll be used in every campaign."

"I want to be on a lipstick," says Sadie, suddenly turning with determination. "A lovely bright lipstick."

"She should be on a lipstick," I say firmly to Malcolm Gledhill. "And you should name it after her. That's what she would have wanted."

"I'll see what we can do." He looks a little flustered. "It's not really my area."

"I'll let you know what else she would have wanted." I wink at Sadie. "I'll be acting as her unofficial agent from now on."

"I wonder what she's thinking," says Ed, still gazing up at her. "That's quite an intriguing expression she has."

"I often wonder that myself," chimes in Malcolm Gledhill eagerly. "She seems to have such a look of serenity and happiness. . . . Obviously, from what you've said, she had a certain *emotional* connection with the painter Malory. . . . I often wonder if he was reading her poetry as he painted. . . ."

"What an idiot this man is," says Sadie scathingly in my ear. "It's obvious what I'm thinking. I'm looking at Stephen and I'm thinking, *I want to jump his bones.*"

"She wanted to jump his bones," I say to Malcolm Gledhill. Ed shoots me a disbelieving look, then bursts into laughter.

"I should be going." Malcolm Gledhill has clearly had enough of us for one night. He picks up his briefcase, nods at us, then swiftly walks away. A few seconds later I can hear him practically running down the marble stairs. I look at Ed and grin.

"Sorry about the diversion."

"No problem." He gives me a quizzical look. "So . . . any other old masters you want to unveil tonight? Any long-lost family sculptures? Any more psychic revelations? Or shall we go get some dinner?"

"Dinner." I stand up and look at Sadie. She's still sitting there, her feet up on the bench and her yellow dress flowing around her, gazing up at her twenty-three-year-old self as though she wants to drink herself in. "Coming?" I say softly.

"Sure," says Ed.

"Not quite yet," says Sadie, without moving her head. "You go. I'll see you later."

I follow Ed to the exit, then turn and give Sadie one last anxious look. I just want to make sure she's OK. But she doesn't even notice me. She's still transfixed. Like she wants to sit there all night with the painting. Like she wants to make up for all the time she lost.

Like, finally, she's found what she was looking for.

TWENTY-FIVE

I've never avenged anyone before. And I'm finding it a lot trickier than I expected. Uncle Bill is abroad and no one can get in contact with him. (Well, of course they *can* get hold of him. They're just not going to do so for the crazy stalker niece.) I don't want to write to him or make a phone call. This has to be done face-to-face. So at the moment, it's impossible.

And it's not helped by Sadie going all moral-high-ground on me. She thinks there's no point dwelling on the past, and what's done is done, and I should stop "droning on about it, darling."

But I don't care what she thinks. Vengeance *will* be mine. The more I think about what Uncle Bill did, the more livid I am, and the more I want to phone up Dad and blurt it all out. But somehow I'm keeping control. There's no rush. Everyone knows revenge is a dish best served when you've had enough time to build up enough vitriol and fury. Plus, it's not like my evidence is going anywhere. The painting is hardly going to disappear from the London Portrait Gallery. Nor is the so-called confidential agreement that Uncle Bill signed all those years ago. Ed's already hired a lawyer for me, and he's going to start formal claim proceedings as soon I give him the say-so. Which I'm going to do as soon as I've confronted Uncle Bill myself and seen him squirm. That's my aim. If he grovels it'll be the icing on the cake, but I'm not that hopeful.

I heave a sigh, screw up a piece of paper, and throw it into the bin. I want to see him squirm *now*. I've honed my vengeance speech and everything.

To distract myself, I lean against the headboard of my bed and flick through the post. My bedroom is actually a pretty good office. I don't have to commute, and it doesn't cost anything. And it has a bed in it. On the less positive side, Kate has to work at my dressing table and keeps getting her legs wedged underneath it.

I'm calling my new headhunting company Magic Search, and we've been running for three weeks now. And we've already landed a commission! We were recommended to a pharmaceuticals company by Janet Grady, who is my new best friend. (She's not stupid, Janet. She knows I did all the work and Natalie did nothing. Mostly because I rang her up and told her.) I did the pitch myself, and two days ago we heard we'd won! We've been asked to compile a short list for another marketing director job, and this one has to have specialist knowledge of the pharmaceuticals industry. I told the HR head that this was a perfect job for us, because, by chance, one of my associates has intimate personal knowledge of the pharmaceuticals industry.

Which, OK, isn't *strictly* true.

But the point about Sadie is she's a very quick learner and has all sorts of clever ideas. Which is why she's a valued member of the Magic Search team.

"Hello!" Her high-pitched voice jolts me out of my reverie, and I look up to see her sitting at the end of my bed. "I've just been to Glaxo Wellcome. I've got the direct lines of two of the senior marketing team. Quick, before I forget . . ."

She dictates two names and telephone numbers to me. Private, direct-line numbers. Gold dust to a head-hunter.

"The second one has just had a baby," she adds. "So he probably doesn't want a new job. But Rick Young might. He looked pretty bored during their meeting. When I go back I'll find out his salary somehow."

Sadie, I write underneath the phone numbers, *you're a star. Thanks a million.*

"Don't mention it," she says crisply. "It was too easy. Where next? We should think about Europe, you know. There must be simply *heaps* of talent in Switzerland and France."

Brilliant idea, I write, then look up. "Kate, could you make a list of all the major pharmaceuticals companies in Europe for me? I think we might spread our net quite wide with this one."

"Good idea, Lara," says Kate, looking impressed. "I'll get on it."

Sadie winks at me and I grin back. Having a job really suits her. She looks more alive and happy these days than I've ever known her. I've even given her a job title: chief headhunter. After all, she's the one doing the hunting.

She's found us an office too: a run-down building off Kilburn High Road. We can move in there next week. It's all falling into place.

Every evening, after Kate goes home, Sadie and I sit on my bed together and talk. Or, rather, she talks. I've told her that I want to *know* about her. I want to hear about everything she can remember, whether it's big, small, important, trivial—everything. And so she sits there, and plays with her beads, and thinks for a bit, and tells me things. Her thoughts are a bit random and

I can't always follow, but gradually a picture of her life has built up. She's told me about the divine hat she was wearing in Hong Kong when war was declared, the leather trunk she packed everything in and lost, the boat journey she made to the United States, the time she was robbed at gunpoint in Chicago but managed to keep hold of her necklace, the man she danced with one night who later became president. . . .

And I sit totally riveted. I've never heard a story like it. She's had the most amazing, colorful life. Sometimes fun, sometimes exciting, sometimes desperate, sometimes shocking. It's a life I can't imagine anyone else leading. Only Sadie.

I talk a bit too. I've told her about growing up with Mum and Dad, stories about Tonya's riding lessons and my synchronized-swimming craze. I've told her about Mum's anxiety attacks and how I wish she could relax and enjoy life. I've told her how our whole lives we've been in the shadow of Uncle Bill.

We don't really comment on each other's stories. We just listen.

Then, later on, when I go to bed, Sadie goes to the London Portrait Gallery and sits with her painting all night, alone. She hasn't told me that's what she does. I just know, from the way she disappears off silently, her eyes already distant and dreamy. And the way she returns, thoughtful and distracted and talking about her childhood and Stephen and Archbury. I'm glad she goes. The painting's so important to her, she *should* spend time with it. And this way she doesn't have to share it with anyone else.

Coincidentally, it works out well for me too, her being out of the way at night. For . . . various other reasons.

Nothing specific.

Oh, OK. All *right*. There is a specific reason. Which would be the fact that Ed has recently stayed over at my place a few nights.

I mean, come on. Can you think of anything worse than a ghost lurking around in your bedroom when you're . . . getting to know your new boyfriend better? The idea of Sadie giving us a running commentary is more than I can cope with. And she has no shame. I know she'd watch us. She'd probably award us points out of ten, or say disparagingly that they did it much better in her day, or suddenly yell "Faster!" in Ed's ear.

I've already caught her stepping into the shower one morning when Ed and I both happened to be in there. I screamed and tried to push her out, and accidentally elbowed Ed in the face, and it took me about an hour to recover. And Sadie wasn't one little bit sorry. She said I was overreacting and she just wanted to keep us company. *Company?*

Ed kept shooting me little sidelong glances after that. It's almost like he suspects. I mean, obviously he can't have guessed the truth; that would be impossible. But he's pretty observant. And I can tell he knows there's something a bit strange in my life.

The phone rings and Kate picks it up. "Hello, Magic Search, can I help you? . . . Oh. Yes, of course, I'll put you through." She presses the hold button and says, "It's Sam from Bill Lington's travel office. Apparently you called them?"

"Oh, yes. Thanks, Kate."

I take a deep breath and pick up the receiver. Here goes my latest salvo.

"Hello, Sam," I say pleasantly. "Thanks for ringing

back. The reason I called is, um . . . I'm trying to arrange a fun surprise for my uncle. I know he's away and I wondered if you could possibly give me his flight details? Obviously I won't pass them on!" I add, with a casual little laugh.

This is a total bluff. I don't even know if he's flying back from wherever he is. Maybe he's taking the *QE2* or traveling by bespoke submarine. Nothing would surprise me.

"Lara," Sam sighs. "I've just spoken to Sarah. She told me that you were trying to contact Bill. She also informed me that you'd been banned from the house."

"Banned?" I muster tones of shock. "Are you serious? Well, I have no idea what that's about. I'm just trying to organize a little surprise birthday-o-gram for my uncle—"

"His birthday was a month ago."

"So . . . I'm a bit late!"

"Lara, I can't give out confidential flight information," Sam says smoothly. "Or any information. Sorry. Have a good day."

"Right. Well . . . thanks." I crash the receiver down. Damn.

"Everything OK?" Kate looks up anxiously.

"Yes. Fine." I muster a smile. But as I head out to the kitchen, I'm breathing heavily and my blood is pumping around fast, all toxic with frustration. I'm sure this situation is terrible for my health. Another thing to blame Uncle Bill for. I flick on the kettle and lean against the counter, trying to calm myself with deep breathing.

Hare hare . . . vengeance will be mine . . . hare hare . . . I just have to be patient. . . .

Trouble is, I'm sick of being patient. I take a teaspoon out and shove the drawer closed with a satisfying *bang*.

"Goodness!" Sadie appears, perched above the dishwasher. "What's wrong?"

"You know what's wrong." I haul my tea bag out roughly and dump it in the bin. "I want to get him."

Sadie opens her eyes wider. "I didn't realize you were so steamed up."

"I wasn't. But I am now. I've had enough." I slosh milk into my tea and dump the carton back in the fridge. "I know you're being all magnanimous, but I don't see how you can do it. I just want to . . . to punch him. Every time I pass a Lingtons coffee shop, I see a great big rack with *Two Little Coins* for sale. I want to rush in and yell, 'Stop it, everybody! It wasn't two little coins! It was my great-aunt's fortune!'" I sigh and take a sip of tea. Then I look up at Sadie curiously. "Don't you want to get back at him? You must be a total saint."

"*Saint* is probably a *little* strong. . . ." She smoothes back her hair.

"It's not. You're amazing." I cradle the mug. "The way you just keep moving forward. The way you don't dwell on stuff. The way you look at the big picture."

"Keep moving onward," she says simply. "That's always been my way."

"Well, I really admire you. If it were me, I'd want to . . . *trash* him."

"I could trash him." She shrugs. "I could go to the south of France and make his life a misery. But would I be a better person?" She hits her slim chest. "Would I feel better inside?"

"The south of France?" I stare at her, puzzled. "What do you mean, the south of France?"

Sadie immediately looks shifty. "I'm . . . guessing. It's the kind of place he would be. It's the kind of place wealthy people go."

Why is she avoiding my eye?

"Oh my *God*." I gasp as it suddenly hits me. "You know where he is, don't you? Sadie!" I exclaim as she starts to fade away. "Don't you *dare* disappear!"

"All right." She comes back into view, looking a little sulky. "Yes. I do know where he is. I went to his office. It was very easy to find out."

"Why didn't you *tell* me?"

"Because . . ." She gives a distant, noncommittal shrug.

"Because you didn't want to admit that you're just as mean and vengeful as me! Come on. What did you do to him? You might as well tell me now."

"I did nothing!" she says haughtily. "Or at least . . . nothing much. I just wanted to have a look at him. He's very, very rich, isn't he?"

"Incredibly." I nod. "Why?"

"He seems to own an entire beach. That's where I came across him. He was lying on a bed in the sun, covered in oil, with several servants nearby cooking food for him. He looked terribly self-satisfied." A rictus of distaste passes across her face.

"Didn't you want to yell at him? Didn't you want to have a go at him?"

"Actually . . . I did yell at him," she says after a pause. "I couldn't help myself. I felt so angry."

"That's good! You *should* yell. What did you say?"

I'm utterly agog. I can't believe Sadie has gone and confronted Uncle Bill on his private beach, all on her own. To be honest, I feel a bit hurt that she left me out. But then, I guess she has the right to seek revenge in any way she wants. And I'm glad she let him have it. I hope he heard every word.

"Come on, what did you say?" I persist. "Tell me word for word, starting at the beginning."

"I told him he was fat," she says with satisfaction.

For a moment I think I must have heard wrong.

"You told him he was *fat*?" I stare at her incredulously. "That was it? That was your revenge?"

"It's the perfect revenge!" retorts Sadie. "He looked very unhappy. He's a terribly vain man, you know."

"Well, I think we can do better than that," I say decisively, putting my mug down. "Here's the plan, Sadie. You're going to tell me where I need to book a flight to. And we're going to get on a plane tomorrow. And you're going to take me to where he is. OK?"

"OK." Her eyes suddenly brighten. "It'll be like a holiday!"

Sadie has taken the holiday theme seriously. A little too seriously, if you ask me. She's dressed for our trip in a backless flowing outfit made out of orange silky stuff, which she calls "beach pajamas." She has on a massive straw hat, is clutching a parasol and a wicker basket, and keeps humming some song about being *"sur la plage."* She's in such a chipper mood I almost want to snap at her that this is serious business and can she please stop twirling the ribbons on her hat? But then, it's OK for her. She's already seen Uncle Bill. She's yelled at him. She's released her tension. I've still got mine, coiled up inside me. I haven't mellowed. I haven't got distance. I want him to pay. I want him to suffer. I want him to—

"More champagne?" A smiling air hostess appears at my side.

"Oh." I hesitate, then hold out my glass. "Er . . . OK, then. Thanks."

Traveling with Sadie is an experience unlike any other. She shrieked at the passengers at the airport and we found ourselves ushered to the head of the queue. Then she shrieked at the check-in girl and I found myself upgraded. And now the hostesses keep plying me with champagne! (Mind you, I'm not sure if that's because of Sadie or because of being in a posh seat.)

"Isn't this fun?" Sadie slides into the seat next to me and eyes my champagne longingly.

"Yeah, great," I murmur, pretending to be talking into a Dictaphone.

"How's Ed?" She manages to get about ten insinuating tones into one syllable.

"Fine, thanks," I say lightly. "He thinks I'm having a reunion with an old school friend."

"You know he's told his mother about you."

"What?" I turn toward her. "How do you know?"

"I happened to be passing his office the other night," Sadie says airily. "So I thought I'd pop in, and he was on the phone. I just happened to catch a few snatches of his conversation."

"Sadie," I hiss. "Were you *spying* on him?"

"He said London was working out really well for him." Sadie ignores my question. "And then he said he'd met someone who made him glad that Corinne did what she did. He said he couldn't have imagined it and he hadn't been looking for it—but it had happened. And his mother told him she was so thrilled and she couldn't wait to meet you, and he said, 'Slow down, Mom.' But he was laughing."

"Oh. Well . . . he's right. We'd better not rush things." I'm trying to sound all nonchalant, but secretly I have a glow of pleasure inside. Ed told his mother about me!

"And *aren't* you glad you didn't stay with Josh?" Sadie suddenly demands. "Aren't you glad I saved you from that hideous fate?"

I take a sip of champagne, avoiding her eye, having a slight internal struggle. To be honest, going out with Ed after Josh is like moving on to Duchy Originals super-tasty seeded loaf after plastic white bread. (I don't mean to be rude about Josh. And I didn't realize it at the time. But it is. He is. Plastic white bread.)

So really I should be truthful and say, "Yes, Sadie, I'm glad you saved me from that hideous fate." Except then she'll become so conceited I won't be able to stand it.

"Life takes us on different paths," I say at last, cryptically. "It's not up to us to evaluate or judge them, merely respect and embrace them."

"What drivel," she says contemptuously. "I know I saved you from a hideous fate, and if you can't even be grateful—" She's suddenly distracted by the sight out of the window. "Look! We're nearly there!"

Sure enough, a moment later the seat-belt signs come on and everyone buckles up—apart from Sadie, who is floating around the cabin.

"His mother is quite stylish, you know," she says conversationally.

"Whose mother?" I'm not following.

"Ed's, of course. I think you and she would get on well."

"How do you know?" I say in puzzlement.

"I went to see what she was like, of course," she says carelessly. "They live outside Boston. Very nice house. She was having a bath. She has a *very* good figure for a woman of her age—"

"Sadie, stop!" I'm almost too incredulous to speak. "You can't do this! You can't go around spying on everyone in my life!"

"Yes, I can," she says, opening her eyes wide as though it's obvious. "I'm your guardian angel. It's my job to watch out for you."

I stare back at her, flummoxed. The plane engines begin to roar as we start our descent, my ears begin to pop, and there's a slight heaving in my stomach.

"I hate this bit." Sadie wrinkles her nose. "See you there." And before I can say anything else, she disappears.

Uncle Bill's mansion is a longish taxi ride from Nice Airport. I stop for a glass of Orangina in the village café and practice my schoolgirl French on the owner, to Sadie's great amusement. Then we get back in the taxi and head the final stretch to Uncle Bill's villa. Or complex. Or whatever you call a massive white house with several other houses dotted around the grounds and a mini-vineyard and a helicopter pad.

The place is staffed pretty heavily, but that doesn't matter when you have a French-speaking ghost by your side. Every member of staff we come across is soon turned into a glassy-eyed statue. We make our way through the garden without being challenged, and Sadie leads me swiftly to a cliff, into which steps are cut, with a balustrade. At the bottom of the steps is a sandy beach and, beyond that, endless Mediterranean.

So this is what you get if you're the owner of Lingtons Coffee. Your own beach. Your own view. Your own slice of sea. Suddenly I can see the point of being immensely rich.

For a moment I just stand shading my eyes from the glare of the sun, watching Uncle Bill. I'd pictured him relaxing on a sun lounger, surveying his empire, maybe stroking a white cat with one evil hand. But he's not surveying anything, *or* relaxing. In fact, he's not looking as I imagined him at all. He's with a personal trainer, doing sit-ups and sweating profusely. I gape, astonished, as he does crunch after crunch, almost howling with pain, then collapses on his exercise mat.

"Give . . . me . . . a . . . moment. . . ." he gasps. "Then another hundred."

He's so engrossed, he doesn't notice as I quietly make my way down the cliff steps, accompanied by Sadie.

"Per'aps you should rest now?" says the trainer, looking concerned as he surveys Uncle Bill. "You 'ave 'ad a good workout."

"I still need to work on my abs," says Uncle Bill grimly, clutching his sides in dissatisfaction. "I need to lose some fat."

"Meester Leengton." The trainer looks totally bemused. "You 'ave no fat to lose. 'ow many times must I tell you thees?"

"Yes, you do!" I jump as Sadie whirls through the air to Uncle Bill. *"You're fat!"* she shrieks in his ear. *"Fat, fat, fat! You're gross!"*

Uncle Bill's face jolts with alarm. Looking desperate, he sinks to the mat again and starts doing more crunches, groaning with the effort.

"Yes," says Sadie, floating about his head and looking down with disdain. "Suffer. You deserve it."

I can't help giggling. Hats off to her. This is a brilliant revenge. We watch him wincing and panting a while longer, then Sadie advances again.

"*Now tell your servant to go!*" she yells in his ear, and Uncle Bill pauses mid-crunch.

"You can go now, Jean-Michel," he says breathlessly. "See you this evening."

"Very well." The trainer gathers up all his pieces of equipment, brushing the sand off them. "I see you at six."

He heads up the cliff steps, nodding politely as he passes me, and heads toward the house.

OK. So now it's my turn. I take a deep breath of warm Mediterranean air and start to walk down the rest of the cliff steps. My hands are damp as I reach the beach. I take a few steps over the hot sand, then just stand still, waiting for Uncle Bill to notice me.

"Who's . . ." He suddenly catches a glimpse of me as he comes down onto the mat. Immediately he sits up again and swivels around. He looks utterly stupefied and slightly ill. I'm not surprised, after doing 59,000 sit-ups. "Is that . . . Lara? What are you doing here? How did you get here?"

He looks so dazed and drained, I almost feel sorry for him. But I'm not going to let myself. Nor am I going to be drawn into small talk. I have a speech to make and I'm going to make it.

"Yes, it is I," I say, in the most imposing, chilling voice I can muster. "Lara Alexandra Lington. Daughter to a betrayed father. Great-niece to a betrayed great-aunt. Niece to a betraying, evil, lying uncle. And I will have my vengeance." That bit was so satisfying to say, I repeat it, my voice ringing across the beach. "And I will have my *vengeance*!"

God, I would have loved to be a movie star.

"Lara." Uncle Bill has stopped panting by now and almost regained control of himself. He wipes his face and pulls a towel around his waist. Then he turns and smiles at me with that old suave, patronizing air. "Very stirring stuff. But I have no idea what you're talking about, nor how you got past my guards—"

"You know what I'm talking about," I say scathingly. "You know."

"I'm afraid I have no idea."

There's silence except for the waves washing onto the beach. The sun seems to be beating even more intensely than before. Neither of us has moved.

So he's calling my bluff. He must think he's safe. He must think that the anonymous agreement protects him and no one will ever be able to find out.

"Is this about the necklace?" Uncle Bill says suddenly, as though the thought has just struck him. "It's a pretty trinket, and I can understand your interest in it. But I don't know where it is. Believe me. Now, did your father tell you, I want to offer you a job? Is that why you're here? Because you certainly get marks for keenness, young lady."

He flashes his teeth at me and slides on a pair of black flip-flops. He's turning the situation. Any minute now he'll be ordering drinks and somehow pretending this visit was all his idea. Trying to buy me, trying to distract me, trying to turn everything his own way. Just like he's done all these years.

"I'm not here about the necklace, or the job." My voice cuts across his. "I'm here about Great-Aunt Sadie."

Uncle Bill raises his eyes to heaven with a familiar exasperation. "Jesus Christ, Lara. Will you give it a rest? For the last time, love, she *wasn't* murdered, she *wasn't* anything special—"

"And the painting of her that you found," I carry on

coolly. "The Cecil Malory. And the anonymous deal you did with the London Portrait Gallery in 1982. And the five hundred thousand pounds you got. And all the lies you told. And what you're going to do about it. *That's* why I'm here."

And I watch in satisfaction as my uncle's face sags like I've never seen it before. Like butter melting away under the sun.

TWENTY-SIX

$\mathcal{I}$t's a sensation. It's front-page news in every paper. *Every* paper.

Bill "Two Little Coins" Lington has "clarified" his story. The big, one-to-one interview was in the *Mail,* and all the papers jumped on it immediately.

He's come clean about the five hundred thousand. Except, of course, being Uncle Bill, he went on at once to claim that the money was only *part* of the story. And that his business principles could still be applied to anyone starting out with two little coins. And so actually the story isn't that different and, in a sense, half a million is the *same* as two little coins, it's simply the quantity that's different. (Then he realized he was on to a loser there and backtracked, but too late—it was out of his mouth.)

For me, the money really isn't the point. It's that finally, after all this time, he's credited Sadie. He's told the world about her instead of denying her and hiding her away. The quote that most of the papers used is: *"I couldn't have achieved my success without my beautiful aunt, Sadie Lancaster, and I'll always be indebted to her."* Which I dictated to him, word for word.

Sadie's portrait has been on every single front cover. The London Portrait Gallery has been besieged. She's like the new *Mona Lisa*. Only better, because the painting's so massive there's room for loads of people to look at her at once. (And she's way prettier. I'm just saying.) We've gone back there a few times ourselves, just to see the crowds and hear all the nice things they say about her. She's even got a fan site on the Internet.

As for Uncle Bill's book, he can say all he likes about business principles, but it won't do any good. *Two Little Coins* has become the biggest object of ridicule since the Millennium Dome. It's been parodied in all the tabloids, every single comedian has made a joke about it on television, and the publishers are so embarrassed, they're offering money back on it. About twenty percent of people have taken up the offer, apparently. I guess the others want to keep it as a souvenir, or put it on the mantelpiece and laugh at it, or something.

I'm flicking through an editorial about him in today's *Mail* when my phone bleeps with a text: *Hi I'm outside. Ed.*

This is one of the many good things about Ed. He's never late. Happily, I grab my bag, bang the flat door shut, and head down the stairs. Kate and I are moving in to our new office today, and Ed's promised to come and see it on his way to work. As I arrive on the pavement, there he is, holding a massive bunch of red roses.

"For the office," he says, presenting them to me with a kiss.

"Thanks!" I beam. "Everyone will be staring at me on the tube." I stop in surprise as Ed puts a hand on my arm.

"I thought we could take my car today," he says conversationally.

"*Your* car?"

"Uh-huh." He nods at a smart black Aston Martin parked nearby.

"That's yours?" I goggle at it in disbelief. "But . . . but . . . how?"

"Bought it. You know, car showroom . . . credit card . . . usual process . . . Thought I'd better buy British," he adds with a wry smile.

He bought an Aston Martin? Just like that?

"But you've never driven on the left." I feel a sudden alarm. "Have you been *driving* that thing?"

"Relax. I took the test last week. Boy, you have a fucked-up system."

"No we don't," I begin automatically.

"Stick shifts are the work of the devil. And don't even get me *started* on your right turn rules."

I can't believe this. He's kept this totally quiet. He never mentioned cars, or driving . . . or anything.

"But . . . why?" I can't help blurting out.

"Someone told me once," he says thoughtfully, "if you're going to live in a country, for however long, you should *engage* with it. And what better way to engage than learning how to drive in that country? Now, you want a ride or not?"

He opens the door with a gallant gesture. Still flabbergasted, I slide into the passenger seat. This is a seriously smart car. In fact, I don't dare put my roses down in case they scratch the leather.

"I learned all the British curses too," Ed adds as he pulls out into the road. "Get a move on, you nobhead!" He puts on a Cockney accent, and I can't help giggling.

"Very good." I nod. "What about 'That's right out of order, you wanker!'"

"I was told 'Bang out of order, you wanker,' " says Ed. "Was I misinformed?"

"No, that's OK too. But you need to work on the accent." I watch as he changes gear efficiently and cruises past a red bus. "But I don't understand. This is a really expensive car. What will you do with it when—" I stop myself before I can say any more, and cough feebly.

"What?" Ed may be driving, but he's as alert as ever.

"Nothing." I lower my chin until my face is practically nestling in the rose bouquet. "Nothing."

I was going to say, "when you go back to the States." But that's something we just don't talk about.

There's silence—then Ed shoots me a cryptic look. "Who knows what I'll do?"

The tour of the office doesn't take that long. In fact, we're pretty much done by 9:05 a.m. Ed looks at everything twice and says it's all great, and gives me a list of contacts who might be helpful, then has to leave for his own office. And then, about an hour later, just as I'm elbow deep in rose stems and water and a hastily bought vase, Mum and Dad arrive, *also* bearing flowers, and a bottle of champagne, and a new box of paper clips, which is Dad's little joke.

And even though I've only just showed the place to Ed, and even though it's just a room with a window and a pin board and two doors and two desks . . . I can't help feeling a buzz as I lead them around. It's mine. My space. My company.

"It's very smart." Mum peers out of the window. "But, darling, are you sure you can afford it? Wouldn't you have been better off staying with Natalie?"

Honestly. How many times do you have to explain to your parents that your former best friend is an obnoxious, unscrupulous total liability for them to believe you?

"I'm better off on my own, Mum, honestly. Look, this is my business plan. . . ."

I hand them the document, which is bound and numbered and looks so smart I can hardly believe I put it together. Every time I read it I feel a fierce thrill, mixed with yearning. If I make a success of Magic Search, my life will be complete.

I said that to Sadie this morning as we were reading yet more articles about her in the paper. She was silent for a moment, then to my surprise she stood up with a weird light in her eye and said, "I'm your guardian angel! I should *make* it a success." And then she disappeared. So I have a sneaky feeling she's up to something. As long as it doesn't involve any more blind dates.

"Very impressive!" says Dad, flipping through the plan.

"I got some advice from Ed," I confess. "He's been really helpful with all the Uncle Bill stuff too. He helped me do that statement. And he was the one who said we should hire a publicist to manage the press. Did you see the *Mail* piece today, by the way?"

"Ah, yes," says Dad faintly, exchanging looks with Mum. "We did."

To say my parents are gobsmacked by everything that's happened recently would be an understatement. I've never seen them so poleaxed as I when I rocked up at the front door, told them Uncle Bill wanted to have a word, turned back to the limo, and said, "OK, in you go," with a jerk of my thumb. And Uncle Bill got out of the car silently, with a set jaw, and did everything I said.

Neither of my parents could manage a word. It was as though sausages had suddenly started growing out of my head. Even after Uncle Bill had gone and I said, "Any questions?" they didn't speak. They just sat on the sofa, staring at me in a kind of stupefied awe. Even now, when they've thawed a little and the whole story is out and it's not such a shock anymore, they still keep darting me looks of awe.

Well. Why shouldn't they? I *have* been pretty awesome, though I say so myself. I masterminded the whole press exposé, together with Ed's help, and it's gone perfectly. At least, perfectly from my point of view. Maybe not from Uncle Bill's point of view. Or Aunt Trudy's. The day the story broke, she flew to a spa in Arizona and checked in indefinitely. God knows if we'll ever see her again.

Diamanté, on the other hand, has totally cashed in on it. She's already done a photo shoot for *Tatler* with a mock-up of Sadie's painting, and she's using the whole story to publicize her fashion label. Which is really, really tacky. And also quite smart. I can't help admiring her chutzpah. I mean, it's not her fault her dad is such a tosser, is it?

I secretly wish Diamanté and Great-Aunt Sadie could meet. I think they'd get on. They've got a lot in common, even though they'd each probably be horrified at that idea.

"Lara." I look up to see Dad approaching me. He looks awkward and keeps glancing at Mum. "We wanted to talk to you about Great-Aunt Sadie's . . ." He coughs.

"What?"

"*Funeral,*" says Mum, in her "discreet" voice.

"Exactly." Dad nods. "It's something we've been meaning to bring up. Obviously once the police were sure she hadn't been . . ."

"*Murdered,*" puts in Mum.

"Quite. Once the file was closed, the police released her . . . that's to say . . ."

"*Remains,*" says Mum in a whisper.

"You haven't done it yet." I feel a bolt of panic. "Please tell me you haven't had her funeral."

"No, no! It was provisionally set for this Friday. We *were* planning to tell you at some stage. . . ." He trails off evasively.

Yeah, right.

"Anyway!" says Mum quickly. "That was before."

"Quite. Obviously things have somewhat changed now," Dad continues. "So if you would like to be involved in planning it—"

"Yes. I would like to be involved," I say, almost fiercely. "In fact, I think I'll take charge."

"Right." Dad glances at Mum. "Well. Absolutely. I think that would only be right, given the amount of . . . of *research* you've done on her life."

"We do think you're a marvel, Lara," says Mum with a sudden fervor. "Finding all this out. Who would have known, without you? The story might never have come out at all! We might all have gone to our deaths, never knowing the truth!"

Trust Mum to bring *all* our deaths into it.

"Here are the funeral directors' details, darling." Dad hands me a leaflet, and I awkwardly pocket it, just as the buzzer goes. I head to the video intercom and peer at the grainy black-and-white image on the little screen. I think it's a man, although the image is so crap, it could equally well be an elephant.

"Hello?"

"It's Gareth Birch from Print Please," says the man. "I've got your business cards here."

"Oh, cool! Bring them up!"

This is it. Now I know I really have a business. I have business cards!

I usher Gareth Birch into our office, excitedly open the box, and hand cards around to everyone. They say *Lara Lington, Magic Search,* and there's a little embossed picture of a tiny magic wand.

"How come you delivered them personally?" I ask as I sign the delivery form. "I mean, it's very kind, but aren't you based in Hackney? Weren't you going to send them by post?"

"I thought I'd do you a favor," Gareth Birch says, giving me a glassy stare. "I value your business greatly, and it's the least I can do."

"What?" I stare at him, puzzled.

"I value your business greatly," he repeats, sounding a bit robotic. "It's the least I can do."

Oh my God. Sadie. What's she been *doing*?

"Well . . . thanks very much," I say, feeling a bit embarrassed. "I appreciate it. And I'll recommend you to all my friends!"

Gareth Birch makes his exit and I busy myself unpacking the boxes of cards, aware of Mum and Dad looking at me, agog.

"Did he just bring these himself, all the way from Hackney?" says Dad at last.

"Looks like it." I try to sound breezy, as though this is a normal course of events. Luckily, before they can say anything else, the phone rings and I hurry to answer it.

"Hello, Magic Search."

"May I speak to Lara Lington, please?" It's a woman's voice I don't recognize.

"Speaking." I sit down on one of the new swivel chairs, hoping she doesn't hear the crunch of plastic. "Can I help?"

"This is Pauline Reed. I'm head of human resources at Wheeler Foods. I was wondering, would you like to come in for a chat? I've heard good things about you."

"Oh, how nice!" I beam over the phone. "From whom, may I ask? Janet Grady?"

There's silence. When Pauline Reed speaks again, she sounds puzzled.

"I don't quite recall who. But you have a great reputation for sourcing talent, and I want to meet you. Something tells me you can do good things for our business."

Sadie.

"Well . . . that would be great!" I gather my wits. "Let me look at my schedule. . . ." I open it and fix up an appointment. As I put the phone down, both Mum and Dad are watching with a kind of eager hopefulness.

"Good news, darling?" says Dad.

"Just the head of human resources at Wheeler Foods," I say casually. "She wanted a meeting."

"Wheeler Foods who make Oatie Breakfast Treats?" Mum sounds beside herself.

"Yup." I can't help beaming. "Looks like my guardian angel's watching out for me."

"Hello!" Kate's bright voice interrupts me as she bursts through the door, holding a big flower arrangement. "Look what's just been delivered! Hello, Mr. and Mrs. Lington," she adds politely. "Do you like our new office? Isn't it great?"

I take the flower arrangement from Kate and rip open the little card.

"To all at Magic Search," I read aloud. *"We hope to get to know you as clients and as friends. Yours, Brian Chalmers. Head of Global Human Resources at Dwyer Dunbar plc.* And he's given his private line number."

"How amazing!" Kate's eyes are wide. "Do you know him?"

"No."

"Do you know anyone at Dwyer Dunbar?"

"Er . . . no."

Mum and Dad both seem beyond speech. I think I'd better get them out of here before anything else crazy happens.

"We're going to lunch at the pizza place," I inform Kate. "Want to come?"

"I'll be along in a sec." She nods cheerfully. "I need to sort a few things out first."

I usher Mum and Dad out of the office, down the steps, and onto the street. An elderly vicar in a clerical collar and robes is standing directly outside on the pavement, looking a bit lost, and I approach him, wondering if he's OK.

"Hi. Do you know where you are? Can I give you directions?"

"Well . . . yes, I am a stranger to the area." He gives me a dazed look. "I'm looking for number 59."

"That's this building—look." I point to our foyer, where 59 is embossed on the glass.

"Ah, yes, so it is!" His face clears and he approaches

the entrance. But to my surprise he doesn't go in. He just raises his hand and starts making the sign of the cross.

"Lord, I call on you to bless all who work in this building," he says, his voice a little quavery. "Bless all endeavors and businesses within, particularly at this time Magic—"

No *way*.

"So!" I grab Mum and Dad. "Let's go and get some pizza."

"Lara," says Dad weakly, as I practically manhandle him down the street. "Am I going mad, or was that vicar—"

"I think I'll have Four Seasons," I interrupt him brightly. "And some dough balls. How about you two?"

I think Mum and Dad have given up. They're just going with the flow. By the time we've all had a glass of valpolicella, everyone's smiling and the tricky questions have stopped. We've all chosen our pizzas and are stuffing in hot, garlicky dough balls, and I'm feeling pretty happy.

Even when Tonya arrives, I can't get stressed. It was Mum and Dad's idea to ask her along, and the truth is, even though she winds me up, she's family. I'm starting to appreciate what that means.

"Oh my God." Her strident greeting rings through the restaurant, and about twenty heads turn. "Oh my God. Can you *believe* all this stuff about Uncle Bill?"

As she arrives at our table, she's obviously expecting a bit more of a reaction.

"Hi, Tonya," I say. "How are the boys? How's Stuart?"

"Can you *believe* it?" she repeats, giving us all dissatisfied looks. "Have you seen the papers? I mean, it can't be true. It's tabloid rubbish. Someone's got an agenda somewhere."

"I think it is true," Dad corrects her mildly. "I think he admits as much himself."

"But have you seen what they've written about him?"

"Yes." Mum reaches for the valpolicella. "We have. Wine, darling?"

"But . . ." Tonya sinks down into a chair and looks around at us all with an aggrieved, bewildered expression. She clearly thought we would all be up in arms on Uncle Bill's behalf. Not merrily tucking into dough balls.

"Here you are." Mum slides a wineglass across. "We'll get you a menu."

I can see Tonya's mind working as she unbuttons her jacket and slings it over a chair. I can see her recalibrating the situation. She's not going to stick up for Uncle Bill if no one else does.

"So, who uncovered it all?" she says at last, and takes a gulp of wine. "Some investigative journalist?"

"Lara," says Dad with a little smile.

"*Lara?*" She looks more resentful than ever. "What do you mean, Lara?"

"I found out about Great-Aunt Sadie and the picture," I explain. "I put two and two together. It was me."

"But . . ." Tonya's cheeks are puffing out in disbelief. "But you weren't mentioned in the papers."

"I prefer to keep a low profile," I say cryptically, like a superhero who vanishes namelessly into the darkness and doesn't need any reward other than doing good.

Although, truth be told, I would have loved to be mentioned in the papers. But no one bothered to come and interview me, even though I straightened my hair especially, just in case. All the reports just said, *The discovery was made by a family member.*

Family member. Hmph.

"But I don't get it." Tonya's baleful blue eyes are on me. "Why did you start poking around in the first place?"

"I had an instinct something was wrong regarding Great-Aunt Sadie. But no one would listen to me," I can't help adding pointedly. "At the funeral, everyone thought I was a nutcase."

"You said she'd been murdered," objects Tonya. "She wasn't murdered."

"I had a general instinct that something was amiss," I say with a dignified air. "So I chose to follow up my suspicions on my own. And, after some research, they were confirmed." Everyone's hanging on my words as if I'm a university lecturer. "I then approached experts at the London Portrait Gallery, and they verified my discovery."

"Indeed they did." Dad smiles at me.

"And guess what?" I add proudly. "They're having the painting valued and Uncle Bill's giving Dad half of what it's worth!"

"No way." Tonya claps a hand to her mouth. "No *way.* How much will that be?"

"Millions, apparently." Dad looks uncomfortable. "Bill's adamant."

"It's only what you're owed, Dad," I say for the millionth time. "He *stole* it from you. He's a thief!"

Tonya seems a bit speechless. She takes a dough ball and rips it with her teeth.

"Did you see that editorial in *The Times*?" she says at last. "Brutal."

"It *was* rather savage." Dad winces. "We do feel for Bill, despite it all—"

"No, we don't!" Mum interrupts. "Speak for yourself."

"Pippa!" Dad looks taken aback.

"I don't feel for him one little bit." She looks around the table defiantly. "I feel . . . angry. Yes. Angry."

I gape at Mum in surprise. My whole life, I don't think I've ever known Mum to actually say she was angry. Across the table, Tonya looks just as gobsmacked. She raises her eyebrows questioningly at me, and I give a tiny shrug in return.

"What he did was shameful and unforgivable," Mum continues. "Your father always tries to see the good side of people, to find the excuse. But sometimes there *isn't* a good side. There *isn't* an excuse."

I've never known Mum so militant. Her cheeks are pink and she's clutching her wineglass as though she's about to punch the sky with it.

"Good for you, Mum!" I exclaim.

"And if your father keeps trying to defend him—"

"I'm not defending him!" says Dad at once. "But he's my brother. He's family. It's difficult. . . ."

He sighs heavily. I can see the disappointment etched in the lines under his eyes. Dad wants to find the good in everyone. It's part of his makeup.

"Your brother's success cast a long shadow over our family." Mum's voice is trembling. "It affected all of us in different ways. Now it's time for us all to be free. That's what I think. Draw a line."

"I recommended Uncle Bill's book to my book club, you know," says Tonya suddenly. "I made eight sales for him." She looks almost more outraged by this than anything. "And it was all lies! He's despicable!" She turns on Dad. "And if you don't think so, too, Dad, if you don't feel livid with him, then you're a mug!"

I can't help giving an inward cheer. Sometimes Tonya's forthright, trampling-over-feet way is just what you need.

"I am livid," Dad says at last. "Of course I am. It's just an adjustment. To realize your younger brother is quite such a selfish . . . unprincipled . . . shit." He breathes out hard. "I mean, what does that say?"

"It says we forget about him," says Mum firmly. "Move on. Start living the rest of our lives without feeling like second-class citizens."

Mum's got more spirit in her voice than I've heard for years! Go, Mum!

"So, who's been dealing with him?" Tonya frowns. "Hasn't that been a bit tricky?"

"Lara's done everything," says Mum proudly. "Talked to Bill, talked to the gallery, sorted everything out—*and* started her own business! She's been a tower of strength."

"Great!" Tonya smiles widely, but I can tell she's annoyed. "Well done you." She takes a sip of wine and swills it around her mouth thoughtfully. I just *know* she's searching for some little vulnerable spot, some way to regain ascendancy. . . .

"So how are things with Josh?" She puts on her sympathetic look. "Dad told me you got back together for a bit but then broke up for good? That must have been really tough. Really devastating."

"It's OK." I shrug. "I'm over it."

"But you must feel so hurt," Tonya persists, her cowlike eyes fixed on mine. "Your self-confidence must have taken a knock. Just remember, it *doesn't* mean you're not attractive, Lara. Does it?" She appeals to Mum and Dad. "There are other men—"

"My new boyfriend cheers me up," I say brightly. "So I wouldn't worry."

"New boyfriend?" Her mouth sags open. "Already?"

She needn't look *so* surprised.

"He's an American consultant over on assignment. His name's Ed."

"Very handsome," puts in Dad supportively.

"He took us all out for lunch last week!" adds Mum.

"Well." Tonya looks affronted. "That's . . . great. But it'll be hard when he goes back to the States, won't it?" She visibly brightens. "Long-distance relationships are the most likely to break down. All those transatlantic phone calls . . . and the time difference . . ."

"Who knows what'll happen?" I hear myself saying sweetly.

"I can make him stay!" Sadie's low voice in my ear makes me jump. I turn to see her hovering right by me, her eyes shining with determination. "I'm your guardian angel. I'll make Ed stay in England!"

"Excuse me a moment," I say to the table generally. "I've just got to send a text."

I get out my phone and start texting, positioning the screen so that Sadie can see it.

It's OK. U don't need to make him stay. Where have u been?

"Or I could make him ask you to marry him!" she exclaims, ignoring my question. "*Too* much fun! I'll tell him to propose, and I'll make sure he chooses a simply stunning ring, and we'll have such fun planning the wedding. . . ."

No, no, no! I text hurriedly. *Sadie, stop! Don't make Ed do anything. I want him to make his own decisions. I want him to listen to his own voice.*

Sadie gives a little harrumph as she reads my message. "Well, I think *my* voice is more interesting," she says, and I can't help a smile.

"Texting your boyfriend?" says Tonya, watching me.

"No," I say noncommittally. "Just . . . a friend. A good friend." I turn away and tap in, *Thanks for doing all that stuff to help me. U didn't have to.*

"I wanted to!" says Sadie. "It's fun! Have you had the champagne yet?"

No, I text back, wanting to laugh. *Sadie, u r the best guardian angel EVER.*

"Well, I do rather pride myself." She preens herself. "Now, where shall I sit?"

She floats across the table and sits on a spare chair at the end, just as Kate approaches the table, looking pink with excitement.

"Guess what!" she says. "We just got a bottle of champagne from the off-license round the corner! The man said it was to welcome us to the area! And you've had lots of calls, Lara; I've written down all the numbers . . . and the post arrived, forwarded from your flat. I didn't bring it all, but there was one package I thought might be important; it's come from Paris. . . ." She hands me a Jiffy bag, pulls out a chair, and beams at everyone. "Have you ordered yet? I'm absolutely starving! Hi, we haven't met, I'm Kate. . . ."

As Kate and Tonya introduce themselves and Dad pours out more wine, I stare down at the Jiffy bag, feeling a sudden breathless apprehension. It's come from Paris. It has girlish handwriting on the front. When I press it, I can feel something hard and bumpy inside. Hard and bumpy like a necklace.

Slowly, I lift my eyes. Sadie is watching me intently across the table. I know she's thinking the same.

"Go on." She nods.

With trembling hands I rip it open. I peer inside at a mass of tissue paper. I push it aside and see a flash of pale iridescent yellow. I look up, straight at Sadie.

"That's it, isn't it?" She's gone very white. "You've got it."

I nod, just once. Then, barely knowing what I'm doing, I push back my chair.

"I just have to . . . make a call." My voice is suddenly grainy. "I'll go outside. Be back in a moment . . ."

I thread my way through the tables and chairs to the back of the restaurant, where there's a small secluded courtyard. I push my way out through the fire doors and head to the far corner, then open the Jiffy bag again, pull out the mass of tissue paper, and gently unwrap it.

After all this time. I'm holding it. Just like that.

It's warmer to the touch than I expected. More substantial, somehow. A shaft of sunlight is glinting off the rhinestones, and the beads are shimmering. It's so stunning I have a sudden strong urge to put it on. But instead I look up at Sadie, who has been watching me silently.

"Here you are. It's yours." Automatically I try to put it around her neck, as though I'm giving her an Olympic medal. But my hands sink straight through her. I try again and again, even though I know it's no use.

"I don't know what to do!" I'm half laughing, half perilously near tears. "It's yours! You should be wearing it! We need the ghost version—"

"Stop!" Sadie's voice rises in sudden tension. "Don't . . ." She breaks off and moves away from me, her eyes fixed on the paving slabs of the courtyard. "You know what you have to do."

There's silence apart from the steady roar of Kilburn traffic coming from the main road. I can't look at Sadie. I'm just standing clutching the necklace. I know this is what we've been chasing and hunting and wishing for. But now we have it . . . I don't want to have arrived here. Not yet. The necklace is the reason Sadie's been haunting me. When she gets it back—

My thoughts abruptly veer away. I don't want to think about that. I don't want to think about any of it.

A breeze rustles some leaves on the ground, and Sadie looks up, pale and resolute.

"Give me some time."

"Yes." I swallow. "Sure." I stuff the necklace into the bag and head back into the restaurant. Sadie has already disappeared.

I can't eat my pizza. I can't make proper conversation. I can't focus when I get back to the office, even though six more calls come in from blue-chip HR managers wanting to set up meetings with me. The Jiffy bag is on my lap; my hand is clutching the necklace tightly inside it and I can't let go.

I text Ed, saying I have a headache and need to be alone. When I get home, there's no Sadie, which doesn't surprise me. I make some supper, which I don't eat, then sit in bed with the necklace around my neck, twisting the beads and watching old movies on TCM and not even bothering to try to sleep. At last, at about five-thirty, I get up, put on some clothes, and head out. The soft gray of the dawn is tinged with a vivid pink-red sunrise. I stand still, gazing at the red streaks in the sky for a few moments, and in spite of everything feel my spirits lifting. Then I buy a coffee from a café, get on a bus, and head to Waterloo, staring blankly out as the bus trundles through the streets. By the time I arrive it's nearer six-thirty. People are starting to appear on the bridge and in the streets. The London Portrait Gallery is still shut up, though. Locked and empty; not a soul inside. That's what you'd think, anyway.

I find a nearby wall, sit down, and sip my coffee, which is lukewarm but delicious on an empty stomach. I'm prepared to sit there all day, but as a nearby church bell strikes eight, she appears on the steps, that dreamy look on her face again. She's wearing yet another amazing dress, this one in pearl gray with a tulle skirt cut in petal shapes. A gray cloche is pulled down over her head, and her eyes are lowered. I don't want to alarm her, so I wait until she notices me and starts in surprise.

"Lara."

"Hi." I lift a hand. "Thought you'd be here."

"Where's my necklace?" Her voice is sharp with alarm. "Have you lost it?"

"No! Don't worry. I've got it. It's OK. It's right here. Look."

There's no one around, but I glance right and left, just in case. Then I pull out the necklace. In the clear morning light, it looks more spectacular than ever. I let it run over my hands and the beads click gently together. She gazes down at it lovingly, puts out her hands as though to take it, then draws them back.

"I wish I could touch it," she murmurs.

"I know." Helplessly, I hold it out to her, as though presenting an offering. I want to drape it around her neck. I want to reunite her with it.

"I want it back," she says quietly. "I want you to give it back to me."

"Now? Today?"

Sadie meets my eyes. "Right now."

There's a sudden blocking in my throat. I can't say any of the things I want to say. I think she knows what they are, anyway.

"I want it back," she repeats, softly but firmly. "I've been too long without it."

"Right." I nod several times, my fingers clutching the necklace so hard I think they might bruise. "Well, then, you need to have it."

The journey is too short. The taxi is slipping through the early-morning streets too effortlessly. I want to tell the driver to slow down. I want time to stand still. I want the taxi to be caught in a jam for six hours. . . . But all of a sudden we're drawing up in the little suburban street. We've arrived.

"Well, that was quick, wasn't it?" Sadie's voice is resolutely bright.

"Yes!" I force a smile. "Amazingly quick."

As we get out of the taxi, I feel dread clasping my chest like iron. My hand is locked around the necklace so hard, I'm getting cramps in my fingers. But I can't bring myself to loosen my grasp, even as I'm struggling to pay the driver with the other hand.

The taxi roars away, and Sadie and I look at each other. We're standing opposite a small row of shops, one of which is a funeral parlor.

"That's it there." I point redundantly at the sign saying *Chapel of Rest.* "Looks like it's closed."

Sadie has drifted up to the firmly locked door and is peering in the window.

"We'd better wait, I suppose." She shrugs and returns to my side. "We can sit here."

She sits down beside me on a wooden bench, and for a moment we're both silent. I glance at my watch. Eight fifty-five. They open up shop at nine. Just the thought gives me a rush of panic, so I won't think about it. Not yet. I'll just focus on the fact that I'm sitting here with Sadie.

"Nice dress, by the way." I think I sound fairly normal. "Who did you pinch that one from?"

"No one," says Sadie, sounding offended. "It was mine." She runs her eyes over me, then says grudgingly, "Your shoes are pretty."

"Thanks." I want to smile, but my mouth won't quite do it. "I bought them the other day. Ed helped me choose them, actually. We were late-night shopping. We went to the Whiteleys center. They had all these special offers on. . . ."

I don't know what I'm saying, I'm just talking for the sake of it. Because talking is better than waiting. I glance at my watch again and it's two minutes past the hour. They're late. I feel ridiculously grateful, like we've been given a reprieve.

"He's rather good at the old bone-jumping, isn't he?" Sadie suddenly says conversationally. "Ed, I mean. Mind you . . . you're not so bad either."

Bone-jumping?

She doesn't mean—

No. *No.*

"*Sadie.*" I turn on her. "I *knew* it! You *watched* us!"

"What?" She bursts into peals of laughter. "I was very subtle! You didn't know I was there."

"What did you see?" I moan.

"Everything," she says airily. "And it was a jolly good show, I can tell you."

"Sadie, you're impossible!" I clutch my head. "You don't watch people having sex! There are laws against that!"

"I just had *one* tiny criticism," she says, ignoring me. "Or, rather . . . suggestion. Something we used to do in my day."

"No!" I say in horror. "No suggestions!"

"Your loss." She shrugs and examines her nails, occasionally shooting me a look from under her lashes.

Oh for God's sake. Of course, now my curiosity is piqued. I want to know what her suggestion is.

"All right," I say at last. "Tell me your genius 1920s sex tip. But it better not involve any weird indelible paste."

"*Well . . .*" Sadie begins, coming closer. But before she can continue, my eyes suddenly focus over her shoulder. I stiffen and draw breath. An elderly man in an overcoat is unlocking the door of the funeral parlor.

"What is it?" Sadie follows my gaze. "Oh."

"Yes." I swallow.

By now the elderly man has caught sight of me. I suppose I am quite noticeable, sitting bolt upright on a bench staring directly at him.

"Are you . . . all right?" he says warily.

"Um . . . hi." I force myself to my feet. "I'm actually . . . I've come to pay a visit to your . . . to pay my respects. It's my great-aunt. Sadie Lancaster. I believe you're . . . this is where . . ."

"Aaah." He nods somberly. "Yes."

"Could I . . . possibly . . . see her?"

"Aaah." He bows his head again. "Of course. Just give me a minute to open up the place, get a few things straight, and I will be with you, Miss . . ."

"Lington."

"Lington." There's a flash of recognition in his face. "Of course, of course. If you'd like to come in and wait in our family room . . ."

"I'll be in in a moment." I give an approximation of a smile. "Just got . . . a call to make . . ."

He disappears inside. For a moment I can't quite move. I want to prolong this moment of limbo. I want to stop us doing this. If I don't acknowledge it, maybe it's not really going to happen.

"Got the necklace?" comes Sadie's voice beside me.

"Right here." I pull it out of my bag.

"Good." She smiles, but it's a tense, remote smile. I can tell she's moved on from 1920s sex tips.

"So . . . are you ready?" I try to sound lighthearted. "These places can be quite depressing—"

"Oh, I'm not coming in," says Sadie nonchalantly. "I'll sit here and wait. Much better."

"Right." I nod. "Good idea. You don't want to . . ."

I trail off, unable to continue—but also unable to bring up what I'm really thinking. The thought that's going around and around my head like an ominous tune, getting louder and louder.

Is neither of us going to bring it up?

"So." I swallow hard.

"So what?" Sadie's voice is bright and sharp as a chip of diamond—and instantly I know. It's on her mind too.

"What d'you think will happen when I . . . when . . ."

"Do you mean, will you finally be rid of me?" says Sadie, as flippantly as ever.

"No! I just meant—"

"I know. You're in a tearing hurry to get rid of me. Sick of the sight of me." Her chin is quivering but she flashes me a smile. "Well, I shouldn't think it'll work for a moment."

Her eyes meet mine, and I can see the message in them. *Don't lose it. No wallowing. Chin up.*

"So I'm stuck with you." I somehow manage a derisory tone. "Great."

"Afraid so."

"Just what every girl needs." I roll my eyes. "A bossy ghost hanging around the place forever."

"A bossy *guardian angel*," she corrects me firmly.

"Miss Lington?" The elderly man pokes his head out of the door. "Whenever you're ready."

"Thanks! I'll just be a sec!"

When the door closes, I adjust my jacket needlessly a few times. I tug at my belt, making sure it's completely straight, buying myself another thirty seconds.

"So I'll just dump the necklace and see you in a couple of minutes, OK?" I aim for a matter-of-fact tone.

"I'll be here." Sadie pats the bench she's sitting on.

"We'll go and see a movie. Something like that."

"Let's." She nods.

I take a step away—then stop. I know we're playing a game. But I can't leave it like that. I swivel around, breathing hard, determined that I won't lose it, I won't let her down.

"But . . . just in case. Just in case we . . ." I can't bring myself to say it. I can't even think it. "Sadie, it's been . . ."

There's nothing to say. No word is good enough. Nothing can describe what it's been like to know Sadie.

"I know," she whispers, and her eyes are like two glittering stars. "Me too. Go on."

When I reach the door of the funeral parlor I look back one last time. She's sitting bolt upright with perfect posture, her neck as long and pale as ever, her dress skimming her slender frame. She's facing directly ahead, feet lined up neatly, with her hands clasped on her knees. Utterly still. As though she's waiting.

I can't imagine what's going through her mind.

As I stand there, she notices me watching her, lifts her chin, and gives a sudden, ravishing, defiant smile.

"Tally-ho!" she exclaims.

"Tally-ho," I call back. On impulse, I blow her a kiss. Then I turn and push my way in with determination. It's time to do this.

The funeral director has made me a cup of tea and rustled up two shortbread biscuits, which he's put on a plate decorated with roses. He's a man with a receding chin, who answers every comment with a somber, low-pitched "aaah" before he gets to the actual reply. Which gets *really* irritating.

He leads me down a pastel corridor, then pauses meaningfully outside a wooden door marked *Lily Suite*.

"I'll let you have a few moments alone." He opens the door with an expert twist and pushes it a little way, then adds, "Is it true she was once the girl in that famous painting? The one that's been in the papers?"

"Yes." I nod.

"Aaah." He lowers his head. "How extraordinary.

One can hardly believe it. Such a very, very *old* lady—
one hundred and five, I believe? A very great age."

Even though I know he's trying to be nice, his words
touch a nerve.

"I don't think of her like that," I say curtly. "I don't
think of her as old."

"Aaah." He nods hastily. "Indeed."

"Anyway. I want to put something in the . . . coffin.
Will that be all right? Will it be safe?"

"Aaah. Quite safe, I assure you."

"And private," I say fiercely. "I don't want anyone
else going in here after me. If they want to, you contact
me first, OK?"

"Aaah." He surveys his shoes respectfully. "Of
course."

"Well. Thank you. I'll . . . go in now."

I walk in, close the door behind me, and just stand
there for a few moments. Now that I'm in here, now
that I'm actually doing this, my legs feel a bit watery. I
swallow a few times, trying to get a grip on myself,
telling myself not to freak out. After about a minute I
make myself take a step toward the big wooden coffin.
Then another.

That's Sadie. Real Sadie. My 105-year-old great-
aunt. Who lived and died and I never knew her. I edge
forward, breathing heavily. As I reach forward, I see
just a puff of dry white hair and a glimpse of dried-out
old skin.

"Here you are, Sadie," I murmur. Gently, carefully,
I slip the necklace around her neck. I've done it.

At last. I've done it.

She looks so tiny and shriveled. So vulnerable. All
the times I wanted to touch Sadie, I'm thinking. The
times I tried to squeeze her arm or give her a hug . . .

and now here she is. Real flesh. Cautiously, I stroke her hair and pull her dress straight, wishing beyond anything she could feel my touch. This frail, ancient, tiny crumbling body was Sadie's home for 105 years. This was really her.

As I stand there I'm trying to keep my breathing steady; I'm trying to think peaceful, suitable thoughts. Maybe even a couple of words to say aloud. I want to do the right thing. But at the same time there's an urgency beating inside me, growing stronger with every moment I stay here. The truth is, my heart isn't in this room.

I have to go. Now.

With trembling legs I reach the door, wrench the handle, and hurtle out, to the obvious surprise of the funeral director, who's loitering in the corridor.

"Is everything all right?" he says.

"Fine," I gulp, already walking away. "All fine. Thank you so much. I'll be in touch. But I must go now. I'm sorry, it's rather important . . ."

My chest feels so constricted I can barely breathe. My head is throbbing with thoughts I don't want to have. I have to get out of here. Somehow I make it down the pastel corridor and through the foyer, almost running. I reach the entrance and burst out onto the street. And I stop dead, clutching the door, panting slightly, looking straight across the road.

The bench is empty.

I know right then.

Of course I know.

But still my legs take me across the road at a run. I look desperately up and down the pavement. I call out

"Sadie? SADIE?" until I'm hoarse. I brush tears from my eyes and bat away inquiries from kindly strangers and look up and down the street again, and I won't give up and at last I sit down on the bench, gripping it with both hands. Just in case. And I wait.

And when it's finally dusk and I'm starting to shiver . . . I know. Deep down, where it matters.

She's not coming back. She's moved on.

TWENTY-SEVEN

*L*adies and gentlemen." My voice booms so loudly, I stop and clear my throat. I've never spoken into such a big loudspeaker system, and even though I did a "Hello, Wembley, one-two, one-two" sound check earlier, it's still a bit of a shock.

"Ladies and gentlemen." I try again. "Thank you so much for being here today at this occasion of sadness, celebration, festivity . . ." I survey the mass of faces gazing up at me expectantly. Rows and rows of them. Filling the pews of St. Botolph's Church. ". . . and, above all, appreciation of an extraordinary woman who has touched us all."

I turn to glance at the massive reproduction of Sadie's painting which is dominating the church. Around and beneath it are the most beautiful flower arrangements I've ever seen, with lilies and orchids and trailing ivy and even a reproduction of Sadie's dragonfly necklace, made out of the palest yellow roses set on a bed of moss.

That one was done by Hawkes and Cox, which is a top London florist. They contacted me when they heard about the memorial service and offered to do it for free, because they were all such fans of Sadie and wanted to show their appreciation of her. (Or, to be more cynical, because they knew they'd get great publicity.)

I honestly didn't intend this event to be such a massive deal at first. I just wanted to organize a memorial service for Sadie. But then Malcolm at the London Portrait Gallery heard about it. He suggested they announce the details of the service on their website for any art lovers who wanted to come and pay their respects to such a famous icon. To everyone's astonishment, they were besieged by applications. In the end they had to do a ballot. It even made the *London Tonight* news. And here they all are, crammed in. Rows and rows of them. People who want to honor Sadie. When I arrived and saw the crowds, I actually felt a bit breathless.

"I'd also like to say, great clothes. Bravo." I beam around at the vintage coats, the beaded scarves, the occasional pair of spats. "I think Sadie would have approved."

The dress code for today is 1920s, and everyone has made a stab at it of some sort. And I don't *care* if memorial services don't usually have dress codes, like that vicar kept saying. Sadie would have loved it, and that's what counts.

All the nurses from the Fairside Home have made a spectacular effort, both with themselves and also with all the elderly residents who have come. They're in the most fabulous outfits, with headdresses and necklaces, every single one. I meet Ginny's eye and she beams, giving an encouraging wave of her fan.

It was Ginny and a couple of other nurses from the home who came with me to Sadie's private funeral and cremation, a few weeks ago. I only wanted people there who had known her. Really *known* her. It was very quiet and heartfelt, and afterward I took them all out for lunch and we cried and drank wine and told Sadie stories and laughed, and then I gave a big donation to the nursing home and they all started crying again.

Mum and Dad weren't invited. But I think they kind of understood.

I glance at them, sitting in the front row. Mum is in a disastrous lilac drop-waisted dress with a headband, which looks more seventies ABBA than twenties. And Dad's in a totally non-1920s outfit. It's just a normal, modern single-breasted suit, with a silk spotted hand-kerchief in his top pocket. But I'll forgive him, because he's gazing up at me with such warmth and pride and affection.

"Those of you who only know Sadie as a girl in a portrait may wonder, who was the person behind the painting? Well, she was an amazing woman. She was sharp, funny, brave, outrageous . . . and she treated life as the most massive adventure. As you all know, she was muse to one of the famous painters of this century. She bewitched him. He never stopped loving her, nor she him. They were tragically separated by circum-stances. But if he'd only lived longer . . . who knows?"

I pause for breath and glance at Mum and Dad, who are watching me, riveted. I practiced my whole speech for them last night, and Dad kept saying incredulously, "How do you *know* all this?" I had to start referring vaguely to "archives" and "old letters" just to keep him quiet.

"She was uncompromising and feisty. She had this knack of . . . making things happen. Both to her and to other people." I sneak a tiny glance at Ed, sitting next to Mum, and he winks back at me. He knows this speech pretty well too.

"She lived 'til one hundred and five, which is quite an achievement." I look around the audience to make sure everyone is listening. "But she would have hated it if this had defined her, if people just thought of her as 'the hundred-and-five-year-old.' Because inside, she was a twenty-three-year-old all her life. A girl who lived her life with sizzle. A girl who loved the Charleston, cocktails, shaking her booty in nightclubs and fountains, driving too fast, lipstick, smoking gaspers . . . and barney-mugging."

I'm taking a chance that no one in the audience knows what barney-mugging means. Sure enough, they smile back politely, as though I've said she loved flower arranging.

"She loathed knitting," I add, with emphasis. "That should go on the record. But she loved *Grazia*." There's a laugh around the church, which is good. I wanted there to be laughter.

"Of course, for us, her family," I continue, "she wasn't just a nameless girl in a painting. She was my great-aunt. She was part of our heritage." I hesitate as I reach the part I really want to hit home. "It's easy to discount family. It's easy to take them for granted. But your family is your history. Your family is part of who you are. And without Sadie, none of us would be in the position we are today."

I can't help shooting Uncle Bill a steely gaze at this point. He's sitting upright next to Dad, dressed in a bespoke suit with a carnation buttonhole, his face quite a lot gaunter than it was on that beach in the south of France. It hasn't been a great month for him, all told.

He's been constantly in the news pages *and* the business pages, and none of it good.

At first, I wanted to ban him from this altogether. His publicist was desperate for him to come, to try to redress some of the bad PR he's had, but I couldn't bear the idea of him swaggering in, stealing the limelight, doing his usual Uncle Bill trick. But then I reconsidered. I started thinking, why *shouldn't* he come and honor Sadie? Why *shouldn't* he come and listen to how great his aunt was?

So he was allowed to come. On my terms.

"We should honor her. We should be grateful."

I can't help looking meaningfully at Uncle Bill again—and I'm not the only one. Everyone keeps glancing at him, and there are even a few nudges and whispers going on.

"Which is why I've set up, in Sadie's memory, the Sadie Lancaster Foundation. Funds raised will be distributed by the trustees to causes of which she would have approved. In particular, we will be supporting various dance-related organizations, charities for the elderly, the Fairside Nursing Home, and the London Portrait Gallery, in recognition of its having kept her precious painting so safely these last twenty-seven years."

I grin at Malcolm Gledhill, who beams back. He was so chuffed when I told him. He went all pink and started talking about whether I'd like to become a Friend, or go on the board, or something, as I'm clearly such an art lover. (I didn't want to say, "Actually, I'm just a Sadie lover; you can pretty much take or leave all those other pictures.")

"I would also like to announce that my uncle, Bill Lington, wishes to make the following tribute to Sadie, which I will now read on his behalf."

There is no way on earth I was letting Uncle Bill get up on this podium. Or write his own tribute. He doesn't even know what I'm about to say. I unfold a separate piece of paper and let a hush of anticipation fall before I begin.

"It is entirely due to my aunt Sadie's painting that I was able to launch myself in business. Without her beauty, without her help, I would not find myself in the privileged position I occupy today. During her life I did not appreciate her enough. And for this I am truly sorry." I pause for effect. The church is totally silent and agog. I can see all the journalists scribbling hard. *"I am therefore delighted to announce today that I will be donating ten million pounds to the Sadie Lancaster Foundation. It is a small recompense, to a very special person."*

There's a stunned murmuring. Uncle Bill has gone a kind of sallow putty color, with a rictus smile fixed in place. I glance at Ed, who winks again and gives me the thumbs-up. It was Ed who said, "Go for ten million." I was all set to ask for five, and I thought that was pushy enough. And the great thing is, now that six hundred people and a whole row of journalists have heard him, he can't exactly back out.

"I'd sincerely like to thank you all for coming." I look around the church. "Sadie was in a nursing home by the time her painting was discovered. She never knew quite how appreciated and loved she was. She would have been overwhelmed to see you all. She would have realized . . ." I feel a sudden rush of tears to my head.

No. I *can't* lose it now. After I've done so well. Somehow I manage a smile, and draw breath again.

"She would have realized what a mark she made on

this world. She's given so many people pleasure, and her legacy will remain for generations. As her great-niece, I'm incredibly proud." I swivel to survey the painting for a silent moment, then turn back. "Now it simply remains for me to say: To Sadie. If you would all raise your glasses . . ."

There's a stirring and rustling and clinking as everyone reaches for their cocktail glasses. Each guest was presented with a cocktail as they arrived: a gin fizz or a sidecar, especially mixed by two barmen from the Hilton. (And I don't *care* if people don't usually have cocktails at memorial services.)

"Tally-ho." I lift my glass high, and everyone obediently echoes, "Tally-ho." There's silence as everyone sips. Then, gradually, murmurs and giggles start to echo round the church. I can see Mum sipping at her sidecar with a wary expression, and Uncle Bill grimly downing his gin fizz in one, and a pink-faced Malcolm Gledhill beckoning the waiter over for a top-up.

The organ crashes in with the opening bars of "Jerusalem," and I make my way down the podium steps to rejoin Ed, who's standing next to my parents. He's wearing the most amazing vintage 1920s dinner jacket which he paid a fortune for at a Sotheby's auction and makes him look like a black-and-white-movie star. When I exclaimed in horror at the price, he just shrugged and said he knew the 1920s thing meant a lot to me.

"Good job," he whispers, clenching my hand. "You did her proud."

As the rousing song starts, I realize I can't join in. Somehow my throat feels too tight and the words won't come. So instead I look around at the flower-laden church, and the beautiful outfits, and all the people gathered here, singing lustily for Sadie. So many diverse people, from different walks of life. Young, old, family members, friends from the nursing home—people that she touched in some way. All here. All for her. This is what she deserved.

This is what she deserved. All along.

When the service finally ends, the organist launches into the Charleston (I don't *care* if memorial services don't usually have the Charleston), and the congregation slowly files out, still clutching their cocktail glasses. The reception is being held at the London Portrait Gallery, thanks to lovely Malcolm Gledhill, and helpful girls with badges are telling people how to get there.

But I don't rush. I can't quite face all the talking and chatter and buzz. Not just yet. I sit in my front pew, breathing in the scent of the flowers, waiting until it's quieter.

I did her justice. At least I think I did. I hope I did.

"Darling." Mum's voice interrupts me and I see her approaching me, her hairband more wonky than ever. Her cheeks are flushed and there's a glow of pleasure all around her as she slides in beside me. "That was wonderful. *Wonderful.*"

"Thanks." I smile up at her.

"I'm so proud of the way you skewered Uncle Bill. Your charity will do great things, you know. And the cocktails!" she adds, draining her glass. "What a good idea!"

I gaze at Mum, intrigued. As far as I know, she

isn't worried about a single thing today. She hasn't fretted that people might arrive late, or get drunk, or break their cocktail glasses, or anything.

"Mum . . . you're different," I can't help saying. "You seem less stressed. What happened?"

I'm suddenly wondering if she's been to the doctor. Is she taking Valium or Prozac or something? Is she on some drug-induced high?

There's silence as Mum adjusts her lilac sleeves.

"It was very strange," she says at last. "And I couldn't tell everybody this, Lara. But a few weeks ago, something strange happened."

"What?"

"It was almost as though I could hear . . ." She hesitates, then whispers, "A *voice in my head.*"

"A voice?" I stiffen. "What kind of voice?"

"I'm not a religious woman. You know that." Mum glances around the church and leans toward me. "But, truly, this voice followed me around all day! Right in here." She taps her head. "It wouldn't leave me alone. I thought I was going mad!"

"What—what did it say?"

"It said, 'Everything's going to be all right, stop worrying!' Just that, over and over, for hours. I got quite ratty with it, in the end. I said out loud, 'All right, Mrs. Inner Voice, I get the message!' And then it stopped, like magic."

"Wow," I manage, a lump in my throat. "That's . . . amazing."

"And ever since then, I find things don't *bother* me quite as much." Mum glances at her watch. "I'd better go, Dad's on his way round with the car. Do you want a lift?"

"Not just yet. I'll see you there."

Mum nods understandingly, then heads out. As Charleston morphs into another 1920s tune, I lean back, gazing up at the beautiful molded ceiling, still a bit blown away by Mum's revelation. I can just see Sadie trailing after her, pestering her, refusing to give up.

All the things that Sadie was and did and achieved. Even now, I feel like I only ever knew the half of it.

The medley eventually comes to an end, and a woman in robes appears and starts snuffing out all the candles. I rouse myself, pick up my bag, and get to my feet. The place is already empty. Everyone will be on their way.

As I head out of the church into the paved forecourt, a ray of sunlight catches me in the eye and I blink. There's a crowd of people still laughing and talking on the pavement, but no one is anywhere near me, and I find my gaze drifting upward to the sky. As it does so often. Still.

"Sadie?" I say quietly, out of force of habit. "Sadie?" But of course there's no reply. There never is.

"Well done!" Ed suddenly descends on me from nowhere and plants a kiss on my lips, making me jump. Where was he, hiding behind a pillar? "Spectacular. The whole thing. It couldn't have gone better. I was so proud of you."

"Oh. Thanks." I flush with pleasure. "It was good, wasn't it? So many people came!"

"It was amazing. And that's all because of you." He touches my cheek gently and says more quietly, "Are you ready to go to the gallery? I told your mom and dad to go on."

"Yes." I smile. "Thanks for waiting. I just needed a moment."

"Sure." As we start walking toward the wrought-
iron gate onto the street, he threads his arm through
mine and I squeeze it back. Yesterday, out of the blue,
as we were walking to the memorial rehearsal, Ed told
me casually that he was extending his assignment to
London by six months, because he might as well use up
his car insurance. Then he gave me a long look and
asked me what I thought about him staying around for
a while?

I pretended to think hard, trying to hide my eupho-
ria, then said, yes, he might as well use up his car insurance, why not? And he kind of grinned. And I kind of
grinned. And all the time, his hand was tightly knit
around mine.

"So . . . who were you talking to just now?" he adds
carelessly. "When you came out of the church."

"What?" I say, a little thrown. "Nobody. Um, is the car
nearby?"

"'Cause it *sounded*," he persists lightly, "as if you
said 'Sadie.'"

There's a beat of silence while I try to arrange my
features in exactly the right mystified expression.

"You thought I said *Sadie*?" I throw in a little laugh
to show exactly what a bizarre idea this is. "Why
would I say that?"

"That's what I thought," Ed says, still in the same
conversational manner. "I thought to myself, *Why
would she say that?*"

He's not going to let this go. I can tell.

"Maybe it's the British accent," I say in sudden inspiration. "Maybe you heard me saying 'sidecar.' I
need another 'sidecar.'"

"Sidecar." Ed stops walking and fixes me with a
long, quizzical gaze. Somehow I force myself to look

back with wide, innocent eyes. He can't read my mind, I remind myself. He *can't* read my mind.

"There's something," he says at last, shaking his head. "I don't know what it is, but there's something."

I feel a fierce tug in my heart. Ed knows everything else about me, big and small. He has to know this too. After all, he was part of it.

"Yes." I nod at last. "There's something. And I'll tell you about it. One day."

Ed's mouth twitches into a smile. He runs his eyes over my vintage dress, my swingy jet beads, my marcelled hair, and the feathers bobbing over my forehead, and his expression softens.

"Come on, twenties girl." He takes hold of my hand with the firm, sure grasp I've got used to. "You did great by your aunt. Shame she didn't see it."

"Yes," I agree. "It's a shame."

But as we walk away, I allow myself one more tiny glance up at the empty sky.

I hope she did.

ACKNOWLEDGMENTS

I would like to thank those who so kindly helped me with my research for this book: Olivia and Julian Pinkney, Robert Beck, and Tim Moreton.

My huge thanks go also to Susan Kamil, Noah Eaker, and all at The Dial Press and Bantam Dell. And, as ever, to Araminta Whitley, Kim Witherspoon, David Forrer, Harry Man, my boys, and the Board.